No Bra Required

By Nikki Ashton

AF378782

To Graham

Thanks for all your help & support

Nikki
x

Dedication

This book is dedicated to those special people who are no longer with me, but I know are up there giving me a helping hand, especially my wonderful Dad and my Pops

3

Thanks go to all my family, friends and work colleagues who have supported and encouraged me (I think the gates are sometime away yet Mr Price), to Jean for the endless cups of tea, to TC for her medical knowledge and lunches, HB for her proof reading, and GTRL for his excellent copy editing (you were right 99.9% of the time!). To my Mum I give extra special thanks for her love, help and support, and lastly, but most importantly, a massive thank you and lots of love to David, for his constant love, pride & encouragement and reminders not to stay up too late writing.

Chapter 1

"Lucy, give me the bobble hat now! I mean it. I'll slap you if you don't hand it over!" Sarah reached across, and snatched at the bright green woolly hat which was pulled down firmly on Lucy Meadow's head. "It even clashes with your hair!"

"Gingerist!" Lucy cried, frowning at her friend.

"You always say its Titian, so I can't be a gingerist, can I?"

"Oh, leave me alone Sarah." Lucy placed one hand on her head and flapped her other at Sarah's arm. It had been two weeks and three days since Simon had gone, leaving Lucy feeling broken hearted, and she hadn't been out of bed, or her bobble hat since.

*

It had been a normal Sunday in May, a late breakfast, an afternoon spent chilling out, Simon reading the papers and Lucy the latest frothy romance that she'd bought the day before. Suddenly, without any announcement, Simon threw the papers to one side, got up and left the lounge. At first, Lucy thought that he had gone to the bathroom or even, unusually for Simon, to make them a cup of tea, but when he didn't re-appear after half an hour, she began to feel slightly irritated. Lucy decided to investigate. She found Simon searching through a drawer, throwing various pamphlets and papers onto the floor.

"Simon why on earth are you making such a mess?" Lucy asked Simon, placing a hand on his back.

"It's got to be here somewhere. You'll need it if the boiler breaks down." He didn't look up at Lucy but carried on searching.

"What, what will I need? Simon, please tell me what *are* you talking about." Lucy shook her head, perturbed by his behaviour.

"If I'm not here, you'll need the guarantee and service documents for the boiler." He looked at Lucy with sadness etched across his face.

"What do you mean 'if you're not here'? You're scaring me now, are you ill or something?" Lucy asked, pulling him into a hug.

Simon pushed her away. "No, Lucy, I'm not ill." His head dropped, and he looked down at his feet that were scuffing the tiled floor. "I'm so sorry Luce, but I'm leaving you. I've met someone else, and I love her," Simon blurted out as he turned and left the room.

Lucy clutched at her chest, fearing that her thudding heart was about to explode. She slid to the floor. "Simon, no you can't," she screamed. "Please, don't Simon, no. You don't mean it. I know you don't." Bile rose in her throat, and a cold sweat enveloped her body. She scrambled to her feet and ran up the stairs. Simon was in their bedroom packing his clothes into a suitcase.

"It doesn't matter Simon. I forgive you. You've made a mistake, and we can get over it." She grabbed at the clothes in his suitcase, and started pulling them out, and throwing them onto the bed.

"Lucy, stop it!" Simon grabbed both her wrists and pushed her away. "It's over. I'm sorry."

"It can't be. You can't just throw five years of marriage away for some fling with someone you hardly know." Fighting to catch her breath, tears rolled down Lucy's face.

"It's not a fling. I love her." Simon paused and turned his face away from Lucy. "It's Jenny from work. We've been seeing each other for a while and…well it's got serious, so I'm sorry Lucy."

"Her! You hate her, you said she was a cow. Please Simon, just give me another chance, I'll do whatever it takes." She grabbed his arms, her eyes pleading for him to change his mind.

Simon removed her hands and moved away. "She's pregnant Lucy, so I'm sorry, there's nothing you can do to make me change my mind."

Lucy's heart broke when he'd said he was leaving, but now it had been ripped from her chest and stamped on. She howled like an injured animal as she collapsed onto the bed. Simon simply continued packing, without even a glance, or any offer of comfort.

*

When Lucy and Simon married they had wanted to start a family as soon as possible, so eighteen months after their wedding, their daughter Lottie was born. She was a beautiful, chubby, baby, always smiling and very rarely crying and they both adored her. One terrible night, when Lottie was almost six months old, Lucy had gone to bed before Simon. She didn't look in on Lottie for fear of disturbing her, but an hour later was woken by the sound of Simon screaming. Lottie wouldn't wake up. She didn't have an illness. Nothing went undetected. Lucy and Simon did nothing wrong; their beautiful baby girl was the victim of Sudden Infant Death Syndrome.

Doctors had said the possibility of it happening another time would be minimal. Every precaution would be taken for Lucy and Simon's other babies, to ensure it didn't. Lucy couldn't take that chance. She couldn't go through that again. She couldn't handle a child, which they'd created from love, being snatched from them. Simon had agreed that it was too much to bear, and so they'd decided that they would create a fantastic life for themselves without any more children.

*

As Lucy watched Simon, she couldn't understand how distant he'd become. He didn't seem to care that this was killing her that she was reliving the agony of losing their daughter all over again, as well as losing him, her husband, and the love of her life. Lottie had barely been gone three years, but he was willing to move on and replace her, replace Lucy too.

"Simon," she whispered. "What about Lottie, did she mean nothing to you?"

Simon faltered for a moment. "I loved Lottie, but she's gone Luce. You need to try to accept it too."

"We agreed Simon…you agreed that we wouldn't have any more children."

"It's what you wanted Lucy, I just wanted what you wanted." He looked at Lucy, unshed tears for his beloved daughter, glistening in his eyes.

"You could have told me how you felt. You didn't need to go and get someone else pregnant. I would have listened." Sitting up, Lucy wiped her face against the back of her hand and sniffed loudly.

"Would you? Would you honestly Lucy? I don't think so, and besides…" Simon stopped speaking, and looked inside his wardrobe.

"Besides what…Simon?" Lucy asked.

Simon sighed deeply, turning back to her. "Besides Lucy, I just don't love you anymore." With that, Simon picked up his suitcase and left the house and hadn't contacted Lucy since that day.

*

Sarah's sigh broke Lucy's thoughts. "Please Luce, we're worried about you. Lying in bed for two weeks can't be healthy."

"And two days," Lucy corrected her.

"Okay for two weeks and two days, whatever length of time it is, it's not healthy. Even your mother has been ringing me to find out whether you've surfaced, or not. The local press thinks that it's a hostage situation, you've been up here so long." She smiled at Lucy, hoping for a reciprocal grin, but there wasn't one.

"I don't want to get up. I don't want to leave the house, and I certainly don't want my mother around here. If you let her in with your key, or even get her to call me, I would never speak to you again." Lucy closing her eyes and pulling the bobble hat further down on her head, disappeared under the duvet.

Sarah shook her head and sighed. "Okay, I'll leave you for today, but I *will* be back tomorrow, and please seriously think about having a shower - you stink."

Lucy sat up from under the duvet, sniffing at her armpits. "No, I don't...do I?" She sniffed again. "Phew you're right I do. Okay, I might have a shower when you've gone. Anyway, why are you so tarted up for a Wednesday afternoon?"

Lucy couldn't see Sarah blush in the dim light of the curtained bedroom. "I'm meeting Ben."

What Sarah didn't elaborate on was that Ben, her husband, had booked a hotel room, and they were going to pretend that he'd picked her up in the bar before going upstairs for some rampant sex. The breakdown of Lucy and Simon's marriage has scared them both, knowing that they rarely had time for each other now that they had two young sons, Noah aged 4 and Milo aged 10 months, they had decided that changes should be made to avoid going the same way as their close friends.

Lucy, sensing that her friend wasn't telling her the whole story, gave her a small smile and squeezed Sarah's hand gently. "Well, have a good time, and give my love to Ben, and the boys."

Sarah smiled back. "I'll do both things Luce, now, please get up, have a shower, and eat something. Crisps and digestive biscuits are not a staple diet."

"Okay." Lucy surreptitiously pushed the empty family bag of crisps under her pillow. "Now go, I'll be fine."

Sarah kissed Lucy on the cheek, and with her face etched with concern, she left the room. She knew that Lucy was stubborn, and if she continued pushing her Lucy would stay in her bed, and her bobble hat, for the rest of eternity.

After an hour of contemplating whether to take Sarah's advice or not, Lucy decided that she would get up and have a shower. She may even change the sheets from the bed; the smell of Simon had disappeared anyway. All she could smell now was her own stale body, cheese and onion crisps, and coffee. Lucy looked around the usually pristine bedroom. She grimaced at the numerous coffee mugs that had made rings on the wooden floor, and the pile of ripped up photographs next to the bed. On her third day of isolation, she hauled a box of photographs from the bottom of her wardrobe and had systematically ripped Simon, or his head, out of them all. The only one that she hadn't touched was the one in the mirrored frame next to her bed. It was of the three of them - the day after Lottie had been born - and she and Simon looked extremely happy, and so in love with each other, and with Lottie. She couldn't bear to rip the photograph as it reminded her too much of her beautiful daughter.

Lucy sighed as she heaved herself out of bed, and dragged herself to the en suite. She turned the shower on, full blast, and undressed as the hot water created a cloud of steam around her. Eventually, after staring into the water for about five minutes, she stepped under it and let it run over her body. She hoped that somehow it would wash not only the smell away, but all her troubles and unhappiness. Lucy soaped herself and shampooed her hair until finally she felt clean and smelled a lot sweeter. She felt a little calmer now, and decided that she was ready to leave the bedroom. After dressing in a track suit, Lucy tied her long hair into a ponytail - she had considered pulling the bobble hat on, but it had started to make her head itch. As she made her way downstairs, Lucy realised that she felt hungry, for something more than crisps and biscuits. She knew that Sarah had done some food shopping for her yesterday. She sighed as she thought of Sarah. She was such a loyal friend, and Lucy had treated her appallingly this last couple of weeks. She'd shouted at her, called her a smug bitch because her own marriage was so successful, and at one point, Lucy had even thrown a book at her. She didn't deserve a friend like Sarah, but they'd been friends since college and been through a lot together: the death of Sarah's mother, the loss of Lottie, the "scandal" of Lucy's gay dad, too many boyfriend troubles to mention and now this.

Lucy opened the fridge door and looked inside; Sarah had clearly surpassed herself. It was full of lots of tempting foods, including Parma ham, eggs, salad and smelly cheese plus a variety of fresh fruit. Lucy pulled out some eggs and cheese to make an omelette, avoiding a large enticing Cornish pasty that she'd noticed on the top shelf. As she reached inside the cupboard for a bowl, her mobile rang. Lucy glanced at it, tempted to ignore the call, but it was a blocked number and something inside her, stupidly, thought that it may be Simon, ringing to say he'd made a mistake.

Lucy quickly answered it. "Hello Simon, is that you?" she asked, her voice full of anguish.

"Don't be so ridiculous Lucy, why on earth would that stupid man be ringing you?" The clipped tone on the other end of the line replied.

Lucy felt both disappointment and anger.

"Mother, what do you want?" she asked, pushing the heel of her hand against her forehead.

"Charming greeting for your own mother, I must say. I wanted to check how you were and to see whether you were out of that stinking pit yet."

Lucy didn't answer, but took a deep breath and started to count to ten. Her mother infuriated her, and any conversation they had invariably ended in a screaming match. Annabelle, Lucy's mother, had made it blatantly obvious that her two daughters, Lucy and her sister Sophie were merely accessories. At least, they had been when they were cute little babies, but as they grew older, she decided that they were nothing more than a nuisance. It was when Lucy was nine, and Sophie seven, that Annabelle passed all significant care of the girls over to her husband, Gerald. As a middle-class family living in a detached house, in a

Cheshire market town, Annabelle didn't understand why the girls couldn't have a nanny. Gerald insisted that he wanted to be part of his daughters' upbringing and not just a bystander while someone else made the crucial decisions about their lives. He also made the point that the house was a modest detached property, not a mansion. He didn't earn millions in his job as an English Lecturer at the local university, and most importantly Annabelle, or Annie as she had been christened, was herself from a council estate in a nearby town, so maybe she was getting ideas above her station. Hating to be reminded of her humble beginnings, it was from this point that Annabelle left the marital bed - not that there had been much action there for at least five years - and took various lovers whom she flaunted in front of Gerald at every opportunity. Gerald was not in the least bothered. When the girls were old enough to understand, he was finally able to reveal to them what he'd known for a long time: he was, in fact, gay. Annabelle had tried to turn the girls against him, saying some unpleasant things about Gerald, but it didn't work. Neither Lucy nor Sophie was surprised at Gerald's news, and certainly weren't going to take their mother's side over his. Gerald's 'coming out' actually gave Lucy some kudos at college with the drama students who for some reason thought that Gerald would love The Sound of Music, and show tunes. Annabelle, however, played the 'hard done by' wife at every opportunity, and tried to create a scandal. Caring little how Gerald, or their daughters, would feel she would allow it to leak out to the most indiscreet people, those whom she knew would gossip. Then when Lucy was in the second year of her teaching degree at university, Gerald told Lucy and Sophie that he had met someone with whom he wanted to spend the rest of his life; Richard, who was the university's new librarian. Both girls were thrilled, even more so once they'd met Richard. He was a kind, considerate man, who adored their beloved father. Annabelle, on the other hand, despite having had a string of affairs over the last eleven years, insisted upon a divorce, on the grounds of Gerald's adultery. She made Gerald's life a misery, to such an extent that, after a year of arguing and being harassed by Annabelle and her cronies, Gerald and Richard

decided to move to County Durham. It was far away from Annabelle but also, unfortunately,

from the girls. Sophie was desperate to move to London to study photography, so she didn't

mind too much, but Lucy never forgave her mother. She had gone to university locally so that

she could be near her dad, and now Annabelle had driven him, and Richard, away.

*

"Lucy, are you actually listening to me?" Annabelle's shrill voice screeched into

Lucy's ear.

"Yes mother, do I even have a choice?"

Annabelle tutted loudly, "No, Lucy you don't. Now open the door and let me in. I

know that you are in the kitchen because I can see you. I'm outside the back door."

"How did you get around the back? You haven't climbed over the gate have you?"

Lucy moved towards the back door and peered through the frosted glass.

Annabelle's laugh tinkled on the other end of the phone. "Don't be so bloody foolish.

I still have a gate key from when you asked me to water your plants, when you went on

holiday."

"That was five years ago," said Lucy. "Why do you still have the gate key?"

"Oh for goodness sake Lucy, stop being bloody pedantic, and open this door now. This

summer drizzle is playing havoc with my bob."

Lucy could see through the glass that her mother was smoothing down her hair. She

sighed as she turned the key and cut the call off - she had no choice but to let her in.

"You'd better come in then," she said swinging the door wide open.

"Oh goodness what an absolute fright you look, you really are a foolish goose."

Annabelle gasped as she continued to pat her hair.

"Oh for fucks sake Mother, stop it with the home counties words and accent. You sound like a pissing Enid Blyton adventure!" Lucy couldn't help herself, she prided herself on not swearing in front of the older generation, but her mother was an exception, she was enough to make the Pope scream a barrage of obscenities.

Annabelle stopped in her tracks and held on to the work surface as if to steady herself. "Well I have never been so insulted," she cried.

"You obviously don't get out much then," screamed Lucy. "What do you want anyway? It's not as if you care about me or what's happened, you hated Simon."

"That's not true, I didn't hate him. I didn't think that an accountant was good enough for you, that's all."

"Crock of shit Mum. You said, 'He has a pin head and squinty eyes and looks as though he should live in a caravan'. Were they or were they not the words you used to describe him when I brought him home to meet you?" Lucy remembered that day eight years ago as clearly as though it was yesterday. They had met at a quiz in a pub where Simon had been drinking with his mates, and he had helped Lucy, Sarah and another friend, Karen with some of their answers. After the quiz, he'd offered them a drink, and Lucy had been mesmerised by his dark brooding looks and wavy black hair.

"I did no such thing. As I remember, I told you that he'd break your heart one day, and I've been proved right." Annabelle studied her nails, a satisfied smile upon her face.

"No, you didn't and even if you did, there's no need to be so smug about it, just because you were right. Christ Mum, you make up your own version of events and repeat it so much that you actually end up believing it. Dad and Granny have always said that half the stories that you've told Sophie and me, aren't true. No wonder you have such an unhealthy relationship with both of us. Sophie even moved to South Africa to get away from you and hasn't been home to see you in over three years."

"She hasn't been to see you either, just your bloody father, and his camp little friend."

"Mum, don't be so rude about Dad and Richard. Anyway, I did see Sophie, about eighteen months ago, admittedly only for an hour on Crewe Railway Station, but she had a really important meeting in London, and it was the only chance we could get." Turning her back to Annabelle, Lucy flicked on the kettle.

"I do hope you're not making instant, it's absolutely ghastly?"

"Firstly, I'm making tea, secondly I'm not making you anything, and thirdly, it's ghastly, not GHARSTLY, there's no bloody r in it!"

"I'll make my own then. You do have fresh coffee don't you?" Annabelle asked, oblivious to Lucy's tone.

Lucy sighed as she opened a cupboard and pulled out a pack of ground coffee that she threw at her mother. Annabelle just managed to catch it, and held it at arm's length in case it marked her extremely expensive cream suit.

"Cafetiere?" Annabelle asked.

"It's behind you, next to the microwave. Seriously, though Mum, what do you want? You've not cared about me since I was nine years old, so why now?" Lucy dropped a tea bag into a mug, ignoring the tut of disgust from Annabelle who only ever used Indian leaves. Lucy pushed a spoon across the work surface towards her.

"Contrary to popular belief, I do care about you Lucy; you *and* Sophie. I gave birth to you after several hours of agony, so of course I care about you,"

"I do believe you screamed "Get this thing out of me now. I want a caesarean." With a variation on the same theme when you had Sophie, and don't say you didn't because Granny told me that."

"Huh, my own mother even turned on me." Annabelle shook her head.

"What, like you turned on us?" Lucy muttered.

"Do grow up Lucy; you're not a mother, so you don't know how hard it can be." As the words came out of Annabelle's mouth, even she, queen of the sharp tongue and snide comments, realised that she had gone too far. She put a hand to her mouth. "God, Lucy I'm sorry. I honestly didn't think."

Lucy wanted to punch her in her stupid, over made up, over botoxed face. "Just get out," she cried. "I never, ever, want to see you again. How could you, I hate you?" Lucy sobbed, tears rolling along her cheeks.

"Please Lucy, I am sorry. Look hit me if you like, but don't touch my nose; I paid over £3,000 for it."

The invitation was too powerful for Lucy. She swung an open palm at her mother's face, landing it on her right cheek. A bright red hand print appeared almost immediately. Annabelle didn't even flinch.

"Well, I deserved that," she said quietly, her eyes bright with tears. "So, let's talk about getting you back into the land of the living, what do you intend to do next?"

Lucy couldn't help but smile. Only Annabelle could take such a whack and act as though it had never happened. Fleetingly Lucy felt a little bit of respect for her, albeit grudgingly. She shook her head.

"I honestly don't know Mum. I honestly don't."

Chapter 2

Annabelle finally left after an hour, an hour in which Lucy had contemplated quietly how it would be possible to kill her mother and get away with it. Cutting up her body and melting it in acid appeared to be the safest way. Although Annabelle had annoyed and hurt Lucy beyond belief during that hour, even Lucy had to agree that it was about time she started to pull herself together. Annabelle had pointed out that Lucy needed to get a solicitor otherwise what would stop Simon from insisting she move out of the house so that he could move the 'bitch' in. Lucy realised it probably wasn't that simple, but just thinking about another woman living in her house, with her husband, made her feel sick, not to mention that their child would be sleeping in Lottie's room probably. Lucy wasn't quite sure that she could continue to live in the house anyway as there were so many memories. However, she still wasn't ready to make that decision yet, but at least she could find out what her rights were.

Once Lucy had seen Annabelle drive off down the road, she heaved a sigh of relief. Why did she allow her mum to make her feel so inadequate, angry and bitter? She had tried to forgive Annabelle for virtually abandoning her and Sophie, but she couldn't. She had lived in the same house when they were children, but a 'morning' over breakfast was the only contact they'd had, everything else was done by Gerald. He washed their clothes, he fed them, and he did their hair and attended every school event. He was a mother *and* father rolled into one and Annabelle never genuinely seemed to care, or feel any guilt about it. Sophie had fared considerably better than Lucy over their mother relinquishing her parental duties. She was a confident child with a bit of Annabelle's hard edge to her, plus it was a lot easier for her to rebel with only one parent taking any notice. Sophie was the one who smoked, who drank alcohol underage, who stayed out late at night, and who usually did what she wanted to do. Yet it was a regular occurrence for Gerald to blow up and ground her for a few weeks. During this time, while Sophie rebelled, Lucy spent a lot of time with their father. She felt sorry for him, and wanted to keep him company, and their bond grew greater, hence Lucy's reason to go to the local university, at which Gerald lectured. Annabelle spoiled that too, and made life extremely difficult for Gerald and Richard. She would cause arguments, and turn up at Richard's house at all hours, when she knew Gerald was there, and cause a scene on the street. She also encouraged her friends and acquaintances to ostracise them. Gerald was even "black balled" from both local golf clubs, and had to resort to the council run 'pitch and putt' to play his beloved sport. There were so many things that Lucy hated about Annabelle, yet somehow she had made sense about Simon and what he could do with the house.

*

After eating an omelette, Lucy looked up a local solicitor, by logging on to her computer. She spoke to a Mr Devine who chatted to her briefly about her situation, and then arranged her an appointment for later that week. He had been extremely helpful, and Lucy was glad that she had taken her mother's advice, for once. Then she decided it was time to call her dad. He knew about Simon leaving because Sarah had telephoned him, but Lucy hadn't spoken to him about it herself. Lucy recalled when she had told Gerald that she and Simon were to be married. It had been one of the few times they had ever argued. Gerald had said that he liked Simon, but something inside had told him that he would hurt Lucy one day. Gerald had told Lucy to be careful, and to be absolutely sure before they booked a wedding, which had agitated Lucy. She couldn't understand why he didn't want her to be happy. However, that was the whole point, as he told Lucy, he wanted her to be happy, he just wasn't sure that Simon was the right man for the job.

"Hello, Gerald Falmer speaking."

17

The familiar voice brought tears to Lucy's eyes as she pictured her dad. She knew his grey hair would be neatly trimmed, and he was probably wearing a tank top, and a shirt and tie, as he always did.

"Hi Dad, it's me," she whispered, tears now falling silently down her cheeks.

"Lucy my baby, how are you? God I'm glad you've called me I've been so worried about you." Gerald cooed on the other end of the phone.

"I feel like crap, to be honest Dad. I can't believe he's gone." Lucy sniffed loudly as her nose began to run. She pulled a tissue from her pocket and wiped her eyes and nose. "She's pregnant Dad, how could he let that happen after what we went through with Lottie?"

"I know darling. I know. Have you spoken to him since? Do you know where he's living or what he's going to do next? Have you been to see a solicitor?" He asked lots of questions, his voice full of concern.

"I haven't heard anything at all. Sarah's Ben doesn't even know where he is, and they are supposed to be close friends. Funnily enough I've just contacted a solicitor this morning, and I'm going to see him in a couple of days." Lucy again sniffed, this time running the back of her hand across her nose.

"That's good. I know it's hard to hear sweetheart, but I think if she's pregnant you have to accept that he's not coming back."

"I know Dad, but I miss him so much." Lucy started to sob uncontrollably, the mixture of hearing her dad's voice and thinking of the inevitable was just too much.

"Lucy sweetie, please stop crying, come on, calm down," Gerald responded in a soothing tone until eventually the crying subsided. "Listen Lucy, I have something to tell you. I didn't want to worry you, but I think there may be a solution to a problem that I have."

"Dad, what's the matter, is something wrong?"

"Look don't worry it's nothing serious, but you know Richard, and I were supposed to be going to Australia for six weeks to see his sister?"

"Yes," Lucy replied, worried despite Gerald telling her not to.

"Well I can't go because... you see the problem is Luce... well I've broken my leg." Gerald laughed.

"Dad, why didn't you tell me, when did it happen, and why on earth are you laughing, it's not funny?" Lucy chided her father.

"I only did it last week, and I just thought that you had enough to worry about, sorry." Gerald apologised.

"How did you do it?" Lucy asked, sighing deeply.

"I fell off a chair, when I was cleaning the bedroom windows."

Lucy gasped; her father and Richard lived in a cottage with sash windows that were as high as the ceiling.

"You could have killed yourself, what were you doing cleaning them? They're enormous Dad."

"Well someone has to do them, they won't just clean themselves," Gerald replied.

"More to the point, why were you standing on a chair, and not a pair of step-ladders? Dad, sometimes for an educated man you genuinely are lacking in common sense."

"Okay Annabelle!" Gerald chuckled on the other end, knowing that likening Lucy to Annabelle would annoy her.

"Hmm hilarious, I don't think! Anyway, if you can't go to Australia what are you going to do, will you lose all your money?"

"Well that's what I was going to say. I can't go, but because I've got a doctor's note from my GP, I can have the money back for my flight. Richard, on the other hand, wouldn't. So I've been trying to persuade him to go. It's been nearly six years since he saw his sister."

"He should go, but I can understand him not wanting to leave you. Oh Dad, I'm so sorry, you were looking forward to it so much." Lucy sighed. She was a little cross that her dad hadn't told her about his fall before now, but understood why.

"That's my point sweetheart, how about you come over and look after me? It will give you some time to think and get your head together, and it would give Richard peace of mind. Plus it's not as though you have to worry about work, is it?"

Lucy was a primary school teacher, up until a year ago. She'd loved her job, but after losing Lottie, she just didn't have the passion for it anymore. She had decided to reassess her life and take an indefinite sabbatical. Simon had been supportive and had encouraged Lucy to resign if it were what she genuinely wanted. So for the last eleven months, she'd worked as a volunteer in a local charity shop, and it was a job that made her feel happy and fulfilled.

"Well, I suppose it would be okay with the shop. Mrs Edwards is always saying how quiet we are. Oh I don't know Dad. I've got such a lot to sort out, and I need to be here."

"Do you honestly need to be there Lucy? If Simon does come back for the rest of his stuff, do you truly want to be there?" Gerald wanted Lucy with him, to protect her. It didn't actually have anything to do with him needing help; he could manage perfectly well with the help of friends and neighbours. "Go and see your solicitor, listen to what advice he gives you, and then decide. Richard isn't going until next Saturday, but you could come midweek and spend some time with him before he goes away. I know that he would love that, and to see you settled in. What do you think?"

Lucy thought for a few seconds, before responding. "Okay, I'll speak to Mr Devine and let you know on Friday evening after my appointment. How will you manage though Dad, if I don't come, and will Richard refuse to go?" Lucy suspected that Gerald needing help was possibly a ploy to get her there, as her father was an extremely resourceful man.

"I'll make sure he goes don't worry, I can always hire a nurse," Gerald lied, crossing his fingers.

"Okay Dad, let me think about it."

"Okay sweetie I'll speak to you later in the week. Lots of love to you, Lucy."

"You too Dad, love you loads." Lucy ended the call and stared into space. Perhaps it was a good idea to get away for a while, spend some time with her dad. She would see what Mr Devine had to say first.

The following Friday evening Lucy sat at the dining room table and stared at her mobile. She was still undecided about what to do - should she go and stay with her dad, or wait here hoping for Simon to come home? She realised that thinking about him coming back was ridiculous, there was no way he would leave Jennifer 'bloody bitch face' Grayson now that she was pregnant. He was an honourable man, she thought, then realised if he'd been honourable he wouldn't have shagged Jennifer 'bloody bitch face' Grayson in the first place. She sighed deeply and spun her phone around on the table top. She thought back to Mr Devine, and the advice he gave her. He had been kind and sympathetic to Lucy's situation and explained what her options were: buy Simon out, let Simon buy her out, or sell the property. One thing that he had insisted was that Lucy should take her time to make her decision, particularly as neither Simon nor his solicitor had contacted her. One thing that he said he would do immediately was to contact Andrew to insist Simon continue to pay for the mortgage, assuming Simon was still using Andrew as his solicitor as they had no forwarding address for him. He also advised Lucy to contact the bank and let them know what the situation was. She needed to try to make sure that she continued with the mortgage payments if Simon stopped. Lucy had sighed with relief, at least she wasn't going to be made homeless, and she had enough money from what Grandpa had left her to pay the mortgage for a year if necessary.

Mr Devine had been a genuinely lovely man, very attractive too, and obviously madly in love with his beautiful wife, and his baby boy. Lucy had spotted a couple of photographs on his desk, one of a very pretty, dark-haired woman kissing an extremely cute baby, the other a really happy picture of a wedding. His wife and a blonde woman appeared to be bridesmaids and Mr Devine and another man were hugging them closely while all of them were smiling widely, and laughing, with the bride and groom. They were such happy pictures that Lucy couldn't help but comment on what a lovely family he had. Mr Devine had almost burst with pride as he told her that Billy was six months old, with his mother's gorgeous looks. Lucy had left his office almost in tears, inexplicably because she was so happy that Mr Devine seemed happy.

Her thoughts went back to her decision, Lucy's phone continued to spin, more slowly now. She slammed her hand down on it. She'd decided. She was going to stay with her dad. The house would be okay for a few weeks. Brian next door would mow the lawn, pick the post up and generally keep an eye on the place for her, and if Simon did cruelly move in with Jennifer then she would come home and bloody well move in with them. Lucy laughed weakly at the thought, it was great being brave when you have a large gin inside you and the worst-case scenario hasn't happened, but she knew, deep down that she would never be able to watch Simon with Jennifer and their child, so it was a ridiculous idea to contemplate. She picked up her phone, and pressed the picture of a smiling Gerald and Richard looking up at her.

"Hello, Gerald Falmer."

"Hi, Dad, it's me. You'd best get Richard to make up the spare room I'm coming to stay for a while.

Chapter 3

The following Tuesday Lucy pulled onto the gravelled drive of her father and Richard's home, and she smiled for the first time in days. She loved this house, and the fact that her dad was there to give her a big cuddle made her just a little happy; if she could actually be truly happy ever again. As she got out of the car the large black front door burst open, and Richard came bounding out to greet her.

"Lucy sweetheart," he called, his arms open wide. "God, we're so glad you decided to come. Your dad has been like an excited puppy all day waiting for you. How was your journey?" he asked, pulling her into a tight embrace.

"Fine thanks Richard. I stopped for about half an hour at Lancaster, so it wasn't too bad. How are you anyway? Excited about your trip I'll bet?" She hugged her 'step-father' back and kissed him on his rosy cheek. Like her father, Richard was tall with steel grey hair, but he had a goatee beard and, like Gerald, he insisted on wearing a shirt and tie daily; neither of them did casual.

"I am, and I'm not," he sighed. "I don't want to leave your dad but can't wait to see Wendy, my sister. Anyway come on, come inside and let's get you settled."

As she walked through the door, Lucy suddenly felt a sense of calm and security. The smell of cinnamon mixed with fresh flowers floated through the air, and the cloud that had hung over her for the last two weeks or so lifted slightly. As she stood in the hallway Lucy could see into the kitchen, she smiled as there, bubbling away on the hob, was a pan of Gerald's famous mulled wine, his favourite tipple that was never limited to just Christmastime. As she recalled many drunken sessions courtesy of the aforementioned wine, she heard Gerald's voice calling.

"Lucy I'm in here, come on hurry up."

Lucy turned and ran into the lounge and threw herself at Gerald, who was sitting on the overstuffed floral sofa with his leg resting on a foot stool. "Oh Dad," she cried burying her face into Gerald's tank top. "I've missed you so much."

"Oh sweetheart, I'm so glad you're here at last. Come on sit down next to me and tell me all about it while Richard gets you a lovely glass of mulled wine."

Three hours later, after a meal of homemade bread, ham and olives and more mulled wine, Lucy felt decidedly more relaxed. She was curled up on the huge love seat next to the unlit fire while Richard and Gerald lolled tipsily on the sofa. Both were listening intently to her tales of woe.

"So, what does this Jennifer 'bloody cow face' Grayson look like?" Richard asked Lucy, before popping another olive into his mouth.

"Bitch face Richard, get it right," Gerald corrected.

"Sorry, what does Jennifer 'bloody bitch face' Grayson look like?" Richard repeated the question.

"That's the trouble," sighed Lucy. "She's beautiful." She took another sip of mulled wine. "She has this bloody hair thing going on, you know it hangs in luxurious dark waves down her back. Admittedly, it's all sewn to her sodding scalp, but it's beautiful. In fact, I don't think there is much about her that is real. I've only met her once, at a Christmas party, and she was wearing an amazing electric blue dress that was practically cut to the navel at the front, and then down to the top of her bottom at the back. You could virtually see her bum crack." Lucy shook her head, trying to eliminate pictures of Jennifer from her mind. "She has acrylic nails, *and* her tits have been done, they're definitely blow ups."

"How do you know that?" Gerald smiled at his daughter, who was finally starting to lose her frown.

"Because, when she was dancing they didn't move Dad. They were totally still, actually nothing from her tits up moved she's had so much work done."

"Really, or are you just feeling a tad bitchy?" Gerald asked.

"Of course I feel bitchy, but it's still the truth. She's nothing like me at all. I mean I like to look after myself, but she is primped to perfection. I bet she never has bed hair or morning breath."

"Lucy you are naturally beautiful. You don't need to primp yourself as you call it." Gerald smiled, looking lovingly at his daughter's very long, russet coloured hair, deep green eyes, and the tiny smattering of freckles over her nose.

"Huh, you have to say that you're my dad. I'm a ginge that goes very frizzy in the rain and extremely freckly in the sun. She's just perfect Dad."

"If she's so image conscious it begs the question why she allowed herself to get pregnant, surely it's going to ruin her figure." Richard commented as he plumped the cushion under Gerald's leg.

"Oh she'll just have bloody surgery to have the fat removed." Lucy waved a hand at Richard dismissively. "The rumour at the Christmas party was she'd had some of her back teeth removed, to make it look like she had high cheekbones, but I don't know how true that was."

"Well she sounds positively horrible," said Gerald, smiling at Lucy warmly. "If Simon can't see how plastic she is then it's his hard luck and dare I say it, you may find that you're better off without him." He quickly continued, anxious not to create a pause for Lucy to fill with crying. "What do you plan to do for the next six weeks?"

"Well, I planned to look after you of course! That's why I came, that's why you wanted me here, isn't it?" Lucy frowned at Gerald. Over the last few hours, she'd noticed that he'd been perfectly capable of getting himself around the house with his crutches. He even helped Richard put the supper together; obviously not so disabled by his broken leg.

Gerald grimaced as he looked at Lucy. "I may have got you here under some slight pretence. Please don't be cross," he exclaimed, noticing the frown on his daughter's face. "I wanted to see you so much, and I knew that Annabelle would be worse than useless probably. With Sophie in South Africa, I didn't want to put the entire burden on Sarah!"

"Oh I'm a burden am I?" Lucy tried to sound annoyed but was smiling. "Dad, of course I'm not cross. I had an inkling when you first asked me to come. I understand why you did it, and I'm glad you did because I do feel much calmer in the few hours that I've been here."

"Well thank God for that," Richard announced. "I for one thought that'd you'd hit the roof, but your dad was adamant that you should come and stay, however, I'm glad you have my darling girl."

"Thanks Richard, but as for what I'm going to do while I'm here, well I have no idea. I'm obviously not needed to baby sit Dad all day, so I'll need something to fill my time."

"I've been thinking about that," Gerald said, his eyes bright with anticipation. "You know that Richard works part time at the Doctors surgery, well Gladys was going to fill in for him, but her sister Enid has got shingles, which means that Gladys needs to look after her resulting in there being no one to cover for Richard, so how about you do it?"

"Me? Dad what do I know about working in a doctor's surgery? I'm an ex-primary school teacher, who volunteers in a charity shop, for goodness sake."

"Believe me Lucy, the differences between children and patients are probably minimal." Richard laughed.

"What if I cock it up? It won't look good on you Richard." Lucy wasn't entirely certain she wanted to spend her time here working. Plus she wasn't quite sure that she felt like talking to strangers just yet.

"Well we've spoken to the practice manager, Elspeth, and she suggested that if you go in with me for a couple of hours, Callie, the full time receptionist, will show you the ropes." Richard enthused. "You would only be working three mornings, Monday to Wednesday from eight until midday. Margery the other part time receptionist works the other days, and the doctors and staff are lovely. You'll fit right in, darling." Richard held his breath, hopeful that Lucy would agree as she needed to be distracted for a while.

"Well you've got this all worked out haven't you?" Lucy smiled as Gerald and Richard both nodded enthusiastically. "Okay, on one condition, if it all turns out horribly wrong you owe me a pair of diamond earrings." Lucy wanted a pair since she'd been a child, and it was a long term joke between them that she'd never been a good enough daughter for Gerald to buy her any.

Gerald reached across and held out his hand. "Okay, let's shake on it. If your time here and working at the surgery turns out to be a disaster, one pair of diamond earrings is yours. Deal?"

"Deal." Lucy agreed and shook his hand. "Okay, well I'm off to bed that mulled wine has made me extremely sleepy." Lucy stood up and kissed her father and Richard tenderly on their cheeks.

"Night, sweetheart and hopefully sleep well," called Gerald as Lucy disappeared from the room.

"Well, you pulled that one off." Richard leaned across and took Gerald's hand. "I didn't think that she'd go for it."

"I know, but if it keeps her occupied and stops her thinking of Simon and Jennifer 'bloody bitch face' Grayson, then it will be worth it. I can't stand the thought of her being so sad. I just had to get her away from there."

"I know Gerald. The main thing is she's here now, so let's hope it helps."

Chapter 4

On the night that she arrived at her father's house, Lucy slept more soundly than she had in weeks. There were no terrible dreams about Simon, or tossing and turning endlessly trying to get to sleep. She got into the huge, comfy, king-sized bed and was fast asleep within ten minutes. The following morning she didn't wake until gone nine, and when she did she felt calm and rested. As she lay staring at the ceiling for a few minutes, Lucy heard her father and Richard pottering around downstairs. The smell of cooking bacon and rich coffee wafted under the bedroom door. Lucy lowered her feet onto the deep pile carpet, stretched, stood up and took her dressing gown from the hook on the back of the door.

She padded down the oak staircase listening to Gerald and Richard talking and laughing as they prepared breakfast in the kitchen. She walked in and smiled. Lucy loved the large kitchen with its stone floor and whitewashed walls. A farmhouse table stood at one end, with seats for eight people, and on top of it, a china jug full of wild flowers. Shaker style cupboards were painted a beautiful dove grey, and at the vast patio doors - now opened on to the large, flower filled garden - hung a thick, rich grey fabric, smattered with sprigs of lilac wisteria.

"Good morning sleepy head." Richard turned around from the large range cooker, a modern replacement for the old Aga that he and Gerald could never master. "How did you sleep? I'm guessing fairly well."

"Really well thanks," said Lucy. She kissed her dad and Richard on the cheek. "Hmm something smells good." She leaned over Gerald's shoulder, looking to see what he was turning over on the grill.

"I thought that you were looking a little skinny and needed a good old Gerald Falmer breakfast." He beamed at his daughter and kissed the tip of her nose. "Now go and sit down, and I'll bring it over when it's ready, well, Richard will," he laughed, nodding at the crutch in his left hand.

"Not too much Dad, I know what your portions are like. I'll be the size of a house, by the time I go back home." Lucy sat down at the table and played with a flower in the vase. "What time did you two get up?" she asked.

"Ooh I've been up since seven. I like to go for a run early morning, but your dad got up about eight. He likes his bed more than I do." Richard came across and placed the condiments on the table. "Would you like coffee or tea, sweetheart?" he asked as he ruffled Lucy's, already messy, hair.

"Erm tea please, unless you've already made coffee then that's fine."

"No, if it's tea you want, then its tea you shall have. Listen Lucy, I'm working the afternoon shift just for today, with you being here, so we thought that maybe you'd like to come into work with me. I could introduce you to Callie, in readiness for your first day on Monday. We could spend an hour meeting everyone, and then…well this magnificent town of ours is your oyster, how does that sound?" Richard put a couple of tea bags into a small teapot for one.

"Yes that's fine Richard. So, what is Callie like, is she a typical doctor's receptionist then?"

Gerald laughed over at the cooker. "What, an old dragon that thinks she's a doctor, without the training?"

"Oi cheeky," Richard scolded. "I'm a doctor's receptionist don't forget. No, she's not what you'd call "run of the mill", is she Gerald?"

"No, let's just say Callie is slightly different. Right it's all ready to eat, so if you could take the plates over Richard that would be great."

As they walked into the surgery later that day, Lucy was amazed at how modern it looked. An LED screen scrolled above the reception desk announcing the wait time for each doctor, intermittently beeping and displaying the name of the next patient. The waiting area in front of the reception was a series of chairs around low, round tables loaded with magazines. In a corner was a play area for children with a toy kitchen and collection of toys and books. The floor was a gleaming hard wood, covered with a large, multi-coloured, striped woollen rug. A percolator bubbled away in the corner, making strong, fresh coffee. Behind the reception desk, Lucy could see what looked like a state-of-the-art computer system. There was a lack of filing cabinets, and cardboard wallets of patient's notes that she would have expected in a small town's GP surgery.

"Callie," Richard called, moving behind the reception desk. "Where are you?"

"Here I am Rich pet, here I am."

Suddenly, from a door at the back a vision of unconventionality appeared, gleaming broadly and holding her arms out to Richard.

Callie's bleached blond hair was tied up on the top of her head with a massive pink bow, tendrils of hair escaping down the sides and at the back. She wore enormous, round, pink, spectacles, bright pink lipstick and a white, cotton, gypsy dress with a huge pink bow at its waist, the elasticated shoulders of which were pulled down to reveal pink bra straps. Lucy surveyed her carefully taking in every inch of Callie's eccentricity, right down to the pink clogs on her feet.

"Why Rich pet, is this the lovely Lucy I've heard so much about?" she asked in a broad, Geordie accent. She hugged Richard to her large bosom.

"Yes," Richard mumbled, trying to extract himself from Callie's cleavage. "Lucy meet Callie Robertson."

"Hi Callie," Lucy uttered, holding out her hand to Callie.

"Hey pet there's no standing on ceremony here. We don't do that shaking hands clart. Come on, give us a hug."

Then it was Lucy's turn to be engulfed into Callie's chest. She looked over Callie's shoulder to Richard and mouthed the word "clart" quizzically.

"It basically means shit around here," he answered.

"Why pet you need some fattening up, I reckon, don't you Rich?" asked Callie holding Lucy out in front of her. "I know you're broken-hearted love but don't let the bastard turn you into a skinny minnie. You need to show him what he's missing. My cue to put the kettle on and cut some cake, I'll be back in a tick pet." With that, she disappeared through the door that she'd first appeared at.

"And that my dear is Callie." Richard smiled at Lucy and rubbed her arm gently. "She's an absolute darling, and you will get used to her."

"So, she knows why I'm here?" Lucy frowned at Richard. "Does the whole town know?"

"I can't lie to you Luce if Callie knows, then possibly most of the patients do. However, I didn't tell her on purpose. She heard me talking to your dad, when he came in for his check-up with Dr Bryce. Sorry sweetheart, but it was an accident."

"It's okay Richard. It's not that I'm ashamed of it. Well I suppose I am a little, but I just don't want to have to keep reliving it all the time. God I hate Simon, and sodding Jennifer 'bloody bitch face' Grayson!"

"I know, but just try to forget about them for a while, and maybe life won't be so bad here."

Lucy smiled tenderly at Richard, glad that her dad has found someone so kind and compassionate. "I'll try Richard, I really will."

"Well while Callie is making some tea, I'll introduce you to the rest of the staff. Dorothy the cleaner should be in and so should Dr Bryce, Dr Kindler and Nurse Gaffney. Elspeth, the Practice Manager, is off this week, and Margery you will probably meet next week. How does that sound?"

"Erm.... Okay... Yes... Fine." Lucy muttered hesitantly. She suddenly felt quite shy about meeting a lot of new people, but it had to be done, and she was sure that they'd all be very kind and pleasant.

"Callie," Richard called through the door at the back of the reception. "I'm just going to give Lucy a guided tour, give me a shout if it gets busy."

Lucy looked around the waiting area where one man sat reading a woman's magazine - this must be the healthiest town in the country she thought.

"Right Luce, Dr Kindler first, he's an absolute sweetie, a little archaic in his ways but the old patients love him." Off Richard trotted with Lucy following closely behind.

After meeting the staff, except for Dr Bryce, who was with a patient, Lucy felt a lot more at ease. Everyone seemed lovely and, as she had hoped, very kind. Lucy had watched in awe as Ellen Gaffney, the practice nurse, had cajoled a young child who was adamant that they weren't having an injection. Ellen distracted the small boy with a "knock, knock" joke while she jabbed him with the needle, all finished before she'd even reached the punch line. Lucy realised that despite being a little gruff around the edges, she was, in fact, a very kind and experienced nurse whom she knew she was going to like. Dorothy, the cleaner was just as pleasant, although a bit scatty. She had cleaned the same window three times while chatting to Richard and Lucy, mainly about her varicose veins.

"Callie, is Dr Bryce free yet?" Richard asked, manoeuvring his way back around the reception desk.

"Anytime now. Mrs Bright has been in for twenty minutes already." Callie grinned widely at Richard, who in turn grinned back.

"Blimey she's obviously come up with something special today if she's managed twenty minutes in there. Mrs Bright has a thing for Dr Bryce," Richard explained to Lucy. "She comes in at least twice a week with some ailment or other, insisting on only seeing him."

"He's pretty tasty you see pet." Callie's eyes narrowed, and her lips pursed as she thought of Dr Bryce.

"Oh right," said Lucy, not really sure how to respond. She couldn't care less whether he did his surgery in the buff every day. Simon was all she wanted, and she knew she was never going to get him back, so men were off the agenda for the foreseeable future.

"Oh here she is now. Okay Mrs Bright all sorted are you?" Callie smiled warmly at the rather busty blonde woman who had just appeared from the corridor leading to the consulting rooms. "Another appointment pet, or has Dr Bryce sorted you out, and seen to you good and proper this time?"

Richard almost spat his tea across the reception desk, as Callie poked his shin with her foot.

"No, I don't need another appointment thank you. Dr Bryce feels that I need to give it a week or two, and see how I feel." Mrs Bright shook her head despondently. "I'll ring if I feel any worse," she said, turning to leave.

"Right pet no problem. You take care then."

Callie and Richard burst out laughing as soon as the large glass door swung shut behind Mrs Bright.

"Christ when is the poor woman going to realise he's not bloody interested in her? She's got to be about sixty, yet thinks a lovely young man like Dr Bryce would fancy her.

Eeeh I don't know! Some women just never know when to give up, do they?" Callie shook her head as she punched something into the computer.

"And who would that be you're talking about then Callie?" a voice asked.

Lucy, who was leaning against the reception desk, turned to see who was speaking. If she hadn't been using it for support, she may well have fallen over. Standing in front of Lucy was the most beautiful man she had ever seen. Dr Bryce smiled enigmatically at them, long lashed, dark-brown eyes shining brightly beneath a dark fringe. Lucy felt a thunderbolt in the pit of her stomach. Her heart began to beat a thudding rhumba in her chest, and embarrassingly she felt an excited twitch in her groin. It was ridiculous, only moments ago she'd been grieving for the loss of her philandering husband, whom she loved more than life itself, then this ludicrously handsome, sexy man appears, and she feels every nerve ending in her body reacting to him.

"You must be Lucy?" he asked, holding out his tanned hand.

Lucy just stopped herself from licking her lips as she took it and shook it gently. Even his hands were sexy, and thoughts of them all over her body made her skin tingle as a heat swept over her.

"Hello," she mumbled, acutely aware that her breast was heaving rapidly if a size 34B breast could heave. It was mostly the padding of her bra that was heaving if she were honest.

"So you're going to help us out while Richard is off on his holiday, is that right?" Dr Bryce asked as he nodded towards Richard. "Well, it will be nice to have a new face around, not that we won't miss Richard because we will, won't we, Callie?"

"Yes pet we will," Callie replied, who despite her earlier description of Dr Bryce, now seemed unaware of his magnetism. She simply carried on typing at the computer.

Richard, who had noticed Lucy's reaction to the doctor, smiled behind his mug of tea. He watched Lucy, who watched Dr Bryce as he joined them behind the desk.

Lucy tried not to stare as the doctor went to a spare computer and stooped over it, one hand resting on the desk as the other typed away on the keyboard. His dark charcoal trousers, which rested on narrow hips, strained slightly against an obviously tight bottom as he leaned over. His pure white shirt pulled across his back as he stretched to retrieve a file close to the computer. Lucy could clearly make out the two lines of muscles, either side of his spine. His shirt sleeves rolled up to the elbows, revealed tanned forearms, a thin leather band on one wrist and a heavy silver watch on the other. Lucy shuddered involuntarily as he ran a hand across his dark hair, cut short on the sides and slightly longer on top.

He suddenly turned to face her and placed his hands on his hips, his shirt pulling across his wide, taught chest. "Right, I'm off out now. I've got a few house calls to make. It's been nice to meet you Lucy, and I look forward to working with you over the next few weeks." He now turned to Richard. "Have a great time Richard, and don't forget to use plenty of sunscreen, that Australian sun is more powerful than you think."

"I will Dr Bryce, don't worry." Richard smiled and placed a hand on the doctor's shoulder.

"Good, that's excellent. Callie you can get me on my mobile if you need me, otherwise I'll see you tomorrow. Enjoy the rest of your day everyone." With that, he disappeared back down the corridor to his consulting room.

As Ed Bryce shut his consulting room door behind him, he let out a deep breath. Richard hadn't told him how beautiful his step-daughter was. Those gorgeous green eyes and that luscious russet coloured hair that flowed down her back. God, there was also the overpowering desire to smell her, and to kiss those freckles on her nose. He'd had to pretend to put some notes on the computer, just to stop him from doing either. Ed hadn't thought it possible to feel such a physical reaction to someone in the space of a five-minute meeting, but the slight strain in his trousers told him that Lucy had definitely affected him. When Richard told him about Lucy and her problems he'd expected that she would be introverted and dowdy, feeling deeply sorry for herself. However, she seemed anything but that. Admittedly she'd only said hello, but her eyes were bright, and to Ed it looked like anger behind them, not sorrow, and that excited him. And those breasts, and long legs in those skinny jeans, they were…bloody hell. What was he thinking? This woman had been dumped on from a great height by her husband, and here he was imagining what she would look like with no clothes on. Ed shook his head and pulled at his trousers to try and loosen his crotch. He desperately tried not to think about what he would like to do with her, should he ever have the pleasure of seeing her without any clothes on. Ed collected his bag and left the surgery through the back door, making a pact with himself to steer clear of Lucy. The last thing he needed was a relationship, least of all with a woman who was probably hurt and angry; it could be a recipe for disaster.

"So," Richard said to a rather flushed looking Lucy. "That's Dr Bryce, what do you think?" He looked at her intently, he wasn't sure that a man was what Lucy needed right now, but the attraction between the two of them had been palpable. Lucy was obviously flustered, and he'd worked with Ed long enough to know when he was feeling uncomfortable, plus he'd seen the rubbish that Ed was entering on the computer and was pretty sure that they didn't have a new patient called "Mr Lance Allot".

"He seems very nice," Lucy replied, lowering her head so that neither Richard nor Callie could see her blushing.

"Yes he is. He's worked here about three years now. He's thirty-four and single. He's a local man. His family still lives in the area, but he lived in Manchester for a while." Richard tidied up the desk, not looking at Lucy as he spoke.

"Oh right." She wasn't sure what else to say. She didn't want to appear to care, but she couldn't ignore how he'd made her feel.

Lucy couldn't recall Simon, her husband whom she'd had a child with and given a vow to love forever, making her feel that way when they'd first met. How was it possible that a man, to whom she'd only said hello and met for five minutes, could make her feel so alive, especially when the love of her life had recently destroyed her heart? Perhaps it was simply nature's way of making her feel good about herself again. It was just a sexual attraction. There was no denying he was a handsome man, but he wasn't Simon, and it was Simon that she wanted, it was her old life that she wanted back, but Lucy couldn't help thinking how delicious it would be to find out whether Dr Bryce really was as good as he looked.

Chapter 5

At eight o'clock, tired after a long house call waiting for Social Services to assess one of his patients, Ed pulled up on his drive and couldn't help but think about Lucy once more. Thoughts of her had buzzed through his mind all afternoon. He'd tried to think of other things like football or beer, but a picture of Lucy, with her beautiful green eyes, would invade his thoughts every time. He had never felt such a reaction before, not even Katie had made him feel like that. Katie whom he'd thought had loved him as much as he'd loved her, but she obviously hadn't and had broken his heart.

"Hi darling." A pretty silver-haired lady dressed in trousers and t-shirt, standing on tiptoe watering a hanging basket next to the front door, greeted Ed with a large smile.

Ed got out of his car and advanced towards her, pulling a hand through his already messy hair. "Hi Mum, sorry I'm late. Are you okay?"

"I'm okay thanks dear, apart from the fact that your bloody father is driving me mad, as usual. For some unknown reason, he decided that he wanted to mow your lawn today, a pretty normal activity you might think except that he wanted to do it nude!" Georgina Bryce shook her head and tried not to smile.

"What? Totally nude?" Ed asked, laughing at the thought. "Why on earth would he want to do that?"

"It's your father Ed, why does he do anything? Anyway come on in dinner is almost ready. I thought that we'd stay and eat with you as you were late getting back. You can tell us how your day has been over dinner."

Ed followed Georgina into the house, and wondered whether he *could* talk about his day without sounding like a sex mad pervert.

"Evening Dad," he said as he met his father coming down the stairs. "What's this I've heard about you naked mowing?"

Jack Bryce shrugged his shoulders and screwed his face up as Georgina disappeared down the hall. "It was a beautiful day, and I didn't want to get all hot and sweaty, so what's wrong with that? I knew she'd have to tell you. The mafia leaves a horse's head in the bed of people like her - bloody grass!"

"I heard that," Georgina shouted from the kitchen.

"Ears like a bloody bat as well." Jack hugged his son. "Did you have a good day Ed, and did you encounter any interesting diseases that you can tell us about over dinner?"

"No sorry Dad, although a patient did have to have a boil lanced today." Ed put his doctor's bag down on the floor and placed his foot on the bottom stair. "I'm just going upstairs but when I come down I'll tell you about that if you like, although maybe not if Mum's made custard for pudding."

"Ooh I don't know it might make her custard more palatable."

"I heard that too!" Was Georgina's response.

After dinner, Ed and his parents were drinking coffee, and talking generally about their day, sitting in the lounge. It was all perfectly pleasant until Georgina changed the subject.

"Listen Ed, I think you should know I'm going to have to go to America for a couple of weeks." Georgina frowned, studying Ed's face for a reaction.

He didn't respond immediately but stared blankly into his empty coffee mug. "Why?" asked Ed, looking at his mother with narrowed eyes. "Why do you have to go?"

"Katie isn't well, and Luke needs help with the children. They have no one else out there, Ed." Georgina looked at Ed with a sad smile, willing him to understand. "He's my son too Ed, and they're my grandchildren," she pleaded.

Ed ran a hand through his hair. "I know that Mum, and don't want you to have to choose, but it still hurts. What about you, Dad, are you going too?"

Ed looked over at his father, who had now taken hold of Georgina's hand. "No son, I'm not." Jack shook his head. "I will never forgive them for what they did to you and Nate, and while I understand why your mother wants to go, I don't necessarily agree with her. Anyway, I couldn't go I've got my annual fishing trip next week."

"Have you told Nate yet?" Ed asked. His eyes were full of sadness.

"No darling, I thought I'd better tell you first, and check what you wanted me to do?" Georgina sighed.

"We'll tell him you're going on holiday. I don't want him to know that you're going to see his mother." Ed coughed and looked away, trying to hide the tears that were stinging his eyes. Nate, his beautiful six-year-old son, was his life, and he hated the thought of anyone or anything hurting him as his mother Katie had.

*

Ed and Katie had met when Ed was doing his residency in Manchester. Katie was in a bar that Ed and his work colleagues frequented after work, she had slipped in her high heels, spilling a sickly looking red cocktail all over Ed. She'd apologised profusely and offered to buy him a drink, but as Ed was on his way home after a long day, he'd suggested that she met him there the following evening instead. Katie (who had spilt the drink over Ed on purpose – she'd spotted him the week before and found him extremely sexy) agreed. They met up the following night, and then the next three nights, and that was it for Ed. Katie was the one that he wanted to spend the rest of his life with. They married within eight months, when Katie fell pregnant with Nate. It hadn't been part of their plan so soon, but Ed loved Katie and couldn't have been happier. And they were happy, for nearly two years until Luke, Ed's brother, came to stay during the summer while he tried to get an English football club to sign him. Luke was a semi-professional footballer in the American minor leagues, and was dangerous and exciting, everything that Ed wasn't, everything that Ed couldn't be because he was still studying to become a GP. Two months into Luke's visit Ed's world came crashing down around him. Nate was rushed into the hospital with suspected meningitis. When Ed ran on to the ward to see Nate, the nurse told Ed that his brother and sister-in-law were waiting in the family room. Ed thought it was strange, but figured the nurse had just misunderstood the relationship between Katie and Luke. He bounded in expecting to have to comfort his wife, only to find his brother had beaten him to it. Ed's son was desperately ill, and his wife was kissing his brother in the next room.

Ed hadn't seen either of them since Katie absconded to America with Luke the following day, leaving her dangerously sick son behind. Fortunately, Nate didn't have meningitis, just a viral infection, but it took nearly a month for him to recover, which was when Georgina stepped in to help. It was subsequently decided that Ed and Nate would move to live with his parents in their large detached house, in County Durham. Then a year later, once he'd qualified as a GP, Ed joined the town's practice and bought a house of his own for him and Nate.

It was a horrible time in Ed's life, and if he hadn't had to concentrate on getting Nate better, as well as working hard to provide for them both, Ed thought that he would have been happy to throw himself under a bus. He'd considered going to America to try to win Katie back but what was the point. If she could leave her young son while he was so ill, Ed patently had nothing to offer that would change her mind. After a while, Ed's sorrow turned to hatred of both his wife and his brother. All he knew now was that they were married and had three-year-old twins, Amelia and Louie. Nate didn't suffer too much from Katie's desertion. He'd cried for her at first, but after a month in the hospital under the care of nurses, Ed and Georgina, he soon stopped, and now never asked whether Mummy was coming to visit this year.

*

"Ed," Georgina broke Ed's thoughts. "I am sorry you know, but Luke asked for my help."

"It's okay Mum," Ed softened now. He knew none of this was her fault. "I'll need to get some help with Nate for after school though, especially as Dad won't be here either."

"I can cancel my trip if that would help?" Jack leaned forward and touched Ed's knee gently.

"God no, don't be daft Dad. I can drop him off at the breakfast club just after eight and then get someone to pick him up from school and stay with him until I get home at five. I'm sure Callie can rearrange my appointments and Dr Kindler won't mind if I juggle my hours a little."

"But who are you going to ask to help after school?" Georgina asked. "Oh, I'd better tell Luke that I can't go, he did rather drop it on me."

"No Mum it's OK, I'll ask Callie in the morning. She knows everyone and everything in this town. She's bound to come up with someone. I can always ask Ollie's mum if she'll take him home for tea for a couple of nights," Ed thought aloud and then frowned. "Argh no I can't. His little sister's got the mumps, so Ollie is staying with his grandmother. Having Nate as well wouldn't be fair on her. Not to worry I'll sort something. Anyway, I'd better go up and check that he's okay. I promised that I'd tuck him in, won't be long." Ed rubbed his tired eyes and wearily made his way upstairs.

"Oh Jack I feel awful," Georgina sighed, after a few minutes.

"Don't be silly, it's Luke and Katie who should feel awful. Ed's really suffered over what they did to him, in fact, I think Luke's betrayal hurt him more than Katie's because, let's face it Georgina, how *do* you get over your twin brother running off with your wife?"

Georgina shook her head. "I know Jack, but Luke's my son too, and he needs my help."

Chapter 6

The following Monday morning Lucy walked along the high street towards her new place of work, with a stomach that was crowded with butterflies. The thought of making a total mess of the job was making Lucy nervous, but she was especially jittery about seeing Dr Bryce again. She hadn't stopped thinking about the effect that he'd had on her all weekend, and on Saturday night, she'd even had an erotic dream about him. She'd woken up all hot and sweaty and blushing profusely. It was extremely filthy. How could this be happening, she was supposed to be heartbroken and sad, not feeling like a nubile teenager lusting after the hottest boy in town? As she rounded the corner, the butterflies in her stomach did a decidedly more energetic flying routine. On the car park were three cars; a bright pink Fiat Uno, and two identical large saloons, both doctors were evidently in.

"Morning pet," Callie called as Lucy walked through the glass door. "Did Richard get off okay, and are you all set and ready to go?"

Lucy nodded and placed a hand on her stomach. "Yes he did thanks. I think I'm ready, but I'm a little nervous though." She smiled weakly at Callie, who today was dressed in an off-the-shoulder pink jumper and multi-coloured leggings with yellow wedge sandals.

"Hey there's no need to worry, everyone here is lovely, not normal mind, but lovely. Now listen, before we start is there anything else you want to ask? I think you got the computer part down to a tee last week pet, so I don't see any problems there."

Lucy shook her head. "No, I think I'm fine, as long as you don't mind me asking questions."

"Why no, of course not pet. Okay, so we're all set for when the hordes arrive, however before then I want to ask you something?" Callie smiled at Lucy and rubbed her arm gently.

"Okay, what is it?" she asked warily.

"I hope you don't think I've spoken out of turn, but the thing is Dr Bryce has a little problem that he needs sorting out, and I thought of you."

Lucy thought of a whole host of problems that she'd love to sort out for Dr Bryce, which made her hot and flustered. Luckily, Callie was sorting the post and didn't appear to see the new crimson complexion that Lucy was now sporting.

"What sort of problem?" asked Lucy, fanning herself.

Callie now turned to face her. "I don't know whether Richard mentioned, but Dr Bryce has a little boy, Nate. He's six and absolutely adorable, a mini version of Dr Bryce, really."

Lucy shook her head. "No, Richard didn't say," she almost growled. But then why would he, she thought, and what business was it of hers?

Oh well, even if she was interested in fulfilling any of the fantasies that she'd suddenly started having, Dr Bryce was a definite no-go area now. He had a child and an ex-wife or ex-partner, and besides, her feelings for Dr Bryce were probably because of her need for physical contact. She loved Simon.

"Oh perhaps he forgot," Callie said breaking Lucy's thoughts. "Anyway, his mum helps him to look after Nate, but she's going away for a couple of weeks. So he needs some help, after school mainly, and he asked if I could think of anyone and well, I thought of you." Callie beamed proudly, both arms crossed over her ample bosom.

"Me!" Lucy gasped. "I don't even know him. Why would you suggest me? I could be a murderer for all he knows, and what about his wife or partner or whatever the child's mother is can't she have him…God she's not dead is she?" Lucy put a hand to her mouth in horror.

Callie smiled and shook her head. "No pet, she's not dead, although I reckon Dr Bryce had wished her so on many an occasion. No, she's not around, she left him when Nate was a toddler and hasn't been back since, not even to see Nate. He doesn't talk about what happened. I mean, I know most things around here, but I canna get that out of him under any circumstances. Anyway, he knows you're no murderer, you must have been checked you're a teacher for goodness sake."

"Ex-teacher," Lucy corrected. "I don't think I can Callie, it's a lot of responsibility. I don't know him very well, and what if Nate didn't like me? So, I'm sorry I can't do it." Lucy shook her head vigorously.

"He'll pay you," Callie insisted. "And it's just for a couple of weeks, two hours at most after school. He's changing his surgery hours to make sure you don't have to work too late. I'll tell him yes shall I?"

"Callie no, I can't!"

"Eeeh Lucy pet, there's no such word as can't. I think it'll do you good to keep your mind off things, and let's face it, you might get to spend some time alone with Dr Bryce." Callie grinned wickedly and shivered. "Ooh how lovely."

Time alone with Dr Bryce was exactly what Lucy was afraid of. He made her tingly all over and have naughty thoughts when she was supposed to be broken hearted. How could she possibly think those things about someone when she was so devastated by the breakdown of her marriage? Then there was the fact that a child was involved. She hadn't shied away from children since Lottie died. Far from it, she'd thrown herself into her role of Godmother to Noah and Milo wholeheartedly. She had been a teacher for goodness sake, but being responsible for a child on a one to one basis, for no matter how short a time, was a different thing altogether. What if she started to care for him, especially as his mother wasn't around? What if something happened to him, and she blamed herself, just as she'd initially done with Lottie?

"Right, I'll go and tell him then." Callie didn't even pause to allow Lucy to protest.

"Callie, you can't bulldoze me into doing this. I don't want to," Lucy cried pulling Callie back by her arm.

"What exactly are you afraid of pet?" Callie's smile was kind as she gently squeezed Lucy's hand.

How could she explain all the things she was fearful of? How Dr Bryce made her feel after one short meeting, or that she may grow attached to his child, or perhaps her marriage hadn't actually meant that much if she kept imagining herself in Dr Bryce's arms.

"There you go," said Callie, taking Lucy's silence as positive. "Nothing. I'll let him know that he has a new part time nanny for a couple of weeks."

Callie left Lucy opening and closing her mouth as she wondered whether Callie was either deaf, obtuse or both.

"Oh…erm…well that's great Callie, thanks. I guess you'd better ask Lucy to come in so I can talk it through with her." Ed, blushing slightly, looked at his computer screen. "My first patient isn't due for a half hour."

"Okay then pet, I'll send her in." Callie disappeared taking Ed's empty coffee mug with her.

Ed had asked Callie for her help on finding someone to look after Nate, but never in a million years had he expected her to suggest Lucy; Lucy of the pert breasts and peach of a bottom. He'd tried to say he hardly knew her, but as Callie had pointed out, she must have been CRB checked as she had been a teacher, and her afternoons were free, so there was no problem. There was a problem though; he hadn't stopped thinking about her since he'd met her last week. Not all the time, but certainly when he was alone in his king-size bed at night. It was a while since he'd had a woman in his bed. Granted, when he'd first moved back here he'd seen a handful of the local single ladies, but nothing serious. They were dinner dates mainly, a couple of them being one night stands when Nate was staying over with Georgina and Jack. The longest relationship he'd had was a girl called Hannah, whom he'd met on a medical conference about six months ago. She'd lasted the whole week of the conference, but they'd both agreed that her living in Portsmouth wasn't conducive to a relationship, something that Ed had been quite relieved about. Well, it was too late now Callie had sorted it all out with Lucy, so he would have to avoid spending any time alone with her, because if he did he wasn't sure he would be able to resist kissing her.

"Ah well," he said to himself. "You never know I may feel differently about her today."

A knock at the door roused Ed, and he suddenly felt extremely nervous. She was just a woman for goodness sake. He'd seen many of them naked, professionally and personally, so what was the issue.

"Erm come in," he coughed, trying to clear his throat that suddenly felt dry and constricted.

"Hi." Lucy came in slowly, her eyes not meeting Ed's. "I believe you wanted a quick chat."

Christ, Ed thought. I do feel the same way; she's gorgeous. Lucy's long slim legs and perfect little body made his heart pump faster and made him want to groan in appreciation.

"Yes, please sit down." Ed stood up until Lucy was seated.

Lucy bowed her head as she started to talk. "It's all happened a little quickly, Callie only mentioned it about ten minutes ago, so I've not had a chance to think it through yet." Lucy looked at him finally, and felt herself almost drown in his eyes.

"Oh," said Ed a little confused. "I was under the impression that she'd asked you over the weekend, and you'd had a couple of days to think about it. Don't you want to do it?" He suddenly felt disappointed, even though he knew he should avoid any contact with her.

Lucy looked at his dejected face and the pulse in his neck that she could see just see above his open collar. Her eyes moved across to his Adam's apple and she suddenly had a strong desire to kiss it. She crossed her legs rapidly, frightened that Dr Bryce might actually realise what was going on between her thighs.

"No, I'm looking forward to it," she found herself saying. "It will be great."

Ed sighed and visibly relaxed into his chair. "Great, thank you so much. It's a bit of a last minute thing I know, but my mum, who helps look after Nate, has to go away for a couple of weeks, and the people that I'd usually call on just can't help out, so you're a life saver."

"No problem," Lucy mumbled, worried at how intense this crush on Dr Bryce was becoming.

"Well I guess you should meet Nate, and obviously there are a few things we need to discuss, so how about you come over to dinner tonight, about seven, is that okay?" As soon as he'd said the words Ed wished he hadn't. What was he doing inviting her over to his house to spend time alone with him, and what if she wore that denim mini skirt that she had on now, how would he be able to take his eyes off those slim, tanned legs?

"Lovely," replied Lucy, equally as surprised that she'd agreed, and without any hesitation whatsoever.

"So all sorted then," Callie smiled at Lucy, who had just told her that she'd agreed to look after Nate; not that Lucy had any real say on the matter.

"Hmm all sorted. Who've we got first today then?" she asked, eager to change the subject.

"Oh dear it's Mr Presley." Callie shook her head. "Well we may as well drop you in at the deep end Lucy. He's due in about five minutes."

"What's so bad about Mr Presley?" Lucy asked, giggling at Callie. "I hope that you're not stitching me up here."

"Oh you'll find out pet, don't worry."

Five minutes later Lucy was watering the plants when the glass door into the practice was flung open, crashing against the wall. She looked up sharply as it was pushed open with such force that she expected to see a crack in it. There standing before her was Mr Presley - Lucy guessed that he hadn't been *born* Mr Presley but now actually thought he was *the* Mr Presley.

"Hello there liddle darlin'"

Mr Presley stood sideways on as he posed in the doorway in tight black trousers and shirt that was open to his navel. His head was slightly inclined as he looked Lucy up and down. With him, he carried a white tasselled scarf that he was using to mop his brow, but he was sweating so much that black hair dye was running down the side of his face, leaving rivulets in his deep brown foundation. On each finger were enormous coloured glass rings and stuffed down the front of his shirt was a chest wig, or at least that was what Lucy thought it was. She was mesmerised by him, silent and in awe until she looked at his feet. Elvis was wearing a pair of brown, Jesus Sandals and purple socks. It was at this point that Lucy stifled a screaming laugh. She chewed at her bottom lip and hoped desperately that Callie would rescue her. Callie, however, was watching from a safe distance behind the rubber plant on the reception desk, laughing silently; not at Mr Presley - she was used to him - but at Lucy, who was obviously trying hard to keep it together.

"I have an appointment with the Doc honey, Doc Bryce to be precise. Hey I'm a poet, and I didn't realise it." Mr Presley smiled and winked at Lucy.

Laughter tears pricked at the corner of Lucy's eyes as Mr Presley got the rhyme wrong and she turned away, aware of how unprofessional it would be to laugh in his face.

"Ooh I'm sorry," she spluttered. "I've got a really bad cough." She almost squealed.

"Hey now honey you'd best see the Doc yourself. Don't ya think?" Mr Presley moved towards her in what could only be described as a strut while at the same time marking the beat of his footsteps by clicking his fingers.

"Hmm maybe," said Lucy rushing past him towards reception. "I'm sorry Callie, can you see to Mr Presley please, I need a drink of water?" She rushed behind the desk, with her head down to hide the tears of laughter rolling down her face.

"Sure pet, hello there Mr Presley and how are you today?" Callie the epitome of professionalism smiled warmly at Mr Presley.

"Not too good honey, I'm here to see the Doc about those pesky piles of mine."

"Oh right pet; smashing. So can you confirm your full name and address for me, just for security reasons because of course, I know it's you." Callie leaned across and scuffed him playfully on the arm.

"Huh huh, sure honey. My full name is Roger Elvis Presley, 87 Cedar Road."

"That's great Mr Presley if you'd like to take a seat and wait until your name flashes up on the screen."

"Sure can honey, thank yer very much."

Lucy who had been listening from behind the staff room doorway, now exploded, imagining him curling his lip as he said it. Callie joined her and shut the door, both of them trying not to laugh too loudly.

Gradually, after a few minutes, Lucy calmed down. "Oh my God," she gasped breathlessly, "that's the funniest thing I have ever seen. Please tell me that's a joke. He doesn't actually dress and act like that all the time does he?"

Callie shook her head, wiping the tears from her face. "Oh yes pet that's Mr Presley's regular attire, unless he's going through his GI period, but you can always rely on the Jesus Sandals. His wife buys them for him."

"He's married?" Lucy asked incredulously, unsure whether anyone woman would put up with that.

"Oh aye, he's been married to Pi Pen for about three years now."

"What!" Lucy started to laugh once more. "Oh please stop it Callie, don't, I think I might wet myself. His wife isn't called Pi Pen, is she?"

Callie nodded "Yes, she is pet. He met her at an Elvis convention in Benidorm. She was performing as Jailhouse Rock Elvis."

Lucy's laughter grew louder and more intense as she thought of Mr Presley and Pi Pen. "You're joking aren't you?" she asked, breathing heavily as she paused from laughing

"No pet I'm not, it's all true. I tell you something else he went out with a Susan Boyle tribute act before he met Pi Pen."

Lucy now laughed hysterically and lost control of herself, and, unfortunately, her bladder.

Ten minutes later Ed appeared in the staff room, a huge smile upon his face.

"Well ladies, just to let you know Elvis and his piles have now left the building."

"Oh no, please don't, not again." Lucy moved toward the door desperate to get away from anymore Elvis badinage. She was exhausted from laughing so hard.

"What's that rustling sound?" Ed asked as Lucy walked past him.

"Paper knickers," informed Callie without looking up from her magazine.

Ed merely nodded and followed Lucy out. "You've been well and truly 'Presley-ed' then." He said gazing at her, thinking that she looked even more beautiful than usual with a smile upon her face.

"Yes I suppose I have," Lucy giggled and wiped her eyes again. "Is every day like this here?"

"Not every day, although working with Callie is never dull. You may actually get to like it here, in our little corner of County Durham."

"You never know," she replied looking at him from under her lashes. "There are benefits."

"Well," said Ed placing a hand on her cheek, wiping a stray laughter tear with his thumb. "You've certainly added some beauty to the place." He then disappeared, back to his consulting room.

Lucy's heart was now beating in double time as she watched his perfect bottom moving enticingly as he walked away. God, how could she have just flirted with him, and why did he have to flirt back? She couldn't possibly have supper with him now. However, the thought of it excited her more than she could imagine. She felt her cheek where he'd touched her and shivered with delight. Things were getting a little messy a little too quickly. She'd only been here an hour, and they were already flirting!

In his room, Ed was certainly feeling the heat too. As he shut the door behind him, he collapsed against it letting out a blast of air.

"Oh my God," he whispered. "What am I doing? Flirting with her and asking her to dinner, you are asking for trouble Ed Bryce, you really are."

The rest of Lucy's day passed uneventfully until, at midday, it was time for her to go home. She didn't think that she'd made too many mistakes, although eighty-year-old Mrs Platt almost got an appointment for a smear with Nurse Gaffney when she actually wanted her in growing toe nails sorted; otherwise she'd done well, so Callie said. As she let herself into the house, she wondered what her dad had been up to, the smell of baking answered her question. She went through to the kitchen, to find him checking on a fruit cake.

"Hi Dad," she said kissing him on the cheek. "You really didn't need my help did you?" She smiled and pinched his cheek.

"Well we've already established that I lied sweetie, but it's my prerogative as your dad," he replied kissing her back. "So how was your first morning then?"

"Well entertaining, to say the least. I met Mr Presley and wet my knickers."

Gerald gave an enormous belly laugh. "Hahaha, poor old Roger, how is he anyway?"

"Fine, which is better than I was. Anyway, I have a bone to pick with you, why didn't you or Richard tell me that Dr Bryce had a son?"

Gerald looked at her quizzically. "I don't know, but what difference does it make?" He now smiled at her; Richard mentioned the buzz of electricity between Lucy and Ed.

"Well none really, other than Callie has bloody well roped me in to being his sodding nanny for a couple of weeks while his mother is away on holiday."

"Oh right." Gerald turned his head to hide the smile that touched his lips. "So you didn't have a choice about the matter then?"

"Dad, you know what Callie is like, of course I didn't have a choice. Anyway, I'm going around for dinner this evening to meet his son, and talk about it." Lucy turned away, and nonchalantly picked at some grapes in the fruit bowl.

"Right," Gerald said his smile widening. "Shall I wait up or not?"

"Dad!" Lucy almost screamed, hitting him playfully on the arm. "It's nothing like that I'm still grieving for my marriage, and am certainly not interested in a relationship."

"Of course darling, I totally understand. By the way, Sarah called, so perhaps you'd better ring her before your date and discuss tactics." Gerald ducked as Lucy threw a grape at him.

"Hi Sarah it's me." Lucy greeted her friend feeling brighter than she had in weeks.

"Hiya how are you? You sound pretty perky" Sarah sighed, thankful that Lucy seemed happier than when she'd waved her off on her trip up north.

"I'm okay thanks. Covering for Richard has been fun, to say the least." For the next ten minutes Lucy regaled the tale of Mr Presley, smiling and laughing again as she recalled her morning.

"Oh dear," Sarah giggled. "He sounds hilarious, and it's good to hear you laughing. What about the people you work with, what are they like?"

"Ah well there's a tale to tell there as well."

"Oh sounds interesting."

Lucy sighed deeply and told Sarah all about Callie and then how she'd coerced her into becoming Dr Bryce's part-time nanny.

"Well it would be something else to keep you busy and keep your mind off Simon." Sarah responded cautiously. "But I can understand why you'd be annoyed at almost being forced into it, or is something else bothering you?" She was greeted with silence. "Luce, I've known you for far too many years, so I know when something is troubling you. Is it because of the little boy, are you worried about looking after him? Luce we've talked about this before and anything that happened wasn't your fault you know."

"I know Sarah, it's not that. It's just…well I feel guilty even saying it." Lucy screwed her face up and rubbed her eyes.

"Go on say it I'm not going to judge you," Sarah pleaded.

"You might when I tell you that I absolutely fancy the arse off Dr Bryce." Lucy frowned expecting Sarah to tell her to stop being stupid. She was three weeks out of a five-year marriage and shouldn't even think of another man this soon.

Sarah laughed loudly on the other end of the line. "Go Lucy!" she cried. "I was dreading what you were going to say. Oh my God Luce, what's he like?" Sarah asked excitedly.

Lucy stood up and started to pace the room. "*Sarah,* this is not a good thing you know. I've just lost the love of my life to Jennifer 'bloody bitch'…"

"Yeah, yeah I know, 'bitch face' Grayson. He's not dead Lucy, he left you for a pregnant Barbie Doll."

"Don't you think it's too soon? I shouldn't even have been looking at Dr Bryce like that, never mind be having erotic dreams about him…shit I didn't mean to tell you that bit." Lucy chewed at her bottom lip as she ran a hand through her hair.

"You didn't?" Sarah gasped. "Oh please, spill the gory details."

"No, Sarah I will not, anyway it makes me blush." Lucy now gave a little giggle.

"That dirty was it, blimey! So what does he look like, gorgeous, or is it just because he's a male and you've not encountered a trouser snake for a while?"

"Yes he's gorgeous," Lucy confirmed. "He's really stylish and has beautiful brown eyes, with these really long lashes that I would die for. From what I can tell he has a fantastic body, and even his forearms are sexy, they are tanned and just…well they're really manly and ooh just…well just sexy." Lucy shivered as she thought of Ed, before continuing with her description. "His hair is dark brown and is quite short at the side, but then longer on top, and it kind of sticks up in a messy but trendy way." Lucy let out an involuntary moan.

"So you've not studied him much?" Sarah gasped. "Christ Luce, he sounds flipping gorgeous. What's he like as a person…Lucy are you still there?"

Lucy was day-dreaming, recalling the way Dr Bryce had touched her cheek. "What, sorry, yes I'm still here. What did you say I couldn't hear you?"

"I said what's he like as a person?"

"Well, from the short time that I've spoken to him, really nice."

"Nice, nice is a crap word to describe someone you obviously want to get down and dirty with. Right, I'm going to get a cup of tea, I'll ring you back in ten minutes, and I want to know every detail."

An hour later and Lucy told Sarah everything about Dr Bryce, including their little bit of flirting earlier in the day.

"So, what should I do Sarah?"

"Honestly?"

"Yes honestly?" Lucy replied, sighing deeply.

"Okay you're right it may be too soon for a relationship, but it's not too soon for some sexy time." Sarah laughed loudly. "Seriously Luce, if you fancy him that much just damn well get it over and done with, and have sex with him to get him out of your system. He obviously fancies you too after what happened today, and if he's a single parent that hates his ex then it may be all he wants too."

"But what if I do go for it and either he's not interested, which makes me look a complete and utter dick, or I end up really falling for him and it's not what he wants, which again makes me look a complete and utter dick, or he ends up falling for me and it's not what I want, and he looks a complete and utter dick?"

"Hmm that's a lot of dicks there! Look it may be the chance you need to take, but please don't miss out on this because of Simon." Sarah's tone was soft and full of concern for Lucy.

"What, in case I think he's coming back? I don't Sarah. I know he's not coming back, but it would still feel a little like cheating on him, we *are* still married."

Sarah was silent for a few seconds. "Ben saw Simon and Jennifer yesterday, Lucy. He bumped into them in town," she said quietly.

"Oh, right, what did he say?" Lucy's heart started to beat faster. Her hands started sweating, and her stomach started churning.

"Well put it this way, she's much more pregnant than you, or I, thought."

"H-h-how far?" Lucy stammered.

"Well Ben said Simon was extremely shifty, but she let it slip that she only had a month to go. I'm sorry Lucy, but he's obviously been playing the doting husband with you while she's been sitting at home knitting booties for the last six or seven months."

Lucy felt numb as a lump grew in her throat - what a liar he'd been. "We had regular sex right up until he left, bloody good sex as well," she whispered. "He's such a fucking coward, how could he do that to me? How could he carry on with our normal life, while all the time knowing he'd be leaving me as soon as he'd grown some balls?"

"I'm sorry Lucy. I really am. If it's any consolation Ben told me that she looked a little rough, and wasn't exactly blooming."

Lucy laughed emptily, the numbness now replaced by anger. "Well one good thing has come out of knowing that, I certainly don't want him back now, the lying bastard. The cheating was bad enough, but that's one bloody whopping lie. God I hate him," she blasted.

"So," Sarah asked excitedly. "Does this mean you'll shag Dr Bryce then?"

"*No, it doesn't*. I may not care about Simon anymore, but I do care about myself, and I can't risk getting hurt again. I'll go to his house tonight and be the true professional, and not look at his arse once!" Lucy laughed with Sarah joining in.

"Well that's good, but if I were a betting woman, I'd put money on the doctor giving you an internal before the end of the summer!"

"Sarah, you are disgusting. I'm going. I've got to get ready to go out, and so I'll speak to you soon."

Sarah giggled. "Okay. But Lucy, don't forget to have a good wash - if you know what I mean?!"

"Bye Sarah." And with that, Lucy cut Sarah off, shaking her head but smiling.

Lucy had felt sick when Sarah had mentioned Simon, and Jennifer. The thought of them together, living her life, knotted her stomach and made her heart ache. Her life had obviously been a lie, seemingly for a long time if Jennifer 'bloody bitch face' Grayson was that pregnant. Lucy felt tears on her cheeks as she hugged her knees to her. She rocked backwards and forwards, thinking of how cruel Simon's actions were. He'd lied to her, he'd let her believe that he loved her and loved their lives, yet all the time was planning his future with someone else. Lucy felt a ball of torment growing in her chest as the crying got louder. Taking large gulps of air loud sobs wracked Lucy's body, until she couldn't breathe hardly. Her previous life truly was over, and she and Simon were totally finished. She wouldn't ever take him back, even if he asked, even if he begged, which she knew he never would. Gradually, her breathing returned to normal as the howling subsided until eventually she sniffed loudly and wiped her tears away with the back of her hand. Simon had broken her heart, but she had to move on somehow and maybe looking after Dr Bryce's son would help her to do that, at least it would keep her occupied. Fuck Simon, she wouldn't let him ruin her

life; she was a strong woman and would damn well prove that to everyone, not least herself.

Chapter 7

Lucy had followed Dr Bryce's directions to his house, and just before seven stood at the end of his drive, wondering whether she was able to go through with the evening. Suddenly, the choice was no longer hers to make. The front door swung open to reveal a casually dressed Dr Bryce.

"Hi," he called. "I saw you standing there and thought that perhaps you weren't sure whether this was it or not. Please, come in." He beckoned Lucy up toward him

Lucy took a big intake of breath as her feet crunched on the gravel. She looked at him steadily as she approached. His stylish work wear and leather shoes was replaced with faded jeans, a white cotton T-shirt and bare feet; even his feet were sexy, she thought. She was also glad that she'd changed into jeans, a loose white shirt and flip flops. Gerald had almost persuaded her to wear something more formal as it was practically an interview. She'd then noticed the glint in his eyes and realised he was mocking her.

"Come in and meet Nate." Dr Bryce stood aside to let Lucy in.

"Thanks Dr Bryce," she whispered.

"Call me Ed, please there's no need to be formal," Ed said smiling.

"Okay, thanks Ed." Lucy edged past, cautious not to touch him.

"If you go through to the kitchen, down the hall and to the left, Nate should be in there, finishing his dinner before bed."

Lucy felt a flutter of panic in her chest; Nate wasn't having dinner with them.

Ed watched her carefully as she moved down the hall. She looked so pretty and fresh and smelled delicious. Her hair was piled up on top of her head in a messy bun, with pieces escaping in a seductive, just got out of bed look. Her scarlet painted toe nails only added to her sexiness.

Lucy hovered in the doorway of the kitchen until Ed was behind her. She could feel the heat from his hand in the small of her back, although he wasn't actually touching her.

"Please go through," he urged. "Nate, this is Lucy, Lucy this is Nate."

If Lucy had fallen utterly in lust with Ed, she now fell utterly in love with his six-year-old son. He was the most gorgeous little boy. He had his father's colouring and equally messy hair, although it was a longer, trendy style. His cheeks were rosy pink, and his eyes were the darkest brown and round as saucers as he looked up from his spaghetti hoops on toast.

"Hi," he said, averting his eyes a little as a slight blush crept over his face.

"Hello Nate pleased to meet you." Lucy held out her hand.

Nate smiled widely now, displaying large gaps where his top teeth should be. Lucy wondered how cute one kid could be.

"Nice to meet you too," said Nate, shaking her hand. "Are you going to look after me while Nanny is on holiday?" Nate asked. His brief shyness and spaghetti hoops had been forgotten as he spun around on his stool to face Lucy. Ed put out a hand to stop him as he was in danger of spinning off. Lucy laughed and smiled warmly at Ed.

 "Yes I am if that's okay with you?" she said.

Nate thought about it for a few seconds and then did a spin back to his food. "Yep, okay."

Ed laughed and turned to Lucy. "And that is Nate; short and very sweet, in every way." Ed ruffled his son's hair. "Let's have a chat while Nate finishes his dinner, then once I've got him into bed we can eat? Is that okay?"

"Hmm," Lucy nodded. The mere ruffling of his son's hair sent her crush on Ed into orbit.

Ed led the way back to the lounge and indicated for Lucy to sit on the large leather sofa. A glass of wine was already waiting for her.

"You do like white wine, don't you?" he asked, suddenly concerned.

"Yes, I do thanks. You have a beautiful house, by the way," Lucy commented trying hard not to stare at Ed. "It's lovely and bright." Lucy looked around the lounge. The walls were clean and crisp, painted in a pale green. On the wooden floor was a thick purple rug and at the large, bay windows were purple and green striped blinds. Apart from a couple of framed photographs of Ed and Nate, and a hurricane lamp on top of the fireplace, there were no womanly touches to the room.

"Yes, we like it," Ed said. We've been here, oh, about three years now, I guess. We lived with my parents for a while, when I first came back from Manchester, but as much as I love them, I just needed my own space."

"I know what you mean. I love staying with Dad and Richard, but I'm not sure I could do it for longer than six weeks. We get on, and I adore them, but there's nothing like doing what you want to do when you want to do it is there?" Lucy picked up her drink and took a sip, taking a peek at Ed over the top of the glass.

"Hmm," he said, now taking a drink from his beer bottle. "If you want to watch TV in the nude you can." Ed's neck coloured as he realised what he'd just said.

Lucy also blushed as images of Ed watching TV in the nude flitted through her mind. "Exactly," she said taking a larger sip.

"So," Ed coughed nervously. "Well, I guess we need to talk about your looking after Nate. I know we've not done this formally or anything, but I would like to pay you. Plus there are a few things you need to know about him and a few little guidelines, if you don't mind."

"Of course not, I understand. Children are very precious." Lucy eyes involuntarily filled with tears, she dropped her head so Ed couldn't see.

"Okay, but to be honest there's not much. Firstly, if Nate needs disciplining over anything, then you're the expert, so I'm happy for you to do that. Go for it, if it's use your manners, or eat your tea, but obviously if it's anything more serious let me know, and I'll sort it."

Lucy nodded. "Okay."

"Right, well I don't expect you to cook for me, although I do like to eat with Nate whenever possible. If I know that I'll be home in time I'll call you, and I can cook, and you're welcome to join us anytime, by the way."

"Oh okay, that's no problem." That wouldn't be happening often, Lucy thought.

"The final thing is my ex-wife." Ed dropped his head and ran a hand through his hair. "I need to tell you all about her, and why I don't want her anywhere near Nate, not that she's likely to come here. She has her own life in America." Ed went on to tell Lucy all about Katie and Luke and how they'd broke his and Nate's hearts.

Lucy looked at Ed totally shocked by what he'd told her. "So, she didn't even ask to have Nate with her?" Lucy watched Ed's crumpled face and sad eyes and took a deep breath; she would do anything to have her daughter with her.

He shook his head. "No. She said that it was best that he stayed with me, thank God. You know what's ironic, it's that she's ended up with a carbon copy of the life she hated, the life she couldn't wait to leave behind."

"Why, what was so bad it?" Lucy asked.

"Well, when we met Katie was only twenty-three and a bit of a party girl, but within a few months was pregnant, and I think she blamed Nate for spoiling her fun. You see I was always working shifts at the hospital, so she had to cope with Nate on her own for most of the time." Ed sighed deeply.

"That must hurt then that she now seems happy to live a family life."

Ed laughed emptily. "Hah, just a bit, especially as Luke is a carbon copy too; we're twins you see."

Lucy stared at Ed wide eyed. "Blimey, I thought going off with your brother was bad, but that's a double whammy."

"I suppose, but we're nothing alike, he was obviously just more exciting." Ed smiled, but it didn't reach his eyes. "Anyway, I don't care anymore, it's Nate I care about."

"Does he ever ask after her?" Lucy put a hand to her mouth. She couldn't help but think of her own much loved, greatly missed daughter now as tears pricked her eyes.

"He did at first, but after a month away from her he was used to Katie not being there. While Nate was ill I either worked or sat at his bedside, and if I wasn't there then my mum was. She was brilliant, and when he came out of hospital she carried on being brilliant, she'd spend hours driving up and down the motorway. Then I saw how tired she looked, and it wasn't fair on Dad either, left at home alone for half the week, so that's when we moved up here. So there you have it," Ed said his voice a little brighter now. "I thought it best to tell you, rather than hearing the version that the crowd outside the school gates has come up with. I know Callie would like to know the truth, but I'd prefer it if you didn't tell her. As much as I love her she's a little loose in the tongue area, and I never want Nate to be told that his mum left him but chose to have two more children that she does live with."

Lucy smiled at Ed, full of sympathy for him. "I promise no one will hear it from me. Do you think that she'll ever come back, even just to visit Nate?"

Ed shrugged as he took a swig from his beer. "Who knows?" Ed was suddenly up out of his chair and reaching behind a book from the shelf behind him. "This is a picture of her, I kept it for Nate. It's only one I have," he said, passing a colour print to Lucy.

Lucy held the print gently in her fingers and gazed down at the gorgeous woman staring up at her. "She's beautiful," she muttered looking at long dark hair framing a perfect face with almond eyes and full lips.

"I thought Nate looked like you, but I can see that he has his mother's mouth and nose."

"Well, she may be beautiful from the outside, but that's all," murmured Ed huskily, taking the photograph from Lucy. "Anyway enough about me, what about you, how are you coping after what's happened?"

"Blimey," Lucy giggled. "Don't tell me you know all about my philandering husband as well, but I suppose if Callie knows why should I be surprised that you do too?" She smiled widely, letting Ed know that she wasn't annoyed.

"To be fair, at risk of getting him into trouble, it was Richard. I think he wanted me to know the truth as you were going to be working at the surgery."

"Oh, so you only let me work at the surgery because you felt sorry for me?" Lucy joked.

Ed smiled and shook his head. "No, not at all, maybe he just thought that I could look after you." He eyed Lucy from over the lip of his bottle, a small smile upon his mouth.

"Hmm, okay so what did he tell you?" Lucy felt hot, was he flirting with her again?

"Just that your husband left you for a woman from work, and that she was pregnant."

Lucy felt relieved that Richard hadn't mentioned Lottie. That was part of her life that she didn't want to share with strangers. "Yep, that's about it, I suppose."

"At least there were no children caught in the crossfire," Ed said putting his bottle down and standing up. "Talking of which, I'd better check on Nate and get him off to bed.

He thinks if he's quiet I'll forget about him and he'll be able to watch Eastenders in the kitchen. I'll be back in a few minutes, and then we can eat."

"Okay, no problem." Lucy smiled up at Ed as he left the room.

She thought about what he'd told her and how it affected him and Nate. Lucy was amazed how any woman could leave their child voluntarily like that. To spend just one more day with Lottie would be her dream. Lucy felt herself blush as she thought of Ed; it also amazed her that his wife could leave him too. He was extremely sexy, and so adorable with Nate. His brother would have to have been something special, because Ed appeared to be the perfect package, but then who was she to judge. She hadn't even noticed that her own husband had been leading a double life for months. Lucy blew out a breath of air. This was going to be so hard, not the job - that would be pretty simple compared with a class of 30, eight-year-old children, or a shop full of aged bargain hunters. It would, however, be difficult being near to Ed. It would be hard work not to throw herself at him and not to beg him to ravish her.

After about fifteen minutes, Lucy heard Ed's tread upon the stairs and realised that he'd gone along to the kitchen. She picked up her wine glass and his half-drunk bottle of beer and went to join him.

"Here you go," Lucy said, passing Ed his drink. "Is there anything I can do?"

"No nothing at all. You sit down, it's all ready. It's only chicken and salad, I hope that's okay. My culinary skills aren't bad, but not too adventurous." Ed grinned at Lucy over his shoulder and after a few minutes turned to her armed with two plates of food, and some knives and forks.

Lucy smiled as he placed the plate in front of her. "Thank you," she said.

"It should fill a space," he responded, reaching up into a cupboard for salt and pepper, before sitting down.

They ate in silence for a few minutes until Ed broached conversation with Lucy. "So why don't you tell me a little about yourself? Obviously Richard has told me about your current situation, but what about you? What do you like and don't like?" He didn't look up but carried on eating.

Lucy was thankful he wasn't looking as she was blushing. She couldn't say to him "you, you are what I like."

"Ooh," she said, pulling herself together. "What do I like? Well I like chocolate cake, white wine, romantic novels, people who make me laugh, Oasis and beetroot sandwiches."

Ed looked at her now and laughed. "Okay, I didn't expect a shopping list, but at least I know we have a couple of things in common: Oasis and beetroot sandwiches. I bloody well love them both. What's your favourite album?"

"Well I'm a traditionalist it has to be 'What's The Story', I just love 'She's Electric'."

Ed dropped his knife and fork with a clatter on to his plate. "No way, that's my all-time favourite song. In fact, I used to sing it to Nate when he was little, to try to get him to sleep."

"Really? I used to sing…" Lucy stopped abruptly. She realised that she was about to tell Ed about Lottie, and she wasn't ready for that yet. "Erm I used to sing it to my friend's little boy." She took a gulp of her wine. "What a coincidence." She dropped her head, not wanting Ed to see the tears in her eyes.

"Well at least I know you won't ruin my son's ears with crap music while you're looking after him," Ed joked.

Lucy looked up now and smiled. "I promise not to play any Bon Jovi."

"Urgh, please no!" Ed held up his hands and shook his head vigorously.

"Simon loves them and made me listen to their whole back catalogue once." Lucy grimaced as she remembered one extremely long November day.

Ed laughed loudly and went to the fridge. "Sorry Lucy, but I think you might be better off without him with awful music taste like that." He turned to look at Lucy, realising what he'd just said. "Oh God, I'm so sorry, I shouldn't have said that." He shook his head and bit his bottom lip.

Lucy grinned, amused at his comment and the look of horror upon his face. "It's okay. You're right he does have awful taste in music, he was a massive fan of Westlife too!"

They laughed loudly together as Ed filled her wine glass up again, and opened himself another bottle of beer.

"Okay," said Ed as he paused from laughing. "What about the rest of your family, what are they like? I know about your dad and Richard obviously. They're both really good guys, but I believe you have a sister too."

"Hmm," Lucy nodded. "Sophie, she's a couple of years younger than me and lives in South Africa. She's a magazine photographer. She's lovely and talented, but, unfortunately, I don't get to see much of her. South Africa is so far away, and she works all over the country, so even if I could afford the fare, or the time to go there, it's difficult for Sophie to be around long enough to have any visitors. The only other family I have apart from Dad and Richard is my mother, but the less said about her the better." Lucy played with the table cloth as she thought about the last time she saw her mother.

"Oh dear, I won't ask any more about her then. We all have family members that we'd prefer not to discuss, don't we?" Ed smiled at Lucy, but it failed to reach his eyes.

"So, what about you?" Lucy asked to change the subject. "What made you want to be a doctor, is it a family occupation?"

"No, not at all. My mum was a librarian, and my dad was a builder who made a good living building bespoke properties and exclusive housing developments. It's the only thing I ever wanted to be, right from Nate's age. The best Christmas present I ever had was a plastic doctor's kit when I was seven."

"So you were destined to be a doctor then?"

"Not at all. I wasn't naturally bright. To get the grades that I needed I had to study really hard, all the way through my education. Unlike Luke, he only ever wanted to be a footballer and was naturally gifted at it; that and chasing girls."

There followed a brief silence until Ed coughed and pushed his chair back to take their empty plates to the dishwasher.

"I can wash those for you," Lucy offered.

Ed shook his head. "That's what the dishwasher is for, don't be silly. Can I get you anything else? I didn't make a pudding sorry. They're not in my repertoire."

"That's okay. I'm quite full thanks." Lucy smiled at Ed before taking another sip from her wine.

"Oh that's good" Ed turned away from Lucy.

God he wanted her so much, and if she looked into his eyes she would surely see they were full of lust. She looked gorgeous tonight, and her smile lit up her whole face, but he sensed that she was holding something back from him. He sighed as he stacked the dishwasher, she was evidently still hurting badly, and there was no way that he could make a move on her, no matter how much he wanted to.

Lucy watched Ed as he bent and stretched to fill the dishwasher. Blimey, he was fantastic, his body was to die for, and when he'd stretched up for the salt and pepper, she could see a tight stomach with a thin line of hair leading down into his jeans. The way that he loved his son was adorable, but his ex-wife and brother had obviously broken his heart beyond repair, just as Simon had broken hers. There was no way that she could act on this stupid crush that she had on him, even if they just had some 'sexy time' as Sarah had suggested, it would stupid to risk another broken heart.

After Ed had made them some coffee they talked for another hour about Nate, his life as a doctor, Oasis, Lucy's experiences as a teacher and books that they both enjoyed. Finally, Lucy stifled a yawn, and she suddenly felt extremely weary.

"Sorry, am I boring you?" Ed asked as he smiled at Lucy.

"God no, I'm just tired. I've not worked for three weeks and getting up early this morning was a bit of a killer." Lucy yawned once more and stretched her arms out to her sides. "I'm sorry, again."

"I understand," muttered Ed, desperately trying to avoid staring at her breasts that were now straining against her white cotton shirt. "Will you be okay walking back on your own, or would you like me to get a taxi for you?" Ed asked.

"No, I'll be fine it only takes ten minutes, at the most."

"Well I don't think there's anyone dangerous around here, but even so I'd prefer to ring for a taxi for you." Ed replied his concern growing.

"Honestly don't worry, it's only just gone nine-thirty. Anyway, I can do my judo moves on anyone who tries to attack me. I'll have to show them to you some time." Lucy involuntarily went into flirting mode, looking up at Ed through her lashes and holding his gaze.

Ed felt a slight stirring in his jeans. He quickly thought of clowns, always guaranteed to dampen his ardour.

At the front door, when they said goodbye, there was a brief moment when Lucy thought Ed was going to hug her, but he patted her on the back instead.

"Anyway, good night," he said moving his hand from Lucy's back to scratch his head.

"Yes, good night and, well I'll see you in the morning." Lucy thrust her hands into her jeans pocket as she suddenly had an urge to run them through his hair!

"Yes, see you tomorrow."

Ed closed the door, as soon as Lucy walked off down the street. He rubbed both hands up and down his face as he flopped down onto the bottom stair. He actually wasn't sure now that this arrangement was a brilliant idea. How on earth was he going to get her out of his head while working so closely with her, not only at the surgery but at home too? He was going to have to think about an awful lot of clowns in the next few weeks. Perhaps the more he saw of her the less enticing she would become, but somehow Ed doubted it if his current erection and dirty thoughts were anything to go by.

As Lucy walked home, she shivered as she thought of Ed. He was so gorgeous, but he didn't appear to realise it, which made him even more attractive. She thought about his deep brown eyes, like pools of melted chocolate, and how they had shone brightly when he spoke about Nate. She thought about his stomach under his white T-shirt and his perfect backside, and then she thought about what he might look like naked, and she shivered again. Her nipples were standing to attention just at the thought of him; imagine if he actually touched her! She shook her head and tried to banish such thoughts from her mind, but they just wouldn't go away.

Chapter 8

The next morning, when Lucy arrived at the surgery, Callie told her that Ed had gone out on a home visit. He'd gone to one of the local nursing homes and would be back after lunch. Lucy felt disappointed, unless he returned to the surgery before she finished for the day, she wouldn't see him until tomorrow.

In bed, the previous evening, she'd thought about him constantly, realising that she actually did like him, not just because he was gorgeous and had a fantastic body. He seemed to be a lovely person, he was funny, he adored his son, and he was engaging. Lucy thought about their brief moments of flirting, wondering whether he was attracted to her too, but then banished the thought from her head; it was merely some gentle flirting, nothing to get excited about.

As Lucy tidied the reception desk, somewhat dejectedly, Callie tapped her on the shoulder proffering a mug of tea.

"So, how did your meeting with Dr Bryce go pet?" asked Callie, taking a sip from her own mug.

"Oh it was good, thanks. I met Nate, and then Dr Bryce, and I talked it through, you know what would happen on a daily basis, that sort of thing." Lucy averted her eyes, not wanting to meet Callie's gaze, in case she saw the blush on her cheeks.

"Nate's a canny bairn isn't he?" Callie enthused. "Dr Bryce loves the bones of him, and they're like best friends, but I suppose it's because it's just been him and Nate for so long. Did he mention Mrs Bryce, the ex-wife, at all?" Callie asked nonchalantly as she flicked on the computer.

Lucy shook her head. "Not much, just that she wasn't part of Nate's life. He didn't offer any more information, and I didn't ask for any." Lucy put her tea down and moved to the desk to greet a patient, putting a stop to any further questioning from Callie.

The morning passed quickly, with a bout of flu hitting the town and only Dr Kindler on duty they worked non-stop. Between them, Callie and Lucy fell naturally into a system, Callie booking patients in as they arrived, and Lucy taking repeat appointments and new ones over the phone.

Despite being busy, every time the glass door had swung open Lucy looked up, hoping that it might be Ed returning earlier than expected. It never was, and so by midday, she had resigned herself not to see him.

"Do you want me to stay a little longer, Callie?" asked Lucy, glancing at the clock that read five minutes past twelve.

"What's that pet?" Callie looked up from the computer, having just booked in another flu sufferer.

"Shall I stay to help you out, or at least until you've had your lunch?"

"No, don't be silly. The rush is over, there's only Mr Gregg and Evie Francis to go in now. You get yourself off, unless you want to wait here?" She looked at Lucy and smiled.

Lucy blushed slightly and shook her head. "No, I just thought you might like some help."

"No, we only take emergencies between twelve and two, so I'll be able to grab some lunch no problem."

"Shall I run out and get you something then?" Lucy was conscious that she was now starting to sound a little desperate, but she *was* desperate, desperate to see Ed.

"I've brought a salad with me pet, so no need." Callie continued typing, not letting Lucy see the smile on her face.

"Oh, okay, if you're sure. I'll be off then." Lucy shrugged her shoulders and started to walk back to the staff room to collect her bag.

"Okay then," called Callie, now grinning. "You seem a bit anxious to stay for some reason pet?" she whispered to herself, giggling softly.

A few minutes later, Lucy reappeared with her bag, and the glass door swung open. In rushed a decidedly out of breath Ed.

"In a hurry pet?" Callie asked, without looking up from her typing. "I don't know what it is about this place today, everyone is desperate to be here, I wonder why."

"Oh, erm hi Callie. I was just conscious that I'd been out for so long," Ed explained, rubbing his chin.

"No longer than usual." Callie smiled broadly and winked at Ed. "Mr Gregg, you can go into Dr Kindler now," she called to the waiting patient. "I'm just off to the ladies Lucy, so I'll see you tomorrow, unless you're still here when I get back of course."

"No, no, I'm going now," Lucy spluttered, looking down and rummaging in her bag as she tried to hide her pink cheeks.

"Oh hi Lucy, sorry didn't see you there." Ed scratched his head and moved behind the reception desk.

He placed his bag on the floor and checked the computer to look at the afternoon appointments. Ed only had three; all pretty straightforward follow ups, but he studied them for longer than necessary. Finally, after a couple of minutes he sighed and turned to Lucy.

"Ah well, not too bad an afternoon," he said, picking his bag up from the floor. "So, are you off now then Lucy?"

"Hmm, yes," she replied, still searching for nothing at all in her bag as a delaying tactic. "I'm just looking for my…you know…my, ah here it is." Lucy pulled a nail file from her bag.

"Right, great." Ed looked a little perplexed. "Anyway, do you have any plans this afternoon?" Ed was in turn, trying to delay Lucy.

He just had to look at her a little longer, Ed thought, in that tight blouse and pencil skirt. And there were no flip-flops on her feet today, but extremely sexy killer heels. Ed suppressed a groan as he imagined Lucy, in his bed, wearing nothing else but the black stilettos.

Lucy broke his thoughts. "Nothing exciting, just the supermarket with Dad, which in his current condition could take hours," she giggled.

"Oh okay. It's just I'm taking Nate to Flatts Woods after school and then for a burger, so wondered if you'd like to come with us? You know, to get to know Nate, before next week." Ed blushed as he looked down at his feet.

"Yes, that would be lovely," Lucy sighed, gazing at Ed. "What time and where?"

God did she sound too forward, Lucy wondered. She hadn't even thought about it, but just said yes straight away. What was it about this man? Her head was telling her to stay away from him, it was too soon after Simon, but her heart was saying, "Just go for it, and give him as many signals as you can that you want him."

"You would? Brilliant. That's great." Ed beamed at her, and then coughed nervously. "Well I'll pick you up about four thirty from your dad's house, is that okay?"

"Fine, I'll see you then." Lucy smiled broadly.

As Callie reappeared, her face spread into a large grin as she saw Lucy still hadn't left. "You still here Lucy, don't you want to go home? I can't think for the life of me what the attraction of this place is," she said winking at Lucy.

Lucy blushed, fleetingly flicking her eyes towards Ed. "There's no attraction Callie, I'm just devoted to the cause."

"You're devoted to something pet, but I doubt very much it's this place. Anyway, Dr Bryce how are you this morning?"

With that, Lucy waved goodbye and scuttled out complete with a crimson face.

By the time Lucy had reached home, she had convinced herself that the trip to the woods was a bad idea. How could she possibly even consider it when she lusted after Ed so much? Lucy decided to ring Sarah for advice, although she knew what her friend's advice would be - go for it!

Lucy was right, when she'd spoken to Sarah and told her about dinner last night, and the trip to the woods, Sarah had laughed loudly, and her well thought out advice was – "There are no guarantees in life, so either shag him, or keep it professional and just see where it goes, but stop being a fanny about it."

At four thirty, having taken Sarah's erudite comments to heart, Lucy stared through the lounge window, waiting for sight of Ed's car. Gerald didn't say anything when she'd told him where she was going, he merely smiled, nodded his head and told her to take an umbrella as they'd forecast rain. He then spent half an hour composing an email to Richard, keeping him updated of the situation.

A few minutes later, Lucy recognised Ed's car at the end of the drive. She shouted goodbye to Gerald, grabbed her keys from the hall table and left the house. As she shut the door behind her, Lucy wondered whether she looked okay, she certainly hoped that she did as she had spent long enough deciding on what to wear, finally choosing a pair of white, ankle grazer, skinny jeans, a white T-shirt, black converse pumps, and she carried a black-and-white striped cardigan.

As Lucy walked towards the car Ed let out a long sigh, she looked stunning. Her hair hung loosely over her shoulders and down her back, and her body looked fantastic in the tight jeans and T-shirt. Then it struck Ed, how happy and relaxed Lucy looked as she waved at him, it made her even more beautiful. He wanted her so badly, and this trip to the woods was something that Ed had thought of, off the cuff, this afternoon, just to get to spend some time with Lucy. Nate had been thrilled about the burger but wasn't quite as enamoured with the woods. They had a large garden that he could play football in, so why did they have to go walking in the woods, but Ed had managed to persuade him that it was a brilliant idea. Plus Nate had seemed pleased when Ed had told him that Lucy was going with them.

Lucy smiled and waved at Ed as she approached the car; she felt happy to see him and was now looking forward to the next few hours. Her stomach flipped as Ed gave her a huge smile, he looked gorgeous. She shivered involuntarily at the thought of spending time with him. Sarah was right; she should see where things went and try not to worry about it.

"Hi," Lucy said, opening the car door. "Hi Nate, how are you?" she asked, turning to the back seat.

"Hi Lucy. I know you're a girl, but can you play football because I've brought my ball with me?" Nate thrust his orange football towards her.

Lucy giggled and took the ball from Nate. "I'm not very good, so perhaps you could be on my side, to help me."

"Hmm, okay. Would it be fair Daddy, if we both played against you?" Nate leaned forward and tapped Ed on the shoulder with his little hand.

"I think it would be okay Nate, but I'm not sure that there is anywhere we can play football. If there is, we'll play, but I'm pretty certain that I'll beat you both, what do you think Lucy?" Ed turned to Lucy, who was now gazing at him.

"Ooh, I'm not so sure about that, are you Nate?"

"No way, we will win 21 – nil."

Ed threw his head back and laughed. "Okay, let's go then and see what happens," he said, thrusting the car into gear and driving off.

Twenty minutes later and the three of them were wandering through the woods. Ed had been right, there wasn't actually anywhere for Nate to play football, so Lucy and Ed walked together as Nate dawdled behind, sulking at having to leave his ball in the car.

Lucy and Ed waited for him intermittently, urging him to join them, but Nate just jutted out his bottom lip and carried on dragging his feet. Ten minutes into the walk, Nate got bored with sulking and ran past them, shouting for Ed to catch him. Ed chased him for a couple of minutes and then fell back to walk in step with Lucy, leaving Nate to run against the late-afternoon wind.

"Look at him," Ed sighed. "He doesn't have a care in the world."

"Except for having to leave his football in the car," Lucy replied, buttoning up her cardigan. They were walking along a path covered by vast trees, all blocking out the watery sun. "He certainly doesn't seem to be affected by not having his mum around anyway. You've obviously done a great job."

Ed smiled and shook his head. "I can't take all the credit; my mum has been brilliant with him. The problem is of course she isn't getting any younger, and I can't expect her to help out for much longer. She's raised her children, she shouldn't have to help me to raise mine," he said, smiling ruefully.

"I'm sure she doesn't mind, at least she gets to keep you both close, rather than in Manchester." Lucy watched Nate in the distance.

"Unlike her other grandchildren." There was a suggestion of bitterness in Ed's voice. "She's hardly ever seen Amelia and Louie; two or three times at most I think. Dad has never seen them."

"Really? Why not?"

"He doesn't agree with what Katie and Luke did to me, especially Katie leaving Nate as she did. Dad signs cards and speaks to the children, and occasionally Luke, on the phone but can't bring himself to visit them with Mum."

"So, how do you feel about your mum visiting them?" Lucy asked, noticing deep ridges across his brow. God she wanted to kiss his frown away.

"It always hurts at first, when she says she's going to visit, but I can't blame her. She didn't speak to Luke for a long time, but it was hard for her. He's her son too, and she felt torn all the time. So, one day I just told her to pick up the phone and call him."

"Blimey, that's very big of you," replied Lucy. "I don't think I would have been that nice about it."

Ed rubbed his eyes. "It's my argument not hers. She was heartbroken by not speaking to Luke; Katie, however, is another matter. From what I gather she barely speaks to her. She only really talks to Luke - Nate, don't run too far ahead please - Katie and Luke turned our lives' upside down, and Mum can't forgive either of them, but Luke is her son, so he gets a free pass on this one."

Nate started to come back towards them, his cheeks bright red from running up and down the pathway. "Daddy can we have a running race to that big tree stump up there, please?" he pleaded as he pointed in the distance. "Lucy you have to race too?"

Lucy put her head on one side, frowning as she contemplated Nate's idea. "Okay, if I have to...GO!" Then off she flew, racing ahead of both Ed and Nate.

"That's cheating," Ed called after her. "Quick Nate, she's going to win."

Father and son raced after Lucy, their laughter escaping into the air as they ran. Lucy looked over her shoulder, to see where they were, Ed was gaining on her more quickly than Nate, who was running in the rear, calling for Ed to wait for him. Then suddenly, Lucy found that she was being hoisted in the air and carried, at some pace, back to where they'd just run from.

"Put me down," she squealed, unable to stop herself from giggling.

"Run Nate, run," shouted Ed, now passing his son running in the opposite direction.

"This is cheating," Lucy cried.

"You cheated first." Ed was laughing now as he carried on running for several feet, until eventually he dropped Lucy, with a thud, onto the grass verge of the pathway.

Not wanting to hurt herself, Lucy hung on for dear life, pulling Ed over on top of her. Lucy pulled in a sharp intake of breath, because with Ed on top of her Lucy's body felt electrically charged, ready to respond to him. It was as though he'd flipped a switch inside her, as waves of excitement churned in her stomach and then bubbled down between her legs, her whole body was tingling, desperate for his touch, and she was almost sure that she could feel something hardening against her!

"Brilliant," said Ed, breathing heavily from his exertions. "I think Nate may win now. Sorry am I hurting you?" he asked, suddenly aware that he was lying on top of her. He looked down at Lucy and tried not to sigh, she smelled so good and looked extremely beautiful; her red hair fanning out over her shoulders, contrasting with the dark-green grass verge. He felt as though every nerve ending in his body was being set alight as a slow, insistent throbbing began to grow in his groin.

"It's okay," she said breathlessly. "I'm fine."

Realising that if he didn't get off her soon, Lucy would be patently aware, of how much he liked her in that position, Ed stood up and held his hand out for her. He looked in the direction of Nate, who initially had stopped running to watch them for a few seconds before carrying on in the direction of the tree stump in

"Come on, we'd better get Nate something to eat before he starves."

"Thanks," she said allowing Ed to pull her up. "I've really enjoyed myself this afternoon."

Their eyes locked as they stared at each other intently, the electricity between them fizzing through the air as Ed held Lucy's hand in his.

"Good," Ed finally replied huskily, before running off in the direction of Nate.

Lucy watched as he picked up Nate, under his arm, and spun him round, father and son laughing loudly. A warm glow flowed through her body as she decided that she was going to like working for Ed.

Once Ed had spun Nate around a couple of times he dropped him to the ground, and now breathless from exertion and laughter they waited for Lucy. She finally caught up with them, patting grass and twigs off her jeans as she approached them.

"Sorry about that." Ed said, laughing at her. "You're not too dirty are you?"

"No," Lucy said breathlessly, "I'm fine."

"You cheated Lucy," Nate joined in now, smiling widely.

"I know, and I'm sorry Nate. I promise not to cheat next time, if we come again that is." Now she was looking up at Ed, from underneath her eyelashes.

"Oh I'm sure we will," Ed replied. He was breathing deeply now, desperately trying not to kiss her.

"Can we go now please?" Nate interrupted the lustful thoughts of both Lucy and Ed. "I'm hungry."

"Well actually," said Ed. "I was wondering, how about going to see Nanny instead of going for a burger?"

"Is she making fish pie? Because if she is; I don't want to. Urgh it's disgusting." Nate licked out his tongue and shook his head.

Ed laughed and ruffled Nate's hair. "No, it's meat and potato pie."

"Oh okay," Nate replied and he skipped off back down the pathway.

Ed and Lucy laughed as they watched him run away from them.

"Is that okay with you?" Ed asked as he drew a line in the soil with his toe.

"No problem, you can just drop me off at Dad's." Lucy ran a hand through her hair.

"No, no," he protested. "You're invited too. I told Mum we were going for a burger, and she insisted that we go there instead, so she can meet you. She's quite protective of Nate you see."

"Oh blimey, what if she doesn't like me or think I'm good enough for her son, erm her grandson?" Lucy blushed, hoping that Ed hadn't noticed her slip of the tongue.

He didn't appear to. "God, no she'll be fine. She's lovely, and I'm sure that she'll like you."

"I don't want to intrude though."

"I've told you, it was her idea." Ed looked at Lucy expectantly, waiting for her reply.

"Oh…okay then if you're sure."

"Great, that's brilliant. Come on then, let's catch Nate up." Ed went to catch hold of Lucy's hand but quickly thrust it into his hoodie pocket instead.

"Okay," Lucy sighed, feeling nervous already.

As they pulled up on the drive, Lucy felt her stomach lurch and her hands start to sweat. What if Mrs Bryce didn't like her and insisted that Ed find someone else to look after Nate? She was actually looking forward to it now as Nate was such a lovely little boy.

"Are you okay?" Ed asked. "You look a little scared. Nanny isn't that bad is she Nate?" Ed laughed as he turned to Nate, who was unbuckling himself in the back.

"She's okay. She shouts at Grandad a lot but never me and Daddy." With that, he jumped out of the car.

"Now I feel worse," moaned Lucy. "You two are obviously her golden boys."

"Believe me, she still tells me off from time to time. Come on, she won't bite." Ed opened his door as he smiled at Lucy.

"Let's hope not," she muttered to herself.

"Mum, Dad, anyone in?" Ed shouted as he stepped into the large hallway.

"In here love," came the reply.

"She's in the kitchen," Ed explained, nodding towards a door on the right. "Come on through. Hi, Mum," he said to Georgina's back as she stood at the sink, washing a pan.

"Hi love, are you okay?" She turned to face her son. "Hello dear." She now looked at Lucy and wiped her hands on the tea towel slung over her shoulder.

"Mum, this is Lucy Meadows."

"Pleased to meet you Lucy." Georgina took Lucy's hand and shook it firmly.

"Hello, pleased to meet you too Mrs Bryce." Lucy gave what she hoped was her most winning smile.

"Georgina, please, Mrs Bryce makes me sound like my mother-in-law, and if you'd ever met her you'd understand why I don't want to be like her - dreadful woman." Georgina's laugh tinkled in the air. "Anyway, sweetheart, how are you?" she asked Nate, hugging him to her.

Nate hugged her back. "I'm okay Nanny," he replied, now escaping from her arms.

"Listen Nate, how about you go and introduce Lucy to Grandad," Ed said, turning Nate towards the door.

"Okay, come on then Lucy, let's get this over with." He caught hold of Lucy's hand and pulled her out of the room as all three adults laughed at his precociousness.

"Ed," Georgina hissed. "Why didn't you tell me that you were bringing Lucy for tea?" Georgina slapped Ed on the arm with her tea towel.

"I know I'm sorry. I asked her to come for a walk and burger, to get to know Nate a little more before she looks after him next week. I'd forgotten that you'd asked us for tea until it was too late. There's plenty isn't there, or is that a silly question?" Ed whispered as he hugged Georgina.

"Good job I don't understand portion control isn't it. So, why did you feel the need to bring your babysitter home for tea then, is there something I should know?" She smiled at Ed, standing, on tiptoe, to ruffle his hair.

Ed blushed as he pulled his head away. "No Mother, there isn't anything that you need to know. I just thought that you might like to meet her, seeing as she'll be looking after your favourite boy."

"Ah, but which one?" Georgina asked, moving over to the oven.

"Nate, obviously." Ed snapped back. "Mum, don't even think it. She's just come out of a marriage and isn't ready for a relationship. Nor am I for that matter."

"Ed don't be so ridiculous, you've been single for nearly four years, so of course you're ready. And," she whispered as she moved back to Ed, "it's obvious that you fancy her, and I'll bet you £100 that she fancies you. Just because I'm your mother it doesn't mean I don't know about sex, your father and I…"

"Urgh no, don't say anything else, please!" Ed cried, sticking his fingers in his ears.

"Stop being such a baby, anyway she seems lovely. She's very pretty." Georgina looked at Ed, who was now gazing into the distance.

"Hmm, more than pretty I'd say," he replied, distractedly.

"Is that so?" said Georgina smiling at her son.

"Grandad, tell Lucy about when you fought with General Custard," Nate said, scrambling on to his grandfather's knee.

Jack Bryce winked at Lucy. "You mean General Custer, well you know Nate I'm not supposed to tell anyone about that. It's top secret, Lucy would have to take the oath before I can tell her."

"Shall I go and get the book then?" Nate asked as he started to climb down from Jack's lap.

"Hey, hey, no hang on," said Jack, pulling Nate back. "You have to know someone for a little while before you let them take the oath. She might be a spy," he stage whispered in Nate's ear.

Nate nodded solemnly and tapped his nose with his finger. "I understand, I understand."

Lucy giggled behind her hand as Jack turned away, not wanting Nate to see him laughing.

"I understand too Mr Bryce," Lucy said gravely. "You need to be sure that you can trust me first."

"Exactly," said Jack. "Now shall we go and see what Nanny and Daddy are up to?"

"Ok." Nate jumped down from his perch and ran off in the direction of the kitchen.

"He's a lovely little boy." Lucy smiled widely at Nate's disappearing back. "I'm really looking forward to looking after him."

"He's very precious to us. I believe you know about Katie and our other son, Luke?"

Lucy nodded. "Ed told me about it, yes."

"It was a terrible business and knocked poor Ed for six. Anyway, it will do them both good to spend some time with someone other than me and Georgina. If truth be told," Jack said, lowering his voice. "Georgina mollycoddles them both, a bit too much, so don't be afraid to kick some butt while you're helping out."

"I understand," said Lucy, mimicking Nate's nose tapping of a few minutes earlier.

Jack laughed heartily and patted Lucy on the back. "I think I'm going to like you. Come on then, let's go and get some dinner before Nate eats the lot."

87

Chapter 9

Lucy had been looking after Nate, alongside working at the surgery, for over a week, and everything was going well. Her mornings were spent at the surgery, usually with much hilarity, thanks to Callie and the throng of strange and wonderful patients who visited every day. Her afternoons, from three, were spent playing pirates with Nate, supervising play dates with visiting friends or doing his reading and homework with him. Ed was generally home between five and five thirty, which meant that he would cook for himself and Nate. Lucy was so scared that he would ask her to stay for dinner she normally had her bag on her arm and keys in hand as Ed came through the door.

Dinner at his parent's house had been lovely, a thoroughly pleasant evening, spent laughing and joking within the bosom of, what appeared to be, a real happy family. Ed had sat opposite Lucy at the table, and she couldn't help but gaze at him as he talked animatedly with his father about football. As she watched him, she thought about what had happened in the woods, when he had lain on top of her. She was convinced now that she had felt something hard, and not imagined it as she first thought, she touched the top of her thigh where it had touched her and shivered. Lucy crossed her arms, to cover her erect nipples as she imagined him lying on top of her, totally naked, the excitement bubbling inside her. After dinner, Ed gave her a lift home, and all the way Lucy wondered whether he might kiss her. He didn't; Ed simply thanked her for a lovely afternoon, and evening, and said he'd see her at the surgery the following day. Somewhat disappointed, Lucy had waved goodbye to him and Nate as they disappeared around the corner.

Now that she'd had time to think about things, Lucy realised it was probably a good job that he hadn't kissed her. It would only make things messy. She was going home in six weeks or so and, no matter what Sarah said, Lucy didn't think she could have Ed as just a "shag buddy" while she was here. She knew that if anything happened between them that would be it, she would be smitten, and she couldn't stand the chance of having her heart broken again. However, she would then see Ed looking gorgeous, and momentarily think "oh what the hell".

Georgina had left for America a couple of days after Lucy had met her, but she rang every afternoon almost, to speak to Nate. For the first couple of days, Ed had seemed a little grumpy during surgery, barely speaking to anyone, but then he'd had a long phone call from Georgina and seemed to have snapped out of it by the time he'd arrived home. He'd apologised and said he'd been worried about his mother, but having spoken to her he now felt he could relax a little. Lucy thought that it probably had more to do with his brother and ex-wife, but didn't feel it was her place to ask for any other details.

As she thought about the last week, Lucy suddenly realised that it was almost two forty-five, so she should go and collect Nate from school. It was only a five-minute walk from Ed's house, so she left her mini parked on the drive.

As Lucy approached the school, she sighed. The usual gaggle of mothers and grandmothers were gathered at the school gates tearing their latest victim to shreds. As an ex-teacher, she knew what it was like, the ones who stood apart, not wanting to join in the gossiping, were usually the subject of all manner of criticism and rumour. Over the last week, Lucy had tried to steer clear of them all, but because Ed was the handsome doctor and because Lucy worked for him, they were all desperate to pump her for information on him. By the time Nate came out of school every day, Lucy felt as though she'd been interrogated, to such a point that she was mentally exhausted.

"Hi," she said, nodding her head at the group as she stopped a little way from them.

"Hi Lucy. How are you?" Karina, the mother of a chubby little blonde-haired boy called Bradley, asked.

"Fine thanks. Are you all okay?" The gaggle nodded in unison.

"How's Dr Bryce?" asked Beverley, a rather large, sweaty woman, who appeared to have a least one child in each year group in the school.

"He's fine," Lucy replied, turning her back slightly to avoid further questioning.

This was what it was like every day. They started off asking how she was, how Ed was, and then they would close in around her, in a pincer movement, like a crack SWAT squad about to take down the enemy, encircling her so there was no escape, before firing questions at her.

"Does Dr Bryce have a girlfriend?"

"Do Dr Bryce and his ex-wife get on?"

"Does Dr Bryce actually have an ex-wife, or were the rumours true that Nate was from a surrogate?"

Lucy could see out of the corner of her eye "Big Bev" as she had nicknamed her, was moving towards her, actually, Lucy heard her legs rubbing together before she spotted her. Lucy smiled and then fished in her bag for her mobile, hoping that would deter Big Bev, but she'd obviously been sent on a mission. The rest of the gaggle were all nudging each other and whispering behind their hands as they looked in Lucy's direction. Lucy certainly didn't want to have to answer any questions so grinned at Bev and said.

"Must make a call, sorry."

She thought about pretending, but knew that, with her luck, her mobile would ring out while she was supposed to be on a call. She rang her Dad's number, safe in the knowledge that his friend Monica had picked him up earlier and taken him to her house, in Durham, for a couple of days for a change of scenery.

Eventually, the machine kicked in, and Lucy started to gabble away to her father's recorded voice. Bev muttered under her breath and shaking her head, returned to the group of disappointed women. Lucy smiled at them as she talked to the machine about absolute drivel for two or three minutes until the school bell rang and chattering children surged out from every doorway, racing excitedly across the playground towards the gate.

After a few minutes, most of the children were disappearing with whoever had come to pick them up, but there was still no sign of Nate or Bradley, Karina's chubby little boy.

"Where the bloody hell is he?" Karina moaned, to no one in particular.

"Nate is usually one of the first out," responded Lucy, slightly worried. She started to walk toward the door for Nate's year group.

As she got a couple of feet from the door, it was pushed open by Nate's teacher; Mrs Bushnell. Lucy didn't like her much. It wasn't professional jealousy, she was too set in her ways. Apparently Mrs Bushnell had taught most of the parents too, and was now almost ready to retire. Nate had told her only yesterday that Mrs Bushnell had called Dylan Foster "a stupid buffoon", not a nurturing and encouraging term of endearment for a six year old, Lucy thought.

Mrs Bushnell moved into the playground pushing Nate and Bradley by their shoulders. She stopped just in front of Lucy and beckoned Karina over with a long, bony finger, her square chin jutting out.

God, thought Lucy, she didn't look happy at all. "Mrs Bushnell, is there a problem with Nate?" Lucy asked.

"The problem with Nate is that he is an extremely naughty boy, Miss, erm, sorry I seem to have forgotten your name."

"It's Lucy," Nate butted in, looking up at Mrs Bushnell.

"It's Mrs Meadows, I'm Nate's child minder while his grandmother is away." Lucy smiled at Nate and got down on her haunches in front of him. "What's the problem Nate?" she asked. "Why is Mrs Bushnell cross with you?"

"I've told you what the problem is, he's been disobedient." Mrs Bushnell bent down and pushed her face in front of Lucy's.

"What about my Bradley?" Karina, who had been silent so far, now stepped forward and poked Mrs Bushnell in her bony shoulder.

"I'll thank you not to touch me Mrs Biggs, but for your information, he's been disobedient too. They are a pair of fiends"

Karina and Lucy now both stood tall in front of Mrs Bushnell, hands on hips, affronted at her name calling of the children.

"Why what have they done that is so bad that they should be called fiends?" Lucy asked, as she stepped towards the teacher and held her hand out to Nate. "Nate, come here, and tell me what happened please."

Mrs Bushnell nudged Nate forward but placed her hands on Bradley's shoulders. "Go on tell her."

"I needed a flag for my pirate ship, that's all," Nate looked up at Lucy with his enormous brown eyes and gappy smile.

"What happened then, did you use the wrong paper or something?" Lucy asked.

"No, he didn't, he used something else he wasn't supposed to." Mrs Bushnell now edged Bradley forward and then turned him around.

"Bleeding hell," Karina cried. "Look at his new trousers." The whole seat area of Bradley's trousers was missing, revealing a pair of Ben 10 underpants. "He's cut the bloody arse out of them." Karina rushed forward and dragged Bradley to her for a closer look.

Lucy's hand flew to her mouth. "Oh dear, I'm sorry Karina. I'm sure that Dr Bryce will pay for a new pair."

"Anyway, what about my Bradley, why is he a fiend?" Karina asked, suddenly remembering what the teacher said.

Mrs Bushnell didn't speak but now turned Nate around by his shoulders.

"Bradley!" Karina cried. "You bloody little bugger."

"Oh dear," groaned Lucy. "I think we may have to call that quits."

Nate also revealed his underpants, as the whole backside of his trousers was also missing.

"I needed a flag too," whimpered Bradley, wiping his nose on the sleeve of his jumper.

"Oh dear," Mrs Bushnell sighed. "Please just get these boys home, they've been given inside playtime for a whole week, and if anything like this happens again then the punishment may see them excluded from the farm trip in three weeks."

"A little harsh," Lucy muttered, pulling Nate towards her. "They're only six for goodness sake, and how on earth did they get hold of scissors that cut material?"

"Firstly, they took them from my desk drawer while I was helping another pupil, and secondly they sneaked off into the book cupboard to do it, so they knew it was wrong. I'm sorry you think I'm being harsh but do you understand how difficult it is to teach delinquent children like this?" Mrs Bushnell folded her arms across her chest as she turned to Lucy.

"Actually I'm a teacher myself, on a sabbatical at the moment."

"Well surely you understand that this sort of behaviour should be nipped in the bud. Why do you think we are a nation of ASBO teenagers, because their behaviour wasn't nipped in the bud when they were children?" Mrs Bushnell pinched her fingers together, to demonstrate how she would "nip it in the bud."

"Well I hardly think that they are fiends, or delinquents in the making. It's just two six year old boys, using their imagination and their initiative. Yes, they were wrong, and I'm sure that both will be punished by their parents, but there was nothing nasty or malicious in what they did. Don't you think that you're overreacting a little? Also, I'd prefer it if you didn't use the term fiend or delinquent when speaking about Nate, or Bradley for that matter.

It's that sort of attitude that helps to create our ASBO society. Tell children long enough and often enough that they're bad, and they'll believe you and start acting like it. So can I ask you to refrain from using such words please, Mrs Bushnell?" Lucy looked Mrs Bushnell directly in the eye as she spoke.

"That's told you," said Karina, grabbing hold of Bradley's arm and dragging him from the playground.

"Come on Nate, let's get you home." Lucy took hold of Nate's hand and walked toward the gate.

"Thank you Lucy," he whispered, before pulling her hand up to his lips and kissing it.

Lucy felt her heart would melt for this beautiful, mischievous little boy, and wondered how his mother could leave him.

"Hmm, well I don't think you'll thank me when I tell your dad what you've been up to." She smiled to herself and squeezed Nate's hand gently.

"Right, so let me get this straight." Ed was standing in front of Nate, hands on hips. "You cut the backside out of Bradley's trousers for a sail, and he cut yours out for a sail too, is that right?"

Nate nodded solemnly. "Yes Daddy."

Ed ran a hand across his eyes and sighed, before flopping down onto the sofa.

"Are you okay Ed?" Lucy peered at Ed and frowned. "You look a little pale."

"I don't feel well at all. I think I might have the flu." Ed closed his eyes and pinched the bridge of his nose with his thumb and forefinger.

Lucy instinctively felt his head against the back of her hand, and then snatched it away quickly. "Erm, you are burning up, so maybe you're right. Perhaps you should go to bed."

"I can't I've got Nate's dinner to sort out, perhaps when he's gone to bed." Ed tried to stand up, but flopped back down again, his skin was now pale and sweaty.

"I think you should go now. I can get Nate something to eat and put him to bed." Lucy looked at Ed closely. His eyes were now closed as he rested his head against the sofa. "Look, why don't I stay the night. You don't look well at all."

Ed shook his head. "No, honestly Lucy I'll be okay. I just need a couple of hours to sleep."

"I know that you're the doctor, but I've seen enough ill children in my time as a teacher to know that you're not well. I can take Nate home with me to get some clothes while you get yourself off to bed."

Ed opened one eye and grimaced as he looked at Lucy. "Are you sure, it would help to know Nate is being looked after? The spare bed is already made up."

Lucy fought the urge to smooth Ed's unruly hair down, his colourless pallor took nothing away from his handsome face. "Go on," she urged. "Get yourself up to bed, I'll pop up and see you when I get back. Is there anything you can take?"

"Just a couple of Paracetamol and a glass of water would be great, they're in the medicine cupboard in the utility room."

"Okay, just give me a minute." Lucy made for the door, but she suddenly realised that Nate was sitting quietly on one of the armchairs. "Are you okay Nate?" Lucy asked as she knelt down to look closely at his worried face.

Nate nodded solemnly, his eyes brimming with tears. "Is Daddy okay?" he asked, almost in a whisper.

"I'm fine Nate, honestly." Ed sat up and leaned forward to grab Nate's hand. "It's flu, that's all."

"Daddy just needs to get some sleep, but I'll be here to look after you. Is that okay with you?" Lucy hugged the small boy to her. As she did, Ed's hand that was holding on to Nate's brushed her breast.

Ed dropped Nate's hand, as though it was burning his fingers. "I'd best go up, I'll get some water and tablets on my way," he said, pulling himself up from the sofa. "Night, night, Nate and I'll see you in the morning." He rubbed Nate's head as he shuffled toward the door.

Nate watched until Ed closed the door behind him. "Daddy will still be here tomorrow, won't he Lucy?" The tears that pricked his eyes moments before now slid down his little cheeks.

"Oh darling of course he will." Lucy stroked his head tenderly. "He really does just need a long sleep."

"But when I wasn't well my mummy went away," Nate gasped as sobs now started to escape from his body.

The words were like a knife through Lucy's heart. This poor child, she thought, must think that any illness meant that someone was leaving. How could Katie have done this to this sweet, sensitive boy, and Ed and his parents must have worked so hard over the last three years to make sure that he felt protected and secure?

"No one is going anywhere Nate. I promise. Daddy is going to bed, and I'm going to stay over and look after you. So, come on, you get your shoes on, and we'll go to my daddy's house and pick up some clothes and things for me, then we'll come back and have some tea and look after daddy, how does that sound?"

"Okay," Nate whispered, wiping his face on his hands. "Can I make Daddy a get-well card?"

"Wow, that's a brilliant idea. We'll do that after tea. Now off you go and get your shoes."

Nate had been quiet all the way to Gerald's house, but as soon as Lucy announced that she would make burgers and waffles for tea, he became a little brighter. They'd had tea and made Ed a card, and after Lucy persuaded him that it would be better to give it to Ed in the morning Nate went off to bed fairly happily. As she cleared away all the craft things, Lucy realised that she hadn't checked on Ed. She went into the kitchen and poured some iced water into a glass and took two more tablets from the packet that he'd left next to the sink.

With trepidation, she climbed the stairs. Once on the landing, she paused and listened carefully, she could hear Nate's soft snoring coming from his room. Relief flooded through Lucy; if he were sound asleep Nate must feel less anxious than he had earlier. She walked across the landing and passed the spare room, where she was staying, before reaching Ed's bedroom door at the front of the house.

She'd been in his room a couple of times before, once to put some shirts in his room that his ironing lady had returned, and another time to find his wallet when Ed had called to say that he couldn't find it. The room had been clean and tidy, in a manly sort of way - the bed wasn't made in pristine fashion, and Lucy had itched to rearrange the curtains that had been pulled open haphazardly.

Lucy now opened the door quietly and peeked into the darkened room, just making out Ed's body under the duvet. As her eyes adjusted to the dimness, she picked her way across the floor, dodging Ed's discarded clothes that he'd been wearing earlier. She placed the glass and tablets on the bedside cabinet and gently shook Ed's shoulder as she perched on the very edge of the bed.

"Ed," she whispered. "I've brought you some more water and Paracetamol. I think you should take them."

Ed roused slightly and turned over to face her. "Hi," he muttered through chattering teeth. "God, it's cold in here?"

Lucy shook her head, grateful that she was only wearing a cotton T-shirt in the warmness of the room. "I think it's you. It's actually quite hot in here. Do you want another blanket or something?" Ed shook his head as Lucy turned on the bedside lamp.

"Is that too bright?" she asked.

"No, it's fine." Ed pulled himself to a sitting position, allowing the duvet to fall, revealing his bare, tanned chest.

Lucy let out a small gasp. Despite his obvious illness, Ed looked incredible, his chest was perfectly formed, his bare arms muscular, and she could see a thin line of hair popping up from underneath the duvet. The pathway to pleasure, she thought.

"What? What's wrong?" Ed asked, alarmed.

"N-n-n-nothing," she stammered. "You just look really pale in the lamplight. Here, take these." She took the tablets and water and passed them to him.

Ed took them from her, swallowed the tablets with a large gulp of water, and then passed the glass back to Lucy. His fingers touched hers as she took it from him, and Ed felt a jolt through his body. Despite his aching limbs and fever, his desire to drag her into his bed was growing by the second.

"Has Nate gone to bed?" he asked, trying to change his focus.

Lucy nodded as she folded her arms, aware that the sight of Ed's bare chest and touch of his fingers had woken her nipples up, at this rate, she was going to have to nickname them Corporal Left and Corporal Right, they stood to attention so often these days.

"Yes all tucked up and snoring away," she said, deciding not to tell Ed about Nate's worries earlier.

"That's good. I think I may have to have tomorrow off. Even if it's just a 24 hour thing, I don't want to pass it on to my patients."

"That's a good idea, I'd stay in bed if I were you."

"It just means that I can't take Nate to school, so could you, please?"

"Sure, no problem." Lucy nodded as she played with the edge of the duvet distractedly. She just wanted to gaze at his body and drink in his beauty with her eyes. Even lying there in his sick bed, he was turning her on.

"Can you ring Callie and tell her you'll be late, and ask her to rearrange my non-urgent patients? Also, could you let Dr Kindler know? It's too late for him to get a locum for tomorrow, but if this carries on for more than a day he might be able to get our usual locum Sally, on standby." Ed shuffled down under the duvet now and pulled it under his chin.

Lucy almost sighed with disappointment at his disappearing chest. "Sure, no problem, I'll go and call her now."

"No," he said, rubbing a hand across his eyes. "Not just yet, tell me what exactly happened with Mrs Bushnell, and tell me what I should do about Nate. I don't know whether it's the right thing to punish him now, the moment seems to have passed somehow."

"Let's talk about that when you're feeling better. If you want me to, I can tell him that you said he can't play video games for a couple of nights, how does that sound?"

"Hmm, good idea, whatever you think," said Ed sleepily, his eyes now heavy.

Lucy leaned over and turned off the lamp. "Okay, I'll tell him tomorrow. Now you get some sleep and shout me if you need anything, I'm just next door." Lucy blushed in the darkness as she realised merely a couple of feet of brick would be separating them all night.

"I know, let's just hope I don't sleep walk," Ed said huskily as his eyes now closed fully.

Lucy giggled quietly as she thought of a naked Ed walking into her room, God she'd never let him leave the way she felt at that moment.

"Night Ed," she whispered getting up from the bed as she heard the same soft snoring that had come from Nate's room earlier.

The next morning Lucy woke after a fitful night's sleep. The noises about the house were unfamiliar to her, the mattress was a little hard, and the room was too hot because she couldn't open the window, but mainly she was desperate for Ed, who was only a few feet away. Lucy had contemplated just going and getting in bed with him, but then wondered whether forcing oneself on a semi-comatose man with a high temperature was classed as assault, she certainly didn't want to risk a court case, imagine the scandal!

She lay in bed for a few minutes, and then leaned over to pick her watch up; it was 6:30 am. Lucy decided to get up and prepare Nate's breakfast before she woke him. She got out of bed, and picking up her clothes, made her way to the bathroom to shower. As the hot water streamed over her body Lucy realised that she hadn't thought about Simon for over forty-eight hours, not once had he entered her thoughts, not even an evil thought about how she'd like to punish him had come into her head. The knowledge of this made her feel lighter, perhaps she was finally moving on.

"Huh, finally," she muttered. "It's only been nearly four weeks, not four years. How can I feel so together about it?" With no one to answer her, Lucy reached across for the shampoo, hoping Ed didn't mind her using it. Lucy started to sing loudly, scrubbing away at her scalp with vigour.

Ten minutes later and Lucy was out of the shower and drying between her toes, with her foot up on the side of the bath, when the door swung open and in walked a sickly looking Ed.

"No, get out!" Lucy cried as she spun her head around towards the door. Suddenly, a sharp pain shot up the side of her neck and into her ear. "Ahh, my God I think I've broken my neck." One of Lucy's hands went around her neck while the other flapped around trying to find the towel that she'd just dropped.

"Let me see," Ed moved forward to examine Lucy's neck, and then remembered that she was naked. "Sorry, sorry, are you okay?" he cried, now closing his eyes and standing still.

"No, it really hurts, do you think I've broken it?" Lucy groaned as she tried to turn her head back.

"I doubt it." Ed replied, taking a crafty look at Lucy's backside through squinted eyes.

Christ it was perfect he thought, just right for grabbing hold of. He then quickly thought of Coco the Clown as a tent started to form in his pyjama trousers.

"You've probably just strained it. You need to get some ice on it if you have. Give it a couple of minutes, and then see whether you can move your head without any pain in your neck." Ed turned his back to Lucy. He had thought of a whole family of clowns, but this erection wasn't budging.

"Okay, thank you." Lucy whispered. "Do you think that you could go now?" Lucy was conscious that her backside was still sticking into the air. She'd managed to grab the discarded towel and was now wrapping it around herself.

"What, oh yes, sorry. Only do you think you'll be long because I'm dying for a pee?"

"WHAT?" Lucy roared.

"No…okay, not to worry, I'll go to the one downstairs. It's just I feel, so weak…it's fine I'm sure I'll manage." Ed couldn't see Lucy's face but had a feeling that she wasn't smiling. "You take your time."

"Idiot," Lucy muttered, once she heard the door close behind him.

Tentatively, she turned around and slowly sat down on the toilet seat, trying hard not to move her head. After a couple of minutes massaging her neck with her fingers, Lucy felt the pain ease slightly. Very carefully she moved her head from side to side, anticipating another sharp pain, but there wasn't one. There was still a dull ache in Lucy's neck, but she guessed that she hadn't strained it too badly.

After an awkward ten minutes, trying to dress without moving her neck too much, she gathered her wet hair up, on top of her head and made her way to Nate's room, gently knocking at the door.

"Nate," she called softly as she popped her head around the door. "It's time to get up."

Nate stirred and rubbed his nose furiously before stretching his legs and arms. "Okay," he mumbled, yawning loudly.

"Do you need me to help you get dressed?" Lucy asked, not sure how much Nate did for himself.

He shot up in bed, his messy hair like an untidy bird's nest on his head. "No way!" He cried. "I can wash and dress myself."

Lucy smiled and giggled quietly. "Okay, I'll see you downstairs in a few minutes. What would you like for breakfast?" she asked.

"Cornflakes, please. Now can I have some privatesee?"

"Yes you can have some *privacy*," Lucy corrected him. "I'll see you downstairs in a few minutes." She closed the door and moved toward the stairs.

Once downstairs Lucy was surprised to see Ed, he was pouring cereal into a bowl with NATE emblazoned on it.

"What are you doing down here?" she asked Ed's back. "You should be in bed. Anyway, I thought that you were too weak to come downstairs." She was suddenly embarrassed, remembering that Ed had just seen her backside in its full glory.

"I know. I do feel really rough, but it's the least I can do after you almost broke your neck." Ed smiled, still turned away from Lucy. "But broken...well it's rather dramatic." He now turned to face her with a large smile, a smile as big as he could muster as he felt so ill.

"It was really painful, and as for you, Mr "I'm too weak to go downstairs for a pee," you big baby. Anyway, get yourself back to bed, you look terrible."

"I think I will if that's okay." Ed's smile now turned into a frown. He wiped his brow with the back of his hand. "Oh, I almost forgot," he said, pausing at the door. "Nice glutes, by the way." With that, he disappeared, giggling quietly to himself, but wincing as his whole body ached.

Lucy couldn't help but smile herself as she recalled the earlier bathroom incident. A few minutes later Nate rushed into the room, his school jersey tied around his waist.

"Excuse me young man, what is that?" Lucy pointed at the offending jumper.

"My jumper." Nate looked at Lucy, as though she were stupid.

"Yes I know that, but why is it tied around your waist? Put it on properly please."

Nate sighed heavily and rolled his eyes. "Okay."

"Thank you. And while I think about it, your dad has said no video games for the next two days because of yesterday's trouser incident."

"I thought Daddy was poorly." Nate frowned as he hauled himself up onto a stool at the breakfast bar.

"He is, but that doesn't mean he can't give orders. I'll probably be looking after you again tonight, so once you've had tea, we will do some reading, but no video games, okay?"

"Okay, can I have my cornflakes now please?" Nate asked, swinging backwards and forwards on the stool.

"Yes Nate you can." Lucy smiled and rubbed his head. She was beginning to adore this little boy and was going to be sad when her two weeks of looking after him were over.

After dropping Nate off at school, Lucy finally got to the surgery by 9:30 a.m. Luckily, the waiting room was fairly sparse of patients, and Callie appeared to be coping admirably without any help.

"Hi Callie," said Lucy, breathlessly. "I'm so sorry I'm late. I was hoping to be here just after nine, but Nate's teacher needed to speak to me." Lucy shrugged off her jacket and took it into the staff room.

When she came out of the room, Callie was looking at her quizzically, tapping a biro against her front teeth. "What did she want?"

She was nothing if direct, Lucy thought, but she wasn't about to spill the beans that Dr Bryce's son had been misbehaving. Anyway, Mrs Bushnell had wanted to apologise for the calling Nate and Bradley idiots, Lucy's comments had obviously hit home. However, their punishment still stood, plus they were on litter duty instead of doing P.E. later today.

"Oh she just wondered how Dr Bryce was." Lucy was careful not to call him Ed at the surgery.

"Oh right," Callie nodded slowly. "And how is he pet, any better this morning?"

"No, not really." Lucy started busying herself with the post that was still waiting on the desk.

"He did get up but, erm he didn't feel well at all." Lucy blushed as once more she remembered Ed and herself in the bathroom.

"When did he get up then, this morning or last night?" Callie smiled at Lucy as she sucked at the end of the biro. She evidently wanted to laugh at her double entendre.

"I will ignore that Callie. It was this morning, and he got up out of bed and came downstairs."

"Oh right. You didn't fancy helping him to sweat it out then?" Callie couldn't help herself now and laughed heartily, forgetting about the biro, she nearly choked on it. "Oooh, huh, huh." Pulling the biro out of her mouth, Callie was laughing and coughing at the same time.

"Callie stop it, please. Dr Bryce and I have a purely professional relationship, nothing more." Lucy looked at her sternly as she passed Callie her mug of tea.

"Ooh thanks," she croaked, sipping the now cold tea. "You must admit you do fancy him though, don't you pet?"

"No!" Lucy hissed, conscious of the three patients waiting. "I've only just split up from my husband, of course I don't fancy Dr Bryce. It's far too soon, it wouldn't be professional, I'm still grieving for my marriage, and I…"

Callie lifted the palm of her hand to stop Lucy. "Alright, alright, forget I said anything, but to be honest pet, I think you'd make a smashing couple."

Lucy sighed heavily and shook her head. "I'll deal with this patient, you go and make a fresh pot of tea." She pushed Callie gently towards the staff room.

"In a few minutes pet, I'll just stay in case you need help with anything."

Lucy furrowed her brow, why would she need help, Callie told her she'd picked everything up quickly? Lucy shrugged her shoulders, and then smiled at the waiting patient.

"Hello sir, can I help you?"

The small, grey haired man smiled at Lucy and then smoothed his greasy fringe down on his forehead.

"I'm Mr Drake, and I'd like to make an appointment to see a doctor please." He said, in an exceptionally nasally voice.

"Well I'm afraid we have nothing available today Mr Drake, unless it's an emergency, we're a doctor down you see. I can do tomorrow morning at ten-thirty, is that any good?" Lucy looked at the little man and smiled.

"Well *you* may be able to help." Mr Drake said, smoothing down his hair once more. "It's this you see, what do you think it might be?" He started to fumble about with his fly, and before Lucy could stop him, he'd moved around to Lucy's side of the reception desk and presented his penis on the flat of his hand.

Lucy almost choked as she held on to the desk. "Well I think it might be a penis," she spluttered. Looking for help she turned around to Callie, perhaps a little too quickly as she felt a twinge of pain in her neck. "Oww," she cried.

"I know that," he said. Ignoring Lucy's obvious discomfort he leaned forward and poked her in the shoulder. "It's the thing at the end of it that I'm not sure about. Do you think you could take a closer look?"

Callie now stepped forward to come to Lucy's aid. "Come on Mr Drake, we've talked about this, you can't keep exposing yourself pet, particularly when there's nothing wrong with it."

"But I can assure you there is. *LOOK*!" he insisted, taking a step forward and pulling it toward Callie and Lucy so that they could get a closer look.

"No, don't!" Callie picked up her ruler and smacked Mr Drake's arm. "Put it away."

"I will not put my penis away, there is something wrong with it, can you not see?" The little man stamped his foot like a small child, his appendage disappearing momentarily as he let go of it, quickly he took hold of it again and placed it back on his palm, adamant that he wasn't going to be fobbed off.

Lucy had now composed herself, slightly, and realised that he wasn't going to be moved until someone looked at it for him.

"Shall I get Dr Kindler?" she asked Callie, who was now standing hands on hips, equally adamant that Mr Drake would remove his silly little dick.

"I want someone to look at it now!"

"Dr Kindler is busy so please put it away." Callie insisted.

"No, I won't."

"Yes you will. I'll hit you again if you don't." Callie raised her ruler.

"No, Callie, don't." Lucy grabbed the ruler from her and sighed heavily. "I'll look at it. He's not going to go unless someone does is he, so I'll take one for the team."

"He does this all the time Lucy, don't let him have his own way."

"Please Callie, let's just get it over and done with. Right, hold still while I take a closer look." As she leaned forward, Lucy held her breath, worrying irrationally that it was going to explode. Suddenly, she started to giggle.

"What do *you* think it is?" she asked the strange little man, before holding a hand over her mouth.

"Some sort of cyst?" He seemed genuinely concerned as his eyes watered.

"It's not a cyst."

"What is it?" Callie asked, now leaning her head next to Lucy's and peering at Mr Drake's willy.

"It's a piece of sweet corn." Lucy managed to say, her teeth gritted to stop herself from laughing.

"Sweet corn." Mr Drake and Callie chorused.

"Yes sweet corn, so I suggest you go home and give it a complete wash. Now, if you wouldn't mind removing your penis from our reception it would be much appreciated."

After spending the next half hour spraying the reception area and Callie's ruler, with antiseptic, Lucy actually found the situation quite amusing. Callie hadn't stopped giggling since Mr Drake had left with his tail between his legs, so to speak, and every time Lucy had looked up from her scrubbing and spraying, it had set Callie off.

"Finally," Lucy sighed. "I feel as though I've washed him away, disgusting little man. Does he really come in and show it to you regularly?"

Callie was now starting to calm down as she sipped her mug of tea. "Oh aye pet, every couple of weeks or so he comes in with it hanging out. To be honest, I think it's the only airing it gets."

"Urgh, he needs reporting." Lucy scratched her head and grimaced.

"He doesn't have nits pet, just a penchant for getting his cock out. Anyway, I canna report him, his brother is the desk Sergeant at the station, it wouldn't get anywhere and what would it achieve? He's not harming anyone. I usually just give him a smack with my ruler, and he's on his way."

"Well, not today he wasn't. He was adamant that I was going to look at it for him. I tell you something, I'll have some tales to tell when I get back home." Lucy giggled as she recalled both Mr Presley and Mr Drake.

"Are you still going home then, Lucy? Don't you fancy staying around here, be near to your dad pet?" Callie finished her tea and moved towards the staff room.

Lucy shrugged. "I don't know, I hadn't really thought about it. I've got my house and my friends back in Cheshire." Lucy called to Callie through the open, staff room door.

"Aye, I suppose, but you've got a couple of nice little jobs here now." Callie said, re-emerging with her jacket.

"Hmm but they're only temporary…Callie why have you got your jacket? You're surely not cold are you?"

"No pet, sorry I forgot to mention I needed to pop out for a couple of hours. I'll be back before you need to go. We've only got a couple of patients this afternoon, and one of them is for Ellen. Howay, here she is now. Hello hinny, busy morning?" Callie smiled warmly at a frazzled looking Ellen.

"Ooh God if you only knew. Why don't some of these women take bloody precautions? I've just delivered Shirley Hawkins eighth child. The little bugger must have been anxious to come out, I only just got there in time. Mind you when you've dropped seven before, it must be pretty easy. It was like a bag of laundry down a chute…anyway morning Lucy, how are you my love?" Ellen asked, flopping down onto a chair behind the desk.

"Oh Lucy's had the pleasure of Mr Drake this morning." Callie started to giggle again. "Anyway, I'd best be off. See you later."

"Bye Callie, I'll give you a call later…so Mr Drake hey Lucy. What did you think about his little fella then?" Ellen asked while watching Callie leave. She now turned back to Lucy. "Anyway, how's Dr Bryce is he any better?"

"Not really, well not when I left him this morning." Lucy felt her colour rise as she thought about Ed.

"Oh dear, poor Dr Bryce. You'll have to soothe his brow when you get back." Ellen winked at Lucy, before swinging the chair around to the computer at the desk to look at the appointments. "So, just Craig Mason's blood sugar tests this afternoon then." Ellen stood up and yawned. "Oh well, no rest for the wicked, when he gets here send him in, please, Lucy."

"Okay," Lucy said to Ellen's back. "I'll bring you a cuppa through in a minute."

"Bless you my child." Ellen replied, doing the sign of the cross.

By 2 p.m. Callie still hadn't returned, and Lucy was getting anxious, she'd said that she'd be back by noon. Lucy hoped that she was okay. Furthermore, she had to pick Nate up at 3 p.m., and it took at least fifteen minutes to get to school at this time of day.

The afternoon had been quiet, without drama or incident. Dr Kindler popped out of his room for a cup of tea and a quick chat, but had subsequently disappeared again to do some paperwork while things were quiet. Ellen saw her patient and afterwards went home to get some sleep; she had another expectant mother having a home birth, in slow labour.

Then, just as Lucy was about to try Callie's mobile, she rushed in through the door looking hot and sweaty. Her hair was dishevelled and her top on back to front.

"Hiya, I was getting worried about you." Lucy said, looking Callie up and down. "Been having some afternoon love have you?"

"No, you dirty minded little devil. I've been having a bad back, so have been for physio', but I'm okay." Callie smiled and rubbed Lucy's arm. "I'm sorry that you've been on your own so long. I bet you're starving aren't you?"

"No, I'm fine. I had some fruit in my bag, so I ate that. Are you sure you're okay, is your back hurting now?"

"Eeh pet stop fussing. Like I said, I'm okay," Callie sighed, looking Lucy's slim frame up and down. "And fruit, for lunch you say, no wonder there's nothing of you. Anyway, you get yourself off, and I honestly am sorry pet."

"Callie, stop worrying about it, I was just worried about you. Anyway, I may as well stay for a little while and then go straight to school."

"Okay pet but go and get a cuppa in the staff room.""

"I'm fine thanks, do you want one?" Lucy asked, flicking through a magazine.

"No, not long had one. So, what are your plans for the rest of the week, no surgery tomorrow for you pet?"

Lucy almost forgot that she'd done her three days of work. The time was going so quickly, and Georgina would be home in eight days, then her time with Ed and Nate would be over.

"I don't know, I guess it depends how Ed, sorry Dr Bryce is."

"Oh Ed is it?" Callie smiled as she nudged Lucy playfully.

"It just seemed strange to call him Dr Bryce when he isn't on duty, he told me to call him Ed, in fact, he insisted." Lucy nudged her back. "Stop stirring it, nothing is going on and nothing will in the future."

"Okay, pet, if you say so." Callie looked at Lucy and smiled. "But if you believe that, then you're a bigger fool than Mr Presley."

By 3:30 p.m., Nate and Lucy were back home, and Nate was kicking his shoes off at the front door. There had been no confrontation with Mrs Bushnell today, so Lucy assumed that Nate's day hadn't involved any misdemeanours on his part.

"Can I go up and see Daddy, please?" he asked, one foot already on the bottom stair.

"Okay, but if he's asleep try not to wake him." Lucy picked up Nate's shoes and discarded school bag and put them into the cupboard under the stairs.

After half an hour, while Lucy was preparing a salad, Nate reappeared now dressed in tracksuit pants and a hoody.

"Daddy said can you go up and see him?" Nate flopped down on to the sofa in the dining area. "Can I watch T.V., please?" he asked, already pointing the remote control at the wall-mounted television.

"Okay, just until dinner is ready and then afterwards we will do some reading." Lucy smiled warmly at Nate, cute as he was his punishment still stood.

Lucy walked slowly up the stairs, wondering what Ed needed and worrying that his chest would be bare again. She wasn't sure she could refrain from touching him for much longer. She'd left a bottle of water and packet of Paracetamol next to his bed this morning, perhaps he'd run out of one, or both.

Once outside his door Lucy knocked gently, hoping that he would have a T-shirt or pyjama top on.

"Come in," Ed answered, rather huskily.

Lucy gave a sigh of relief, he was wearing a T-shirt. "Hi, Nate said that you wanted to see me."

"Hi," Ed looked at her intently. She looked beautiful he thought. Her hair was tied up in a bun, revealing her slim neck and her deep green eyes peeked at him from under long dark lashes. She was wearing a simple, long sleeved, T-shirt with skinny jeans and on her feet were pink, fluffy slippers. Ed thought that she looked tired, tired but beautiful.

"How's your neck?" he asked, conscious that he was staring at her.

"Oh, fine thanks," Lucy replied, instinctively putting a hand to it.

"Oh that's good. Anyway, I just wanted to say thanks, for looking after Nate, and me. I really appreciate it." Ed gulped. It was hurting his throat to talk.

"No problem, I don't mind. Is your throat sore? Nate and I could go out and get you some lozenges if you like?"

"God no, load of rubbish. Some salt water would be great, or some watered down antiseptic, there's some in the medicine cupboard. But before you go though, can I ask you something?" Ed paused to take a sip of water.

Inexplicably Lucy's heart started to thud like a bass drum in her chest. "Y-y-yes, what?" she asked.

"Well as thank you, I was wondering…God how do I say this without sounding like I'm coming on to you, because I'm not, it's just that I'm really grateful for all that you've done…but well, I was wondering if you would like to come to the annual NHS dinner with me next Saturday evening…just as friends of course." Ed hadn't meant to sound so pathetic, but he was anxious not to frighten Lucy. He knew that she was nowhere near ready for a relationship, but he genuinely wanted to take her as she deserved a night out.

Lucy, her colour rising, lowered her head. She began playing with a tendril of hair that had fallen down from her bun. "Oh that's really kind of you, but what about Nate. Your dad won't be back until the Sunday, and your mum on the following Wednesday, who will you get to look after him?"

"Dr Kindler's grand-daughter, Amy, has done some babysitting for me before, I'm sure she'll do it." Ed coughed and then groaned, his throat felt as though he were swallowing razor blades.

Lucy moved over to the bed and looked more closely at Ed. "You look terrible, let me go and get that salt water for you. Do you need anything else?"

Ed shook his head and coughed weakly. "No, that's fine. So, what do you think, about the dinner I mean?"

Lucy surprised herself with her quick response. "Okay, that would be lovely, thank you. Now let me get you that water." Lucy turned away to hide the blush that was at her cheeks.

As she turned to leave Ed reached out and grabbed her hand. "Thanks Lucy, I don't know what I would have done without you today, and I'm glad that you're going to come with me to dinner. They're quite a good night usually."

"Okay, now you get under the covers, and I'll be back in a few minutes."

As she made her way back down the stairs, Lucy couldn't believe that she'd said yes. What was she doing to herself? She kept agreeing to do things that put her in close contact with Ed, having dinner with him, working for him, staying overnight to look after him and

Nate and now this, the NHS dinner. She fancied him like mad, but the old question cropped up once more, wasn't it was too soon after Simon to feel like this?

After Nate had done some reading, Lucy said that he could watch T.V., just for half an hour before bed, giving Lucy time to call Gerald. She left him a message on his mobile yesterday, to say she was staying over to look after Nate, but now felt the need to speak to him in person.

"Hi Dad," she said breezily as Gerald answered the phone.

"Hello darling, how are you? How's Ed, I got your message?" Gerald was smiling on the other end. He liked Ed and thought he might be just what Lucy needed.

"He's still not well Dad. I'm going to have to stay at least another night. Your house is fine though, well, it was when I drove past earlier. It's all locked up, and the alarm is on."

"Oh that's okay, not that I'm worried about it. Anyway, anything exciting happening there?" Gerald asked.

"No, nothing much happening, I'm afraid. Although, I did have a run-in with Nate's teacher, Mrs Bushnell." Now she thought about it Lucy was a little embarrassed. She hated it when parents shouted the odds at her, plus she wasn't even Nate's parent.

"Really, why was then that?" Gerald asked, settling himself further in his chair, ready to hear Lucy's tale.

Lucy recounted the trouser incident and Mrs Bushnell's name calling of Nate and his friend.

"So I know it was wrong, and everything I hate about parents, but I couldn't help myself," Lucy explained, expecting a telling off from her father for being rude.

"Well if you thought it justified, but maybe you'll appreciate the 'horrible parents' a little more now." Gerald laughed, imaging Lucy telling Nate's teacher off. "Funny though isn't it, you know that you feel so protective of him already?"

Lucy's brow furrowed. "I suppose so, but I'd react the same way for any child."

"I'm not saying you wouldn't, and Nate is a terrific kid. I totally understand why you felt it necessary to protect him. So, what about Ed, I know he's ill, but how are you coping being around him?"

"Hey, what do you mean?" Lucy blushed, surely her dad hadn't realised that she was lusting after Ed, she'd hoped that she wasn't that obvious.

"You know what I mean Lucy. I'm your dad, I don't miss anything. I've seen a change in you since you've been working for him, *and* young lady, I've seen that glint in your eyes whenever you speak about him."

Lucy shook her head vehemently. "Dad, seriously, you don't know what you're talking about. There is no way I fancy Ed," she whispered, frightened that Nate might hear. She looked across at him, but he was still engrossed in a quiz show on the T.V.

"Rubbish," Gerald admonished. "Of course you do, crikey Lucy you're only human, he's a good looking man. Oh, sweetheart I do worry about you."

"What are you worried about me for?" Lucy frowned, unsure what Gerald could be worried about.

"I worry about you because you're obstinate Lucy. You can't see what's in front of you, and if you can you're too stubborn to admit it. Ed is perfect for you, so just ask him out on a date, or whatever it is you youngsters do these days." Gerald sighed.

"Dad, for one I would hardly call myself a youngster, and for two, what on earth makes you think that I want to go out on a date with him, or him with me for that matter?"

"It's obvious that you like each other, so why wouldn't you want to go on a date with each other?"

Lucy sighed and shook her head, a small smile touching her lips. "If, and that's a massive if, I did fancy Ed, well I wouldn't do anything about it because it's just too soon after Simon. Plus I think Ed is still heartbroken over his wife, so he's not ready either."

"What a load of rubbish, too soon after Simon. Seriously, Lucy, life is too short to spend worrying about time, it's just a number. Do you think that Simon worried whether it was too soon to jump into bed with Jennifer 'bloody bitch face' Grayson? No, he bloody well didn't, so why should you?" Gerald was quite animated now, banging his fist down on the arm of the chair. "As for Ed, I'm pretty sure that believe it or not, Ed has had sex in the last three years. He doesn't come across to me as a man heartbroken over his ex-wife."

"Okay Dad, keep your hair on," Lucy giggled. "I hear what you're saying, but don't you think people will think I'm being a bit reckless, or more to the point stupid?"

"Sod what people think or say, it's your life. And if it doesn't work out, well you're stronger than you think, you'll get over it."

"I know Dad, and I know you just want what's best for me, but it's all a bit scary."

"Lucy my darling, life is scary. I worried about you marrying Simon, and I know it's different, but I just don't worry about the thought of you being with Ed." Gerald sighed heavily. "Sweetheart, I just want you to be happy. I want you to step out there and take life by the scruff of the neck and enjoy yourself."

Lucy exhaled as she thought about Gerald's words.

"Okay Dad, I will, I'm just not sure how big the steps will be."

Chapter 10

When Lucy called Sarah later that evening, her news of the dinner had been met with squeals of delight.

"What are you going to wear?" Sarah asked excitedly. "You should go shopping and buy something fabulous, something so sexy that he won't be able to resist you."

"Hang on; I haven't decided whether I'm going to go yet." Lucy frowned as she played with the hem on her T-shirt.

"I thought that you just said that you'd agreed to go." Sarah was perplexed.

"Yes I did, but I may change my mind, I might make up an excuse."

"Lucy," Sarah moaned. "Don't be so silly; go to the bloody dance for goodness sake."

"Sarah, don't have a go at me, please, I know it's stupid, but all this business of fancying someone other than my husband is a bit scary."

"The husband you're separated from because he's got a pregnant girlfriend, don't forget. Ah Luce, please don't be scared, it's meant to be fun." Sarah's tone softened. "What are you scared of anyway?"

Lucy heaved a sigh. "I don't want to go through it all again. It's too boring and complicated. Anyway, we've talked about it before, so you know why. Dad gave me a good talking to though, and I am erring more on the side of going, at the moment."

"Good old Gerald, I say. Okay, let's work under the premise that you're going, what are you going to wear?"

Lucy giggled, imagining Sarah rubbing her hands together at the thought of picking an outfit for her. "Listen, do you want to meet in Newcastle for the day, and go shopping? In fact, you could stay over if you like. Dad has plenty of space, and I'm sure Ed will feel better in a couple of days so I won't need to be here for Nate."

"A shopping trip, of course I'll come. Saturday would be better for me, because of the boys. Ben won't mind. He's just had a golf weekend in Scotland. What time shall I meet you?"

Lucy smiled, aware that Sarah was beyond excited about the prospect of a shopping trip. "It's up to you; you'll need to check the times of the train first."

"Okay, I'll do that as soon as I put the phone down, and then I'll text you the time. God, I'm so excited now. Not only do I get to shop with someone else's money, but we can have a lovely lunch, a gossip, and maybe I'll get to meet the good-looking Doctor." Sarah started to laugh.

"Don't you dare embarrass me while you're here."

"I won't." Sarah giggled again.

"I mean it Sarah, I won't be happy if you do," Lucy scolded, deep furrows forming on her brow.

"Okay, okay, I promise." Sarah sighed. "I'll text you later with the time I get into Newcastle."

The following Saturday morning, Lucy sat in the station cafe. She sipped hot, black coffee as she waited for Sarah's train to arrive. The day after speaking to Sarah on the telephone Ed had been feeling much better. He wasn't quite well enough to go back to work, but could look after Nate, and so Lucy packed up her overnight bag and went home after taking Nate to school. Ed was extremely grateful for the extra hours she'd put in while he'd been ill, and insisted that she take the Friday off. As the weather had turned to rain, Lucy had spent the day doing nothing but reading and watching rubbish TV chat shows with warring families. At 3 p.m., when she would pick Nate up from school normally, Lucy realised how much she already missed him. It was going to be hard when Georgina came back and picked up the reins again. However, Lucy also realised it wasn't just Nate that she was missing, but Ed too.

By the time Gerald arrived home later that evening, Lucy was glad to see another human being that wasn't insisting on a DNA test because 'my girlfriend cheated on me with my brothers, wife's uncle!' Gerald had suggested that they share a bottle of wine, and Lucy told him all about the last few days with Ed and Nate. He didn't comment, just nodding and smiling as Lucy had talked.

Lucy looked at her watch; it was 11:25. Sarah's train would be arriving in a couple of minutes. She drank the last of her coffee, picked up her bag and made for the platform.

Among the crowd of people jumping from the train, Lucy could see Sarah desperately trying to drag her overnight case behind her. People were pushing past Sarah, who was tugging at the bag that was obviously stuck.

"Here, let me help you." Lucy laughed as she reached out to drag Sarah's case off the train.

"Oh thank you," Sarah sighed, hugging her friend to her chest. "I had visions of having to leave it on the train, stupid bloody thing."

"More haste less speed, I think the phrase is," said Lucy hugging her friend back. "Did you have a good journey?"

"Hmm, apart from having to leave so early." Sarah tutted and took the case from Lucy.

"I thought you left at eight, that's not too early."

"It is when Saturday is normally your lie-in. Anyway, let me look at you. You look fab sweetheart. The northern air is doing you the world of good."

Lucy blushed slightly as she slapped at Sarah's arm. "Ah, don't be silly. I don't look any different than I did three weeks ago, when I last saw you."

"Oh you do. Remember back then there was a green bobble hat stuck on your head."
Sarah laughed as she ruffled Lucy's hair.

"No, I didn't, I'd actually taken it off by then. I have to admit though, it is lovely here
– away from Simon, and you know who." Lucy took hold of Sarah's arm and steered her
toward the station exit.

"I need to drop my bag at left luggage before we hit the shops. A little retail therapy is
just what the doctor ordered," Sarah said, smiling at Lucy.

Nearly two hours later and Lucy and Sarah finally took a break for lunch. Lucy already
had the perfect dress, according to Sarah, and now just needed shoes to match. Sarah even
persuaded her to buy some new underwear to match the beautiful ivory, lace dress that she'd
bought. Lucy had argued with Sarah about the underwear. It was expensive, and as Lucy had
pointed out she didn't *actually* need a bra. She wasn't exactly well endowed.

"Okay," Sarah said, pausing from eating her salmon. "You've officially got just over
three weeks left here, so do you think you'll sleep with the good doctor in that time?"

"*Sarah*, you're obsessed with my sex life. All we've done is a little flirting." Lucy
shook her head and gave Sarah a withering look.

"Well if it was me, I probably would." Sarah shot a smile at Lucy before continuing to
eat her lunch.

"Oh there's a shock!" Lucy replied sarcastically

"I just think it's worth considering, although you've not said much about him since I
got here, you've not gone off him have you?"

"No, there's just nothing to say about him." Lucy put her knife and fork down and
pushed her plate away.

"So you do still fancy him then? Come on Lucy, you fancy him like mad don't you, and from what you've said he seems to fancy you too." Sarah grinned as she poked Lucy in the shoulder.

Lucy held her hands up in submission. "Okay I admit I do fancy him and after spending a few days with him, and Nate, well…I fancy him more than ever. I can't stop thinking about him." Sitting back Lucy felt relieved that she'd finally admitted it aloud. "Happy now?"

"Hallelujah!" Sarah smiled and shook her fists in the air. "I never thought you'd admit it. So, does that mean you may actually let him see that new underwear you've just bought?"

"Sex really is all you think about isn't it?" Lucy blushed and drank some of her wine. "Look, I think he may like me, he's definitely flirted with me, but it's the same old question – is it too soon?"

"Honestly, no I don't think it is. I know on the telephone I said to sleep with him and be done with it, but having seen how well you're doing, I think you'd cope if you had a relationship with him and it didn't work out. Plus, if you're honest, your marriage hasn't been brilliant for a long time. I know it sounds harsh, but think about it."

Lucy dropped her head and sighed again. She had to admit that Sarah was right. "I think I kidded myself that we were happy all this time, but I've thought about it a lot, especially the last few days. You're right; things hadn't been brilliant since Lottie…not as happy as they should have been, anyway. But, that doesn't mean that Ed is the man I should be with, or will be with for the rest of my life. We may have flirted a little, but that's as far as it goes. I can't base my future on a bit flirting, the twitching in my knickers and chapel hat peg nipples," she said as she smiled at Sarah.

"Even thinking about moving on is a massive step forward though, Luce. No one is saying he's going to be the one, but it might be fun finding out." Sarah took a sip from her drink, before coughing to clear her throat. "Anyway, there's something else I need to tell you."

"What, something exciting I hope."

"Depends how you look at it. Simon and Jennifer have had a little boy." Sarah paused waiting for a reaction; Lucy merely nodded for Sarah to continue. "He was born two days ago, about two weeks early, and he's called Caleb."

Lucy downed the rest of her drink and was silent while she took in the information that Sarah had just given. Finally, she was ready to speak.

"How did you find out?"

"He rang Ben."

"Where are they living, do you know?"

"They're living in Jennifer's house, in Knutsford. Apparently, when Ben saw them in town, a few weeks ago, they'd been to visit Andrew, his solicitor."

"He hasn't contacted me, or my solicitor." Lucy played with the salt cellar as she mulled the information over in her head.

"Actually, he may have Luce," Sarah interrupted her thoughts. "I've got a pile of letters here for you. When I knew I was coming over, I called in on Brian to pick up your post." Sarah reached down to her handbag and pulled out a ream of letters, held together with an elastic band. She passed them over to Lucy.

Lucy flicked through them quickly, finally stopping and pulling a white envelope free of the band. Across the top was emblazoned "McCartney, James & Munroe"- Simon's solicitors. She ripped open the envelope, pulled out the letter and read it. After a few minutes, Lucy refolded it, put it in the envelope and popped it into her handbag with the rest of her post.

"Well?" Sarah leaned forward and took hold of Lucy's hand.

"He wants a divorce, no massive shock there. He wants to sell the house but is willing to give me two-thirds of the profit. Unless of course, I want to buy him out, and then he wants a third of the equity, which is probably about twenty-five thousand pounds." Lucy sat back in her chair and indicated to the waiter for two more drinks.

"I'm assuming the grounds for divorce are his adultery?"

Lucy shook her head. "You're joking aren't you? No, he's gone for unreasonable behaviour, apparently we have no common interests – twat!"

"No way!" Sarah was astonished. "He can't do that, you were having sex up until he left, isn't that a common interest. I bet Jennifer 'bloody bitch face' Grayson doesn't know that!"

Lucy laughed emptily. "I don't care anymore, Sarah. Like you said, I need to move on and if agreeing to that means that I can, then so be it. I'll call my solicitor on Monday. A copy has apparently gone to him. Thank you," Lucy said, looking up at the waiter as he placed two more glasses of wine on the table. "I suppose he's being quite generous only asking for a third of the equity, he could have asked for a third of the value."

"Bloody hell Lucy," Sarah spluttered. "Generous is the least he can be after what he's done to you. So what are you going to do, sell or buy him out?"

"Until I speak to my solicitor I don't know. I have to be honest though, my heart is saying, sell up and make a fresh start. Anyway, where am I going to get that much money from?"

"Re-mortgage, ask your dad?" Sarah winced. Neither were particularly attractive options.

"Hah, neither," Lucy echoed Sarah's thoughts. "How can I get a mortgage when I don't have any income? I can't ask my dad and Richard. It wouldn't be fair, and I have no way of paying them back. Even if I get another job teaching, most of my salary would go on the mortgage. My savings from when Grandpa died amounts to about twelve thousand pounds, but that would still leave a massive chunk of money to find. No, I think I'm going to have to sell up, get a job teaching if I can, and then either rent or buy something small."

"Oh sweetheart, I'm sorry. He's really messed your life up hasn't he? Maybe you should think more seriously about staying. You could stay with your dad for a while until you get a job, and then you'd have a lovely lump sum to put down on a cottage in the town."

"Hmm." Lucy nodded. "It's an option, but places in Dad's town aren't cheap, but at a push I may be able to manage it. Anyway, let's not think about that now. I've got shoes to buy for this dinner that I may not even go to."

"Lucy!" Sarah practically snarled at her.

"I'm joking; of course I'm going to go. I haven't spent nearly two hundred pounds on a dress that I'm not going to wear. Come on drink up; let's spend some money while I still have some."

Later, that evening, Lucy and Sarah were back at the house enjoying some dinner and a bottle of wine with Gerald.

"So Sarah, did you manage to spend any money this afternoon, or was it just Lucy?" Gerald leaned forward and filled Sarah's glass.

"I did manage a lovely pair of shoes and matching handbag, but generally, it was Lucy splashing the cash. She's going to look amazing, by the way." Sarah grinned at Lucy.

"Really," said Gerald winking at Sarah. "Amazing enough to knock Ed sideways?"

"Dad!" Lucy scuffed Gerald's arm. "Stop encouraging her. She's talked about him all afternoon and hasn't even met him."

"Well we can always rectify that. Pass me my mobile please." Gerald pointed to his phone.

"What are you doing Dad?" Lucy looked shocked. "You're not ringing Ed are you?" She passed Gerald his phone tentatively.

"No, don't be silly. I'm going to ring Mike the taxi man. Go and get ready girls, we're going down to the pub."

"Ooh how exciting, do you think Ed will be there?" asked Sarah, getting up from her chair and clapping her hands.

"He's often in The Well on a Saturday night, so there's a good chance." Gerald started to punch out the numbers on his phone. "Mike, hi there, Gerald Falmer here. Can we have a taxi in, oh let's say, a half hour? Excellent see you then, thanks Mike. Right off you go. You've got half an hour to beautify yourself." Gerald nodded at Lucy. "Sarah, can you help me upstairs, so I can have a quick wash and brush up?"

"Sure no problem. Go on Luce, hurry up." Sarah pointed to the door. "Get up those stairs and get ready, I can't wait to see the gorgeous doctor."

"Do I have a say in this?" Lucy asked.

"No!" Gerald and Sarah chorused together.

"Dad it's packed in here, you're going to get knocked about?" Lucy held on to Gerald's arm as she scanned the room looking for a chair.

"There's a table over there," Sarah shouted above the chatter and clinking of glasses. "Lucy you help your dad, and I'll go and save the table."

"Okay, come on Dad. Be careful, it's really crowded." Lucy manoeuvred her father by the arm around the crowded bar.

"I'm fine Lucy, I'm not disabled I've only broken my leg." Gerald smiled kindly at Lucy, whom he could tell was nervous about the possibility of seeing Ed.

"Okay sorry, I was just trying to be helpful," she said holding a chair out for him. "There you go. I'll go to the bar, what do you both want?"

"Let me come too, please." Sarah said excitedly, hoping that Ed may be at the bar.

"It doesn't need both of us, you go if you're that bothered." Lucy frowned at Sarah and flopped down onto a chair next to Gerald.

"Oh, okay," Sarah replied sulkily. "What would you like Gerald?"

"A pint of bitter please, any kind will do."

"What about you, frosty knickers?" Sarah asked Lucy, poking her in the shoulder.

"White wine please, and make it a large one."

Smiling at Lucy, Sarah walked away giggling to herself.

"What's wrong Lucy?" Gerald asked, knowing full well what the problem was. "Not worried about seeing Ed are you?"

"You know I am; it makes me look like a stalker Dad. He's bound to think I've come in here just to see him."

"Not necessarily, your friend is over to see you, so why wouldn't you bring her to the busiest pub in tow..." Gerald didn't finish, as was suddenly distracted by something in the distance. "Oh I think Sarah wants you," he said, a huge smile upon his face as he tried to stifle a laugh.

Sarah was near the bar, waving wildly at Lucy and pointing at a dark-haired man standing next to her. "Is this him?" she mouthed

Lucy, highly embarrassed, dropped her head into her hands. The dark-haired man had now turned to Sarah and was looking at her quizzically; it wasn't Ed.

"Is she with you?" A voice asked next to Lucy.

Lucy lifted her crimson face to see Ed standing next to her chair. "Oh hi," she whispered, wishing that she was anywhere but in the pub with her batty friend pointing at total strangers.

"Ed, how lovely to see you. Are you feeling better?" Gerald asked, holding a chair out and indicating for Ed to sit down.

Ed shook his head. "No, I can't stay Gerald. I'm here with my friend, Rob. But, I am feeling much better thanks. Did you enjoy your visit to your friend's house?" All the time he spoke to Gerald, Ed surreptitiously looked at Lucy. Noticing how pretty she looked in her navy-blue shirt and white trousers.

"Hmm I had a lovely time. Monica spoiled me rotten. So is it a big night out tonight, or just a few drinks, you could ask your friend to join us too?"

"No, we're only having a couple. Rob's wife is cooking us dinner, Nate is already over there. We've had our orders to be back by nine." Ed smiled and glanced at Lucy.

"So, I believe that you are taking my daughter out on Saturday evening. She's been out shopping today for the perfect outfit, haven't you Lucy?" Gerald didn't look at Lucy but smiled at Ed.

"Yes Dad, I have," she replied through gritted teeth. "The idiot at the bar came with me to buy it."

"Oh great, fantastic," Ed scratched his head furiously. Feeling flustered he still avoided Lucy's gaze. "Is she a friend from home then?" he enquired.

"Unfortunately, yes she is. She's staying over until tomorrow." Lucy groaned inwardly, Sarah was on her way back from the bar.

"Ooh, hello," Sarah said, putting the drinks down on the table. "I'm Sarah, Lucy's friend, and you must be Dr Bryce." She held her hand out to Ed.

"Please call me Ed," he said, shaking her hand. "Anyway, I'd better get back to Rob; it looks as though he's been served, at last. Great to see you all, and I'll see you on Monday at the surgery Lucy."

"Okay Ed, goodnight."

"Night Ed," cooed Sarah, winking at Lucy.

"Goodnight Ed. See you soon," Gerald said, leaning forward to pick up his drink.

"Crikey Luce, you never told me he was that gorgeous. Flipping heck, he's top banana and look at his bum in those jeans." Sarah leaned out of her chair and ogled Ed as he made his way across the pub.

"Please just let me die now," Lucy groaned. "Sit back in your seat and stop staring at the poor man." She pulled Sarah by the arm. "Did you have to make it so obvious that we've been talking about him?"

"What…what did I say?" Sarah was aghast and thought that she had been extremely subtle.

"He saw you pointing at the guy that you thought might be him, and how could he fail to see you wink at me when he said goodnight, you made it so bloody obvious? How can I face him on Monday, he must know I fancy him now? I blame you entirely Father, you sodding well made us come here." Lucy took a drink from her wine and flopped back in the chair.

"Don't be silly, we're just out for a Saturday night drink. Where's the harm in that?" Gerald laughed and nudged Sarah.

"Plenty when it's with bloody Laurel and Hardy." Lucy said, taking another large sip of wine.

"So that's her then," said Rob as he looked at Lucy over Ed's shoulder. "You didn't say she was ginger."

"So what if she is, anyway I would say the colour is russet. Well, what do you think?" Ed was inexplicably nervous about seeing Lucy in the pub.

"Honestly… pretty tasty, and there's no danger of her drowning, although, in my opinion, I'm guessing it's more to do with the bra than natural assets, but you're the doctor, you'd know."

Ed sighed and shook his head. "Do you know Rob, I thank God every day that you sat next to me on that first day at Infant school? Anyway, how can you tell from here, actually don't answer that? Rob, you can stop looking now, thank you." Ed poked Rob sharply in his stomach. "I can't believe she's in here."

"It's the local pub man, and she's living locally. What did you expect?" Rob shook his head and sighed. "What's wrong with you, you've gone all jittery?"

"I know. I feel like a bloody teenager about to ask a girl out on a date." Ed took a large gulp from his beer.

"I thought that you already asked her out on a date."

"No, it's not a date. It's a thank you for looking after Nate last week when I was ill."

"Will you be aiming to get her into bed at the end of it…if so, then that's a date."

Ed shook his head. "Of course I won't be trying to get her into bed. We've discussed this, she's had a bad time, and it wouldn't be appropriate."

"Well a good shag may just be what she needs." Rob laughed at the look of horror on Ed's face. "The look on your face! You really do have it bad don't you mate?"

Ed sighed again and nodded. "Unfortunately, I think I do, and I don't know what to do about it."

Chapter 11

Lucy looked at her reflection in the mirror of her dressing table and smiled. She had just put on the tall, slender heeled nude coloured shoes that she had bought, and was now standing back to look at the result. The dress was nipped in at the waist, sleeveless and had a long zip all the way down the back, and Lucy had to admit it was stunning. She couldn't help but be pleased with the way it accentuated the curve of her small, but pert breasts and narrow back, and showed off her toned arms. Lucy had taken her hair up into a sleek bun, and the only jewellery she wore were a pair of drop pearl earrings. Lucy was really glad that Sarah had persuaded her to buy the dress, shoes, handbag, and the underwear. She felt fantastic, ladylike and elegant and hoped that Ed thought so too.

Lucy smiled as she thought of Sarah. They'd had a seriously good time together the previous weekend. The shopping trip, seeing Sarah, and the evening at the pub with Gerald, had all been fantastic, and Lucy had thoroughly enjoyed herself, despite the letter announcing Simon's intention to divorce her and the embarrassment of seeing Ed in the pub, and Sarah making it obvious that he was their sole reason for being there.

This last week at work, both at the surgery and looking after Nate, had been pretty uneventful. There were some lingering looks between her and Ed, but nothing X-rated and there certainly wasn't any flirting. Even Callie was unusually quiet, not making any meaningful comments or cracking any double entendres.

Although she was used to high heels, Lucy made her way downstairs with some trepidation. Ed was waiting for her, and the last thing that she wanted to do was to fall and make a fool of herself. Once at the lounge door she took a deep breath and slowly opened it. Lucy saw Ed standing with his back to her as she peeked around the door. He was talking to Gerald, who was in his favourite chair, his leg up on the footstool.

"Ah, here she is." Gerald beamed as he noticed Lucy in the doorway. "Wow, you look gorgeous, doesn't she Ed?"

Ed turned slowly and for a moment didn't speak, but just looked at Lucy. He felt a lurch in his stomach, and his heart started to beat faster as he drank in her beauty. This was different from how he'd seen her before. It wasn't with lustful eyes that he now looked at her, no clowns were needed. He didn't just want her body, he wanted all of her. She was so beautiful, and Ed desperately yearned to be a part of her life.

"Erm yes Lucy, you look nice," he finally said, groaning inwardly. Nice really didn't cover how she looked.

Lucy was aggrieved; disappointed that 'nice' was all be could manage. "I guess we'd better go then," she said, bending down to kiss Gerald on the cheek.

"Yes, we don't want to be late." Ed replied.

"Have a good time both of you." Gerald smiled at their disappearing backs.

As Lucy got into the passenger seat of Ed's car, she flicked down the visor, quickly checking her reflection. Nothing had changed from when she was upstairs feeling fantastic, ladylike and elegant. Apparently, her outfit just wasn't Ed's 'cup of tea'.

Ed got in beside her and turned over the engine. "I hope you enjoy it tonight. It won't all be medical talk, I promise. Although, Dr Kindler does get carried away when he's talking about the common cold." He twinkled a smile at Lucy as he moved the car down the road.

"That's okay, I'm sure I'll cope. Who are we sitting with, do you know?" Lucy wondered, hoping it would be someone she knew from the surgery.

"Oh it'll be a practice table. Dr Kindler and his wife Mary; Ellen and her partner Greg; plus Elspeth and her husband, Brendan."

Suddenly, Lucy felt as though she'd only been invited to make up the numbers. "Oh I see, shouldn't you have invited Callie instead of me then? She's the full-time receptionist, I'm just helping out."

Ed glanced at her and frowned. "No, why would I? This was a thank you, to you, for the extra time you put in with Nate last week."

"I just thought that as it was a practice table, that…" Lucy wasn't sure she could put into words what she thought. How could she say, 'I thought that you fancied me and this was a forerunner to you asking me out properly?'

Ed suddenly realised that Lucy had got totally the wrong idea about his invitation.

"Honestly it's not like that Lucy. I really did ask you as a thank you," he stressed.

"It's okay, ignore me, I'm being stupid." Lucy, still unsure whether he meant it, fell silent and stared through the window.

She felt awkward now, she had been convinced Ed had wanted her to come because he liked her and found her attractive, but now she felt as though she was merely making up the numbers.

As Lucy was turned away from him, Ed stole a glance in her direction. Her arms were crossed, her shoulders were tensed, and the way her lips were pinched together in a thin line, he could sense that she wasn't relaxed; and he guessed it was probably because of his 'nice' comment. She'd obviously gone to a lot of trouble, she looked gorgeous for God's sake, and he like an idiot had practically described her efforts as mediocre. Plus, somehow he'd made her think he'd invited her out of duty – Christ far from it, he'd been desperate for tonight to come around, just to spend some time with her.

Ed coughed nervously. "Erm I have to say Lucy, you really do look lovely tonight."

Lucy now looked at him, but there was still no smile. "Yes you said, thank you."

"Well I didn't actually put it very well in the house, did I? And I promise you, this invitation wasn't just to make up the numbers; I've been looking forward to it all week." Ed said, a beseeching look in his eyes.

Lucy unfolded her arms and allowed a small smile to appear on her lips. He looked so apologetic, she couldn't stay cool with him.

"Anyway," she said after a few moments silence, "how do these evenings pan out?" Lucy was desperately trying to change the subject.

Ed laughed and shook his head. "I have to be honest they're more okay than brilliant. There's a four-course dinner usually, followed by a disco. However, you should be warned I'm not a pretty sight on the dance floor."

Lucy starting to relax now, smiled. "I'm sure that I can teach you a couple of steps."

"I'm sure you can," replied Ed watching Lucy sneakily, once again marvelling at how beautiful she looked. What a tit I am, he thought. 'You look nice', Christ no wonder she looked disappointed.

"The problem is," Lucy interrupted Ed's self-criticism, "I'm not sure I can teach anyone sober how to do The Macarena."

Ed laughed, envisioning himself dancing in a line of other doctors, with Lucy at the head teaching them all. "Oh don't worry I don't intend to be sober, I'm going to leave the car at the hotel. So I should be dancing like a professional by the end of the evening."

"That will remain to be seen." Lucy said, giggling quietly to herself.

They continued with their journey for another ten minutes until Ed finally pulled into the grounds of the hotel. As Ed parked the car, Lucy realised that she was feeling apprehensive.

"Blimey, I feel quite nervous," she thought aloud.

"Don't be," Ed replied, undoing his seatbelt. "Everyone is really nice, honestly." He almost groaned aloud – there was that word again. "Oh look, there's Ellen and Greg." Ed jumped out of the car and walked quickly around the car and opened Lucy's door.

"Oh thank you," she said looking up at Ed from under her long lashes. "Very gentlemanly, I must say."

Ed laughed. "Make the most of it; I may not be very gentlemanly after a few drinks."

"I'm counting on it," Lucy whispered, but just loud enough for Ed to hear.

Ed, feeling the familiar sensation of lust for Lucy, thought that there was probably safety in numbers if he were to avoid kissing her right there and then, so he called across to Ellen. "Ellen, wait up, we'll come in with you," he shouted.

"Oh hi there. Hi Lucy," Ellen called waving at them both. "I need the ladies, so wait for us in reception." She and Greg rushed up the steps to the hotel, leaving Ed and Lucy alone on the car park.

"Okay," said Ed watching Ellen disappear. "We may as well go in then. After you." They walked toward the hotel, the gap between them diminishing with each step.

The evening had been as Ed described; the food had been unexciting and there had been a vast amount of cheesy party music played. However, Lucy and the rest on the Springfield Practice table enjoyed it immensely. Lucy had got to know Ellen and Elspeth better, finding they all had the same sense of humour, and Mrs Kindler, a retired solicitor, had been exceptionally kind, offering her advice on her divorce. However, the main reason that Lucy had enjoyed herself was because she'd talked and laughed with Ed, at great length. She tried to teach him The Macarena as promised, but he was pretty hopeless. He was the worst dancer in the line of around fifteen people who were following her lead. They'd jumped about to a couple of Oasis tracks and even did Sambuca shots, at the instigation of Dr Kindler. Who would believe that a sixty-year-old doctor could be such a bad influence?

"Oh my God," Ed gasped, "that was disgusting, what did you say it was called?"

Lucy started to laugh as Ed pulled out his tongue and grimaced. "It's called a 'Slippery Nipple'," she replied, knocking the rest of her own drink back.

"It's bloody awful." Ed picked up his bottle of beer, taking a swig to wash down the sickly liquid.

"Lightweight, oops sorry," gasped Lucy falling against Ed. "I think that last one may have been my cue to drink some water,"

Ed gently held Lucy's arm to steady her, his fingers lingering on her soft skin as their eyes fixed on each other. His heart beat rapidly, and his stomach flipped as he fought hard not to kiss her. This couldn't go on, he thought, if he didn't kiss her soon he was pretty sure he'd internally combust. He'd never felt so attracted to someone before.

Lucy was also feeling highly charged. Her skin tingled at Ed's touch, and a hot flush enveloped her body as she was mesmerised by how handsome he looked in his tuxedo. She couldn't believe that she'd only just noticed. She'd been so worried about her own appearance, and Ed's apparent lack of enthusiasm for how she looked, Lucy hadn't thought about how gorgeous he looked this evening. 'God how shallow am I?' she thought.

"Are you okay," Ed whispered, moving closer to Lucy.

"Yes," her reply was barely audible.

Suddenly the electric atmosphere was broken.

"Hey come on you two, it's 'The Row Boat Song'," Ellen had appeared at Lucy's side, and was now pulling them both toward the dance floor.

The moment was gone, and as they tore their gaze away from each other, Lucy and Ed followed Ellen to join the rest of the party sitting on the floor, shaking their torsos in time to the music.

"Have you enjoyed yourself dear?" Mrs Kindler moved up to the spare chair next to Lucy a little later in the evening.

"Yes, it's been great. Oh and thank you for your advice earlier, I'll certainly make sure that I speak to my solicitor about it." Mrs Kindler hadn't offered any different advice than Mr Devine, Lucy's solicitor, but Lucy hadn't wanted to appear rude and say so.

"Are you enjoying working at the practice, working for Ed?" The older lady didn't look at Lucy but played with her glass.

"Yes and Dr Kindler." Lucy added. "It's been good. I'll be sorry when Richard wants his job back. But," she sighed, "I've got to go home at some point."

"Not necessarily, I'm sure that you could make a decent life for yourself here. There would be a few people sorry to see you go." Mrs Kindler said as she glanced up and smiled at Ed who was standing over at the bar, watching them intently.

Ed had been plucking the courage up to ask Lucy to dance for the last ten minutes, but every time he'd tried to approach her someone else would jump into the seat next to her. Ed knew that he should go over there and ask her, and stop being such an idiot, but the double whisky he'd just knocked back still hadn't made him brave enough. Ed ordered another, and knocked that back too, giving him just the extra edge that he needed. The alcohol suddenly had the desired effect, because as he watched Lucy talking to Mrs Kindler, Ed made his mind up there and then; he wasn't just going to ask her to dance, he was going to ask her out; he wanted them to have a relationship, on whatever level she was ready for. They'd had a fantastic evening, after the false start, and it had become evident to him as the evening went on how badly he wanted her. Ed didn't know if Lucy felt the same way, he thought she might after the incident at the bar earlier, but he'd never know if he didn't ask.

"Right Edward," he said to himself. "Get a grip, grow a pair, and go and get her."

As he approached the table Lucy and Mrs Kindler were still deep in conversation, so Ed stood for a moment, listening to them talk.

"So, I know it may seem a huge decision, so soon after your husband leaving, but life goes on dear. Oh I think someone may want to steal you for a dance." Mrs Kindler nodded her head towards Ed, whom she had just noticed standing next to the table.

"Oh hello." Lucy gulped as she stared at him.

"I thought that you could give it one last go at teaching me how to dance." Ed said, holding his hand out to Lucy.

She smiled and nodded. "Okay, but don't embarrass me again, please."

As she took hold of Ed's hand, Lucy felt her whole body tingle at his touch. Not only did she feel sexually excited by him, but she felt safe with her hand in his. She felt as though it was meant to be there, nothing felt strange about holding hands with him. Lucy tightened her fingers around Ed's and gave his hand a little squeeze. Ed turned his head and gave her a dazzling smile, as if acknowledging that he felt the same way.

As they approached the centre of the dance floor the music suddenly changed, and a slow number started to play. Lucy's legs turned to jelly as Ed turned around and pulled her to him.

"We shouldn't really waste a classic song like this, should we?" Ed started to move his feet and unexpectedly they were in time to the music. He danced Lucy through a crowd of people to the other side of the dance floor, as far from their table as possible.

"I didn't realise you liked Marvin Gaye." Lucy looked at Ed intently as they now shuffled in one spot.

"I love him. He's a very wise man." Ed replied, his eyes scouring every part of Lucy's face.

"In what way is he wise?" Lucy's breathing started to get faster as Ed's lips moved closer to her ear.

"As the man says – let's get it on." Ed's voice cracked with nerves, worried that he was about to make a fool of himself.

"P-p-pardon," Lucy gasped, her heart thumping and her chest rising and falling rapidly. She drew in a shuddering breath as Ed's palm touched her face.

"You heard me, didn't you?"

Lucy nodded silently, biting her bottom lip and staring up at Ed with large eyes.

"So?" he asked. "Do we agree with Mr Gaye?"

Lucy nodded again, her whole body aching for him to kiss her. "Yes," she whispered.

"Excellent." Ed's lips brushed against Lucy's as he cradled her face in both hands. It seemed like hours that their lips were locked together, but it was actually only moments before Ed pulled away. Lucy left deflated, wanting more kisses, almost collapsed into his arms. The kiss had been magical and had taken her breath away.

Ed laughed as he tightened his grip around Lucy's waist. "Are you okay?" He frowned and tilted his head to look intently at Lucy. "Only you look a little strange."

Lucy smiled and exhaled slowly. "Hmm, I'm fine. In fact, I'm more than fine."

Ed suddenly looked concerned. "Are you sure, only I don't want you to think I'm taking advantage because you've had a drink, and I don't want you to think I'm saying this because I've had a drink. Although to be honest, it's the drink that's given me the courage." Ed smiled down at Lucy. "Also, I know that it's quite soon after your husband, but I just had to say something. You look so beautiful you know, more than beautiful, although I can't think of another word that describes how gorgeous you look."

"Nice," Lucy laughed.

"I did try to apologise for being such an idiot," Ed replied a deep furrow across his brow.

"I'm only joking, don't worry. As for you taking advantage, well I don't think you are, and I agree, it isn't long after Simon, but it feels right. But..." Lucy paused and looked down at her feet.

"What?" Ed was alarmed. "Please don't say 'but nothing can happen between us' I couldn't stand that."

Lucy shook her head and smiled. "No, I wasn't going to say that, I was just going to say, can you sort your dancing out? There's nothing more unattractive than a man who can't dance."

Ed pulled Lucy to him, both his arms wrapped around her, holding her tightly. "For you, I'll do anything, but Lucy," he said now holding her away from him. "We will take this as slowly as you want. I don't want to risk spoiling what I think could be a fantastic thing."

"Thank you, but to be honest all I've been able to think about lately is getting into bed with you, so slowly isn't how I want to take it." Lucy blushed and covered her face with her hands. "Argh, I can't believe I've just said that, I think I'll have to blame the drink," she groaned through her fingers, astounded at her own forwardness

Ed gently removed her hands. "It's seeing Mr Drake's penis that has made you so brazen," he said trying to sound serious. "Honestly if it's him you want, then just say."

"No, thanks. I'm quite happy with you; at least, I think I could be."

"No matter how long this lasts I will try to make you happy." Ed whispered softly.

"What do you mean by 'no matter how long it lasts'; don't you expect it to last very long?" Lucy asked, somewhat dejected.

"That's not what I said," Ed looked concerned. He took hold of Lucy's hand and pulled her toward the door. "We need to find somewhere quiet to talk."

After a few minutes of opening doors in the hotel reception, Ed found an empty dining room, already set for breakfast. He led Lucy over to a table and pulled two chairs out.

He sat and dragged Lucy down next to him. "Lucy, I'm not looking for just one night of sex. I really would like us to see where it could go. But, I also know that you are due to go home in three weeks. Three weeks aren't long enough for you to make any life-changing decisions, and I wouldn't expect you to. So that's what I meant when I said, no matter how long it lasts…does that make sense?"

Lucy nodded and smiled. "It does, but I don't have to go back straight away."

Ed lifted Lucy's hand and kissed it. "Why don't we see how things go over the next three weeks before you make any decisions?"

"Okay, but what do we do now?" Lucy asked, looking at him coquettishly.

Ed leaned forward and kissed her again. His fingers stroking Lucy's cheeks as their lips touched, and their tongues explored as they kissed urgently. Lucy moved her hands up and down Ed's strong thighs as she pushed herself closer to him. Finally, very slowly Ed pulled away, gazing intently into Lucy's eyes.

"What would you like to do now?" Ed asked, smiling widely.

"Well my dad is a light sleeper, and you've got Nate to think of. So as much as I'd love to go to bed with you, I think we may have to wait just a little longer." Lucy couldn't believe she was being sensible about it. Ed's kisses were fantastic, and she was desperate for more of him, but tonight just couldn't be that night.

Ed hung his head and ruffled his hair. "Argh, you're right I know, but I'm not sure I can wait much longer. Do you realise how long I've wanted you?" He gazed up at Lucy.

Lucy shook her head. "No, how long?"

"Since the first time I saw you, does that sound cheesy?"

"Nope." Lucy smiled and kissed Ed's cheek. "I felt the same way. I just kept telling myself it was too soon after Simon, and that I shouldn't be attracted to you."

"I know this has happened very quickly, but it feels right. Time is just a number you know."

Lucy started to giggle. "That's just what my dad said."

"You've talked to your dad about us?" Ed started to laugh too. "I thought I'd been able to hide how I felt."

"So did I, but Gerald is rather more astute than either of us give him credit for. Oh and Richard, and don't forget Callie."

"What, they know as well?" Ed looked at Lucy incredulously.

Lucy nodded. "Hmm, I'm afraid they've all been dropping little hints."

Ed shook his head and sighed. "I should have guessed Callie would know. I'm sure she's a witch. Oh well, there's no need to try to keep it quiet then."

"Perhaps we shouldn't say anything to Nate just yet, let's see how things go first." Lucy whispered.

"Hmm I think that's probably best. Listen, my dad is back tomorrow, and I know Nate has missed him a lot, so how about I take him over there to see Dad, once I've picked my car up? It would give us some time alone. You come over to the house for around midday, and just let yourself in if I'm not there."

"That's sounds perfect." Lucy started to giggle. "It seems a little naughty though."

"Well we'll have to see about that. Come on we'd better go back; otherwise they'll all be wondering where we've gone." Ed glanced at his watch. "The taxi will be here in about fifteen minutes."

Lucy leaned in and kissed Ed tenderly, running her hands through his hair, and moving her lips down to nibble his ear.

"Well, let's hope that the next twelve hours fly by," she whispered.

Ed groaned. "I'm going to be counting the minutes I can assure you."

Ed and Lucy finally stopped kissing as the taxi stopped at the end of Gerald's drive.

"Here you are, is this the right address love?" The taxi driver turned to Lucy, who was pulling herself away from Ed.

"Yes it is, thank you. I'd better go," she whispered to Ed. "Thanks again for tonight, it was wonderful."

Ed tucked a stray hair behind Lucy's ear, his fingers lingering on her cheek. "My pleasure and I'll see you tomorrow." He kissed her once more.

"Are you ready love, only I've got another job five miles away in about twenty minutes?" The taxi driver sighed and started to drum his fingers on his steering wheel.

"Yes, sorry. Okay, I'm going, and I'll see you tomorrow." She quickly landed a kiss on Ed's mouth before opening the car door and getting out. "Bye," she mouthed through the window as the taxi sped off up the road.

Quietly letting herself into the darkened, silent house, Lucy felt the excitement build in her stomach for what may happen the following day. All thoughts of Simon and concerns about the timing were banished with Ed's kisses. Lucy felt happy and enthusiastic about the future, for the first time in months.

Chapter 12

After a restless night, Lucy wandered downstairs to find Gerald making a pot of tea.

"Morning sweetheart, did you enjoy the party last night? I didn't hear you come in." Gerald put an arm around Lucy's shoulder as she rested her head on his.

"We had a great night Dad," she sighed.

Gerald kissed her head. "That's good, so why were you moving about all night? I heard you come down here a couple of times."

Lucy turned to Gerald and frowned. "Sorry, I thought I was being quiet. I couldn't sleep and figured some hot milk might help, but, after two cups I was still awake."

"Come on, sit down and tell Daddy all about it with a cup of tea. Can you take the tray over to the table, please love?"

Lucy picked up the tray and followed her father. She sat down next to him and flopped back in her seat.

"Okay, go on." Gerald said as he poured the tea.

"Well I might as well spit it out. Ed and I kissed last night, and have decided to see how things go…you know, as a couple." Lucy put her hand to her mouth and looked at Gerald wide-eyed. "I can't believe I've just said it, I can't believe it happened." Her face then broke into a smile.

Gerald beamed and taking Lucy's hand gave it a squeeze. "That's fantastic news Luce. I'm extremely happy, for both of you. So what's with the restless night and glum face this morning?"

"Because I'm worrying about what happened. What if Ed's changed his mind this morning, now he's sober? What if I get hurt again, and what if people think I'm terrible for getting into another relationship so soon after Simon?" Lucy put her head in her hands and groaned.

"Well, if Ed has changed his mind, which I doubt, he's not worth bothering about. If you get hurt again, then you *will* get over it. You got through Lottie dying, and you've got over Simon leaving you for his pregnant girlfriend. I've said it before, you're much stronger than you think, and it may be you that ends things with Ed, have you thought of that?" Gerald put his hand up to stop Lucy butting in. "Finally, who on earth would think you are a terrible person for being happy? Some people wait years for a second chance at happiness, you are a lucky young lady to find it within a couple of months. We can't mess with fate Lucy." He sat back and sipped from his tea.

"I know I'm being stupid, aren't I? I just couldn't stop worrying during the night." Lucy shrugged and smiled at Gerald.

As she drank her tea Lucy's phone beeped in her dressing gown pocket. She pulled it out. It was a message from Ed.

Morning gorgeous x I can't wait to see you xx

Lucy started to giggle as she read, and then re-read Ed's message. All the time Gerald looked at her expectantly.

"Oh for goodness' sake Lucy, I don't want to pry, but just tell me what's put that smile on your face?"

Lucy thrust her phone at Gerald and squealed with delight. "He hasn't changed his mind."

"Apparently not, but then I didn't expect him to. So, you're meeting up later are you?"

Lucy nodded enthusiastically. "Yeah, I'm going over at lunchtime."

"So are you going to tell Nate?" Gerald poured himself another cup of tea.

"No…actually, I probably shouldn't be telling my dad this, but Ed is taking him over to spend some time with his dad. He's back from his fishing trip today."

"Okay, perhaps you're right; you shouldn't be telling your dad. I don't need to know anything else." Gerald laughed heartily.

"I'd better get ready," Lucy said, glancing at the kitchen clock. "I said I'd meet him at his house at twelve."

Gerald almost spat his tea out. "Crikey Lucy, it's only eight-thirty," he exclaimed.

"God that late, I'd better get going," she gasped, drinking down the last of her tea. "Thanks for the tea Dad." Lucy kissed Gerald on his forehead and rushed out of the room.

At midday, Lucy had been waiting in Ed's kitchen for ten minutes. She went to the hall to check her reflection, for what was probably the twentieth time. She'd left her hair loose and worn a deep purple blouse, black pencil skirt and her black stilettos. She did wonder if it was too formal an outfit, but it made her feel sexy and confident, and so decided to keep it on.

Just as Lucy was reapplying her lipstick, she heard Ed's car pull up on the drive. She ran back into the kitchen, planning on looking nonchalant and unruffled when Ed walked in. However, as soon as she heard the door open she couldn't help herself but rush into the hall.

Ed's eyes lit up as he saw Lucy. "God, you look gorgeous."

As he stepped toward her, Lucy ran to him, throwing herself into his arms. Ed's mouth was on hers as Lucy clung to him, desperate for his kisses, pushing her body against his. Ed kissed Lucy's neck as she held her head back, her fingers now trembling against his face. Her hands travelled up his T-shirt as she marvelled at the sweetness of his taste, feeling the tightness of his muscles. They kissed more urgently, getting more desperate for each other.

Ed started to kiss her hair, her ears and back down to her neck again. Lucy shuddered with desire for him.

"We should probably move away from here. People may see us through the glass in the door," Ed whispered into Lucy's ear.

Lucy backed up the hall into the kitchen, and within moments was pulling Ed's T-shirt over his head. She ran her hands across his shoulders and chest, then down to his flat, toned stomach. Ed slowly removed Lucy's blouse, kissing her neck and shoulders as he let it fall upon the floor.

"No bra to waste time with," he said cupping her pert breasts.

"The advantages of having little ones," Lucy giggled. "No bra required."

"They look perfect to me." Ed bent his head to take one of Lucy's erect nipples into his mouth.

The blood pounded in Lucy's head as she pulled Ed to her by his belt loops. Feeling his evident arousal, she unfastened the button of his jeans and slipped down the zip. He wasn't wearing any underwear.

"Great minds," she groaned reaching inside his jeans.

Ed moaned with delight as he undid Lucy's skirt and pushed it down her slender legs. First stooping to kiss her mouth, he then pulled off her underwear and his own jeans. Finally naked he dropped his head to kiss her stomach.

As Lucy started to step out of her shoes, Ed looked up and shook his head. "No, leave them on," he said. "You wouldn't believe the fantasies I've had about those shoes."

Lucy laughed and placing her foot back inside the shoe, pulled Ed's head up to hers so that she could kiss him.

Ed then scooped Lucy up, and with her legs wrapped around him, he carried her to the rug in the dining area, and laid her gently on it. Lying together they started to explore each other's bodies, rolling over and breathing rapidly as they moved closer to each other. Eventually, Lucy guided Ed inside her, unable to wait any longer. They moved quickly and in unison, both holding tightly to the other, and revelling in their mutual desire, finally culminating in a cry of ecstasy, first from Lucy and then Ed.

They lay together, entwined, gasping as their breath gently slowed down. Ed smiled at Lucy and kissed her tenderly.

"That was amazing," he said, nuzzling her neck.

"I can't believe it," Lucy whispered. "I tried so hard to tell myself it wasn't right, and that I shouldn't feel this way about you."

"Well thank God you didn't try hard enough." Ed leaned with one elbow and looked down on Lucy. "Seriously though, you don't regret it, do you?"

Lucy shook her head. "Nope, not one bit."

Ed gazed into Lucy's eyes and kissed her tenderly. "Shall we go upstairs, where it's more comfortable?"

Lucy nodded. "That sounds great," she giggled.

They made their way up the stairs, running at first, impatient to be with each other once more. However, the sight of Lucy's bare bottom was too much for Ed, and as they reached the landing, he wrapped his arms around her waist and pulled her around to face him.

"God you're beautiful." He made love to her again, but this time more languorously. Finally, on reaching Ed's room they collapsed back onto his bed, lying together and listening to each other's breathing for a while.

"Ed, there's something I need to ask you." Lucy finally whispered as she reached up to kiss him.

"What is it?" he said, pulling himself up into a sitting position.

"Is there any chance, at all, that we could do that again?" Lucy ran her finger along the deep V of his pelvis, her touch rousing Ed once more.

Ed laughed. "You're bloody insatiable, insatiable and sexy...oh my God," he groaned as Lucy's hand moved down the inside of his thigh.

Lucy looked up at him seductively. "If you like that, just wait and see what else I can do."

Leaning across a sleeping Ed three hours later, Lucy checked the time on his bedside clock.

"Ed," she whispered, shaking him gently. "Ed wake up, it's nearly four o'clock."

"Hmm," Ed mumbled pulling Lucy to his chest. "We've got ages yet," he said kissing her forehead.

"What time are you picking Nate up?"

"I said I'd go about five, so there's no need to rush." Ed's fingers started to circle Lucy's nipple.

"You sod," she whispered, her body starting to tingle all over, again. "That's not fair. We need to get up. You need to go and get Nate."

"You're right," Ed sighed. "I do need to get up...so shut up and kiss me." He rolled Lucy onto her back and started to kiss her passionately.

After a few minutes of responding to Ed, Lucy started laughing and pushed him away. "No, enough Dr Bryce. Get out of this bed, get dressed and go and collect your son."

"Aaww, I love Nate, but I don't want to pick him up yet." Ed sat up and smiled down at Lucy. Her smile had disappeared, but her eyes twinkled wickedly. "You're not going to give in are you?"

"No, I'm not. He's got school tomorrow, and I'm sure your poor dad is shattered."

"Okay, okay, I'm getting up." Ed got out of bed, yawning and stretching.

Lucy feasted her eyes on his naked body and almost pulled him back in beside her. He had a broad chest, slim hips and a sculpted pelvis with a fine trail of downy hair. Lucy desperately wanted his strong, tanned, sinewy arms to hold her tightly. Feeling a throbbing in the pit of her stomach, Lucy knew she had to get out of the bed and away from Ed; otherwise she'd undoubtedly drag him back into it for another three hours.

"What are you looking at?" Ed wondered, tweaking Lucy's nose.

"You. Get some clothes on quick, before I change my mind." Lucy put her feet on the floor and leaned over, searching for her shoes.

"They're here." Ed held her high, black shoes from the end of his fingers. "Sure I can't persuade you to put them back on again?"

"I'm sure you could, but you shouldn't. You seriously need to go and pick Nate up."

"I know I do, and I'm going." Ed leaned across the bed and kissed Lucy's shoulder. "Are you going to hang around and wait until I get back, or do you want to come with me?"

Lucy turned to Ed. "I didn't think we were going to tell him yet? Don't you think we should wait a little while?"

Ed shrugged. "I don't know, why do we need to wait? After today, I think we both know how we feel, or did I imagine hearing 'Oh God Ed, you're so good', and 'Oh Ed, do that again.' Well did I?" He laughed at the blush that was creeping up Lucy's neck.

"No, you didn't imagine it, but we have to think of Nate. It might be too much for him, his part-time Nanny suddenly becoming daddy's girlfriend." Lucy placed her hand on Ed's cheek. "I'm sorry, but you can't take the teacher out of the girl."

"I know you're right, but I'm happy. Can I tell my dad at least?"

Lucy grinned. "If you want to…do you want to?"

Ed nodded enthusiastically. "God yeah, he'll be chuffed for me, pulling a classy, gorgeous girl like you."

"Okay," Lucy laughed. "I suppose I'd better tell my dad too, oh and Sarah. She'll kill me if she thinks I've been keeping things from her."

Ed smiled as Lucy stood up and padded across the bedroom to the door. He couldn't believe how fantastic the afternoon had been. Their bodies had fitted so well together, and they instinctively knew what each other wanted. He gazed at her body, with its tight bottom, tiny breasts and long, slim legs. Her face was beautiful, yet the smattering of freckles on her nose also made her cute. Ed frowned as he suddenly realised that she only had three weeks left here, and he knew in that instant that he must do whatever was necessary to entice her to stay.

Lucy left Ed upstairs to get dressed. She knew if she didn't it would delay him from going to pick up Nate. She was now dressed and folding Ed's clothes that had been discarded earlier. As she picked up his T-shirt, she held it to her nose and breathed in his scent, reliving the afternoon in her head. Never before had she experienced the sort of orgasms that she'd had this afternoon. Even with Simon, when they had their best sex ever, she never felt the way she had today. She had felt a shuddering and intensive jolt that had been painful almost, full of emotion that brought Lucy to tears nearly. She sighed happily, glad that she hadn't continued to worry about the timing. She was also grateful that the alcohol had given Ed the confidence to take the initiative last night and move things to where they both obviously wanted to be.

As Lucy contemplated everything, Ed came behind her and wrapped his arms around her waist, resting his chin on her head.

"Are you okay?" asked Ed, kissing her neck.

"Yes." Folding her arms across her chest, Lucy held on to Ed's forearms. "Knackered, but happy. What about you?"

"The same, in fact, I still can't quite believe it. Can you say, 'Oh God, Ed you're so good' one more time to prove I wasn't dreaming it?" Ed laughed as Lucy slapped at his arm.

"Don't get too big headed. Anyway, if I'm not mistaken I do believe I heard you say, "Yes, yes, oh God yes" on several occasions." Lucy turned to face him and snuggled into Ed's chest. "I wish we could have stayed in bed."

"I did try to persuade you." Ed kissed the top of Lucy's head before pulling away. "I'd better go," he said threading his fingers through Lucy's.

"I know, me too. Dad will be desperate for the gossip."

Ed looked shocked. "You're not going to tell him are you?"

"I tell him everything." Lucy grinned at the look of horror on Ed's face. "I'm joking; obviously I'll leave out the details. Anyway, what do we do about tomorrow at the surgery? Do we tell everyone or wait until Nate knows?"

Ed shrugged. "I'm more than happy to tell everyone, but if Nate doesn't know, then perhaps we should wait. It might be quite exciting having clandestine meetings in the staff room and drugs cupboard." Ed laughed as he landed a kiss on Lucy's lips. "Go on then get going," he said, smacking her bottom.

"Okay, I'll see you at work in the morning Dr Bryce. Goodnight." Lucy kissed him, giving his groin a gentle rub as she did so.

"*Lucy,*" Ed groaned as thoughts of 'Coco the Clown' filled his head.

"Well hello there," Gerald said, grinning at Lucy as she walked across the lounge. "I'm guessing from that huge smile upon your face that you've had a good afternoon."

Lucy kicked off her shoes and sank onto the sofa. "Amazing Dad. Absolutely bloody amazing."

"That's good, and that my dear is all I want to know."

"That's all you're getting anyway." Lucy smiled to herself, remembering the afternoon.

"Are you a couple then, can I ring Richard and tell him that his instincts were right?" Gerald shifted on his chair, re-positioning his leg on the foot stool.

"Yes we are, and yes you can tell Richard. We're not telling anyone at the surgery though, so please don't let it slip to Callie. Ed wants to wait until he's told Nate, but he's going to tell his dad this afternoon."

"There is one other person you'd better tell, and that's…"

"Sarah, yes I know. I'm going to have a bath and ring her from there. Is there anything you need before I go up? This call could take a while if I know Sarah."

Gerald grinned and shook his head. "No, thanks for asking darling. Shall we eat dinner at about seven? Will that give you enough time?"

Lucy laughed as she got up from the sofa. "I think so, but don't you do anything. I've abandoned you enough today, so I'll cook tonight. Chilli okay, or would you prefer something different?"

"Yes chilli sounds great. Go and have your soak and say hello to Sarah for me."

As Lucy left the room, Gerald reached for his mobile. He couldn't wait another couple of hours for Richard to wake up. He'd have to text him now to let him know Lucy's news.

"Hi Luce, how are you, how was the dinner?" Sarah asked excitedly.

"I'm great thanks. In fact, I'm fantastic so that should tell you how good the dinner was." Lucy let out a little scream of delight.

"Aaargh," Sarah yelled back. "Tell me, tell me, tell me."

"Okay, give me chance. Well, it didn't start too well, seeing as Ed just said I looked 'nice.'"

"What, you looked gorgeous in that photograph that you messaged to me. 'Nice', bloody hell what a tosser!"

"Don't worry, it gets much better."

"So he's going to tell his dad when he picks Nate up." Lucy finished, turning the hot water tap on with her toe.

"Oh my God. I'm so happy for you Luce. How do you feel?"

"Happy, obviously. I did have some doubts during the night, but after today…well I've no doubts at all." Lucy smiled as she thought of Ed.

"So, was he any good?" Sarah was always straight to the point.

"*Sarah*!"

"Don't pretend you don't want to tell me. If you can tell me about having a wee in a plastic cup while watching The Chemical Brothers, then you can tell me what sex with the doctor was like. Oh, just hold that thought…Ben, you'll never guess what; Lucy only shagged the doctor this afternoon. I know, quite a few times apparently. Ooh tea please… right I'm back, carry on."

"Sarah, did you just tell Ben that I've had sex with Ed?" Lucy sat up in astonishment, slopping water over the side of the bath.

"Yes, I tell Ben everything. He just came in to ask me if I want a cup of tea. Anyway, stop changing the subject, what was the sex like?" Sarah tutted on the other end of the line.

"Don't tut at me, you've just told your husband, Simon's friend, that I've had sex with someone else while still officially married. If Simon found out it could cause problems with the divorce." Lucy slipped back under the water where it was warmer.

"Ben won't say anything, he's not speaking to Simon anyway."

"Why not?" Lucy asked.

"Don't go mad, but do you remember last summer when Simon booked us that surprise spa weekend?"

"Hmm."

"Well Ben found out today that it was so Simon could go to Barcelona with Jennifer." Sarah winced expecting Lucy to scream and shout, but she was silent. "Lucy, are you still there?"

"Yes, just thinking what an absolute dick head he was…is. How did Ben find out?"

"The dick head actually told him, in fact, Ben said he was boasting about it. Ben was livid, not just because it was a shit thing to do to you, but also because he'd involved me."

"I'm not surprised Ben was mad. If I'd found out I might have thought that you were in on it." Lucy shook her head, wondering what else she was going to discover about her husband.

"That's what Ben said. Anyway, enough of trying to change the subject. What about the sex?"

"Oh for goodness' sake Sarah. If you must know it was brilliant, more than brilliant. I've never had an orgasm like it…well like them before."

"Crikey, I've heard some of your 'fantastic' orgasms when we were at college, so it must have been good. Better than dick head as well, hmm that's excellent."

Lucy couldn't help but laugh. "Yes, better than dick head and despite everything, he was pretty good at sex. It was probably the only thing he was decent at in the house, he couldn't cook, and he was terrible at DIY. We generally had to pay more money to get someone in to put his cock ups right."

"Don't get me started on what husbands can or can't do Lucy. I adore Ben, but he tried to cook lunch today, as a treat for me, but he burnt two pans in the process. The carrots were pure mush, the potatoes rock hard and the chicken was so undercooked I thought it was going cluck at me and walk off the plate." Sarah started to giggle.

"You should know better than to ask a man to cook more than one thing at once. You know they can't multi-task. Actually, that's a lie; they can watch porn and wank at the same time!"

Sarah roared with laughter. "Oh Luce, I do miss you, but that doesn't mean I want you to come home. You need to stay there and keep having bloody amazing sex, for as long as you can."

"What if the sex is always amazing, what do I do?"

"Bloody well stay where you are," Sarah roared. "Don't you dare come back here? So, is there anything else you can tell me about the Love God's technique, anything that I could pass on to Ben?"

Lucy's laugh echoed in the bathroom. "No, there isn't, I'm not giving any trade secrets away. Let's just say I think he probably got an A star in gynaecology at medical school."

Sarah sighed heavily. "Oh you are a lucky bitch, although I'm not complaining, it's just lovely to hear you so happy. Let me know what you decide about coming home, I know it's a massive decision, but perhaps you should think about staying there, for a bit longer at least."

"I'll keep you informed, but if things stay this great then I don't think I'll be coming home just yet. I promise to let you know what I decide though."

"Okay, well take care and I'll call you later in the week. Mwah." Sarah blew a kiss over the phone.

"Thanks Sarah. Oh and Sarah…."

"Yes?"

"Please don't let Simon find out about Ed. I don't want him knowing my business, and I also don't want Ed dragged into anything."

"No problem Luce, neither of us will breathe a word to anyone. Bye and speak to you again soon."

"Bye."

Lucy reached up and put her phone on the window sill before lying back in the water once more. Before the conversation with Sarah, she hadn't considered what Simon might do if he found out about Ed. It did worry her a little, but ultimately, she wasn't the one with a new baby with someone else. The thought of Simon's baby brought a frown to her face. At some point, she would have to tell Ed about Lottie, and she wasn't sure how she would cope having to revisit that terrible time. The other thing that troubled her was also telling Ed that she didn't want any more children. She didn't know if he wanted more children in the future; it wasn't something you discussed with your new partner during an afternoon of sex. However, if things did progress and got serious between them, it was another difficult conversation they would have to have.

Chapter 13

"Good morning ladies, how are you today?" Ed smiled as he leaned against the reception desk. "Did you enjoy your weekend Callie?"

"Yes thanks pet, how was the dance?" Callie looked up from her paperwork and smiled at Ed. "Lucy says it was okay, but the beef was a little tough."

"Hmm, that probably just about sums it up to be honest. Is there a possibility of a cup of tea please Lucy? I didn't get the chance before I left home."

"Yes no problem, I'll bring it through in a couple of minutes. Callie, do you want one?" Lucy enquired, standing with her back to both Ed and Callie.

"No thanks pet, I had one before I came out this morning. You should get up earlier in the morning Dr Bryce, all this rushing around and not having any breakfast isn't good for you. Which you should know, as a doctor." She wagged her finger at Ed.

"I know, but I had a late night and didn't want to get out of bed this morning. Extra strong I think, please Lucy." He walked away, a huge grin on his face, having omitted to tell Callie that he and Lucy had been talking over the phone until almost 2 a.m.

A few minutes later Lucy tapped on Ed's consulting room door. Her heart was beating fast at the idea of being alone with him, if only for a few minutes.

"Come in," he shouted.

"Your tea, Dr Bryce."

As she walked in with the tea, Ed moved swiftly from behind his desk to take the mug from Lucy and put it onto his desk. As the door shut behind her, he pulled Lucy into his arms, and started to kiss her neck, running his hands through her hair.

"God I missed you in my bed last night," he whispered.

"I know, I couldn't sleep because I was thinking about you." Lucy could feel her body respond to his kisses. She pulled away, breathless. "No, we can't, not here."

Ed groaned as he readjusted his trousers. "I know, and I'm sorry. That was totally unprofessional of me. You look beautiful today, by the way," he murmured into her ear.

"So do you." Lucy gazed at Ed, wide-eyed. "I'd better get back before Callie suspects something."

"If she doesn't already, she's cannier than she looks."

Lucy moved away from Ed, and winked at him as she opened the door. "I'll bring you your post when it arrives Dr Bryce."

Ed winked back and mouthed "I can't wait."

When Lucy got back to the reception desk, she found Elspeth, the Practice Manager, talking to Callie. On Saturday night, there had been no indication that anybody knew what had happened between her and Ed, but Lucy was still suspicious that Elspeth may have said something to Callie.

"What are you two gossiping about?" she asked the two women as she approached them.

"I was telling Callie about the dance, and agreeing with you that the meal wasn't up to much." Elspeth started to flick through the letters that had just arrived.

"Hmm, it wasn't the best, was it? We had a good time though." Lucy nudged Elspeth and started to giggle. "Especially when Dr Kindler lined up the Sambuca shots for everyone."

"Ooh don't remind me. I had a very bad head on Sunday. How did you feel?" Elspeth asked Lucy, frowning at her.

"I was fine, great, in fact."

"I'm so glad you enjoyed yourself pet. You deserve a bit of fun. What about Dr Bryce, did he enjoy it?"

Lucy felt herself blush, but luckily, Callie was aiming the question at Elspeth, so didn't notice.

"I think so, although Lucy did try to teach him and a few others how to do The Macarena, but to be honest he was pretty rubbish." Elspeth laughed as she started to walk away. "Anyway, I'd better get on with some work. I've got to review the accounts, urgh I hate my life."

"Oh dear, never mind pet, we'll bring you a cuppa along soon." Callie now turned to Lucy. "So, pretty uneventful evening then by all accounts. Oh well never mind, Mr Drake is in later this morning, that'll spice our lives up a little, although I think he's only got a sore throat today."

Callie disappeared to the staff room, and Lucy heaved a sigh of relief, she and Ed didn't seem to be the subject of gossip, just yet.

For the rest of the morning, Lucy and Ed hardly saw each other. The surgery was extremely busy, and so Ed was tied up with patients. He'd had no post so Lucy couldn't use that as an excuse to see him. By midday, Lucy was getting agitated that she now wouldn't get to see him until the evening as her shift would soon be over.

"What's wrong pet?" Callie asked, tapping Lucy on the shoulder. "You've had a face like a kipper for most of the morning."

Lucy coloured up. She hadn't thought her disappointment had been obvious.

"I'm fine thanks Callie, probably just a little tired."

"Even Mr Drake didn't bring a smile to your face. You'd better get to bed early tonight,"

Lucy did now smile; she sincerely hoped she would be in bed early.

"You're right Callie," she replied, removing her smile to look serious. "I'll make sure I do."

Suddenly Lucy's heart missed a beat as Ed appeared from his consulting room. He glanced at Callie, ensuring that she was busy, before winking at Lucy and giving her an enormous smile.

"Is that you finished for the morning Dr Bryce?" Callie asked, looking up from the computer.

Ed nodded and smiled at her. "Yes my next patient isn't until two, so I'm going to go home for a couple of hours. I've got a few personal calls that I want to make, plus I've forgotten my lunch, I was in such a hurry this morning."

"Okay no problem. Dr Kindler will be back from his house call in a few minutes, but if I need you I'll give you a call."

"I'll see you later then Lucy," said Ed, nonchalantly flicking through some leaflets on the reception desk.

"Sorry, oh yes, see you later. Would you like me to feed Nate for you?" Lucy tried to sound as casual as possible.

"Erm, yes please if you don't mind. I shouldn't be late, but he needs an early night tonight, he didn't go to bed until nine last night."

"Okay, will do. Right Callie, shall I make a cup of tea, I've got half an hour before I leave?"

"No, I'm fine pet. In fact, you may as well get off now. There's no one else booked in this morning. You walked in today, didn't you?"

"Yes, why?" Lucy asked.

"Well you could get a lift with Dr Bryce, couldn't she?" Callie looked at Ed inclining her head toward Lucy.

"No, don't be silly. It only takes me ten minutes to walk. You go Dr Bryce, I'll be OK."

"If you're sure." Ed picked up his bag. "I'll get going, see you later Callie."

After five minutes of tidying the reception desk, Lucy sighed and moved over to Callie.

"I'll go home now Callie, is that okay?"

"Yes pet, of course it is. I'll see you tomorrow, have a lovely afternoon." Callie smiled at Lucy.

"Bye Callie, you enjoy the rest of the day too."

Once outside, Lucy started to walk quickly in the direction of Ed's house. She hoped that she'd read his signals correctly, and he would be waiting for her. As she was about to cross over the road, Lucy heard the beep of a car horn. Initially she ignored it, she couldn't imagine anyone would be beeping at her; but then it went again, lasting a little longer and more insistent than the first burst. Lucy turned around in the direction of the noise; parked down a side street was Ed, waving at her with a huge smile on his face.

Lucy ran across to the car and jumped in. "I didn't realise that you were waiting for me. I was going to make my way to your house."

Ed pulled Lucy to him and kissed her. "That would take you too long," he sighed "Let's get going."

A mere five minutes later and Ed was letting them into the house.

"Do you think anyone will be watching us?" Lucy asked as she looked around cautiously.

"So what if they are?" Ed turned and smiled at her. "The neighbours know that you're looking after Nate, so it's not unusual for you to be here."

Ed opened the door, and Lucy followed him in, pausing as he stooped to pick up the post. Pushing the door closed with one hand, Lucy pinched his bottom with the other.

"Sorry," she said as she started to giggle. "I couldn't resist it, it's so gorgeous."

Ed placed the letters on the window sill and grabbing Lucy's hand pulled her up the stairs. "I can't resist you for much longer either."

Once in the bedroom it didn't take long for them to remove each other's clothes, before falling onto Ed's bed and making love frenetically.

"Oh my God," gasped Lucy, leaning back onto her hands. "That was amazing."

Breathless, Ed reached up and pulled Lucy down to him and kissed her. She rolled off the top of him and flopped on the bed next to Ed, exhausted.

"You are bloody fantastic, do you know that?" Ed leaned over and kissed Lucy's nose.

"I don't know about that." Lucy lifted Ed's arm and pulled it around her as she snuggled up to him.

Ed moved closer. "Yes you are, and I don't just mean in bed. Look how strong you've been about the split from Simon."

Lucy started to laugh. "You wouldn't say that if you'd seen me in my green bobble hat a few weeks ago. Let's just say you probably wouldn't have looked twice at me, never mind treated me to an afternoon of sex."

"What on earth are you talking about?"

"Well when Simon first left I stayed in bed for over two weeks, wearing my pyjamas and a bobble hat the whole time." Lucy buried her face against Ed's chest. "God I'm so embarrassed about it now, I was such a bitch to Sarah, and the smell was awful."

"Hmm nice." Ed laughed and lifted Lucy's chin with his finger. "I bet you still looked beautiful."

"Nah, I can promise you I didn't." Lucy took Ed's hand and kissed his palm, before interlocking her fingers with his.

"Anyway, at the risk of spoiling the atmosphere, have you thought about what you're going to do about Simon?" asked Ed.

"Well actually, he's decided for me. He's asked for a divorce and wants me to buy him out of the house, or sell it." Lucy sighed.

"Oh, I'm sorry; it can't be an easy time for you."

"No, Ed don't be. I've learned a few things about him recently that make me realise that he's a complete and utter dick head. Actually that's a lie, I think I already knew he was a dick head, but ignored it."

Ed leaned on his elbow and looked at Lucy intently. "In what way was he a dick head?"

"Well, he was a great husband at first, attentive, caring and loving but then when..." Lucy stopped and closed her eyes.

"When what sweetheart?" Ed traced his finger along Lucy's trembling chin. "What's wrong, are you okay? He didn't hurt you did he?"

Lucy shook her head and took a large breath. She needed to tell Ed about the most distressing event she'd ever experienced. It was still very early in their relationship, but she wanted him to know, and even if this didn't last, she knew Ed would understand.

"Simon changed," she began, a ragged breath shuddering from her mouth. "Simon changed once our daughter died."

"Oh God Lucy, I'm so sorry." He wiped Lucy's tears from her cheek with his hand. "I don't know what to say, that has to be the worst thing that can happen to a parent."

"It's okay, I don't talk about it usually, but I wanted you to know. She was beautiful and perfect, and nearly six months old. She wasn't ill, she didn't have anything wrong with her, but I put her to bed one night, and she just didn't wake up." Lucy smiled sadly at Ed. "Her name was Lottie."

Ed tightened his arms around Lucy and kissed her forehead. "Oh baby, that must have been terrible. Christ, I just can't imagine what you've gone through." Ed shook his head and blew out a blast of air. "How long ago was it, unless you don't want to talk about it anymore?" His face was full of concern.

She shook her head. "No, I'm fine, better than I thought I'd actually be. I was dreading telling you, but it's okay I want to talk about it, about her."

"If you're sure." Ed pulled Lucy to him and hugged her tightly.

"Yes, I'm sure. It was three years ago, and I was a wreck for months afterwards. I lost interest and passion in my job, which is how I ended up working in a charity shop, and I think I probably lost interest and passion in Simon for a while."

"Surely you're not condoning him having an affair, are you?" Ed asked.

"No, not at all. What he did and how he left hurt me so much. I couldn't believe that he'd been so bloody careless and got her pregnant, especially as we'd agreed that we wouldn't have any more children."

"What never?" Ed asked. "Why did you decide that? Were you scared that it would happen again? I mean I totally get it, but that's a huge decision to make."

Lucy nodded. "That was exactly it, in fact, I was petrified. She was so beautiful and precious, and I just can't stand the thought of that ever happening again, it would probably kill me. We discussed it over and over, and both agreed it was the best choice to make."

"Which makes the fact that Simon is starting a new family an even bigger blow then, I guess," said Ed.

"When he first left I was absolutely floored by it all, I felt as though I would die without him. But, as the weeks have gone on, I've realised that I was actually angry with him. Angry because he'd lied about how he felt for the last three years, angry that he didn't trust me, or our relationship, enough to tell me how he felt, but most of all angry that he could replace Lottie so easily." As she finished Lucy wiped a stray tear from her cheek.

"When Richard told me about you, he said you were heartbroken, but that day I met you I could tell that you were angry, it showed in your eyes." Ed stroked Lucy's face tenderly and hugged her closer.

After a few minutes, Ed finally broke the silence that had fallen between them. "You know it was probably really hard for him to tell you. The thought must have crossed his mind that you would think that he was replacing Lottie. I'm not sticking up for him, but it must have been tough for him too."

Lucy sighed as she thought about Ed's words. "Maybe, but at the time I was hurting and couldn't see past that he'd replaced us both." Lucy rubbed her hands across her eyes, wiping the last of her tears. "Anyway, whatever feelings I did have for Simon have completely gone."

Ed started to laugh. "Since you met me and received the Ed Bryce special loving you mean?"

Lucy hit his arm playfully. "Don't get too big headed doctor, but yes you obviously do have something to do with it. But, I've also found out a few things about Simon that prove what a shit he's been for a while, and if I'm honest with myself, has been since Lottie died." Lucy went on to tell Ed about the things she learned from Sarah, plus other things that Simon had done during their marriage, which at the time she'd explained away, not wanting to admit that her marriage wasn't perfect.

"God you're right he is a shit" Ed looked horrified at Lucy's story of the spa break.

"Hmm, I know, Lottie's death should have brought us closer, shouldn't it?" Lucy looked up at Ed with wide, questioning eyes.

Ed nodded. "I agree, but who knows what he was going through." He pulled Lucy to him and enfolded her in a tight hug. "Thank you for trusting me enough to tell me."

Ed looked at Lucy and realised that he wanted to hold her forever, and protect her from anything else horrible that may happen. He thought about their relationship and knew that, despite only being together a couple of days, she was extremely important to him.

Lucy shifted in Ed's arms "What time is it?" she asked. "You have to get back to the surgery soon."

Ed looked at his watch. "It's just gone one; I'm okay for another half hour."

"That's good," said Lucy snuggling up to his chest again. "You ought to get some lunch before you go back though."

Ed shook his head. "I'm not hungry, are you?"

"No, I couldn't eat a thing." Lucy smiled up at Ed.

She genuinely couldn't eat; she had a steady flutter of butterflies in her stomach when she was with Ed, he made her feel safe and she trusted him. Lucy also knew that she had to make a decision soon about going home, but while she was here with Ed, feeling happy and safe, she didn't want to think about it.

Two days later Lucy had made her last trip to school to pick Nate up. Georgina had arrived home from America earlier in the day, so would be resuming her care of Nate the following afternoon.

"Are you excited about seeing your Nanny later, Nate?" Lucy rubbed Nate's head as they walked up the drive.

"Yes, she might have a present for me. I'll miss you though," Nate replied as he smiled up at Lucy.

"Ah, thanks Nate. I'll miss you too."

"You could come and have tea; I think Daddy would like that too."

Lucy started to blush. "Oh really, why?" she asked.

"Because he likes you, he told me that you were a nice lady." Nate didn't seem to be perturbed by Lucy's question.

Lucy let out a sigh of relief, glad that Nate hadn't found out about her and Ed from someone else.

"Well, I think he's a very nice person too. Anyway, what would you like for tea?" Lucy changed the subject.

"Erm, chicken noodles please."

"Okay, we'll see if there are any. If not we'll have to think of something else."

"It's okay, Daddy bought some at the supermarket yesterday, especially for me." Nate nodded sagely.

Lucy laughed as she opened the door. "Okay, chicken noodles it is then."

As they walked into the hall, Lucy thought she heard a noise in the kitchen. It couldn't be Ed; she knew he had a busy surgery this afternoon.

"Hello," she called. "Is anyone there?"

In the kitchen door, Georgina appeared.

"Nanny!" cried Nate running down the hall, into his grandmother's arms.

"Hello, my darling. Gosh I've missed you." Georgina pulled Nate into her arms and hugged him tightly. "Have you been a good boy for Daddy and Lucy?"

"I have been really good Nanny, did you buy me a present?" Nate stood on tiptoe and kissed Georgina's cheek.

"Hi, Lucy." Georgina looked up at Lucy and smiled. "I'm sorry did I startle you? I couldn't wait to see this young man, so Jack dropped me off."

"No, it's okay. Did you have a good trip?" Lucy relieved Nate of his school bag.

Georgina's face darkened, despite a small smile at her lips. "It was okay, thank you." She looked down at Nate and ruffled his hair. "Nate, why don't you go upstairs to get changed and you might find something for you on your bed."

"A present?" Nate smiled widely.

Georgina nodded. "Yes, so off you go. Shall we have a cup of tea?" she asked Lucy. "I think we've got quite a lot to talk about."

Lucy shuffled uncomfortably on the spot. "Oh, okay, yes a cup of tea would be lovely."

Georgina smiled widely and rubbed Lucy's arm. "There's nothing to worry about, I promise."

Lucy followed Georgina into the kitchen, and watched as she made them both a cup of tea. Finally she passed a mug to Lucy, and they both sat down at the dining table.

"So, firstly tell me all about my boys and what they've been up to while I've been away."

Lucy coughed nervously, wondering whether Jack had told his wife about her and Ed.

"Well Ed was ill while you were away, so I stayed, for a couple of nights, to look after Nate, oh, and we had a little incident with Nate's teacher."

"Oh dear, the lovely Mrs Bushnell. Tell me all about it," said Georgina settling in her chair.

After telling Georgina the story of Nate and Bradley's trousers and details of Nate's play dates and homework, Lucy was feeling a little more relaxed. Georgina had barely mentioned Ed to Lucy, so she either didn't know about their relationship, or she was going to wait and grill Ed about it later, either way Lucy was relieved.

"Sounds like Nate has kept you busy. I have really missed him, and Ed and Jack of course, but Nate most of all." Georgina smiled as she poured some tea into her mug. "Would you like any more tea?" She proffered the teapot to Lucy.

Lucy nodded. "Please. So, was your flight back okay, you don't seem to be too jet lagged?"

"I am starting to flag a little to be honest, but I wanted to see Nate and Ed. I called Ed at the surgery before you got here, and he thinks he should be home by four, a couple of patients have cancelled apparently."

Lucy's heart skipped, and her stomach somersaulted at the thought of seeing Ed soon, despite that they'd already managed a brief meeting in the staff room. She smiled as she thought of their secret kiss earlier in the day when Callie had nipped out to get some milk. The last two evenings Lucy had spent here, with Ed, until around midnight. Once Nate had gone to bed they had curled up on the sofa, laughing, talking and kissing until Lucy had reluctantly had to go home. Gerald had been great about Lucy leaving him alone each night, he'd had some friends round to play Bridge on one night, and on the other he had gone to bed early to read a book.

"To be honest I hope he doesn't ask me too much about the trip," said Georgina, breaking Lucy's reverie.

"Oh, did something happen that might upset him?" Lucy tried not to sound overly concerned.

"No, nothing unusual, but just having to tell him about Luke and Katie is always difficult."

"I can imagine."

"It's hard because the children are beautiful, and extremely well behaved. I'm the same as any doting grandmother – I want to talk about my grandchildren."

"Can't you talk to Mr Bryce about them?" Lucy felt for Georgina, it must be hard for her having two sons at loggerheads, but she could understand Ed's aversion to talking about his brother.

"Jack listens to a certain point, but as soon as I mention Luke or Katie he gets really angry. His relationship with Luke is very fragile after what he and Katie did. Don't get me wrong I'm still angry, but I'm not as stubborn as Jack, and a little more forgiving. To be honest with you, Jack and Luke have always clashed, you see Luke's caused us no end of heartache over the years. He was always in trouble at school, and then when he left he was sacked from one job after another, usually because he never turned up, preferring to either play football or stay in bed with his latest girlfriend instead," Georgina explained.

"What about his grandchildren though, Mr Bryce is missing out of being in their lives too?"

Georgina shook her head. "I know that part hurts me too, but he just won't visit them. His answer is they can come and stay here for the summer when they're old enough."

"I can understand his reluctance, but that doesn't make it any easier for you though, does it?" Lucy instinctively reached across and held Georgina's hand.

Georgina smiled and patted Lucy hand, on top of her own. "Oh it is lovely to have someone to talk to, it really is. The other problem I have is that Luke has asked to borrow some money. They're up to their eyes in debt apparently. Luke is an assistant football coach, so he doesn't earn a terrific amount, but they live like millionaires. They both have a car, country club memberships and a nanny stroke house-keeper; none of which they can afford."

"So what are you going to do, if you don't think I'm being nosey?" asked Lucy.

"No, I don't think you're being nosey, but I don't know what I'm going to do either. I can't possibly give them any money without Jack's consent, and I don't think he'll give it. You see before Luke left for the states, we had to pay off a huge debt for him. He'd borrowed an awful lot of money from one of those backstreet loan companies and not made any repayments for four months, and you can imagine how high the interest was. If we hadn't paid it off, knowing Luke he'd have probably gone off to America and just left us to deal with it anyway, he wouldn't actually care what mess he'd left behind. He's totally selfish and never been willing to make sacrifices for anyone, not even Katie and the children, unlike Ed, who worked long hours all the time he was studying because he knew that it would provide a decent life for his family if he did. So, it's a difficult conversation that I'm going to have to have with Jack, but not today, it can wait until tomorrow at least." Georgina sighed and gave Lucy's hand a squeeze.

Suddenly both Georgina and Lucy were alerted by the noise of a key in the front door. Georgina stood up and made her way to the hall to greet Ed.

"Hi Mum," he said, pulling her into a bear hug. "Ooh I'm so glad that you're back."

"Hello sweetheart. I've missed you." Georgina pulled away from her son and looked at him. "Well you don't appear to have lost weight, so Lucy has done a good job looking after you both."

Ed lowered his eyes and hugged his mother again. "Yes, we've been okay thanks. Oh hi Lucy," he said, noticing Lucy through the kitchen doorway.

"Hi," called Lucy brightly. "I'm going to make a fresh pot of tea, would you like one?"

"Oh yes please," replied Ed releasing Georgina from his grip.

"Oh for goodness sake," cried Georgina. "Why don't you two stop pretending that you are just employer and employee? I know all about you both being a couple; did you honestly think your father would be able to keep it a secret all the way home from the airport? He couldn't wait to reveal all the details; I'd hardly got my seat belt fastened." Georgina laughed as she placed a warm hand on Ed's cheek. "So why don't we sit down and you can tell me all about it."

Ed grinned at Georgina and hugged her again. "I asked Dad to let me tell you, but I should have realised he'd wouldn't be able to help himself. The thing is…" he paused looking around to check Nate wasn't in earshot. "We haven't told Nate yet."

"It's okay, Nate's upstairs, he's probably playing his new computer game that I bought for him."

"I just thought, well we just thought that he may find it strange Lucy suddenly becoming daddy's girlfriend."

Georgina smiled. "That's a healthy sign that you are referring to yourselves as 'we'. Come on sit down and let's talk about the best plan of action."

Lucy and Ed spent the next ten minutes telling Georgina all about the last few days, and how they'd fought their feelings for each other, but finally gave up fighting at the dinner.

"Okay, so what about you Lucy, you're due to go home in a couple of weeks aren't you?"

Lucy nodded and held Ed's hand. "I am, but I think I've decided to stay on a little longer, to see how things go."

Ed's lips spread into a broad smile that lit up his eyes. "Why didn't you say earlier?" He said picking up Lucy's hand and kissing it.

"I was going to tell you later, I decided last night, well at about four o'clock this morning to be honest. I woke up suddenly, and it struck me that I wanted to stay. It is okay isn't it?"

"God, yes of course it is," Ed replied. He felt ecstatic that Lucy had made the decision on her own; he hadn't needed to persuade her.

"That is lovely news Lucy, but I need to be sure that you're not rushing into this, so soon after your marriage breaking up." Georgina looked at them both; she was serious, but not stern.

"Well, that's one of the things that stopped me acting on how I felt about Ed. It was pretty much instant to be honest, but I couldn't get my head around it, because you're right it was only three weeks after Simon left."

"Don't get me wrong Lucy, I think you'd be perfect together, but he's my boy, and I *cannot* and *will not* let anyone hurt him again." A shadow passed over Georgina's face.

"Ah bless you Mum, but honestly everything is going to be okay, I know it is." Ed smiled at Georgina as he placed a hand on her cheek.

"Good, so two things to sort out then," said Georgina getting up from the table. "When to tell Nate, and what are we going to do about your dad's birthday? He's going to be sixty-five in three weeks, and I think we should have a party."

Chapter 14

Gerald had been delighted that Lucy had decided not to go home yet. He was confident that his daughter was now happy and enjoying her life once more. He was so confident, in fact, that he'd been persuaded by Lucy, and Richard, to fly out to Australia; once he'd had his plaster removed. Richard was overjoyed at being able to extend his trip by an additional six weeks, and even happier that he was being joined by Gerald. And so, Gerald had jetted off with a promise from Ed that he would take care of Lucy.

Lucy and Ed were also extremely happy and had been able to spend quite a few nights together – thanks to Georgina. She'd said that she had missed Nate terribly and that it would be lovely to spend more time with him, so he'd stayed over with his grandparents quite a few nights over the last week. Lucy and Ed were extremely grateful to Georgina as they both knew that she had recognised their desire to have some time alone.

On the Saturday, after Gerald had flown to Australia, they had also decided to tell Nate that Lucy was now Ed's girlfriend. Not only did they want to be a couple openly at Jack's upcoming party, but they didn't want to risk anyone else letting it slip to Nate. Ed had been quite nervous about telling Nate, not because of his reaction to the situation, or to Lucy, but because Ed knew that Nate would ask questions - he was right to be nervous.

"So, Lucy is going to be your girlfriend and work at the surgery for you." Nate frowned.

"Yes, that's right," replied Ed.

"Well, Callie works at the surgery and is a girl, so is she your girlfriend as well?"

"No, she's my friend and she's a girl, but not my girlfriend."

"But Lucy is a girl and your friend, so why is she your girlfriend?"

Ed turned to Lucy and smiled. "Help me out here please Luce."

Lucy grinned as she stepped forward and sat with father and son at the dining table.

"It's a little different to Callie, Nate." Lucy leaned closer to Nate. "I'm Daddy's special friend, we hold hands and say nice things to each other, and we may go on trips together."

"But Daddy says nice things about Callie too, and he holds my hand, and we go on trips together." Nate smiled at Lucy, cute dimples forming in his cheeks.

"Well Daddy and I kiss, not like he kisses you, and he doesn't kiss Callie at all." Lucy pushed Nate's fringe from his eyes.

Suddenly Nate stood up. "Oh okay, I'm glad Daddy has you as his special friend. Can I go and play now please?"

Ed nodded, unsure what else he could add to the conversation. "Erm yes, off you go."

As he left the room, Lucy and Ed burst out laughing, both now realising that he'd been playing them.

"The little terror," said Lucy leaning over to kiss Ed. "He knew all along what you were saying to him."

Ed grinned. "He knows far too much. Anyway, the main thing is he doesn't seem particularly worried by it."

"Thank goodness. We just need to tell everyone at the surgery now."

The following Monday morning Ed informed Dr Kindler, Elspeth, Ellen and Callie what some of them had already guessed; he and Lucy were a couple.

"Well thank God for that pet. I thought you were never going to tell us." Callie shook her head and smiled. "I'm sick of thinking of reasons to leave you two alone, you should see the amount of milk we've bought recently."

"I told you that she probably knew," said Ed turning to Lucy who was at his side.

Lucy blushed, worried that they'd been too obvious for the last couple of weeks.

"I would have told you Callie, but we needed to tell Nate first," Lucy explained.

"No worries pet, I'm just glad you both realised that you were made for each other."

"My wife said that she thought something was going on at the dance." Dr Kindler shook his head. "I must walk around with my head up my backside, I can't say as I noticed. Oh well, very good, I'm very pleased for you. I'd better get ready for Mrs Pearson; she'll be here in fifteen minutes." As he walked past Lucy, Dr Kindler gave her a warm smile and squeezed her hand.

"I agree," said Ellen. "I'm really happy for both of you." She leaned forward and hugged Lucy tightly.

"Does this mean that Lucy won't be making as many cups of tea though?" asked Elspeth, nudging Ed. "It's been great this last couple of weeks, it's been the perfect reason to go in and see Ed, which means we've all been inundated with cups of tea."

Lucy dropped her head into her hands. "Has it been that obvious?" she cried.

Elspeth shook her head. "No, I must be honest; I thought that you fancied him. I didn't realise something was already going on, don't worry."

"Well you all know now." Ed laughed and put his arm around Lucy's shoulder. "So, there won't be any surprises at Dad's party on Saturday."

"You haven't seen what I'm wearing yet," replied Callie winking at them all.

The day of Jack's birthday arrived with bright sunshine and a pleasant breeze, perfect weather for a garden party. The surprise party was being held at Ed's house, and forty relatives and friends were attending. Ed had wanted to be in charge of the barbeque, but as Georgina pointed out, it would be terrible if everyone was given food poisoning by the local doctor, and so caterers had been hired to provide a buffet.

Lucy had worked alongside Georgina and Ed all day, preparing the garden, hanging bunting and banners and putting up tables and chairs. Her face held a permanent smile as Ed kissed her, or pinched her bottom at any opportunity, neither he nor Lucy embarrassed about showing their affection in front of Georgina.

Since they'd told Nate about them being a couple, Lucy had spent the vast majority of the last two weeks at the house, without Nate being shipped off to his grandparents. They'd had dinner together and, on each occasion, Nate had asked her to read to him before bed, commenting that he preferred it to reading to himself as Lucy could make funny voices for the different characters. In fact, it had been a blissful couple of weeks for both Ed and Lucy.

As Lucy chatted to Georgina about the best place to position the buffet table, Ed watched her and thought that his heart was going to burst out of his chest. Over the last few weeks of getting to know Lucy properly, not just sexually, he realised how funny she was, and how kind and considerate. Georgina had telephoned Ed at the surgery two days ago in a panic because the company supplying Jack's present, of the expensive fishing rod that he'd coveted, had gone bust. So, now there was no gift and there was nowhere locally that could provide one on such short notice. When Ed had explained to Lucy, she immediately started to trawl the internet and make numerous phone calls until she found someone who could help. The next morning Lucy insisted on making the four hour round trip to the Scottish Borders to pick up the rod. Ed knew it wasn't just Lucy trying to make a favourable impression, he'd seen how kind she was with the patients, always helping the elderly and infirm into the consulting rooms. She was attentive to the rest of the staff too, checking if anyone needed anything or would like a cup of tea or coffee, and she was fantastic with Nate, patiently helping with his homework and reading to him in funny voices that made him laugh like a drain.

As Lucy turned and smiled at Ed, the realisation hit him like a punch in the chest; he loved her. Those lustful feelings that he'd had almost eight weeks ago had become much deeper in the past month since they'd become a couple. Ed wasn't sure whether he should tell Lucy yet, she may not feel the same way, and then he would feel foolish. Her marriage had only ended almost three months ago, so how could she possibly feel the same way. No, he would wait and see how things went between them, rather than scaring her off.

"Hi baby," Ed said as Lucy came over and entwined her arms around his waist.

"Hi, are you okay? You look thoughtful, do you want to share?" Lucy stood on tiptoe and kissed Ed.

"Just thinking about tonight, and how much Dad is going to love it. Plus you get to meet Grandma Wilkins, you'll love her." Ed grinned at the look on Lucy's face. "What's the frown for?"

"Because I'm scared about meeting your family. What if they don't like me?"

"They'll like you, what's not to like." Ed cupped her face in his hands. "I swear they are all lovely people. Oh except Grandma Bryce, she's an old dragon."

"Oh shit, really?" Lucy's face crumpled into a grimace.

"Good job she's not coming then isn't it." Ed started laughing as Lucy slapped his arm.

"That's not funny Ed. Anyway, why isn't she coming to her own son's birthday party?"

"Well, put it this way she wouldn't be welcome if she did."

"Oh no, why not?"

"Well we buried her five years ago…Oww, that hurt," Ed cried as Lucy hit him again, but harder than before.

"Ha bloody ha, funny man. Anyway, shouldn't you go and pick Nate up from Ollie's house, it's almost five o'clock and he needs to have a bath before the party starts."

"Okay, bossy boots. See you in about half an hour." He pecked Lucy on the lips and strode off across the garden.

As he walked away, Lucy watched him, a familiar feeling of excitement in the pit of her stomach. God, he was sexy, and the way he made her feel in bed was incredible, but it was more than that, he cared about her and made her feel safe, and she couldn't imagine her future without him.

As Ed turned to wave goodbye, Georgina joined Lucy and smiled widely.

"He's very easy to love isn't he?" she said nodding towards her son.

It only took Lucy a matter of seconds before she nodded and smiled.

"Yes," she replied, "extremely."

"Don't worry," replied Georgina hugging Lucy to her. "Your secret is safe with me."

Ed and Lucy were alone in the house by six o'clock. Georgina had gone home to change and to start the pretence that she and Jack were going to Ed's for a barbeque, Nate had gone to 'persuade Granddad not to wear his shorts', and so had left with Georgina. The caterers were outside setting up in preparation for guests arriving at seven o'clock, half an hour before Jack.

"Do you think that this will look okay?" Lucy held up a mint coloured lace dress. "Or will it clash with the ginger?"

Ed laughed. "You silly woman, you're beautiful."

"I'm bloody ginger still. So, tell me honestly, is the dress okay. I've got another one as back up."

"No, baby that one is perfect, and you'll look stunning in it." Ed pulled Lucy to him and kissed her neck. "You need a shower though; you're all hot and sticky."

Lucy giggled as she felt Ed's obvious arousal pushing against her leg. "Hmm you could be right, the trouble is," Lucy murmured as she unbuttoned Ed's jeans, "so are you and we don't have long before the party, so perhaps we should have a shower together, it will save time."

"Good thinking," groaned Ed pulling Lucy's T-shirt over her head.

"I think I'm a genius to be honest." Lucy kissed Ed and led him to the bathroom.

When Jack arrived at seven-thirty everyone was waiting, drinks in hand, in anticipation of the big reveal. Ed had to smile when he saw that his dad was wearing his shorts, Nate obviously hadn't been successful in trying to convince him otherwise. As Jack, Georgina and Nate walked through the gate into the back garden everyone shouted 'surprise'; and Rob - Ed's friend, blasted a rendition of 'Happy Birthday' from the iPod hooked up to Ed's huge speakers that he'd brought out into the garden.

"Oh my goodness, is this is all for me?" Jack was incredulous.

"Yes darling it is. Happy birthday sweetie." Georgina hugged her husband and kissed his cheek.

"Now can you see why I wanted you to wear trousers?" Nate placed his hands on his hips and sighed.

Jack smiled and ruffled Nate's hair. "I do Nate, and I'm sorry that I didn't listen to you. Oh hello…" Jack wandered off as he recognised a former work colleague.

"Well done Mum," said Ed smiling at Georgina. "I didn't think you'd get him here without him finding out. I must admit when you said you wanted him to have a party I didn't think that you'd manage to fix it all in only three weeks."

"Well I did, thanks to you and Lucy. You've both been a massive help, I couldn't have done it without you," replied Georgina as she kissed Ed. "Where is Lucy, by the way?" she asked.

"Oh she's talking to Callie, over there." Ed pointed in the direction of Lucy talking to what could only be described as a Saloon Girl.

Georgina open and closed her mouth and shook her head. "W-what has she got on?" she stammered.

"Erm I'm not sure whether she thought it was going to be fancy dress, or whether that's something she would wear normally."

They both looked across and stared at Callie's outfit, totally fascinated. She wore a pink and black corset dress with a ruffled hem that was hitched up on one side with a black bow, a black feather boa, long, pink, satin gloves, black ankle boots, and all topped off with a pink ribbon and a feather around the mass of curls piled on top of Callie's head.

"She said she was going to surprise us." Ed started to laugh as Callie had not disappointed them.

"Blimey, you're not kidding," Georgina replied. "Anyway, talking of surprises, has Lucy's arrived yet?"

"Not yet, shouldn't be long though."

"Oh good, anyway I'd better go and mingle and steer your father around otherwise he'll stay with Brian Reid talking fishing all night."

"Okay, I'll go and check Lucy's okay with Annie Oakley over there."

As Ed approached Callie, and Lucy he took the time to look at Lucy. She had been dead wrong about the mint coloured dress. It complemented her colouring beautifully, and showed off her slender legs as it stopped just above the knee. Ed felt the surge in his chest that he'd felt earlier. He couldn't imagine his life without her now, yet it was only four weeks, he only hoped that she felt the same way.

"Hi," Ed said placing a hand in the small of Lucy's back. "Are you two okay, do you need me to get either of you a drink?"

Callie shook her head, spraying downy feathers everywhere. "No, it's okay; Elspeth and Brendan have gone to get some."

"It's a pity Ellen and Greg couldn't make it," said Lucy

"Hmm they've gone to a wedding over in Durham apparently. It's one of Ellen's nieces I think. Talking of people coming here tonight, I've just spotted a surprise for you." Ed nudged Lucy and pointed in the direction of the garden gate.

She looked across and now her face broke into a huge grin. "Sarah, Ben!" she cried and started to run toward them. "What are you doing here?" Lucy pulled them both into a hug. "It's so great to see you both."

"Well Ed had something to do with it," Ben explained as he detached himself from Lucy's arms. "He rang Sarah last week, and so here we are."

Lucy turned to Ed, who was now standing next to her and was shaking Ben's hand.

"Good to meet you," Ed said.

"You too, I've heard quite a lot about you." Ben gave a huge smile and winked at Lucy.

"Hmm, thank you Sarah. Anything I tell you is supposed to be between us."

"Sorry, I just couldn't help myself. Anyway, lovely to see you again Ed."

"You too." Ed hugged Sarah. "I'm really glad that you could make it."

"Ah thank you," said Lucy as she kissed Ed. "That was such a lovely thought."

"I knew that you were missing Sarah, so thought that it would be an ideal opportunity for me to get to know her and Ben and for you to spend some time together."

"Well thank you, it's a brilliant idea." Lucy smiled and hugged Sarah again. "I can't believe you're here, it's so good to see you Ben, I haven't seen you since…well you know when." Lucy's voice trailed off, but the smile didn't disappear. She wasn't sorry about Simon leaving anymore, or the fact that she'd last seen Ben when he'd rushed to her side with Sarah on the day Simon left.

"Ben, let me show you where the drinks are, and leave these two to catch up for a few minutes." Ed led Ben across the garden toward a drink laden table on the patio.

"Oh God, it's so lovely to see you," said Sarah hugging Lucy tightly. "I have to say you look amazing." She lowered her voice to a whisper. "Sex still amazing then I take it?"

Lucy smiled and shook her head. "I'm not saying anything, you'll only tell Ben. Anyway, changing the subject rapidly, how are the boys? I've really missed them."

"They're good, in fact, Noah has drawn you a picture. It's in my overnight bag, so I'll give it to you tomorrow."

"Where are you staying, you could stay at Dad's?"

"All organised, Ed rang your dad and Gerald arranged for us to pick the spare key up from his neighbour," Sarah replied.

"Blimey," Lucy said. "He's thought of everything."

"He certainly has. I tell you Lucy, he's worth holding on to, fantastic in bed and thoughtful. What more could a girl want? So, what's the news from Simon, him of the phallic shaped skull?"

Lucy started to laugh. "Well, Simon has now agreed that we should divorce on the grounds of his adultery. I was willing to go with the 'Unreasonable Behaviour', but Mr Devine didn't think there was enough grounds for that, so he said we should aim for adultery, and unbelievably, Simon agreed almost straight away. Funnily enough, the forms arrived yesterday, so I have to fill them in and Mr Devine will send them to the court, and to Andrew, Simon's solicitor."

"So, how do you feel about it all?" asked Sarah.

Lucy thought for a few seconds. "Okay, I think. It was weird when they arrived, but I'll be happy to see it all sorted. Once they've been filled in and sent to the court I'll be able to move on properly."

"Doesn't the fact that you're with the gorgeous doctor mean that you've moved on anyway?" Sarah asked.

Lucy smiled and glanced in Ed's direction, over by the drink table. "Yes, I suppose so, but I think I need to be Lucy Falmer again before I actually believe it."

"So have you named Jennifer in the divorce?"

"Yes, although Mr Devine told me I can't include the 'bitch face' bit of her name."

"Ah shame, never mind. Let's get some drinks and enjoy tonight and forget about them," said Sarah hugging Lucy again.

"Great idea, and then I'll introduce you to Nate and Ed's parents."

"What about the saloon girl over there? She looks interesting," said Sarah.

"Oh she is. She certainly is."

A few hours later and the party was well and truly underway. Jack was enjoying himself immensely, insisting on showing everyone his new fishing rod and his casting skills. However, the more beer he drank the less skilled his casting became. The buffet was extremely tasty and had been demolished within half an hour, with now only a few lone sandwiches curling up on plates.

Lucy, spotting an empty chair, took the opportunity to rest for the first time that day. Her feet and legs ached, but she truly didn't mind, it had all been worth it to help Georgina and Ed pull off a terrific party. She looked across at Sarah who was in deep conversation with Callie, and Ed who was talking animatedly to Ben about music. Lucy was overwhelmed that Ed had thought to invite them; it was such a lovely surprise.

"Having a rest dear?" Georgina came over and sat next to Lucy. "If your feet are anything like mine they're throbbing."

"Hmm, they are a little, but they're not too bad. It's been a great night though Georgina, Jack's had a fantastic time, not as much as Nate though I must say." Lucy laughed as she thought of Nate moving around the party showing everyone his one and only card trick, where he was supposed to guess which card they'd picked.

"I know, he's loved it. He went spark out when I took him up to bed earlier." Georgina started to giggle. "That card trick wasn't very good though was it?"

Lucy shook her head and joined in Georgina's laughter.

"No, I think he named every card before he got Callie's right. He was funny when he hid behind the garden shed, when Ed wanted him to go to bed."

"I know, he's a little devil, but he was absolutely shattered." Georgina sighed and looked over at Ed and Ben still chatting. "He's had a good time too," she said nodding toward her son. "He seems to like your friend Ben."

"I know they've talked music and football all night." Lucy's eyes gleamed as she followed Georgina's gaze.

Ed caught her eye and smiled, and Lucy's stomach flipped, and her heart beat faster.

"I'm so glad that he's met you, Lucy, he deserves someone who loves him." said Georgina watching Lucy's face.

"It wasn't part of my plan, but yes I do. I just hope it works out for us. I know it's only a few weeks, and I'm sure you're worried that it's still quite soon after the end of my marriage, but I just can't imagine my life without him, but I don't want scare him or put him under any pressure this soon in the relationship."

Georgina leaned to Lucy and taking her hand, squeezed it tightly.

"I don't think you need to worry about anything, Lucy. I know my son, and I'd say he's a smitten as you are. Anyway, I'd think I'd better get the cake out and get Jack to give his speech before he gets too drunk."

"Okay, do you need any help?" Lucy asked.

"No dear, you sit there and have a well-deserved break for a few minutes."

"So it just leaves me to say thank you to my darling wife for this fabulous party. I don't know what I'd do without you sweetheart." Jack put his arm around Georgina.

"I couldn't have done it without Ed or Lucy," Georgina said once Jack had let her go.

"Well you've all been brilliant, so everyone I'd be grateful if you could raise your glasses to Georgina, Ed and Lucy." Jack raised his glass in cheer, followed by the rest of the party that were gathered around to hear his speech.

As everyone broke away to continue partying Ed pulled Lucy to him, and kissed her tenderly.

"Thank you from me too," he said.

"It was my pleasure; I've really enjoyed it, not just tonight, but today helping your Mum."

"I could show you my thanks in another way." Ed whispered into Lucy's ear, while he gently caressed her breasts.

Lucy was immediately aroused and groaned with pleasure. "We'll have to be quick; people will notice we've gone missing."

"Hmm a quickie in the downstairs loo might be quite exciting." Ed caught hold of Lucy's hand and gently pulled her across the lawn toward the house.

Upon reaching the door into the house, Ed turned to Lucy.

"Shall we go upstairs, the loo isn't very romantic is it?" he asked.

Lucy licked her lips and looked at Ed through her lashes. "I never said I wanted romance, at this minute I just want you, wherever it is I don't care."

"Well, I do hope that my arrival isn't going to spoil things for you."

Ed and Lucy both turned to where the voice came from as the owner stepped out from the shadow.

As soon as Ed gasped Lucy knew who the woman was.

"What the fuck are you doing here?" asked Ed dropping Lucy's hand.

"That's a lovely greeting for the mother of your son, I must say."

Chapter 15

Within minutes, Ed had managed to secrete Katie into the lounge, and gathered his parents and Lucy by his side. Lucy had protested at first, insisting that it was a family matter, but Ed had been adamant.

"You're my girlfriend Lucy, and I want you by my side. Please." He looked at her pleadingly

"Lucy, Ed is right, you should be there." Jack placed a reassuring hand on Lucy's shoulder.

Ed smiled at Lucy and kissed her tenderly. The joy that he'd seen in Lucy's face earlier in the night had now been replaced with a look of fear.

"There's nothing to worry about, I promise," he reassured her.

"Come on, let's get in there and find out why she's here," said Georgina striding down the hall.

She pushed open the door to find Katie fingering a silver framed photograph of Nate. Georgina walked over and took the frame from Katie.

"What do you want Katie?" Georgina turned as she heard the door close behind her. Jack stood with his back against the door, arms folded; behind his mother was Ed, clutching Lucy's hand.

"Hello to you too Georgina," Katie responded with a hint of an American twang to her voice.

"Forget about any niceties Katie, like I said outside, what the fuck are you doing here?" Ed's shoulders tensed as he increased his grip on Lucy's hand.

"Well I must say I thought you might all be a little friendlier, but I guess not. Jack, you're a little quiet over there, nothing to say." Katie smirked as she pushed her hair behind her ear.

"I've nothing to say to you Katie, you should know that. Just tell Ed what he needs to know."

Katie shrugged and turned her gaze on Lucy.

"You must be the latest girlfriend. Not your usual sort Ed, I always thought you were a breasts man."

Lucy glanced at Katie's ample chest; they looked perfect and real; much to Lucy's misery.

"Katie, just answer the question," said Georgina moving into Katie's eye line. "What are you doing here?"

"Well if you must know, I've left Luke, and I want to come home. I'm here for Ed and Nate."

Ed enfolded Lucy's hand in both of his, tightening his grip even more so than before. He sensed that she was about to bolt, and he didn't want her to. Apart from wanting her by his side, Ed knew that she needed reassuring that he didn't feel the same way as Katie.

Despite this his heart beat faster, and his stomach felt as though he'd just come off a big dipper ride.

"You have got to be joking," he whispered as he stared at Katie.

"Ed, I think I should go." Lucy's voice was barely audible beside him.

Ed shook his head but didn't look at Lucy, he kept eye contact with Katie, hoping that she would see the hate and anger in his eyes and realise the futility of her plan.

"No, Lucy, she's the one who should go. She's the one not welcome here, not you."

"Ed, you know you don't mean that." Katie took a step toward Ed.

Georgina put a hand against Katie's shoulder to stop her.

"You heard what he said, so go. In fact, before you do just answer me a couple of questions. Does Luke know you're here, and where are the children?" Georgina asked.

Katie sniffed and lowered her head, a sobbing sound escaping from her.

"Luke knows I've left, but he wouldn't let me take the children. He's got them."

"More children you've abandoned then," Jack said from the back of the room.

"It's not like that Jack," Katie said between sobs. "I didn't want to tell you this, but he's been beating me, and I was beginning to fear for my life."

"Huh," Georgina scoffed. "I don't remember there being a bad atmosphere when I was over, and it was only a few weeks ago. You're a liar."

"Does this look like I'm lying?" blasted Katie as she rolled up the sleeve on her blouse.

Her arm was dark blue and yellow, with finger marks running through a large bruise.

"So it's nothing to do with wanting me or Nate, you simply want someone who will rescue you from Luke, and you thought I'd be mug enough." Ed sighed heavily and ran a hand through his hair.

Lucy felt a small sense of relief and relaxed her shoulders. She'd been sure that Ed would suggest she go home while he sorted it out, but the fact that he wanted her to stay made Lucy feel a little more secure. However, when she looked at Katie she couldn't believe that Ed wouldn't want to be with her. Katie was beautiful, her hair was dark and shiny, and her skin golden brown from the American sun. Her dark and sultry eyes looked at Ed in such a way that there was no doubt what she was here for. But Ed was probably right; she just wanted to use him to escape her violent husband.

Lucy squeezed Ed's hand and wrapped her arm around his forearm. "Can I have a word outside please Ed?"

Ed nodded and led Lucy from the room. Once in the hallway he pulled Lucy to him and wrapped his arms tightly around her.

"I don't believe her. I just don't think that Luke would do that. He's a lot of things but not a wife beater." Ed shook his head.

"Look, you've got an awful lot that you need to sort out, and I don't think I should be involved." Lucy placed a palm against Ed's cheek. "This is between you and Katie."

"But, you should be there, you're my girlfriend and I love you…" Ed's colour changed to crimson as he realised what he'd just said. "Sorry, I shouldn't have said that, I wasn't meant to…"

Lucy gasped and then kissed him. "It doesn't matter, I love you too," she said breathlessly.

"You do? Honestly?"

"Honestly." Lucy nodded.

"I thought it was too early to tell you, I thought you'd think I was crazy. I know it's not been long Luce, but I do love you." Ed started to laugh as he held Lucy tightly.

"I know I felt the same, I thought you'd think I was a mad woman, or a stalker."

"God no, well I know you're a mad woman, but a beautiful mad woman. Christ, what a mess, what am I going to do about her?"

"I honestly don't know Ed. You need to think about Nate in all of this if she does want you and Nate back, and she can't have you, she's at least going to want to see Nate."

"I know, but what if it's just a whim, and she lets him down again? I can't take that risk Lucy." Ed moved across the hallway and sat on the stairs.

Lucy placed herself on Ed's knee and wrapped her arms around his neck.

"How about I wrap everything up outside, it's almost eleven, so I'm sure people will be leaving soon anyway. Once they've gone I'll go back to Dad's with Sarah and Ben. Then when you've finished with Katie I can come back."

Ed gazed at Lucy before kissing her passionately. After a few minutes, they broke away from each other, realising that now wasn't the time or place, Ed needed to concentrate on Katie. Just at that moment Jack appeared in the hallway.

"Hi Dad, what's happening in there?" Ed asked.

"She says she has nowhere to stay, so your mother offered her a bed at our house, but I'm not happy about it Ed." Jack rubbed his face with his hands. "What on earth is she doing here?"

"I don't know Dad, but I doubt Luke has been beating her. Lucy has suggested that she break the party up, people will be going home soon anyway."

Jack nodded. "Hmm, just tell them I'm ill or something if you don't mind Lucy."

Lucy smiled and got up from Ed's knee. "Good idea. I'll tidy up outside and then go back to my dad's house." She stooped to kiss Ed. "Ring me when she's gone, no matter what time it is."

"Okay baby, I will. I just hope it doesn't take long to get rid of her."

"Somehow I've got a feeling it might," said Jack shaking his head.

Half an hour later, with the help of Sarah and Ben, Lucy had tidied the garden of plastic cups and plates and empty beer cans. Most people had gathered something was wrong when Lucy had gone back outside. Jack had evidently been enjoying himself and the beer all night, so the story of him being ill wasn't a complete surprise to anyone. Callie and Elspeth wanted to help tidy up, and were a little difficult to get rid of, but Lucy had finally managed it.

"Okay are you ready Luce?" asked Ben putting an arm around her shoulder.

"Yes, I think so. I just need to get my handbag from the kitchen."

"It's okay," Sarah said. "I've got it here, I just picked it up when I took Ed's iPod back in."

"Thanks," said Lucy taking the bag from Sarah. "Could you hear anything?"

"Well there were a few raised voices, but I couldn't hear what they were actually saying."

"God, I hope they don't wake Nate up." Lucy sighed. "Anyway, come on let's go, it's only a few minutes' walk from here."

By 1:00 a.m. Lucy still hadn't heard from Ed and was getting anxious. Sarah and Ben had stayed up with her until midnight, but had both been so tired from their journey they'd had to go to bed. Lucy wondered whether to go back to the house, despite what she'd agreed with Ed, but decided against it. He needed time to sort things out. So, Lucy decided to go up to bed, he wouldn't call her now, it was far too late. Just as she turned the lamp off, Lucy heard a faint knock on the lounge window, pulling the curtain to one side she saw Ed.

Lucy rushed to the front door and swung it open, dragging Ed into her arms.

"Oh God, I was so worried. I didn't think you were going to call me. What's happened?"

Ed kissed her. "I think I need a strong drink and a sit down."

A few minutes later Lucy passed Ed a large brandy and sat next to him on the sofa.

"Well, what's happened, what did she say?"

"Not much more than when you were there. Luke had been hitting her apparently, so she left, and he wouldn't let her take the children. She says she has some money of her own, enough to get here and to live on for a couple of weeks, but that's all. Apparently Luke has frozen the bank account." Ed yawned and rubbed his eyes. "I'm knackered; can I stay here tonight please?"

"Of course you can, but why? Who's with Nate?" Lucy took the glass of brandy from Ed and placed it on the coffee table.

"Dad is, he refused to spend a night under the same roof as Katie, so he's stayed at mine with Nate, and Katie has gone home with Mum. When Katie went to the loo we agreed to say Nate was staying at a friend's house, I couldn't risk her going upstairs and waking him."

Lucy stroked Ed's tired face. "Bloody hell, what a nightmare. Are you going to let her see Nate while she's here?"

"No, no way." Ed shook his head vehemently. "He finishes school for the summer on Friday, and Mum and Dad were going to take him to their cottage in Wales at some point, so Dad is going to take him tomorrow instead, for whatever length of time it takes to get rid of Katie. Mum will join them once Katie's gone."

"God, it's all a bit sudden, they don't have anything packed."

"Mum is sorting it all out. It'll be fine, I promise. Anyway, are you okay, this hasn't upset you has it?" Ed pulled Lucy onto his knee.

"No, I'm fine, just shocked really, but probably not as shocked as you," Lucy replied.

Ed blew out a deep breath. "That's an understatement Luce, it's bloody floored me, I just never thought she'd ever come back, well I hoped she wouldn't."

"How did you feel seeing her after all these years?" she asked, feeling slightly apprehensive.

Ed considered his answer for a few seconds. "I felt fucking angry because she thought it would be that easy to come back and because she ruined Dad's party. I hate that she doesn't seem to care about her son or, for that matter, her other kids that's she's also abandoned. She's a selfish bitch." After a few moments, a smile appeared on Ed's face. "Plus, I hate that she stopped our romantic liaison in the toilet." he said, attempting to lighten the mood.

"I know." Lucy grinned as her fingers caressed Ed's neck. "But the fact I got to hear that you love me, more than made up for that."

"I'm sorry it came out like that, I would have much preferred to have told you in different circumstances, in bed for instance." Ed kissed along Lucy's jaw-line and nibbled at her ear. "You know, it's funny, but I'm not feeling that tired anymore."

Lucy felt Ed's excitement growing and responded to his kisses, a bubbling sensation starting between her legs.

"Tell me now then," she whispered as she unbuttoned his shirt.

"Christ I love you," he groaned as he unzipped the back of her dress and pulled it down to her waist to reveal her bare breasts.

"How much?" Lucy wriggled on his knee, pulling her dress down over her legs before tossing it onto the floor.

"So much it hurts, now you tell me." Ed pulled off his shirt and moaned as Lucy unbuttoned his jeans and slid her hand inside.

"I love you, and now I'm going to show you how much," she whispered in his ear.

"Oh my God, I love it when you show me."

The next morning Lucy and Ed finally woke to the sound of Sarah and Ben, pottering about in the kitchen downstairs.

"Hmm, morning," Lucy yawned and stretched her arms, smiling at Ed lying next to her. "You didn't sleep much last night did you?" she asked.

Ed shook his head and rubbed his eyes. "Not a lot, too much to think about. I'm sorry, did I keep you awake?" Ed kissed Lucy's nose.

"No, I couldn't sleep either. Last time I looked the clock said it was just before six."

"Well you got a couple of hours at least, it's just gone eight now. I'd better get up and go and see Nate, before Dad and he leave." Ed lowered his legs out of the bed and reached for his discarded jeans from the night before.

"Wait for me and I'll come with you," said Lucy throwing the duvet back.

"No, you stay here and spend some time with Sarah and Ben. I'll try and come back as soon as I can, but I need to find out what Katie plans to do," said Ed pulling on his shirt.

Lucy felt slightly dejected, after Ed's declaration of love last night, and some intensely passionate sex, she'd thought that he wouldn't want her to leave his side.

"Okay," she said in a small voice. "Perhaps I'll take Sarah and Ben to The Well for lunch. You'll ring me and let me know what's happening, won't you?"

Ed was looking down at his feet, his head in his hands.

"Sorry, what did you say?" he asked as he turned to Lucy.

"Keep me informed." Lucy said.

"Okay, I'll call you when I can." Ed leaned across and kissed Lucy before grabbing his shoes and socks. "I'm not sure when it'll be though."

"No worries, whenever you can," Lucy replied to his disappearing back.

"Luce, stop worrying he's got a lot on his plate," said Sarah holding Lucy's hand tightly.

"I can't help it Sarah, she's beautiful."

"Seriously Lucy, he's mad on you," Ben said. "He talked about you non-stop, when he wasn't talking about Oasis and Newcastle United of course."

Lucy attempted a smile as she played with the stem of her glass.

She'd brought Sarah and Ben to The Well for lunch, but she was so nervous she'd hardly eaten any of her Sunday lunch but had drunk a large amount of wine. Ed hadn't been in touch since he'd left her bed, and she couldn't help but worry that he'd been bewitched by Katie.

"What makes you think that he's suddenly decided it's Katie he wants?" asked Sarah forking one of Lucy's roast potatoes and putting it onto her own plate.

"Her bloody big charlies for one thing," snapped Lucy.

"Has she got big boobs?" Ben's eyes widened as he looked up from his lunch.

"Ben!" Sarah smacked her husband's arm but couldn't help but smile. "Ignore him Lucy. Ed is a far better man than that; he wouldn't be swayed by a pair of bosoms. Seriously though, why are you so afraid?"

"Well, she does have a fantastic body, plus she's beautiful and she's the mother of his son. He's known me for a couple of months, and he may think he loves me but…oops," she hiccupped.

Sarah held her hand up. "Hang on what did you just say, he may think he loves you. Has he told you that?"

Lucy dropped her face into her hands and nodded. "Hmm," came the muffled reply.

"Again, louder please." Sarah pulled Lucy's hands away from her face.

"Hmm, he's told me that."

OH MY GOD! Lucy that's fantastic, quite quick, but fantastic, don't you think Ben?" Sarah nudged Ben so hard the cauliflower on the end of his fork almost went up his nose.

"What? Oh erm, yes great Lucy." Ben carried on eating his lunch.

"Have you told him?" Sarah pushed her plate away, more interested in what Lucy had to say than her roast beef.

"Yes," Lucy whispered. "I wasn't going to, I thought it was too soon, but I couldn't help it because…well because I do. More wine please Benjamin," she said proffering her glass to Ben.

"It is a little quick, but if that's how you feel, then that's how you feel, and I'm really happy for you. Aren't we Ben?"

Ben paused from pouring wine into Lucy's glass. "What? Oh yes, immensely happy Luce." Ben smiled at Sarah. "What are we happy about, sorry I wasn't listening?"

"Oh just eat your lunch and be quiet," said Sarah moving her chair closer to Lucy's. "To be honest I'm not surprised, anyone who can make you orgasm like you did last night must be a good man. Sorry Lucy, but you need to learn to be a little quieter when you have guests in the house."

"Take care sweetie, and let me know how things go with Katie, promise?" Sarah dragged Lucy into a hug.

"I promise," replied Lucy, muffled by Sarah's chest.

After lunch, Lucy had taken Sarah and Ben for a walk around the town, surreptitiously checking her mobile every few minutes, but there was no call from Ed. Her friends were now leaving, and soon Lucy would be alone with her anxieties.

"Bye Lucy," said Ben kissing Lucy on the cheek. "It'll be okay, I'm positive. He really cares about you."

"Hmm, I know, but I did think I'd have heard from him by now." Lucy swayed slightly as the wine mixed with fresh air started to affect her balance.

"He'll be in touch when he can," said Ben swinging an overnight bag into the boot of the car.

"Ben's right Luce; he's just got a lot to sort out. Anyway, you take care, and I'll give you three rings when we get back."

Lucy laughed at their old habit from when they were teenagers.

"Okay, and thanks for coming both of you. I'm just sorry you couldn't spend more time with Ed."

"No worries, there'll be other times," replied Ben getting into the car. "We've agreed to go and watch Newcastle and City next season, so we'll be up for that."

"Oh and Luce," Sarah called. "No more wine please, you've had enough for one day."

"Okay," Lucy replied, wobbling again.

As Lucy waved them off, her phone started to ring in her pocket. She snatched it out and answered it breathlessly.

"Hi Ed."

"Hi Luce, sorry I've not been in touch all day."

"You sound tired," Lucy replied.

"Hmm, I'm okay. Anyway, I'm really sorry, but I'm not going to be able to meet up with you today."

Lucy's heart started to hammer in her chest. "Oh, okay. How come?"

"I just can't Lucy. Katie is absolutely distraught and refusing to leave. She's almost deranged; I may even have to sedate her."

"Ed she's not really your problem anymore."

"Of course she's my problem," he snapped back at her. "I can't leave Mum to deal with it. I thought you'd understand."

"I do," Lucy said softly with tears pricking at her eyelashes. "I just hoped that I'd see you today."

"Well sorry, you won't. Look I'll see you at work tomorrow."

"Okay, see you then."

"I am sorry Lucy, truly I am." Ed's voice had softened now. "I'll try and call you later, okay."

"Hmm okay. Bye Ed." Lucy's voice caught in her throat.

"Bye."

"Oh Ed…" He'd already gone. "I love you," she whispered to a dead line.

Chapter 16

Lucy didn't have a good night's sleep. She'd had to spend the majority of the night in the bathroom. She hadn't heeded Sarah's advice, and after another bottle of wine and no food, she'd fallen asleep on the sofa and had then been rather sick. The time she did spend in bed she'd been, tossing and turning, thinking about Ed and Katie, and wondering what was happening. Needless to say, Ed hadn't called her again, which made Lucy even more fearful that Katie had got her own way and wormed her way into Ed's bed. Eventually, as the birds started to wake, sleep finally overcame her. It was two hours later that her alarm shrilled that it was time to get up.

Lucy groaned as she stretched over to turn it off. The last thing she needed was a morning at the surgery, but she would see Ed at least, and she didn't want to leave Callie in the lurch. So with all the willpower she could muster, Lucy got out of bed and went to shower, hoping it would wake her up, and make her hangover go away.

By the time she arrived at the surgery, Lucy was feeling a little more human, after her dad's remedy of orange juice, tonic water, a chocolate bar and two Paracetamol. When she saw Ed's car on the car park she also felt slightly more optimistic, things weren't so severe that he hadn't been able to leave Katie.

When she walked in Callie was already behind the desk, flicking through a daily newspaper with one hand, the other rubbing her back.

"Morning Callie." Lucy tried to appear happy and keen to be there. She was sure Ed wouldn't like Callie to know that he had problems; he was an extremely private person where Katie was concerned.

"Ah morning Pet." Callie grimaced as she looked up.

"Is your back hurting again?" Lucy asked concerned.

Callie nodded. "Hmm, and I've got a bad tummy as well, so I don't think I'll be much company today Pet."

"Why don't you go home, I'll manage?" Lucy was worried about Callie, but she also realised that she had more chance of speaking to Ed if she was the only one on reception.

"No, I'll be okay. I've just taken some pain killers, so I'll be mint once they've kicked in."

"Okay, if you're sure. Shall I make us a cup of coffee?"

"Ooh that would be good, and could you get Dr Bryce one, please? He did ask me about five minutes ago. I was surprised you weren't with him to be honest, not had a row have you Pet?" said Callie half smiling, as she dragged a stool over to the desk. "It might ease a little if I sit down."

Lucy, thankful for the change in conversation, went to make some coffee.

A few minutes later and Lucy was knocking on Ed's door with a cup of coffee for him. Her stomach was lurching for fear that he would be withdrawn, or even worse tell her that it was over between them. She'd thought about it all night, and if that was what he decided then she would take it on the chin and move on. Lucy knew that she would go back to Cheshire to lick her wounds, but would not spend weeks in bed with a bobble hat on. If Simon leaving had done nothing else, it had reminded her that she was a strong person and life went on. Of course, she would be devastated, but she couldn't go back to that dark place again.

"Come in," called Ed from the other side of the door.

Lucy opened the door, and with trepidation walked in, averting Ed's gaze, frightened of what she'd see in his eyes.

"Hi," he said quietly.

Lucy looked at him, and relief flooded her body. He was smiling at Lucy, and his eyes were happy to see her.

"Hi," she replied still holding tightly to his coffee mug.

"Come here," he said softly and beckoned Lucy over to him. "I'm so sorry."

Lucy almost ran around the desk, slopping coffee on the floor as she did so.

"I thought you were going to tell me that you were back with Katie." Lucy flung herself into Ed's open arms and buried her head in his chest.

"Oh Luce, I am so sorry I really am. I was just so stressed out, and I couldn't think of anything else other than how I was going to calm her down, and get her away from here." Ed kissed Lucy tenderly as he stroked her cheeks. "I'll never forgive myself for making you feel like that."

"It doesn't matter now, but next time just talk to me, tell me what the problem is, don't shut me out."

"I won't. She's a bloody maniac though Luce, I wouldn't have wanted you near her." Ed broke away from Lucy and pulled her onto his knee as he sat down. "She trashed Mum's spare bedroom, and then threatened to kill herself unless I went to see her. I doubt she would've, but I couldn't have that on Mum's conscience if she'd meant it."

"Oh my God, no wonder you were stressed. Why didn't you ring me though, you didn't stay with her all night did you?" Lucy stroked Ed's face, and she saw how tired he looked.

"Christ no, I finally managed to calm her down about ten o'clock. She went to bed and I stayed talking to Mum until gone midnight. I knew I'd ruined your sleep the night before, so didn't want to do it again, I should have realised that you'd be worried. I'm so sorry."

"Forget it Ed, at least for now. However, I will make you pay, once this is all over." Lucy kissed Ed's cheek and ruffled his hair.

"I wouldn't expect anything less," Ed laughed. "But seriously Luce, I don't know what to do about Katie. She's not budging."

Lucy sighed and shook her head. "I don't know what to suggest. Has she asked to see Nate?"

Ed shook his head. "Nope, not at all."

Lucy gasped. "You are joking."

"No, all she talks about is Luke hitting her, having no money, and I'm sorry to say this, me and her trying again." Ed blew out a heavy breath. "She's bloody deluded."

"I know how much you loved her Ed, is there not a part of you that wonders what it would be like." Lucy dropped her eyes, once again scared of what she may see in his face.

"God Lucy, no way," said Ed raising his voice. "Look at me, Lucy I promise you I don't want her back. I love you." He kissed her passionately as if to prove to Lucy in one kiss how he felt.

After a few minutes, Lucy pulled away, smiling.

"Okay, I believe you," she said softly. "Shall I cook dinner at Dad's tonight?"

"Sounds good, she won't know where to find me," said Ed kissing Lucy's palm.

"Is she likely to come looking for you?" Lucy asked. "Because if you're supposed to be pacifying me, it's not bloody working."

Ed laughed and hugged Lucy to him. "Honestly, I don't know, but the way she's behaving I wouldn't put it past her."

"Well whatever, you don't have a choice now, you're definitely coming home with me tonight Dr Bryce." Lucy got up from Ed's knee and walked around the desk toward the door. "So, you'd better find some ways to make up for yesterday, and be warned I'm not easily pleased."

"Okay, I'll put my thinking cap on."

"Good, be sure you do. See you later."

"See you later. Oh and Lucy."

"Hmm."

"I love you."

Ed rubbed his damp hair with a towel as he padded barefoot across the lawn toward Lucy.

"God, that feels better," he said as he sat on a garden chair. "I really needed that."

"I know, Dad's shower is amazing isn't it? Did you speak to your Mum, by the way?"

Ed nodded and took a sip from the wine Lucy had poured for him.

"Hmm, seemingly Katie has been a lot calmer today. She's just gone up for a bath apparently."

"I feel sorry for your Mum; it must be terrible being stuck with her." Lucy put her feet up onto Ed's knee.

"I know, but she feels obligated to have her stay."

Lucy sighed. "I don't suppose Georgina would trust her in the house on her own, would she?"

Ed shook his head. "No, I've tried to convince her to go and meet up with Dad and Nate, but she won't. She tried to get hold of Luke today, but the Nanny said he was at work and that Katie had gone to visit a friend for a few days, so goodness knows what's going on," Ed sighed. "Anyway, let's not talk about them tonight, how has your day been? I've hardly seen you; it was busy today, wasn't it?"

"I know, it hasn't been that busy since the flu epidemic, when you were ill. I'm worried about Callie though, her back was giving her terrible pain today, and she had a stomach ache. I told her to go home, but she wouldn't, especially when we started to get busy," replied Lucy.

"I'll take a look at it for her tomorrow if she's still in pain, although she's not actually our patient. I think she goes to one in Middleton, near to where she lives. I'll see how she feels tomorrow."

"That would be good, anyway, shall I get you a beer, or are you okay with the wine?" Lucy asked.

"I'll go, do you want one?" asked Ed.

"Please."

As Ed went back into the house, Lucy watched him and felt a warm glow surround her. Except for all this trouble with Katie, life was pretty good at the moment. Ed loved her, she loved him and she was enjoying working at the surgery. Maybe she should move here permanently, Lucy pondered. She had Sarah, Ben and the boys back home, but that was all; Annabelle wasn't exactly a reason to go back!

Lucy closed her eyes and considered her options, enjoying the early evening sun on her face. Suddenly she felt the warmth disappear, thinking it was a cloud overhead she opened her eyes to look; Katie was standing over her.

"How the hell did you get in here?" Lucy demanded as she stood up to confront her visitor.

"The side gate was open. Is Ed here?" Katie turned around to scour the garden.

"You have no right to be here, this is my father's house." Lucy stood on tiptoe as in her bare feet she was at least two inches shorter than Katie, and looked at her eye to eye.

"Hmm, I did wonder how someone like you could own a property like this."

At that moment, Ed reappeared in the garden carrying two bottles of beer.

"Katie, what are you doing here?" Ed marched over to the table and put the bottles down, before placing a protective arm around Lucy's shoulder.

"I needed to see you Ed," replied Katie reaching her hand out to touch Ed's arm.

Lucy couldn't help herself and smacked it away.

"Get off him, he's not yours to touch."

Ed chuckled at the side of her, and then tried to disguise it with a cough. "She's right Katie, don't touch me please."

"You never used to say that. You used to love me touching you, do you remember that night we went down to Flatts Woods in the car and parked up. You loved me touching you in all sorts of ways that night." Katie smiled seductively at Ed.

Lucy snatched her head around to look at Ed, thankfully he didn't seem to be moved in any way by Katie's reminiscing.

"Katie, I'll ask you again, what are you doing here? What on earth do you want me for, and how did you know where to find me?"

Katie sighed heavily and sat down on one of the garden chairs. She picked up Lucy's half empty wine glass and started to drink from it.

"Excuse me, that's mine if you don't mind." Lucy pulled the glass from Katie's hand and tipped the rest of the wine onto the grass.

Ed laughed again beside her.

"God she's a touchy one," said Katie screwing her face up. "When your mother was speaking to you on the phone I heard her ask you if you were staying at Lucy's. It's a small town Ed, I wandered around looking for your car. Anyway, what I want is for you to take me out of that dreadful house of your parents. Can't I stay with you, *please* Ed?" She pleaded.

"No, you can't Katie. I don't want you in my life, never mind in my house. It wouldn't be fair on Lucy either. She's my partner, and I love her, so why would I want to distress her by having you living in my house?" Ed kissed Lucy on the forehead, hugging her closer to him.

Katie's smile fell momentarily, but then was soon back. "I didn't realise it was serious, you never said. You really should have told me last night, and I wouldn't have kept you to myself all evening."

"I didn't because my life is nothing to do with you anymore, and never will be."

Lucy watched Katie's smirk disappear. Suddenly Katie didn't look quite as beautiful as Lucy had first thought. The face and eyes were perfect, framed by that lustrous dark hair, but it was as if something horrible that had been hidden inside had begun to appear on those perfect features.

"Well I hope that you take good care of Ed," replied Katie looking Lucy up and down with eyes full of hate.

"She takes care of me *and* Nate, thank you."

Despite the mention of Nate, there was no response from Katie, not a hint of love in her eyes for the son she hadn't seen for three years.

"What are your plans anyway?" asked Lucy reaching up for Ed's hand that was resting on her shoulder.

"Yes, what are they Katie? You can't stay here forever, and Lucy and I are going on holiday soon." Ed squeezed Lucy's hand.

Lucy recognised what he was trying to do, and went along with the lie.

"Yes, we're going away for almost three weeks, so what's the point of you staying around?"

Katie leaned her head to one side and narrowed her eyes as if she were thinking.

"Well, I guess there's no point me staying here too long then is there? I'll stay with your mum for a few more days until I can convince Luke to wire me some money over, and then I guess I'll have to go to Manchester and see if I can find my lazy, fit for nothing, brother. He'll have to put me up for a while, although I'm sure last time I spoke to him he was living in a squat." Katie sighed and sat back in the chair. "Any chance I can have a glass of wine?"

Lucy looked at Ed and nodded – a steely determination in Katie's eyes showed she wouldn't leave until she'd had a drink; plus Lucy couldn't be bothered to argue.

"I'll go and get you a glass," Ed said. "Cupboard on the left, is that right?" he asked.

Lucy nodded again and watched as he strode off toward the house.

"So Lucy…is it Lucy?" asked Katie leaning her chin on her hand as she looked at Lucy.

Lucy smiled and nodded. "That's right."

"So Lucy, how long have you and Ed been together?"

Lucy thought carefully about how to respond to Katie's question. "Long enough to know that it's the real thing, and long enough to know that I love him, and Nate."

"Well, I'm sure Nate's adorable. Of course, you would love Ed; he's pretty remarkable, bloody good in bed as well if memory serves me right. I believe you work at the surgery for him, how quaint, the lowly receptionist bags the handsome doctor with a gorgeous son, quite a ready-made family for you."

Lucy clenched her hands together tightly to stop herself throwing her beer bottle at Ed's ex-wife. "If that's how you want to look at it Katie, but it wasn't like that."

"Well how was it then? Don't tell me you've been friends for years and one day realised you loved one another?"

"No, we were instantly attracted but did try and stay on a professional footing…Christ, what on earth am I telling you for? It's none of your business." Lucy stood up to go and find Ed, she couldn't stand being in Katie's company any longer, with her stupid accent and humongous breasts.

"No need to get huffy about it honey, but just remember he was mine first, and I intend to get him back, I hope that we're clear on that."

Lucy stopped in her tracks and turned to face Katie. "What about your children. Don't you want them with you as well?" Lucy asked.

"Ed wouldn't want Luke's children here. In fact, he wouldn't want any more children here, even if they were his own. He told me just after we'd had Nate that one child was enough, so how does that fit into your plans?" Katie smiled and examined her finger nails.

Lucy knew that Katie was trying to put her off Ed, but, unfortunately for Katie, her announcement didn't upset Lucy in the slightest.

"Oh well that's understandable. It's a good job that I don't want any either."

If the wind had been taken from Katie's sails, it didn't show in her face.

"It won't be an issue anyway, you'll soon be kicked to the curb when he realises it's me he wants, and Louie and Amelia will be happier with their father anyway." Katie replied.

"You're not worried that he'll get violent with them like he did with you?" Lucy asked.

Katie shook her head. "No. Luke may get a little rough sometimes, but he would never hurt the children."

Lucy shook her head in disbelief. "I'm going to find Ed."

"Before you go, can I ask something, please? If you two are so loved up and serious with each other, why do you live with your dad when your partner has his own house that you could move into...hmm it's been puzzling me that one." Katie stood up. "On second thoughts I won't have that glass of wine, things aren't quite as problematical here as I imagined, plus Georgina will be thinking I've drowned in the bath – well hoping more to the point."

With that, Katie left as Lucy stood with an open mouth watching her go.

Lucy was still frozen to the spot when Ed re-emerged a minute later. He placed a glass of wine on the table as he looked around the garden.

"Where's Cruella de Vil?" Ed asked with a huge smile on his face. "Has she gone to kill some puppies?"

"I wouldn't put it past her," replied Lucy as she sat down. "She's just told me that she you belonged to her first and that she intends to get you back. She means what she says Ed, and I'm worried. I think she knows we haven't been a couple for long, she made a comment about us not living together, and the situation wasn't 'as problematical' as she imagined." Lucy jutted out her bottom lip; Katie was seriously getting on her nerves.

Ed knelt down next to Lucy's chair and took hold of both her hands.

"I'm more than happy for you to move in with me if that's what you want, but I don't want to rush you. Plus, I have to think of Nate in all of this." Ed leaned forward and kissed Lucy tenderly. "But, that doesn't mean I don't love you and want you."

"God Ed, don't be silly, I totally understand, and I totally agree. No matter how much we want to spend every moment together, we can't be selfish. Nate needs to be secure in our relationship as much as we do. I would never, ever, want to put him through what Katie did."

Lucy did understand and agree. As she looked at Ed's face, she knew her feelings were growing deeper by the day. She would love to be able to say they were ready for that level of commitment, but no matter how they felt about each other they had Nate to consider. Plus she needed to get divorced first!

"That Lucy is why I love you," said Ed interrupting her thoughts. "Oh, by the way, your mobile was flashing when I went into the kitchen; I think you've got a missed call. Here you go." Ed reached inside his jeans pocket for Lucy's mobile.

"Oh thanks, it might be Dad ringing to catch up. I'll go inside and ring him from the landline, I won't be long."

"Okay, I'll be here." Ed kissed Lucy as she got up to leave.

As he sat down Ed thought about what had happened earlier, and how Katie had found him. She was right, it was a small town, and if she didn't go soon then maybe a holiday with Lucy was a good idea, he had some time booked off in a couple of weeks. They could take Georgina to Wales and stay there for a few days and then move on to somewhere else with Nate, a family holiday perhaps. Maybe that was too early, maybe they could spend time in Wales and then he and Lucy go on somewhere for a few days. Ed decided he would think about it before he mentioned anything to Lucy. Then his thoughts turned to Lucy. She was being amazing about all this with Katie, obviously she'd been worried, but that was his fault. He should have realised that by him staying away she would fear the worse. She was so different to Katie in many ways, not just in looks, but her demeanour. Ed could see now that Katie had always been selfish and petty, whereas Lucy was kind and compassionate. Ed knew that if this situation were reversed Katie wouldn't have spoken to him for weeks.

After around ten minutes, Lucy reappeared, worry etched on her face.

"Hey, what's wrong?" Ed asked as Lucy sat down next to him. "It's not your dad or Richard is it?"

Lucy shook her head, staring into the distance. "No, it wasn't Dad, it was Brian my neighbour. Apparently Simon has been to the house this afternoon and taken his stuff."

"That's okay, isn't it? Or does it make it all seem a bit final?" Ed took hold of Lucy's hand.

"No, it's not that. I don't care about him, but Brian has a spare key, so thought he'd better check everything was okay once Simon had gone, and well…he's cleared the place. There's nothing left." Lucy looked at Ed with tears in her eyes. "Brian didn't want to snoop too much, but as far as he can see he's taken every stick of furniture."

"Christ Luce, he can't do that, surely? You should ring your solicitor and find out what you need to do."

"I'll call him in the morning. I can't believe he's done that," Lucy whispered. "I've nothing left Ed."

"He probably thought that because he's let you have the house he's entitled to the rest. What a tosser! Did he suggest in any way that's what he was going to do?"

"Nope, he said he only wanted a third of the equity, and that was it. I should have realised it was all too good to be true."

"I don't know," Ed sighed, "between us we've got a real pair of rotten ex partners, haven't we?"

The next morning when there had been a lull in patients, Lucy gave Mr Devine a call to inform him of what Simon had done. He'd been sympathetic but had informed Lucy that unless she could prove that the things he'd taken were gifts to Lucy, or paid for by Lucy, then there wasn't a lot she could do. He suggested that she changed the locks to avoid Simon entering the property again. It seemed a little late if what Brian said was true, there wasn't anything left for Simon to come back for. One good thing Mr Devine had told her was that Simon had paid his half of the mortgage this month – scant consolation though for Lucy, who potentially had nothing left but the bricks and mortar of the house, and her clothes.

Just before she left for the day, Lucy caught up with Ed in the staff room and explained everything to him.

"So, that's it, there's nothing you can do about it." Ed sighed and gave Lucy a hug. "I'm really sorry, you must feel like crap about it."

"It's not the furniture I'm bothered about, it's the other things he may have taken. There were photographs of Lottie, and a few things that were my grandparents. I just don't know if he's taken those as well."

"Maybe Mr Devine is right, maybe you should get the locks changed. Plus, it might not be a bad idea to go home and find out exactly what he's taken. We could go together if you like?" Ed suggested.

Lucy smiled broadly. "That would be lovely Ed, but I don't want you to get involved in all of this. If someone spotted you and told Simon, well you may get dragged into the divorce."

"So what? I'm not bothered."

"But I am," said Lucy. "He's the one that cheated, I didn't and I'm not giving him the opportunity to get off with the responsibility."

"Who's likely to see me and tell him, I thought you said he'd moved out of town?" Ed caught hold of Lucy's hand and interlocked his fingers with hers. "It would be good to have a few days away."

Lucy shook her head. "I can't ask you to do that Ed. A friend of Simon's mother lives a few houses away; she'd spot you for certain she's always twitching at the curtains. Plus she'd revel in telling him or his mother. Anyway, you're busy here, and I want to get it sorted as soon as possible. I've already spoken to Callie, and she said Margery won't mind coming in for an extra day."

Ed's face fell. "Are you going today then?"

"I thought I'd go tomorrow morning and come back on Thursday. It's only one night Ed," said Lucy.

Lucy realised that Ed looked genuinely disappointed that she was going away, even just for one night. She really didn't want to; apart from being away from Ed she didn't want to leave him alone with Katie. She trusted him, but certainly didn't trust Katie.

At that moment, Callie bounded in. "Right pet, all sorted. Margery is more than happy to work tomorrow."

"All sorted then I guess." A frown appeared on Ed's face. "I'd better take you out for a lovely dinner tonight to make up for not seeing you tomorrow."

"Blimey, loves young dream," Callie laughed. "She's only going for one night man."

"I know, but I will miss her." Ed laughed as a blush appeared at his cheeks.

"I'll be back before you know it, but dinner out sounds lovely, thank you."

"Eeh, I don't know pet, I think that should give you an idea about your future. Why don't you put that house up for sale and move here permanently," said Callie as she left the room.

"Maybe she's got a point," said Ed taking Lucy into his arms. "It's something to think about."

"Perhaps," said Lucy smiling. "But we'll see how good dinner is first."

Chapter 17

The inky black sky overhead seemed to indicate that the rain, which had started at the beginning of Lucy's journey at seven-thirty that morning, would continue for a while yet. She hadn't wanted to leave Ed, or his bed. As usual he'd made it difficult for her to leave, making love to Lucy slowly, showing her what she'd be missing that night. But now after an arduous journey, all that was forgotten. Her head fuzzy from concentrating on driving, Lucy shuddered as she got out of the car, amazed at how her mood had darkened from the moment that she turned into the road. As she looked up at her house, it seemed unfamiliar after nearly three months away. Brian's car wasn't on his driveway, so Lucy made a mental note to call on him later, to thank him for looking after the house and garden, but at the moment she was glad that she could look around alone. She approached the front door and put the key in the lock, turning it with apprehension, scared of what may face her on the other side.

The post lay on the floor, so she picked it up and shoved it into her handbag - it could wait until she'd checked the house out.

As Lucy moved down the hall toward the lounge, she sighed with relief. Simon had at least had the decency to leave the coat stand that had belonged to her grandparents. She slowly opened the door into the lounge and gasped at what she saw – or more to the point what she didn't see. Simon had indeed taken everything, even down to the box of matches that were used to light the gas fire and were normally found on the hearth. All that was left was a pile of Lucy's magazines that had obviously been emptied from the now non-existent magazine rack.

Every room was the same, empty apart from the items that Simon evidently didn't want, or belonged to Lucy. He'd left a few knick-knacks and a rocking chair that had been Lucy's grandma's, and in Lucy's wardrobe were the clothes that she'd left behind when she'd gone to stay with Gerald and, to her delight; the large box of photographs was where she'd left it. Then she felt sad as it appeared Simon hadn't wanted any pictures of Lottie, it wasn't as if he hadn't seen them, because he'd taken a vase of his grandmother's that had stood next to the box in the bottom of the wardrobe. Then as she walked into the bathroom Lucy laughed emptily, Simon had taken the towels and even the shower gel from inside the cubicle.

She made her way downstairs and slumped to the floor in the hallway, taking her phone out of her bag to ring Ed.

"Hi Luce," he answered. "How is it?"

"Oh Ed," she cried. "It's awful, there's hardly anything left. I haven't even got a bed to sleep in tonight."

"You *are* joking?" he asked incredulously.

Lucy shook her head. "No, he's even taken the shower gel."

"He can't get away with that, surely there's something you can do."

"I doubt it; I wasn't working, so he paid for everything, so officially everything belongs to Simon. I'm going to have to stay at a hotel tonight, unless Sarah will let me stay there."

"Oh sweetheart, I wish you'd have let me come with you. I don't like to think of you all alone facing that," Ed sighed.

"I'll be fine, I kind of expected it anyway. Simon doesn't do anything in half measures. I'll hang about until I can see Brian and then shoot over to Sarah's."

"Are you going to see your Mum while your home?" Ed asked.

"*No*, anyway it's July, she goes to France with her friend Guy in July. So, if she's not gone already she'll be getting ready to go."

"Surely she'd want to see you though, she could spare you some time."

"Not likely, there's a lot to do to 'look super for Antibes'," Lucy mocked Annabelle's cultivated voice. "She's probably having her back waxed as we speak."

Ed let out a laugh. "You really don't get on do you?"

"No, we do not." Lucy said emphatically. "Anyway, what about you, how's your day been so far?"

They continued talking for another ten minutes until Ed had to see a patient. Apparently Callie's back pain seemed to have eased, but Dr Kindler was suffering with a migraine, so Ed was going to be extremely busy for the rest of the day, and probably into the early evening. Just as they were saying goodbye, Lucy heard a knock at the door.

"Oh, there's someone at the door," she said. "I'd better go. Call me later when you finally finish at the surgery."

"Okay, will do. Speak later and I love you."

"Bye darling, love you too."

Lucy rushed over to the front door and opened it to find a grim faced Brian standing before her.

"I'm so sorry Lucy, if I'd known I would have rung the police or something."

"Come in Brian," said Lucy ushering him in. "Honestly, it's not your fault, and there isn't anything the police could do. Legally he's entitled; it's just morally that he's a shit."

Brian smiled and rubbed Lucy's arm. He was a retired train driver, and he and his wife Maureen were gentle souls and Lucy knew that he would feel dreadful about what had happened.

"This has all been awful for you, hasn't it?" he said. "Simon leaving and now this. How have you been coping?"

Lucy smiled. "Better than I thought to be honest Brian. In fact, so much so I'm thinking of selling up and moving up there permanently." Lucy hadn't actually thought about it since Callie's comment yesterday, but she suddenly realised that it was actually the right thing to do.

"Oh no, Maureen and I will be really sorry to lose you. But, you should do whatever is best for you, and I must say you look much better and healthier than when you left."

"I feel happy to be honest Brian, and maybe Simon has done me a favour by taking everything, it means I can make a totally fresh start."

"Well that's good Lucy you just make sure you keep in touch."

"I will Brian, I promise."

Lucy spent the rest of the day at the house, packing up the remainder of her clothes into the empty suitcase that she'd brought with her – lucky she had, Simon had even taken the spare ones that were in the loft. Everything else that was left was either piled into her car, or if it wouldn't fit in the car Lucy put it in the dining room, ready to collect at a later date. After slipping out to get a sandwich from the local shop, she then rang a locksmith and arranged for him to come and change the locks. She'd paid a large amount of money for him to come that afternoon, but she didn't care, at least Simon wouldn't be able to get back in now. Finally, Lucy found the time to call Sarah to ask if she could stay overnight, which Sarah had been overjoyed at.

"Are you sure it's okay?" Lucy asked as she followed Sarah up the stairs.

"Of course it is silly. There's no way you were staying in a hotel, when there's a spare room here."

"It's a pity the boys aren't here. I would have loved to have seen them."

"They would have loved to see you too." Sarah opened the door to the spare room.

Sarah's in-laws had taken the boys on holiday for a couple of weeks, so Lucy wouldn't get to see either of her godsons.

"How are Ben's parents anyway?" Lucy asked as she unpacked her pyjamas.

"Oh they're great; I don't know what I'd do without them. They help out with the kids such a lot. Anyway, enough of all that, let's get downstairs with a bottle of wine and discuss the men in your life." Sarah hugged Lucy tightly.

"I've lots to tell you Sarah, so we may need quite a big bottle."

Lucy told Sarah the whole story from the Sunday evening, when Ed hadn't been in touch because of Katie, through to Katie's appearance at Gerald and Richard's house. Finally, regaling her tale of Simon taking everything from the house. Lucy had been right, there was a lot to tell and Ben had been despatched to buy another bottle of wine.

"What a pair of slime balls," said Sarah. "It's a pity Simon is with Jennifer 'bloody bitch face' Grayson, it sounds as though Katie would be an ideal partner for him."

Lucy laughed. "With his track record I wouldn't put it past him to try it on with her if, they ever met." Lucy sighed heavily. "There is something else I need to tell you though Sarah, and I'm not sure you're going to like it."

"What?" Sarah frowned.

"Well, I've decided that I'm going to sell up and stay in County Durham."

Sarah's face now broke into a smile. "Lucy, I'm just glad that you're happy. Of course, I'll miss you like crazy, but it's only three hours away, it's not the other side of the world. I just need you to be sure it's what you want, it is isn't it?"

Lucy smiled and nodded vigorously. "It is. I just can't imagine my life any differently now. Going back to the house today made me realise, it's definitely what I want."

"What did Ed say when you told him?"

"I haven't had the chance yet, he's been so busy today. Anyway, I'd rather tell him in person."

Sarah smiled at Lucy as she lifted her glass in cheers. "Well, here's to your new life and I hope that both you and Ed are extremely happy. Will you move in with him then, or buy something together?"

"Blimey Sarah, I don't know until I've spoken to Ed, but I won't be leaving Dad's for a while yet, unless Dad and Richard don't want me there and then I may rent."

Sarah looked at Lucy quizzically. "I thought you meant you were moving in with Ed."

"It's a little soon for that, I'm not even divorced yet. Plus he's got Nate to think of. Besides, even if Ed and I don't go the distance, I love it there. I feel healthier and happier than I have in a long time, even before Simon left."

"I suppose you're right. I'm just excited for you. Whatever you decide I hope that you'll be happy."

"I hope so too Sarah, I really do."

Lucy had called Ed from the motorway services to tell him what time she'd be back, and he was now waiting at his house in anticipation. He hadn't thought that one night apart would be that difficult, but he'd missed her so much. For nearly six weeks, they'd spent almost every night together, even if it hadn't been the whole night. He was supposed to have had a home visit during the two hour surgery break, but Dr Kindler had offered to do it instead, as Ed had covered for him the day before. Ed was grateful for the time to see Lucy and had eagerly accepted.

Lucy was just as excited about being back with Ed, she'd driven the last hour in hot anticipation, eager to tell him her news, and desperate to have his body against hers.

She knocked on the back door as she opened it. "Hi," she shouted. "I'm back."

Ed appeared in the kitchen and gave her a dazzling smile. "Hi baby, God am I glad to see you." He walked towards her, actually how glad was evident in his trousers. "I thought you'd never get here."

Lucy dropped her bag on the floor and allowed Ed to pull her into his arms. Immediately his lips were on Lucy as he kissed her hungrily down the length of her neck, pulling the thin straps of her summer vest off her shoulders until Lucy's breasts sprang free of the white cotton. Desperate for Ed's skin against her own, Lucy pulled at the buttons of his shirt and opening it pulled it from inside his trousers. Once his shirt was opened Lucy moaned with pleasure at the feel of his chest against hers, then as Ed started to circle one of her nipples with his tongue Lucy felt a tingling sensation between her legs. As Lucy rubbed her crotch against Ed's erection, he reached down and pulled up her skirt and felt bare skin.

"Please tell me you've driven all the way here without any underwear on," Ed moaned and he gently squeezed Lucy's buttocks.

"Since the motorway services I have, I wanted to be ready for you."

Ed moved his hand and started to feel between Lucy's thighs, marvelling at how ready for him she was.

"Bloody hell Lucy, what are you doing to me?"

Lucy unbuttoned Ed's trousers and pushed them halfway down his thighs. "I want you now," she groaned into Ed's ear. "I'm ready now."

Ed manoeuvred Lucy towards the dining table and then gently lifted her onto the edge. As he bit gently at her breast he moved her legs apart, his hands lingering at the top of her thighs for a few seconds, and then he pulled Lucy towards him, and moved inside her. Lucy gave a gasp as he entered her and gripped his shoulders as Ed made love to her. They were both so highly charged that, within minutes, they both let out a moan of pleasure, climaxing together.

Lucy and Ed hung on to each other, panting and sweating, their skin sensitive from the intensity of their orgasms. Ed kissed Lucy lazily along her collar bone and then as she leaned back to expose her breasts, his mouth moved down towards her nipples once more.

"Christ Ed, I'm not finished," she whispered taking Ed's hand and putting it between her legs.

As Ed's fingers played with her hard clitoris Lucy could feel her whole body start to tremble until finally she bucked her crotch towards him as she orgasmed once more.

"That's what I call a welcome home," Lucy panted.

"It was worth a night apart," said Ed as he pulled his trousers up. "I need to get a shower before I go back to the surgery. Fancy joining me?"

"I'm not sure my body would stand much more today, but I can always come and wash your back for you." Lucy pulled her straps back over her shoulders and jumped off the table smoothing down her skirt.

Ed took hold of Lucy's hand and pulled her towards the hallway, to make their way upstairs to the bathroom. Just as they reached the bottom step, they heard a knock and then a shout from the kitchen.

"Ed, it's only me. Callie said I could find you here."

"Hi Mum," Ed shouted back, we're just in the lounge.

Ed tried to fasten his shirt quickly, and Lucy started to giggle as he pushed her towards the lounge. He put a finger to his lips that had broken into a huge smile.

"Sshh," he hissed. "She'll know what we've been up to."

Ed pushed Lucy inside the room and onto a chair while he almost vaulted the arm of the sofa and landed, just as Georgina walked in.

"Hi Lucy, how was your trip?" Georgina bent down and kissed Lucy's cheek that was now burning hot and crimson.

"Oh okay, just as I thought, he's taken everything." Lucy tucked her skirt around her thighs, suddenly aware that she wasn't wearing any underwear in Georgina's presence.

"No, gosh that's terrible. Sorry though, you'll have to tell me about it another time, we need to talk." Georgina looked at Ed, who had one hand stuffed inside his trouser pockets while the other tucked his shirt in surreptitiously.

"Why what's wrong? Don't tell me, Katie." Ed shifted uncomfortably as Georgina sat down beside him.

"No, well not quite, but we do need to sort something out. Don't panic, but you're dad isn't feeling well. He's woken up this morning with a sore throat, a headache and joint pain, so he's not sure he can cope with Nate on his own."

"I can go and collect them from the cottage," said Lucy keen to help.

"That's the problem, I don't think that Nate should come back here while she's still around. What do you think Ed?" Georgina asked.

"I agree, I don't want him here while Cruella is, but what's the alternative?"

"Well, it's not ideal, but someone needs to go to them. Your dad may be okay tomorrow, but I don't think we can take that chance."

"I'd go, but I'm not sure I can get the time off just yet. I've got some holidays booked in a couple of weeks, but I don't think we can get a locum in before then. Sally Bennett who normally does it for us is on holiday herself." Ed scratched his head, wondering how to resolve the situation.

"What if I went to stay with them for a few days?" Lucy asked.

"Actually, I think it's best if I go," Georgina replied. "If Ed can't go because of work, well, it should be me. I was supposed to be there anyway, and after all he's my husband."

"You're forgetting one big problem," said Ed. "Katie!"

"Believe me, I haven't forgotten her, unfortunately. I've told her that she's got to go to a hotel, or a hostel or something," Georgina replied.

"And what did she think of that idea, not much I'm guessing?" Ed smiled ruefully.

"She says she doesn't have enough money, so I've offered to pay… for a few nights that's all." Georgina held up her hand as she could see Ed was about to protest.

Ed shook his head. "Mum, no you can't do that. She's not our responsibility, she's bloody Luke's. Plus Dad would hit the roof."

"Ed's right Georgina, I know it's not really anything to do with me, but I honestly don't think that you should offer to help her," Lucy added.

"She'll take advantage Mum, you know she will. The bill will end up in the thousands if I know Katie."

Georgina sighed. "I hear what you're both saying, but I do feel responsible. She's here because of Luke, and she's the mother of my grandchildren. I can't just push her out onto the streets."

"Katie is nothing if not resourceful, she'd manage I'm sure," Ed answered.

Georgina stood up and moved to the door. "I'm sorry darling," she said addressing Ed. "But my mind is made up and I'm going to pay for a hotel for her."

Suddenly Ed also got up from the sofa. "Mum, wait. I'll sort the hotel out."

Georgina smiled. "No, it's definitely not up to you to sort her out, I'll do it."

Ed put a hand on Georgina's shoulder. "Seriously Mum, I want to, I want her out of here more than anyone, so I'll pay. When she gets the money from Luke she can pay me back."

Lucy now joined them "Georgina, I think you need to tell Ed what Luke asked you," she prompted.

Ed looked at her quizzically. "Sorry, what are you talking about?"

"He asked me for money, apparently they're broke. I haven't even mentioned it to your dad as I knew he'd say no." Georgina moved over to the window and stared outside. "That's partly why I feel responsible for Katie, maybe if I'd lent them the money they would still be together."

"That's ridiculous Mum, it's not your fault."

"Ed, you know what Luke is like, he can't handle pressure so maybe that's why he hit her."

Ed moved over to Georgina and put an arm around her. "I don't believe he has hit her, now you've told me that I think it's more likely she left because they have no money."

"So again it's my fault," Georgina argued.

"No, it's *their* fault for spending the money in the first place. We both know how much money he's had, Mum." Ed now turned to Lucy to explain. "When we were kids Dad built four houses, and then sold them at a profit. The money he made was put in trust for us until we were twenty-five, and it was a pretty big amount."

"Obviously not enough though," Lucy replied.

"Obviously, but I know what Luke is like, and if Mum bails him out then I'm damn sure he'll be back in the shit again before we know it." Ed sighed. "Mum, you have to make him take some responsibility. You and Dad have worked hard for your money, your retirement should be about doing what you want, when you want, not worrying about how you spend your money because you've given a huge chunk of your savings to Luke."

"Look I've said before, it's none of my business, but Ed's right, Georgina," Lucy said.

Georgina turned around and smiled at them both. "I know, and I also know if I give him some this time he'll keep asking. I just feel so bad that she's here trying to disrupt our lives, yours in particular, Ed."

"Well don't." Ed thought for a moment. "Listen Mum, go home and get packed to go to the cottage, and I'll sort somewhere out for her to go to. I'll come over later and tell her the good news." He hugged his mother once more.

"I hate putting this onto you, sweetheart," Georgina said.

"You're not, I want to sort it because I want her gone. Now, go home and do as you're told for once." Ed smiled at Georgina and kissed her cheek.

"Okay, I'm going. Oh one thing though you two," said Georgina pausing at the door.

"What?" Ed asked.

"Sorry I interrupted your afternoon sex session."

"Pardon." Lucy almost choked.

"Hey?" Ed cried.

"Well I assume that's why Lucy's knickers are hanging out of her handbag, anyway speak later, bye."

Later that evening Ed and Lucy were on their way to Georgina's to see Katie. Ed had a plan and hoped that Katie would go with it, but if she didn't at least he'd managed to get her a room in a Bed & Breakfast for a few days. That would at least give him some time to try and figure out how to get rid of her once and for all.

"I can't believe you've written her a cheque for ten thousand pounds," Lucy said as Ed pulled onto Georgina's drive.

"Unlike Luke I invested my money in property, and when I sold all three houses, about a year ago, I made a hefty profit, so I can afford it. Anyway, ten thousand is nothing compared to being free of her, so stop worrying." Ed leaned across and kissed Lucy's cheek. "Come on let's get this over with."

Georgina, having seen Ed's car arrive, was at the front door before they'd reached it.

"She's in her room and is refusing to come down." Georgina sighed. "You'll have to go up there I'm afraid. Anyway, what's your plan?" she asked, stepping aside to let them in.

"Well I've been thinking, she won't go without money, so *I'm* going to offer her some, and if that doesn't work I've got her a B&B that she can stay in while she's waiting for her money from Luke, although I'm doubtful that he'll ever send her any."

Georgina looked worried at Ed's response. "A few nights in a hotel is one thing Ed, but offering her a lump sum of money, well that's ridiculous. How much money anyway?"

"Enough to make her think twice about refusing it," Ed replied.

"No, Ed I won't allow it." Georgina shook her head and blocked Ed's way along the hall. "Luke asked me for a huge amount, I can't let you give her that much."

"Mum, I'm offering Katie enough to get her to leave town, how she and Luke sort out their money issues is their business. I'm not about to become the Bank of Ed just for their benefit."

"I'll ask you again, exactly how much money are you offering her Ed and don't you dare try to fob me off?"

Ed dropped his eyes to the floor, knowing that Georgina wouldn't be happy and would agree with Lucy

"Ten thousand," he said, wincing.

"No chance on this earth am I allowing that." Georgina strode down the hall toward Jack's study. "I'll give it to her, I'll just have to suffer the consequences of your dad's reaction," she cried yanking open a drawer and taking out a cheque book.

Ed took it and threw it back into the drawer, before closing it.

"Mum, listen to me, I am doing this, so no more arguments."

"What about you Lucy, what do you think?" Georgina asked.

"I agree with you both, I think it's too much, but Ed is right, I can't see anything less having the desired effect."

Georgina sat down at Jack's desk and was silent for a few minutes. "Okay," she muttered. "You win, offer her the money."

Ed bent and kissed his mother's cheek before turning to Lucy.

"Come on," he said. "I want you to come too, that way she can't pull me into the bedroom and molest me." A broad grin reached across his face.

"Not funny, Edward," Lucy replied following him toward the stairs.

Once upstairs Lucy followed Ed to Katie's bedroom and waited behind him as he knocked on the door.

Katie flung the door open. She was wearing an extremely short t-shirt and a tiny pair of pants. Lucy couldn't help find her eyes drawn to Katie's long, brown legs, and once again her chest. She obviously wasn't wearing a bra, but despite having given birth to three children, they were perfectly shaped and pert. They were so perfect, in fact, that Lucy had a sudden feeling of happiness at the realisation that they obviously weren't real, but blow ups as she and Sarah liked to call them.

Ed to his credit looked Katie in the eye. "I've got this for you." He handed over the cheque.

Katie took it and examined it for a few seconds. "What's this for?" she asked.

"It's money to help you go and find your brother, or whatever you want to do with it," replied Ed.

"Ten thousand pounds, you must really want to get rid of me." She leaned against the door frame and eyed Ed up and down. "Can you afford this?"

"Yes."

"You must think I'm pretty shallow, if you think that I'm only here for the money."

"Well aren't you?" Lucy demanded, moving next to Ed.

Katie shook her head. "No honey, I'm not." She slowly ripped the cheque up. "I'm not here for your money Ed, I can get money from Luke. I came back for you, and if you don't want me then I won't take your money. I'll wait until Luke sends me some, and then I'll go, I promise." Katie smiled at Ed as she dropped the fragments of the cheque into his hand.

"But Luke doesn't have any money, does he? He's asked Mum for a loan."

Katie frowned at Ed. "Sorry, I don't know anything about that, and I can promise you we don't need money from your mother. I'm just waiting for Luke to wire me some." She suddenly sounded agitated.

"Why don't you just take it from me, you can even pay me back if that's what you want." Ed was exasperated now.

Katie shook her head. "Nope, I'll wait for Luke."

Amazed that she'd turned the money down, Ed sighed. "Not good enough sorry, you need to take the money and go."

"I don't need to do anything," Katie drawled. "I've told you, I'll go when Luke sends me some money."

"And I've told you it's not good enough," Ed voice started to rise in his irritation. "You have to leave, so I've booked you into a Bed & Breakfast in town. I've paid for four days, so you've got that long to either get money from Luke, or I'll write you another cheque."

"What happens after four days?" Katie asked, a small smile on her lips. "Do I get thrown into jail?"

"If you haven't left after four days then you can pay the B & B bill, and the ten thousand is no longer an option." Ed folded his arms and stared Katie in the eyes.

After a few moments Katie shook her head and laughed. "Okay, I'll go to the hotel and hope that Luke sends me some cash. I'd better pack I guess, do you want to help me honey?" Katie smile at Lucy.

Lucy shook her head. "No, I'm sure you can manage."

"Be ready in fifteen minutes," said Ed. "I'll book a taxi for you."

"Okay but if *you* change *your* mind, you know where I am." Katie reached across and took Ed's hand to squeeze it.

Ed snatched his hand away. "Don't think this changes anything Katie, I still think you're up to something, so for the next four days, I don't want to see you, unless it's to collect your cheque."

Ed turned and taking Lucy by the hand went back downstairs.

"I can't believe she wouldn't take it," said Lucy when they were back in the hall.

Ed shook his head. "Me neither, I was convinced that she'd jump at the chance. Maybe she doesn't know about Luke's money problems, she'd have taken that money otherwise, especially if she knows that she's unlikely to get any from him. What do you think?"

Lucy shook her head. "I'm sorry Ed, I don't know what to think, I thought the same, that she'd snatch your hand off. But, don't forget she told me in no uncertain terms that she was here for you, so perhaps that's the sole purpose of her visit and the money isn't important."

"If it is then she'll be disappointed, because that isn't going to happen."

"You may believe that, but I'm not so sure Katie does."

After sending Katie to the Bed & Breakfast, and waving Georgina off to Wales, Ed and Lucy went back to his house and fell into bed, exhausted from the evening's events. Ed could sense that Lucy was feeling a little insecure about Katie, so had suggested that Lucy stay with him for a few days; at least until Katie had left for good.

Lucy spent most of the following day weeding the garden and mowing the lawn for Ed, keeping herself busy to avoid thinking about Katie and the current situation. The weather had improved, and the sun was burning brightly with a cool breeze, so once she'd finished working in the garden, she sat outside to read. As she tried to concentrate on her book, Lucy felt a presence beside her. She looked up to see Katie, who was staring down at Lucy over the top of a pair of huge sunglasses.

"What time will Ed be back?" Katie demanded.

"Around six, and what the hell are you doing here, have you come for the money?"

"No, like I said last night, I don't want his money. I want to go into Newcastle, I have an appointment with a lawyer there. My rental car is being picked up this morning, so I was hoping I could borrow his car. Is he not coming home for lunch?" Katie bit her nail distractedly.

"No, not today, but tell me why you're here. Ed told you to stay away unless you came to collect the cheque, and as you haven't then go away."

"Listen for just one minute please, honey. I need to get to Newcastle and I need a car to get there," Katie said the words slowly as if she was talking to child.

"I heard you, so get a train," Lucy said just as slowly. Lucy turned back to her book.

"You could take me, or lend me your car." Katie smiled at Lucy, ignoring the train suggestion.

"I'm not taking you," Lucy spluttered.

"Well, can I borrow your car then?"

"Are you crazy, why on earth would I lend you my car?" Lucy put her book down and glared at Katie.

"Because honey if I miss this appointment it'll take weeks to get another one. I was lucky to get it due to a cancellation. If I do miss it the chances of me leaving sooner, rather than later, will be pretty slim. He's going to get in touch with Luke about the money and our divorce."

The word divorce hit Lucy like a brick between the eyes. She hadn't thought that Katie was that serious about leaving Luke and her children behind.

"You're divorcing him?" Lucy asked. "You didn't say."

"He hit me, and would I really come here for Ed if I was going to stay married to Luke? Get a grip Lucy, if I want to move on, I have to cut Luke loose."

"Does moving on mean having Ed?" Lucy stood up and pushed the chair under the table.

"I told you last night, I'll go as soon as I get some money from Luke. I can see now that Ed will never be mine again, so chill sweet cheeks. Now, can I borrow your car or not?"

Lucy realised that at least she would be able to have lunch with Ed, without worrying whether or not they'd bump into Katie.

"I'll get you the keys, but you'll need to put petrol in it. Do you have any money?"

Katie nodded. "I'm not totally destitute."

"Fine, and be careful in it, because if there's any damage you'll have to pay."

"Whatever you say honey." Katie followed Lucy toward the house.

"And stop calling me honey." Lucy snapped, pleased to be rid of the dreadful woman for a few hours.

At lunch Lucy had thought that she would tell Ed about deciding to stay as she hadn't had the opportunity yesterday, but as soon as she saw him she could tell that he was worried about something.

"What's wrong?" Lucy asked.

Ed had kissed her cheek, taken hold of her hand and just carried on walking towards the pub, without saying anything.

"Sorry Luce, I'm just a little tired. We've had a busy morning, and I didn't sleep terribly well last night." Ed rubbed his eyes.

"You're not worried about Katie, are you?" Lucy could sense it was a little more than tiredness that was affecting Ed.

Ed shook his head. "No more than yesterday, although she's got a bloody cheek asking to borrow your car, especially as I asked her to stay away." He attempted a smile. "But, why am I surprised by anything that she does. Where's she gone by the way?" Ed asked as they crossed the road.

Lucy frowned. "I told you on the phone earlier, have you forgotten already?"

"Sorry, I've been so busy, I hate to say it but I probably wasn't listening properly."

Lucy felt somewhat annoyed, but Ed was right, he had such a responsible job and was extremely busy, but how could he forget something as important as Katie arranging a divorce.

"She's gone to Newcastle; she's managed to get an appointment to see a solicitor about getting a divorce."

Ed suddenly stopped in his tracks. "A divorce?"

"Yes Ed, a divorce. I was shocked too. I honestly thought that she'd go back to him after a few weeks of teaching him a lesson."

"Hmm." Ed carried on walking. "She really is serious then." His voice trailed off.

Lucy glanced at Ed and noticed that he was staring into the distance.

"Are you okay?" she asked, pulling at Ed's hand.

"What, erm, yes sorry. Yes, I'm fine. What do you fancy for lunch anyway?"

"Anything," said Lucy aware that Ed's mind was certainly not on food.

When Lucy arrived back at Ed's house, she was surprised to see her car parked on the drive. It was only three hours since Katie had gone off to Newcastle to see her solicitor, Lucy hadn't expected her back yet. She sighed, wondering whether the visit had been unsuccessful as it had been so short.

"Hello," Lucy said dully as walked into the garden.

Katie was sitting at the table leafing through a magazine. She looked up and gave a half smile to Lucy.

"Nice lunch?" Katie asked.

"Erm, yes thanks."

"That's good. I half expected to find you both here when I got back, Ed always did like a little afternoon sex session. "

Lucy tutted and gave Katie a cold stare.

"What we do is our business, not yours. Did you see your solicitor? I must say I didn't expect you back so soon," Lucy said moving past Katie.

"I see I'm not supposed to enquire after your business, but you can ask about mine. No fair Lucy honey." Katie smiled and wagged her finger at Lucy. "However, if you must know, I saw him, and he's going to start the ball rolling from this end. He thinks I could be divorced within a couple of months."

Lucy looked at Katie quizzically. She knew exactly how long it would take to be divorced, and she was pretty sure it wasn't a couple of months, especially with one of the parties being overseas. However, Lucy said nothing – she didn't want Katie to know that she was getting divorced, or more specifically how only four short months ago Lucy had still been living 'happily' with her husband.

"That sounds quite quick," Lucy commented.

"He's a good lawyer."

Lucy winced; Katie's Anglo-American drawl was starting to grate on her.

"Well, let's hope he gets you some money fairly quickly. So, do you have my keys, you could have just put them through the letterbox." Lucy held her hand out to Katie.

Katie threw the keys nonchalantly in Lucy's direction. "I wanted to be sure you got them back, and I've got nowhere else to go. The old witch at the hotel won't let me stay in my room." Katie flicked her hair back before continuing to leaf through the magazine.

"And that's our problem because?"

"Because you and Ed made me stay there, so just let me hang around here for a while, anyway I want to talk to Ed about something?"

Lucy wondered whether the thought of one more night in the Bed & Breakfast had been enough to break Katie, and she was going to ask Ed for the money. She looked up at the blue sky and sighed.

"Okay, but Ed won't be back for another couple of hours yet."

"That's fine by me, honey." Katie stood up and moved toward Lucy.

"Oh no, I'm going for a bath, you can stay out here; there's no rain forecast."

An hour later Lucy came back downstairs, surprised to hear voices coming from the kitchen. She couldn't be sure, but was convinced it was Ed and Katie. Entering the kitchen she almost froze as she saw them both drinking wine at the breakfast bar.

"Oh hi honey." Katie smiled over the top of her wine glass as she spotted Lucy in the doorway.

"Hi, I didn't know you were home, you're early." Lucy moved over to Ed and kissed him on the cheek.

"Hmm, my last patient didn't turn up. Do you want some?"

Lucy nodded as Ed went to the cupboard to get her a glass. She sat in Ed's seat and looked across at Katie, who winked and smiled.

"So, what were you talking about?" Lucy asked, a lump the size of an apple growing in her throat.

"Oh just old times," Katie answered.

Ed turned to Lucy and smiled as he placed a glass in front of her.

"Ignore her Luce, I found her in the garden when I got home. She wants to know if I can find her a different place to stay, apparently Mrs Trickett is 'an old witch and the bed smells of biscuits'. Anyway, did you have a nice bath?" Ed kissed Lucy on her lips and stroked her cheek. "You smell lovely," he said.

Lucy suddenly felt less anxious because of his touch and his kiss, although all hopes that Katie was here to take the money and run, were evidently futile. "Thanks, and have you found her somewhere else to stay?" Lucy asked before taking a sip from her wine.

"No, he's being mean and won't," Katie said leaning over to give Ed a nudge in his arm.

"Katie, just drink your wine and go." He turned to Lucy. "She helped herself when I had to take a call," he explained, shooting Katie a hard stare.

"I'll start dinner in a minute, I assume that you'll be leaving soon Katie."

"I could stay." Katie exclaimed with a huge grin on her face, and a wink at Lucy

Ed frowned at her. *"No, you can't."*

"Oh and we all seemed to be getting on so well," Katie purred. "Anyway, I'm not hungry, so no need to worry honey, oops sorry, I forgot that you don't like me calling you honey. Lucy it is from now on."

Ed sighed and shook his head. "I need some fresh air, I tell you what I'll go and get us a Chinese take-away and you'd better be gone by the time I get back," he nodded at Katie.

"I don't mind cooking." Lucy caught hold of Ed's hand and drew him to her. "Or we could just go for a walk if you need some fresh air."

"No, I don't want you to have to cook. I won't be long. What would you like?"

"Ooh I've changed my mind, please let me stay, I love Chinese food and I really don't have anywhere to else to go." Katie smiled at both Ed and Lucy. "I promise that I'll behave."

"Oh for God's sake just get her some food," Lucy cried, "She may actually go and leave us alone once she's eaten."

Ed shrugged. "Well it's up to you, but she can eat it in here, we'll go into the lounge."

"But…" Katie started to argue.

"Shut up Katie, that's my only offer, so take it or leave it."

Katie nodded and looked at Ed from under her eyelashes. "Thank you Ed."

"Just tell me what you want," Ed said thrusting a menu under her nose. "And hurry up."

Once Ed left to get the food, Lucy busied herself getting plates and knives and forks ready while Katie read the newspaper. There was no conversation between them, which in itself concerned Lucy. Katie usually took immense delight in annoying Lucy.

Lucy decided to watch the early evening news and was just going into the lounge when her mobile shrilled in her pocket. She didn't recognise the number but answered it anyway.

"Hello," she answered tentatively.

"Is that Lucy, Gerald's daughter?"

"Yes, is there something wrong with Dad?"

"No, sorry dear. I didn't mean to startle you. I'm Grace one of your dad and Richard's neighbours. It's just I've been out in my garden, and I could hear running water, so I looked over the wall and well, there's a lot of water running out from under the back door."

"Oh God, you're joking." Lucy started to look around the room for her car keys. "How much is a lot?" she asked, picking the keys up from the table.

"Well it's rather like a small stream. Your Dad gave me your number when he went away, just in case. I did knock on Hilary's door, because I know she and Frank have a key, but they've not been home all day."

"Okay, thanks Grace, I'll go over there as soon as I can. Bye."

"Oh dear, trouble?" Katie asked without looking up from the paper.

"There's water running from my dad's house. Tell Ed I'll be back as soon as I can." With that, Lucy ran out of the front door and got into her car.

As she turned the corner, she didn't spot Ed on the pavement returning with a bag of take-away food.

When Lucy got to the house, she parked the car and rushed in through the front door. There was no sign of anything in the hallway and she couldn't hear any running water. She went through to the kitchen at the back of the house, but there was still nothing. Then suddenly she heard the water coming from the utility room on the far side of the dining area. The problem was obvious when Lucy opened the door. There was water gushing from halfway down the water pipe that ran from the boiler. The washing machine and tumble dryer were saturated as the water cascaded off them, and various mops, brushes and buckets were floating on the pool of water that had formed. Luckily there was a step down into the utility room, which was why the kitchen and dining room hadn't been affected.

Lucy ran back into the kitchen and opened the cupboard under the sink, quickly finding the stop-cock and turning off the water. She ran back to the utility room and watched, as finally after a few seconds, the water slowed to a dribble.

After briefly surveying the damage, Lucy rang a plumber. He agreed to come around the following morning, telling Lucy that nothing else would happen now she'd turned the water off. He also suggested she turn the electric off before unplugging the washer and tumble dryer. Lucy had tutted at this, pointing out she wasn't stupid. The plumber realised that Lucy was obviously stressed and simply responded by saying he would see her at nine in the morning. Lucy then rolled up her jeans, took her shoes off and paddled into the utility room. She opened the back door and let out the rest of the water, before spending the next hour and a half trying to clean up the mess of soggy carpet and soaked walls. Finally, with some semblance of order restored, Lucy decided to go back to Ed's.

It was almost 8 p.m. by the time Lucy pulled onto the drive, heaving a sigh of relief. She was cold and extremely hungry. She opened the front door and walked down the hallway, the lounge was in darkness, so she went through to the kitchen, thinking that Ed had probably decided to eat with Katie, which troubled her. When she got into the kitchen it was empty, just the light above the cooker was on. She looked around to see two empty wine bottles and a white plastic bag that held a series of plastic take-away cartons. Lucy looked inside, and they were still full of food. Suddenly her heart began to beat faster, there'd only been one wine bottle when she'd left, and why hadn't they eaten the food, but more to the point where was Ed and where was Katie? Lucy moved back into the hallway and towards the stairs. As she placed her foot on the bottom stair, Lucy felt a fear like nothing she'd ever felt before. She knew that whatever was up the stairs would probably break her heart because deep down Lucy knew that Katie had won and that she would find her and Ed together up there. Quietly she crept up the stairs, wiping the uncontrollable tears that were now beginning to slide down her cheeks. At the top, she moved towards Ed's bedroom door, and with shaking hands she opened it and flicked on the light. There, in front of her, was Lucy's ultimate nightmare.

"Hi honey," Katie purred from beneath him.

"Ed, how could you?" Lucy whimpered

"Oh shit, Lucy."

Lucy turned and ran from the room, silent tears flowing unheeded down her cheeks.

Chapter 18

In a trance Lucy drove back to her father's house and packed into a suitcase the clothes that she hadn't taken to Ed's. She wrote a note for Hilary next door, asking her to let the plumber in, and then pushed it into an envelope, along with a blank cheque to pay him, before posting it through her letterbox. Lucy then drove off towards the motorway, and home.

About twenty miles from home, Lucy pulled off the motorway to a service station hotel. It was getting late, she was exhausted both physically and emotionally, plus there was no bed at home for her to sleep in.

Once she let herself into the room, Lucy allowed herself to cry. She curled up on the end of the bed and sobbed. There were no histrionics as there were the day Simon left, just quiet sobbing and an aching heart. Finally, when her head started to pound, Lucy wiped her nose on the shiny, golden throw on the end of the bed and stopped crying.

"No more tears," she said aloud to the empty room. "They are the last tears I will shed for Ed Bryce."

It was almost 1 a.m. and Lucy suddenly realised that her mobile hadn't rung once since she'd left Ed's house.

"You wanker," she cried at the silent mobile. "Huh, obviously you're too busy with Katie to check how I am."

Feeling that tears were about to start again, Lucy remembered her vow and took deep breaths, until finally the feeling subsided. Then she decided to try and get some sleep, hoping that Ed wouldn't appear in her dreams.

At 5 a.m. Lucy was woken by her mobile ringing next to her. She looked at the screen; it was Ed. Lucy felt panic stricken as the mobile rang, and rang. She threw it to the bottom of the bed as if it were a bomb about to explode. Eventually, it stopped, but as soon as Lucy leaned over to pick it up, the mobile started to ring again. This time Lucy turned it off.

"Piss off," she shouted at the phone in her hand. "I don't want to know what your pathetic little excuse is."

Seeing Ed's name flashing on the screen made her heart ache again, and quietly she sobbed, until finally she fell back to sleep for another couple of hours.

By 8 a.m. Lucy was ready to go home. She'd woken with a pounding headache and was now desperate to get out of the miserable room with its hideous blue and gold décor, and off white towels that were hard as cardboard. But before going to her car, Lucy went to the mobile phone store in the service station to get a new SIM. As well as sorting her out with a new SIM the man behind the counter had also deleted Lucy's voice messages for her. He asked if she wanted to listen to them first, but Lucy couldn't stand the thought of having to hear the excuses that Ed had concocted.

Once she was in her car, Lucy brought the mobile to life and went to her contacts. She scrolled through until she found Ed's details.

"Delete," she whispered.

Lucy then realised she had to tell Gerald what had happened, not a conversation she was looking forward to. He would be gentle, supportive and understanding, and Lucy knew he would make her cry. She looked at the clock on the dashboard. It was eight-thirty, so that would make it about 9.30 p.m. in Australia. Lucy cursed as it dawned on her that she now only had a 'pay as you go' SIM, and she wouldn't be able to call him. She would be home in less than an hour; she'd ring him then, which would at least mean she could cry without fear of crashing the car.

"Hi Dad," Lucy said as Gerald answered his phone an hour later.

"Lucy darling, how are you? How's Ed and everyone?"

Tears immediately sprang to Lucy's eyes at the sound of her Dad's voice, and the mention of Ed.

"Well that's what I'm calling you about. We've split up, and I've come back home." Despite the promise to herself, Lucy started to cry.

"*What*? Why, what's happened sweetheart?"

"It's a long story Dad," she whispered before recounting the tale of Katie, and the sordid discovery of her in Ed's bed.

Lucy had been right; Gerald made her cry, as did Richard, who also joined the conversation via speakerphone. Though both were outraged, they were also amazed that Ed would do such a thing. Particularly Gerald who had only agreed to go out to Australia because he was convinced that Ed would look after his daughter.

"I don't understand it Luce," Richard said. "From what your dad has told me, Ed was besotted with you."

"I thought so too, but he was even more besotted with Katie apparently." Lucy sniffed loudly. "Sorry, I promised myself I wasn't going to cry, but it hurts – a lot."

"Right, we're coming home." Gerald's voice cracked.

"No Dad, you're not and please don't get upset. I'll be fine. But, I need you to promise me something, do not, and I mean under no circumstances, contact Ed on my behalf. We are over. Promise me please, both of you."

For a moment the two men were silent.

"I promise," Gerald replied flatly.

"Richard?"

"Okay I promise, but seriously Luce, we'll get the first plane we can," Richard responded.

"*No*, I will be okay. I'm not going to take to my bed with a bobble hat on. Actually I couldn't if I wanted to, I don't even have a bed." Lucy laughed at the absurdity of the situation.

"What?" Richard and Gerald chorused.

"That's a whole other story that is too long and boring to tell you now, so anyway, enough of me, how's Australia?"

By ten-thirty that morning Lucy had bought herself some necessary furniture, enough at least to live in some level of comfort. She was now walking up Sarah's drive, dreading having to re-tell the whole sorry story once more.

"Shit," Sarah cried as she opened the door. "Oh sweetie I'm so so sorry. I honestly thought that he was one of the good ones." Sarah flung her arms around Lucy.

"Erm, how did you know?" Lucy asked, managing to struggle free of Sarah's hold.

"Gerald called me; he didn't think you'd want to have to go over it again. Come on, let's do the only thing we can in situations like this…let's get plastered."

"It's a bit early Sarah."

"Crap, it's after midday somewhere in the world, so it's not too early."

Sarah plonked Lucy down on the sofa and disappeared to get a bottle of wine and two glasses.

"Sarah, I've got to take collection of a bed this afternoon, I can't get drunk," Lucy said as Sarah came back into the room.

"Oh don't worry about that, I'll get Ben to run us around to your house when he pops home for lunch."

"Honestly Sarah, I don't want to get drunk. I don't want to end up crying again." Lucy's face crumpled. All the emotion that she'd been holding in for hours came tumbling out.

"Oh Luce, I don't know what to say." Sarah put her arm around Lucy's shaking shoulders. "Just let it all out, come on have a really good cry."

Finally, Lucy's tears subsided, and she fished a tissue from her jeans and blew her nose.

"Better?" Sarah asked, handing Lucy a glass of wine.

Lucy nodded. "A little thanks. I thought he loved me."

"I think he does sweetie, I just think she's a little unfinished business."

"She's a little bitch," Lucy replied. "It's what she's been after since she got there, and he promised me she wouldn't manage it."

"Well as we know what a man thinks and what his dick thinks are often two different things."

Lucy couldn't help but laugh. Sarah almost always had the ability to make her laugh. Lucy smiled and leaned across to kiss Sarah's cheek and hug her tightly.

"What's that for?" Sarah asked.

"For being you and for being the best friend anyone could ask for."

"That's what I signed up for all those years ago."

"I know, but it's beginning to become a little one sided, isn't it?"

"No, you were there when my mum died, and when Ben almost missed Noah's birth, oh and that time I almost got caught having sex with Danny Brown behind the curtain in the drama studio at college. If it hadn't been for you pretending to faint, his girlfriend would have been bound to find us."

"Well, you've been brilliant recently, so thank you."

"What now then? Are you going to go back there eventually, maybe when your dad gets back?"

Lucy shook her head. "Nope."

"But the other day you said you'd stay, even if it didn't work out between you and Ed, so what's changed?"

"Us not working out and him shagging his ex-wife in front of me is quite different."

"Hmm I suppose so."

"I'm still going to sell the house, but I'm going to get something smaller. I don't need a family house, a small cottage or apartment will suit me just fine." Lucy sighed and dropped her head into her hands. "God, Sarah I'd even started to think about having another baby one day, that's how safe he made me feel." Lucy kept her head down, willing away the tears that were threatening again.

"Oh sweetheart, that's awful, I feel terrible for you, and I'm gob-smacked Luce, I honestly didn't see this coming. He seemed like a genuinely lovely guy, who cared about you a great deal." Sarah shook her head in disbelief.

"I think he did care about me, loved me even, but you're right Katie was unfinished business. I doubt that they'll even stay together, but it's too late for him and me."

"Oh my God," Sarah gasped. "I've just had an awful thought."

"What?" Lucy asked startled by Sarah's gasp of horror.

"What if you never have sex that good again, because he was pretty fucking good wasn't he?"

"You only know that because I told you, I might have been lying." Lucy couldn't help smiling at the thought of sex with Ed, but then her heart seemed to knock on her chest as if to remind her of the situation, and a sadness enveloped her, turning her smile into a frown.

"Christ Lucy, you didn't have to tell me, I heard you don't forget, on the night of the party. I could even hear you orgasm over Ben's snoring, and that's bloody loud when he's had a drink."

"Well, at least I'll have the memories if the next one doesn't live up to standards. Actually, that's another annoying thing, the night I got home from here we had incredible sex on the dining room table, and then he takes Katie to bed the next day. Anyway, what am I saying there'll never be anyone else. From now on I'm going to live like a nun."

Sarah almost spat her wine across the room.

"With a dirty habit maybe," she cried. "Come on, pass me your glass, one more won't hurt you."

Chapter 19

Almost two weeks later Lucy had got some sort of order in the house, all the things she had bought had arrived, and most importantly for Lucy there was a 'For Sale' sign planted firmly at the end of the drive. She'd cried over Ed, and what might have been, but ultimately she realised that it all had probably gone too fast. She'd fallen in love with him too deeply and too quickly, and although Lucy didn't regret their time together, in hindsight she probably should have steered clear of another relationship so soon after Simon. Yes, Ed had helped her get over Simon, but she'd simply replaced one cheating bastard for another, although she conceded Ed wasn't in Simon's league. In some ways she could see how Katie could have beguiled him, she was his first true love, and while she wasn't white washing Ed, Katie had probably laid it on a plate for him. However, Lucy didn't wallow in self-pity, this time she felt stronger and more determined than ever to go on with her life. Ed was just another story to tell.

When speaking to Gerald, daily, he'd expressed feelings of guilt for suggesting Lucy should pursue a relationship with Ed, but as Lucy pointed out, she wouldn't have done if she hadn't truly wanted to, and in any case if Katie hadn't arrived things may well have been different.

There had been no contact at all from Ed, or anyone else in County Durham, because obviously no-one had her new number. Gerald had called Hilary, and explained that Lucy had an emergency back home to deal with, so asked if Hilary could take over looking after the house until he and Richard were back. Hilary had been willing to do so, and informed Gerald that the plumber had now fixed the burst pipe in the utility room.

Richard had called the surgery, on Lucy's behalf, a call that left Lucy feeling guilty. Seemingly Callie was off work, incapacitated by her back, and so Elspeth was helping Margery out with reception. Lucy felt terrible about leaving them in the lurch, without any explanation, but she couldn't talk to anyone about it, especially if they were likely to talk about Ed.

And so, it was almost as though Lucy's life up North had never existed. She'd even managed to get her job back at the charity shop, although Mrs Edwards had taken a little persuading. Finally, she'd agreed that Lucy could come back on a trial basis, and if after that time she'd shown she could be trusted, she may get her full hours back. Lucy couldn't help but smile, she'd missed Mrs Edwards and her superiority complex.

When Lucy got home after an afternoon in the shop, the red light was flashing on the answerphone. She pressed the button and listened to the message as she started to make a cup of tea. It was Richard.

"Hi Lucy, I didn't want to ring you on your mobile, while you were working, so when you get home can you give us a call, please. It's nothing to be alarmed about, but we need to speak to you. It doesn't matter what time, we'll be up early. Bye darling."

Lucy's heart started to beat faster as she dialled the number. What if something was wrong with her dad?

After a minute or so of the international dial tone, Richard answered the phone.

"Richard, what's wrong, is it Dad?" Lucy asked anxiously.

"No, darling, no it's not. I'm sorry I didn't want to upset you." Richard's tone was soothing, yet there was something in the sound of his voice that hinted something was wrong.

"Well, that's good, but something is bothering you, what is it?"

"Ellen called me last night, and don't be too worried, but Callie is ill."

Lucy sat down heavily on the sofa. "How ill?"

"She's got ovarian cancer and has had to have a hysterectomy."

Lucy didn't hear much more of the conversation, all she could think of was darling, vibrant Callie and the laughs that they'd had together. How could this be happening, no-one deserved this, least of all Callie?

"Lucy, are you going to go and see her then?" Richard asked.

"Sorry Richard, what did you say?"

"I asked whether you were going to see Callie. She's been trying to get hold of you, so asked Ellen to call me."

"I didn't let her know my new number. I was being so pathetic about Ed that I cut everyone out of my life that might speak to him." Tears now started to sting Lucy's eyes.

"It's okay, you know now," Richard soothed.

"Is she going to die, Richard?" Lucy's voice broke.

"I don't think so darling, from what Ellen said they don't think its spread. So I'm sure she'll be okay, but she had no idea, she just thought she had a bad back. She's been taking pain killers and stomach tablets for months without telling anyone. She'd not even been to see her own doctor, just a chiropractor, but obviously he wasn't helping. Apparently, it was Ed that suspected it, and got her a consultant's appointment fairly quickly." Richard sighed heavily.

Lucy gasped involuntarily at the mention of Ed's name.

"When was this Richard?" she asked.

"I'm not sure Luce, only a couple of weeks ago. Apparently, Callie has kept it secret, she didn't want anyone to know, but obviously now everyone does."

Lucy ran a hand through her hair. "I need to see her Richard, but I don't want to see Ed."

"Well it's up to you Lucy, but I know she'd love it you went up there."

"I don't understand why she'd want me though. We've only known each other a few months." Lucy stood up and started to pace the room. "Is she in a hospital, or at home?" she asked.

"In hospital, in Newcastle. I'll text you the details. So, will you go?"

"Yes, I should go if it's what Callie wants. I'll go tomorrow. Mrs Edwards won't be happy about me not going into the shop, but who cares."

"Okay sweetheart, and give her our love and tell her we're thinking of her and will see her soon."

As Lucy walked along the sterile hospital corridor the following day, her heart started to beat faster. She was worried about seeing Callie, worried about what to say to her, how to react if she looked ill. Lucy chastised herself; of course she was going to look terribly ill she had cancer for goodness sake.

Once Lucy got to the ward she asked one of the nurses about Callie, and was pointed toward a private room on the right. The door was closed, but Lucy could see through the window that Callie was sleeping. Lucy gasped, Callie was propped up on a pink pillow, with a frill around the edge, her usual pink bow in her hair, and wearing a pink candy striped nightshirt, looking as far as Callie did, pretty normal. As she opened the door, Lucy started crying tears of relief. She ran over to Callie and flung her arms around her.

"Howay pet, what on earths all this crying about?" Callie enveloped Lucy in her arms and hugged her tightly.

"Oh Callie, I'm so sorry. I should have been around for you." Lucy sobbed into Callie's shoulder.

"Well you're here now, pet."

"What do you want me to do, anything at all? I'm here for you." Lucy snatched a tissue from the top of Callie's bedside cabinet.

"I don't need anything Lucy pet, it's Ed that needs you."

Lucy stood up abruptly and placed her hands on her hips.

"But Richard said you've been asking for me," she cried.

"Well, it's the only way I could think to get you here. Once I couldn't reach you on your mobile I didn't know what else to do," said Callie smiling widely at Lucy.

"Are you actually ill?" Lucy demanded looking at Callie through narrowed eyes.

"Oh aye pet, I've had my hysterectomy about four days ago, and then I'll have to have some chemotherapy, but I'll be mint pet, don't you worry. So, less of me, what's gone on with you and Dr Bryce? He's had a face like a smacked arse since you went."

Lucy shook her head in disbelief, here was Callie about to face awful months of treatment for cancer, and all she cared about was sorting out her and Ed. She truly was a remarkable woman.

"You have no idea at all what happened?" Lucy said finally as she pulled a chair nearer to the bed.

Callie shook her head. "No, he's visited me a couple of times, but he won't say anything. You know what he's like, too bloody private for his own good that one."

Lucy thought carefully about what to say. Ed obviously didn't want anyone to know his business, or the fact that he was a cheat, and why should Lucy protect him, but something told Lucy that this was Ed's secret to tell, and she didn't want to be the one to spoil Callie's perception of him.

"Well, there's nothing for me to say, it just didn't work out." Lucy looked down at the floor to avoid Callie's gaze.

"Look at me pet, and then tell me that there's nothing to say." Callie moaned slightly as she shifted in the bed.

"Are you okay?" Lucy asked as she took hold of Callie's hand.

"Howay, I'm fine, now stop stalling me Miss, and tell me what's happened."

Lucy thought for a moment about what to say. She'd have to tell Callie something, but should she tell her the truth?

"I thought he loved me Callie, but I don't think he did. Well, not enough anyway."

"Rubbish, it was obvious he did in the way he looked at you. He's been miserable since you went home. Like I said, I canna get a peep out of him, he's lost weight, he looks tired, and he's awful quiet. That's not a man that didn't love you." Callie reached for Lucy's hand and gave it a gentle squeeze.

"I'm sure he's fine. How are the rest of his family, are they back from Wales yet?" Lucy knew if they were it meant Katie had gone.

"No, they're still there, as far as I know, but they tend to spend the whole summer there anyway. You're asking the wrong person though pet, Dr Bryce and Ellen are the only people I've had contact with for the last couple of weeks. I was pretty much knocked for six when I got my results, and sorry to say I went to ground until I came in here last week." Callie turned and looked away from Lucy.

"I believe it was Ed who spotted what was wrong?" said Lucy breaking the silence.

"Aye, it was just after his Dad's party, so he got a consultant friend of his to see me pretty much straight away. I think he knew though, he's an extremely intelligent man that doctor of yours." Callie's eyes shone with tears.

"He's not my doctor Callie," Lucy whispered.

"Oh Lucy pet, just go and see him for goodness sake. Talk to him, and try to sort things out."

"I can't Callie, you don't understand."

"Tell me," Callie cried. "How can I help if you don't tell me what the problem is?"

"He shagged his wife!" Lucy put a hand to her mouth; she hadn't meant to say it, plus saying it meant it actually happened.

Callie was open mouthed, staring at Lucy.

"His wife, since when has she been back?" Callie pulled herself up into a sitting position.

"Since Jack's party. That's why we had to get rid of everyone pretty quickly." Lucy dropped her head, ashamed at having let it slip.

"So where was she hiding out then? He didn't say anything, you didn't say anything."

"I shouldn't have said anything, I'm sorry Callie, please don't ask me anything else about it."

Callie rubbed Lucy's hand gently. "Lucy pet, I know people think I'm an old gossip, but I won't say anything to anyone. I like you and Dr Bryce, and think you should be together, so anything I can do to help I will. Now, bloody well tell me what happened."

Lucy sighed and shook her head. "Well it was all top secret because of Nate, he didn't want her to see him. She turned up at the party and then stayed with Georgina when Jack took Nate to Wales, and then Georgina had to go to Jack because he was ill." Lucy paused not wanting to continue.

"And?"

Lucy gulped back the tears that were threatening to fall.

"Well then she moved into a B & B," she said finally, "and I moved in with Ed for a few days, and then…"

"And then that's when the deadly deed happened." Callie replied.

Lucy nodded. "Hmm, yes. I caught them at it in Ed's bed. Look Callie, I don't want to talk about it anymore, it's too horrible to think about."

Callie sighed heavily. "Okay pet, but I tell you something I'm shocked. It's just not like him. Would you think about forgiving him?"

Lucy shook her head vigorously. "No. He knew how much Simon hurt me, and then did the same thing, so no I wouldn't."

"Well that's a shame pet, because I think you're made for each other. There may be an explanation you know."

"Oh yes I know what it is; she was his first true love, the mother of his son, oh that's okay then. Sorry Callie, but for me it's unforgivable."

"Eeh, I don't know Lucy, it's heart breaking." Callie shook her head and sighed. "Anyway pet, are you going to be staying at your dad's tonight?"

Grateful for the change of subject Lucy smiled.

"Yes, but I'll come and see you tomorrow before I go home."

"Okay pet that would be lovely. Now tell me everything that you've been doing since I last saw you."

Lucy spent an hour with Callie, and then could see that she was tiring, so decided to go home. As she made her way along the corridor, Lucy took a deep breath. It hadn't been as awful as she'd expected and they hadn't had to talk about Ed too much. A sense of relief washed over Lucy that Callie seemed okay, she was strong and was bound to beat the cancer, and Lucy was sure now after seeing her. Lucy got to the exit, and just as she was about to walk out, she noticed something in the corner of her eye. Someone was watching her. Lucy spun around and almost fell backwards.

"God Katie," she whispered to herself.

Lucy's hand went to her mouth and gazed at her smiling enemy. Katie looked more beautiful than ever. She had a hand pressed to her stomach and was smirking triumphantly. Lucy moved back against the wall, behind a row of wheelchairs, and watched Katie disappear through a set of double doors. As they swung shut Lucy looked up at the sign above them; her heart thudded in her chest as she read the word 'Maternity'.

Chapter 20

As Lucy let herself into the house, she sighed remembering the last time she'd been here – packing up her clothes because…she didn't want to think of why. It hurt too much. She went into the kitchen and spotted a note on the table. It was from Hilary, telling Lucy about the burst pipe. Attached to the note was the plumbers receipt for the replacement piece of pipe and his labour. Not bad for a couple of hours work, maybe she should retrain as a plumber, Lucy thought with a dry smile. Putting the piece of paper to one side, she then made her way to the utility room, and as she opened the door a pungent smell hit her almost immediately. It was caused by a pile of towels on the floor that had clearly laid there for the last two weeks, drying slowly and leaving a smell of wet dog.

"Bloody hell," Lucy cursed.

She remembered piling them in the wash basket on top of the work surface when she had cleaned up the water, so the plumber must have used them and not bothered to do anything with them. Lucy wished now she'd not left Hilary the blank cheque, otherwise she'd definitely be knocking this off the bill.

As Lucy scooped up the towels to throw them into the washing machine, she suddenly felt a sharp pain in the palm of her hand. Pulling her hand away, Lucy was shocked to see a deep cut across her palm, with dark red blood pouring from it.

"Shit!" She dropped the towels, and as she did so a fairly large, rusty nail bounced on the floor and rolled towards Lucy's foot. She tutted, wondering what it was doing wrapped in the towel.

Lucy quickly turned on the cold water tap, and stuck her hand underneath the flow of water. After a few minutes she pulled it away from the tap, but the blood continued to form on her palm. A further five minutes beneath the water made no difference as blood still pumped from the cut. Lucy looked around and saw a couple of clean tea towels; she grabbed them and wrapped them around her hand. She'd been working at the surgery long enough to realise that it may need a stitch, and as the nail was rusty she would also need a tetanus injection, as she couldn't remember the last time she'd had one. Going back into the kitchen Lucy picked up keys and made for the front door. On reaching it, she stopped dead.

"Shit, I can't go to the surgery," she cried running her uninjured hand through her hair.

She didn't know what to do, the surgery was five minutes away, and the nearest A & E was half an hour in the car, but at least Ed wouldn't be at A & E. After a couple of minutes thinking of her dilemma, Lucy noticed that her blood had penetrated both tea towels. She had her answer, the surgery it was.

Lucy pushed open the glass door and took a huge intake of breath, as she crossed the threshold. Margery, who had worked opposite shifts to Lucy, was tapping away at the computer behind the desk.

"Hi Margery," Lucy whispered.

Margery looked up and smiled. "Hello Lucy, gosh I didn't expect to see you here. Richard said you'd had an emergency at home, are you ready to come back?"

"No, I'm not. I came to visit Callie." Lucy held up her hand. "But, I've had an accident with a rusty nail."

Margery winced as she looked at the now sodden tea towels wrapped around Lucy's hand.

"Oh dear, that looks nasty. Take a seat and I'll go and see if Ellen can have a look at it for you, Dr Kindler is busy and Dr Bryce is off this week," said Margery rushing off to see Ellen.

Lucy felt her stomach lurch at the mention of Ed's name, but then heaved a sigh of relief that he wasn't there; but Lucy's heart was heavy with the realisation that he was probably at the hospital, holding Katie's hand.

Lucy hated the fact that the mere mention of Ed's name set her nerves jangling. Oh well, she'd learn to cope with it, she just wouldn't talk about him ever again. Then she gave a hollow laugh, knowing beyond doubt that Ellen was bound to want to talk about him, after all she'd been Callie's sidekick in getting Lucy back into town.

Margery came scurrying back, and nodded at Lucy. "Right go straight through Lucy, she's got a free half hour."

"Thanks Margery, I appreciate it."

When she reached Ellen's room, Lucy knocked before going in. A little nervous at what reaction she'd get, Lucy hesitated in the doorway.

"Oh Lucy sweetheart, it's so good to see you."

Lucy had no need to worry, Ellen rushed forward and grabbed Lucy to her chest.

"Owww," Lucy cried, pulling her injured hand free from in between her and Ellen.

"Sorry, sorry. Come on let me have a look at it then?" Ellen carefully unwrapped the tea towels from Lucy's hand. "Oooh nasty." Ellen winced. "But you're lucky; I don't think you'll need stitches."

Ellen worked in silence for the next few minutes, cleaning and dressing the wound. Finally, she sat back and eyed Lucy up and down.

"Okay madam, before I give you an injection in your arse, tell me what's happened. Why did you bugger off without a word to anyone, and why is Ed looking as though he's sucked a lemon and the pips are stuck in his teeth?"

Lucy dropped her head. "I think you should ask Ed."

"Have done, to be honest I forced him to tell me because I was tired of seeing his miserable jib every day. He told me that he had no idea why you went," said Ellen crossing her arms across her chest.

"Well he's a liar, he knows exactly what he's done." Lucy started to swing backwards and forwards on the stool that she was sitting on.

Ellen grabbed hold of Lucy's knees and stopped her from swinging.

"If it's about Katie, then he doesn't really have a choice."

Lucy now looked up, her mouth wide open as she stared at Ellen aghast.

"He's told you about Katie?"

"That he's given her a roof over her head, yes he has, although he swore me to secrecy. You have to see it from his point of view, she's the mother of his child," replied Ellen as she leaned forward to rub Lucy's arm gently.

"Ah I see," said Lucy nodding her head, irritation building up inside her. "It's a roof over her head he's giving her is it. Okay, so what about the bed, sorry let me re-phrase that, what about the place in his bed?" Lucy was sick of hearing about 'poor old Ed', and she used the back of her hand to rub furiously at the angry tears that had started to fall.

"Sorry," said Ellen, a look of surprise spreading across her face. "What do you mean?"

"They're having an affair Ellen." Lucy sniffed.

"But he's lost without you, it doesn't make sense." Ellen shook her head. "Are you sure?"

Lucy laughed emptily. "Yes, I'm sure." She knew she could say so much more, but simply didn't want to relive that moment again. "Listen, can we not talk about it anymore, please."

"If that's what you want, but honestly Lucy, he looks terrible. He's lost weight, he's quiet and moody. I just can't believe that he'd be like that if he didn't care."

"Please Ellen, no more!" Lucy put her hand up. "No more…just inject me and then forget I ever came here. I need to get on with my life, and he, sorry I mean they, need to get on with theirs."

Ellen sighed deeply. "Okay Lucy. Anyway, how've you been?"

While Ellen gave Lucy a tetanus injection, Lucy talked about her life over the last few weeks, and shared tales of some of the customers who came into the shop. Both women giggled and made general chit chat for about fifteen minutes before Lucy announced that she ought to go before Ellen's next patient arrived.

"You take care," Ellen said, pulling Lucy into another hug. "Think about what I've said, he really doesn't know what he did to make you leave."

"I will take care, but you think about what I said Ellen. He does know, but maybe doesn't want to admit to anyone what he did, maybe that's why he's sworn you to secrecy."

"Okay Lucy, I hear what you're saying, and I will ask him about it."

"Not on my account Ellen, please. Give my love to everyone, won't you?"

"I will, but have you been to see Callie yet?" Ellen asked.

"Yes, I'm going to call again before I go home. Thanks for this, by the way." Lucy held up her bandaged hand. "Take care Ellen."

"You too Lucy, you too."

When Lucy arrived back at the house, she was desperate for a cup of tea and something to eat. An early start and eventful day had left her feeling tired. She yawned and decided that dinner would soon be followed by bed.

Lucy turned the kettle on, and warmed some soup, all the while trying not to think about Ed and Katie and what she'd witnessed at the hospital. While waiting for the soup, Lucy glanced at the calendar, her Dad and Richard would be home soon, it was already the first week of August. Then something about the date struck a chord with Lucy, turning off the hotplate she ran into the hall and picked up her bag. She scrabbled about inside it until finally she found what she was looking for; her diary. Flicking through the pages, her heart started to thud rapidly, beads of sweat formed on her brow, and her stomach kept somersaulting as though it were an Olympic gymnast.

"Oh God, please no," she whispered. "No, no, no, no, no." Frantically she flicked back through the pages again, and again.

"Don't do this to me, please, please don't do this."

Lucy placed a flattened palm against her chest, afraid that her heart was about to burst through it, it was beating so fast. She paced the room a couple of times, and then went back to the calendar and studied it again.

"This can't be right. You can't have let this happen." She picked up her diary. "You. Stupid. Stupid. Woman." Lucy emphasised each word by hitting her head with it.

Then as the enormity of the situation hit her, Lucy's legs began to shake, her palms became clammy, and a chilling sweat enveloped her body. She had to be wrong, it was a mistake surely – but deep down she knew it wasn't.

"Shit, this can't be happening to me." The words were barely audible as Lucy slid to the floor and cried.

Chapter 21

"How can you be pregnant?" Sarah took Lucy by both shoulders and stooped to look up at her face that was staring down at the floor.

As soon as dawn had broken that morning, Lucy had fled back home to Cheshire, forgetting all about her promise to visit Callie again. She needed to see Sarah, for yet more support, and hopefully to find out that she was wrong.

Lucy pulled away from her. "How, well what happens is you have a man and a woman …how the hell do you think it happened?" Lucy tutted as she pushed the heel of her hand against her forehead.

"I *mean* how have you allowed it to happen? You're normally so careful, Mrs Sarky Knickers."

"I don't know, Sarah, I've taken my pill religiously." Lucy pulled herself away and flopped down onto the sofa.

"Are you sure, you didn't forget at all, did you?"

Lucy shook her head and reached inside her bag for her makeup bag.

"No, I wouldn't forget. Here, look, I kept it for some unknown reason," she cried thrusting an empty blister pack at Sarah.

"Hmm," Sarah muttered looking at the pill packet. "So, you take it for twenty-one days and start again seven days later, so when should you have started taking it again?"

"Today." Lucy frowned at Sarah, she knew all this so why was Sarah going over it again?

Sarah's looked perplexed as she contemplated Lucy's problem. "However, yesterday you realised that you'd not had a period in the gap, is that correct?"

Lucy looked at Sarah quizzically. "Yes Miss Marple, but I can tell you "Whodunnit", Dr Bryce did it, in the dining room with his penis!"

Sarah frowned and shook her head. "I am *trying* to make a point here if you don't mind!"

"Okay, make it then," Lucy shouted sulkily.

Sarah continued, ignoring Lucy's tone. "So if you're sure you haven't missed any, there must be another explanation?"

Lucy screwed her face up and shook her head. "So, that's your point, there must be another explanation. Well done Sarah."

"Well I'm not a doctor am I?" Sarah started to giggle. "Hey why don't you ring Ed and ask him?"

Lucy gave Sarah a withering look. "I'll ignore that comment."

"Sorry," Sarah replied solemnly. "Seriously though you need to think really hard about this."

"What difference does it make how it happened, it's happened. I'm up the duff without a paddle!"

"Very true, hey you could sue the pharmaceutical company who made the pill. Perhaps it's a dodgy batch…Lucy, are you listening to me?"

"Oh shit." Lucy was reading a piece of paper that she taken out of the contraceptive packet.

"What?" Sarah peered at the paper.

"Read that bit about being sick. Christ, I'm such an idiot."

Sarah read the part that Lucy pointed at. "Well, were you sick?" she asked.

Lucy nodded. "The day after the party, when you told me not to have more wine. I spoke to Ed after you left, and it didn't go well, so I drank another bottle of wine and ended up being ill as I hadn't eaten anything."

Sarah put an arm around Lucy. "How sick were you?"

"I think I threw up at least twice. Bloody hell, how pathetic am I, getting drunk like that just because my boyfriend didn't ring me?"

Sarah pursed her lips and nodded. "Hmm quite pathetic."

"But I was upset and hadn't eaten anything." Lucy cried, pleading her case. Suddenly she put a hand to her mouth and groaned. "Oh shit, I didn't take my pill the next night either, I took two on the Tuesday evening."

"You plonker, this paper says you're supposed to take them within twelve hours?" replied Sarah, poking Lucy in the arm.

Lucy nodded as she bit her bottom lip. "I know that now."

Sarah sighed and hugged Lucy. "Sorry Luce, but it looks as if you've cocked up, so to speak."

"This is a nightmare," Lucy cried burying her head in her hands. "Let me look at the stick again. It definitely shows a positive result doesn't it?"

Sarah reached behind her for the test and poked it in front of Lucy's face.

"Oh yes, it's very positive. The darkest blue plus sign I've ever seen on a pee stick!"

"Not funny Sarah, *again*." Lucy snatched the test from Sarah and re-examined it, turning it over and over in her fingers as she looked at every detail of the stick.

"It is a real one, just like the rest of them." Sarah pointed to another eight tests that had been discarded on the armchair opposite them. "Look shit happens and, unfortunately, it's happened to you."

"Where's the one that tells you how pregnant I am?" Lucy stood up and started to look through the pregnancy tests that she'd purchased from two different chemists. "Here it is, huh I told you, two weeks. I bet you it was the day I got back from here and he had me on the sodding dining table." She threw the test back with the others, and then sat down again.

"I've always liked the name Country Oak for a baby…no not funny, okay." Despite the sombre mood, Sarah had to smile.

"What am I going to do, Sarah?" Lucy asked tearfully. "How could I be that stupid? The whole point of me taking the pill was so that I had control of the situation."

"I don't know sweetheart, but you were a tiny bit stupid." Sarah held her hand. "Anyway, let's forget about how it happened, it's happened," Sarah replied. "You now need to decide what you're going to do."

"I can't Sarah, I just can't think about it yet. Please don't make me." Lucy let her head fall back and she stared up at the ceiling. "One thing I do know, believe it or not I'm not going to get rid of it."

Sarah asked, "Even though you've been adamant about not wanting anymore children?"

"Yes. Despite everything I've said, and that I'm petrified, I couldn't get rid of it. Sorry, but you're going to have to put up with me being a quivering wreck for the next couple of years," Lucy said smiling weakly.

"That's not a problem, I'll always be here for you, but what about Ed?"

Lucy turned sharply to look at Sarah.

"What about Ed?"

"You need to find out if he's going to be there for you too."

Lucy shook her head and stood up.

"No. I won't be asking for any help from him whatsoever." Lucy started to pick up the used pregnancy tests and throw them into the carrier bag that she'd brought them in.

Sarah put a hand out to stop Lucy.

"Lucy you have to tell him. If not now, at some point."

"Please don't tell me that he has a right to know," Lucy said snatching her hand away and continuing to move the sticks.

"That's not what I meant," Sarah cried. "I was thinking about the help that he should give to you, if not practically then financially."

"I don't need his help. Anyway, he has his own family to care for."

"I know that, but Nate might like to have a brother or sister." Sarah winced expecting Lucy to throw the tests at her.

"Nate will have a brother or sister. Katie's pregnant too."

Sarah gasped and flopped back onto the sofa.

"You're joking," she cried

"No unfortunately I'm not," said Lucy. "He's been very busy has Dr Bryce."

"Are you sure, how do you know?"

"I don't know for definite, but I'm pretty sure." Lucy told Sarah all about seeing Katie at the hospital.

"Hmm, she may not be. You just said you thought she'd seen you, so maybe she just did the old stomach patting thing, and going into maternity to make you *think* she was pregnant." Sarah thought that Lucy was possibly right about Katie, but if Katie was as sly as Lucy said, then it may well be a pretence.

"Maybe, but it doesn't matter anyway. Who cares whether she's having his baby or not."

"Okay, well if you're adamant that you don't want him to know, you're going to have to think very carefully how you do that. He lives in the same town as your father."

Lucy gasped. "Oh shit, I never thought of that, what a bloody mess." Lucy hung her head. "I don't want to think about it anymore today. I need to ring the hospital and leave a message for Callie, she was expecting to see me today." Lucy pulled her mobile out of her bag, and started to look for the number that she'd saved. "She's another one that I'll have to keep it from because there's no way Callie will be able to keep it quiet."

"We'll talk about it tomorrow, because to be honest Luce, I can't see how you can keep this from him for long." Sarah gave Lucy's head a consoling pat as she left to make them both a strong cup of tea.

Chapter 22

By the time Gerald and Richard were due to arrive back from Australia, Lucy's morning sickness had started. She was now almost five weeks pregnant, and even though her doctor had said she was perfectly healthy, and her pregnancy appeared to be progressing well, Lucy panicked about every little twinge and stomach grumble.

They were landing at Manchester Airport, so were going to spend the night with Lucy, and she would drive them back home the next day, but the more she thought about it, the more anxious she became about returning to Ed's home town. At least she was no way near showing, so maybe this was the perfect time to return. If she did happen to bump into Ed, he wouldn't suspect anything.

Once Lucy had visited the doctor and had her pregnancy officially confirmed, it was then that she started to think of Lottie continuously. She kept recalling how she'd felt at this point in her last pregnancy, and constantly comparing it, just in case there were similarities that may indicate that this child may tragically be taken away from her too. While she was shopping, Lucy couldn't help but look at baby clothes, picking them up and holding them against her cheek, wondering what Lottie may have looked like wearing it. All the time Lucy was a conflict of emotions. The idea of another baby, although scary, had grown on her, and she knew that she already loved it unconditionally, yet she felt guilty for feeling that way. Silently she would apologise to Lottie and promise that she'd not forgotten her. Sarah had certainly earned her 'Best Friend Stripes' the last couple of weeks, trying to keep Lucy thinking straight and generally looking after herself.

As Lucy waited in anticipation for the first glimpse of her Dad and Richard, she wondered whether they would spot her secret straight away, or whether she'd be able to manage to hold on to it until they were safely ensconced in her lounge. She smiled and placed a hand on her extremely small bump. Yes, she was scared of what may happen, Ed finding out scared her, and how she would cope as a single mother scared her, but she was also thrilled. As the days passed Lucy's previous mantra of 'no more children', seemed stupid, and she was extremely regretful of the time she'd wasted on all that angst and pain about creating a new life, but at no point though did she regret not having another child with Simon; that ship had well and truly set sail.

Suddenly appearing round the corner Gerald started to speed up as he spotted Lucy.

"Sweetheart," he said engulfing her into a bear hug. "Oh I'm so glad to see you. Are you okay?" Gerald stood back and examined his daughter's face. "You look so pretty, doesn't she Richard?"

"Hello my darling." Richard had now joined them and kissed Lucy as he leaned across the barrier. "Your Dad's right, you do look pretty, I think we expected you to be red-eyed and miserable."

Lucy laughed and kissed Richard's cheek. "I'm fine. I'm done with being miserable over men. Come on let's get you both home so you can fill me in on everything that you've done. You two look pretty good yourselves. Oooh I've missed you both so much."

Once back at Lucy's house, after a takeaway meal, Richard and Gerald were enjoying telling Lucy all about their trip. They'd both had a wonderful time, and looked tanned and healthy; even Gerald's leg had improved with lots of swimming in the family pool.

"It sounds like you've had a brilliant time," Lucy said passing Richard his digital camera back. "And your photos are amazing. I love that one of the bridge and the people walking up the top of it."

"I know, I thought they were absolutely barking mad, but people were queuing up for miles to do it." Richard re-filled his wine glass and beamed at Lucy. "Oh much as I've loved being with Wendy and the family, it's good to be back home and see you."

"Ah bless you Richard, but I've been okay, I promise."

"We would have come home Lucy, if you'd wanted us to. You sounded okay on the phone, but I've been so worried about you, we both have."

Lucy leaned forward and squeezed her Dad's hand. "Dad I do appreciate the thought, but I would have been cross is you'd have come home. Honestly, I've been fine. I won't lie it's not been easy, but let's face it we'd only been together a couple of months, no time at all compared to a five year marriage."

"But you still cared a lot about him, because it was a short length of time doesn't mean your feelings aren't as strong," Gerald replied.

"Have you spoken to Ed at all?" Richard asked, concern clouding his face.

Lucy shook her head. "Nope, and I don't want to. I saw them in bed together and he swore at me for finding them, so what is there to say? What on earth could he say to me that would change all that?"

Gerald shook his head. "Nothing I suppose, but I'm absolutely shocked that he would do that. I truly, truly thought that you two were a perfect match. He cared for you so much, it was obvious."

"We'd both said the 'L' word." Lucy gave an empty laugh. "I should have kept my mouth shut."

"Well if I know Ed he wouldn't have said it if he didn't mean it," Richard said shaking his head. "I honestly don't know what to say to him next week when I go back to work."

"Nothing Richard, it's not your problem and this isn't going to spoil your relationship with him. You have to work for him, and to be honest I think he did love me, but just didn't bank on Katie's determination to get him back."

"I agree with Lucy, Richard. You have to work for Ed, and I also agree that he did love her, so if Lucy wants us to leave it we will. Although, I may have to move to Dr Kindler, I'm not so sure I can be that magnanimous."

"If that's what you want Dad, then that's up to you."

"I think I will have to Lucy, plus I guess I owe you a pair of diamond earrings," Gerald said, remembering his bet with Lucy.

Lucy smiled and shook her head. "I won't hold you to that, don't worry."

"No a bets a bet, I promised you diamond earrings if things didn't work out."

"Seriously Dad, I don't want any, they'd just remind me of what happened all the time."

"I understand sweetheart, but if you change your mind then tell me."

Lucy blew out a deep breath. "Okay I will, but I do have something to tell you now that could make life a little difficult for you."

Richard and Gerald looked at each other quizzically, and then back at Lucy.

"What is it sweetheart?" Gerald asked.

"Okay, despite everything I've ever said, and what I've ever done to avoid this happening, well I may as well just say it. I'm pregnant."

Gerald gasped.

Richard knocked back the rest of his wine, and then reached across for Lucy's which he suddenly realised she hadn't touched.

There was silence for a moment as both men tried to take in the news Lucy had just given to them. Lucy watched them both intently, smiling at the look of astonishment on both their faces.

"Are you two okay?" Lucy asked. "Strong, sweet tea anyone?"

Both shook their heads, with their mouths open wide.

Finally Gerald spoke. "Stupid question, but how?"

"Too much lonely drinking on the night Katie arrived. I ended up being sick and then didn't take my next pill within the recommended time."

"But you've always been extremely careful Lucy, surely something like this has happened before, when you were with Simon, being ill or forgetting your pill I mean?" Gerald shook his head, still unable to believe that six short weeks ago he'd left his daughter in love with her new partner, and adamant that she didn't want any more children – now here she was alone and pregnant.

"I was sick once before, but I guess Simon and I were just lucky. The thought honestly never entered my head Dad. I expect if Ed had known I'd been sick he would have used something, but I didn't tell him. I was too embarrassed about drowning my sorrows and puking like a teenager."

"Am I right in thinking that Ed doesn't know about the baby?" Richard asked.

"Yes you're right Richard…Dad please don't look at me like that." Lucy had glanced at Gerald and seen the look of horror pass over his face.

"Lucy, I will support you in any way possible, but not telling him about his child, well I'm sorry I don't agree. I was forced to move away from you and Sophie, and it broke my heart, it devastated me and you two were grown women."

Lucy had thought about this a lot over the last few days, and her resolve had softened slightly.

"I'm not saying never Dad, just not yet. I can't cope with having to deal with him and Katie just yet. There's something else you need to know."

"Wait, let me get some more wine," Gerald said. "I'm not sure I can take another surprise without alcohol!"

"Okay, are you sitting comfortably?" Lucy asked before preceding to tell them about Katie's pregnancy.

As the weeks passed, Lucy bloomed, growing happier with each day. She had managed to get a part-time job working at an after school play-scheme, and she was enjoying every minute of it. The pay wasn't great, but it was enough with her savings and Simon's continued contribution to the mortgage to get by. At almost eight weeks pregnant she still wasn't showing too much, for which Lucy was grateful. If she were to come through the divorce without any problems, Simon couldn't find out about her upcoming event.

Ed still wasn't aware that he was to have another child, however, Lucy agreed with Gerald that she would tell him and decided that it should be that weekend. Richard had offered to arrange a meeting between them, but Lucy asked him to wait for a couple of days, until she arrived at their house, just in case she chickened out. She hardly spoke about Ed to Richard or Gerald. Richard did tell her he hadn't seen any evidence of Katie, but that Ed was unusually quiet, barely speaking to anyone at the surgery and that he wasn't able to look Richard in the eye. All signs of his guilt, Lucy commented.

Pulling up onto her father's driveway Lucy sighed heavily. It reminded her of doing the same thing just four months ago, then she'd been distraught at the end of her marriage, this time she was here to tell another man that she was going to have his baby.

Gerald opened the door and gathered Lucy into his arms, hugging her tightly.

"Hello sweetheart. How are you feeling? Was the journey okay?"

Lucy nodded and kissed Gerald's cheek.

"I'm fine thanks Dad, a little tired from driving, but otherwise I actually feel really well…apart from morning sickness that is, although even that is easing."

"That's great, come on in, let's get you a cup of tea."

As Lucy entered the house, she sniffed the air and laughed.

"Dad, you disappoint me, no mulled wine on the go." Lucy nudged Gerald and winked.

"We didn't think it was right in your condition. I've made some lemonade instead." Gerald dropped Lucy's bag that he'd taken from her.

Richard appeared from the lounge and moved forward to greet Lucy.

"You look beautiful," he said gazing at Lucy. "Pregnancy suits you evidently."

"Thanks Richard, although I'm not so sure you'd say that if you saw me in the morning when I have my head down the toilet." Lucy laughed and hugged him.

"I thought you said it was getting easier," Gerald exclaimed turning Lucy towards him.

"It is Dad, it's just morning now instead of all day." Lucy's face broke into a huge smile. "Honestly, I feel really healthy, so stop worrying."

"Come on let's sit down," Richard said ushering them all into the lounge.

Once they'd all sat down Lucy suddenly realised that Gerald and Richard appeared anxious about something.

"Okay you two, what's wrong?" Lucy made herself comfy on the chair.

Gerald looked at Richard who nodded.

"Well," Richard began. "I rang Ed…"

"I asked you not to until I got here." Lucy knew that she needed to talk to Ed, but she wanted to do it when she was ready, plus she'd specifically asked her 'fathers' not to do anything until she said so.

"I know you did, but Ellen mentioned that Ed was thinking of going to Wales this weekend, to help his parents pack up before coming home, and well I didn't want you to have a wasted journey." Richard explained.

Lucy conceded that he'd probably done what he thought was best.

"Okay, I understand," she replied still a little annoyed nonetheless. "So, what did he say?"

Richard's eyes darted to the floor. "I only spoke to Katie," he said finally looking at Lucy.

"And?"

"She told me that he'd gone to Wales to bring Nate home and to tell his parents that they were going to be giving it another go and, as you said, she's pregnant with his child." Richard moved across and held Lucy's hand.

Lucy's eyes filled with tears. She realised that Ed's betrayal still hurt, her heart still ached for him, and all these weeks she'd been fooling herself that he meant nothing to her. Suddenly she felt sick, she rushed from the room as bile rose in her throat.

"Are you okay darling?" Gerald asked when Lucy reappeared, ten minutes later.

Lucy nodded, one hand to her mouth, the other resting on her stomach.

"Hmm, it was just a shock to hear it straight from the bitch's mouth."

Gerald brushed Lucy's hair from her face.

"I know Luce, it must have been difficult to hear, even if you already thought that's what was happening. You know, maybe he's only giving it a go because she's pregnant."

Richard added. "Your dad's right Lucy, he does look miserable. He isn't acting as though he's just got back with the love of his life, and is about to have another child with her. You'd expect at least a little smile on his face, but there's nothing but a scowl these days."

"Perhaps he is miserable, maybe he is only going along with it for the child's sake, but the main thing is he's with her, so that's it. I assume then that he's not coming to see me while I'm here?" Lucy asked.

"It was his mobile that Katie answered, so I doubt she'd even tell him I called. I have sent a text as well." Richard shook his head and sighed. "I should have ignored you and asked him at the surgery yesterday, I could have spoken to him in person then."

Lucy smiled weakly, almost wishing now that Richard *had* ignored her, despite being cross with him earlier.

"Don't worry about it Richard. I do need to tell him, but it just isn't going to be this weekend. What did you say in the text?"

"Erm, let me check." Richard pushed some buttons on his mobile. "Ah, here it is." He passed the mobile to Lucy.

"Have left you a message with Katie. Lucy is here this weekend and needs to see you. Please try to come over if you can. Richard." Lucy read aloud. "When did you send it?"

"About ten minutes ago, when you went to be sick," Richard replied. "I'm hoping that he's left for Wales and Katie isn't with him, or has hold of his mobile."

"It's a bloody mess, isn't it?" Gerald sighed. "I should never have gone over to Australia, in fact, I should never have asked you to come here in the first place."

"Don't be silly Dad. I don't regret being with Ed, I just regret how it ended, and that's certainly not your fault. Anyway, I'm absolutely shattered, so I'm going to bed if you don't mind." Lucy rubbed her tired eyes and yawned. "See you both in the morning."

"Night darling," Gerald said and kissed her cheek. "I hope you manage to get some sleep."

"Hmm, me too," Lucy replied. "Me too."

Lucy fell into a deep sleep fairly quickly, even with the sadness that lay heavy in her chest. She had been sleeping soundly for almost two hours, when she was woken by someone shaking her shoulder vigorously. Disorientated Lucy initially didn't realise where she was, and was shocked to see Gerald peering down at her.

"Dad? What is it?" Lucy asked as she pulled herself into a sitting position. "What time is it?"

Gerald looked at her gravely and sat on the edge of the bed.

"Lucy," he whispered. "I'm sorry darling, but there's been an accident."

"What sort of accident, who Dad?" Lucy started to pull her feet out of bed.

"It's Ed sweetheart. Georgina called, he's been in a car accident and it was pretty bad."

On hearing this, Lucy's vision blurred, a cold sweat pricked her, and the room started to move. As darkness enveloped her, Lucy fell into a faint.

Chapter 23

The following lunchtime, Lucy was contemplating whether to visit Ed or not.

After she'd come round, a couple of minutes after fainting, her first thought was to go to him, sod what he'd done. However, Gerald had pointed out that, by the time they'd made the three hour journey to the hospital in Chester, it would be nearly 2 a.m. Also, it would be highly unlikely that they'd be allowed to see Ed anyway. So Lucy had been persuaded to wait until the morning. Through the night though, Lucy changed her mind, and although she wanted Ed to be okay, and was dreadfully upset that he'd been hurt, he wasn't hers to worry about anymore – plus Katie would be at his bedside and she certainly couldn't face her. Gerald and Richard disagreed.

"Lucy sweetheart, Georgina wouldn't have contacted you if she didn't think you should be there. She was quite insistent that we get you over there as soon as possible," Gerald soothed.

"He's right Lucy, she was extremely upset but pretty adamant that you be there."

"I can't Richard, what if Katie is there? Actually there are no 'what ifs' about it, she'll definitely be there. No, I'm sorry, I feel for Georgina and am really worried about Ed, but I'm not going." Lucy wiped the tears from her cheeks with the sleeve of her jumper.

She knew that if anything happened to Ed she'd be heartbroken, because no matter what he'd done she had loved him, still loved him, but he'd cheated on her, and she couldn't forgive him.

Gerald took Lucy's hand and stroked it gently.

"I understand all that Lucy, but what if something happened to him, how would you feel?"

Lucy took a shuddering breath and burst into tears. "I couldn't stand it," she gasped in between sobs. "I love him dad, but I can't forgive him."

"Okay, okay, ssh, come on calm down, it's not good for the baby. I think you should go and have a lie down, and try and get some sleep." Gerald hugged Lucy tightly.

"Yes why don't you go upstairs and get some sleep," Richard added. "I'm pretty sure you didn't get any after we told you last night."

"No, I've only been up a couple of hours," Lucy replied.

"Well why don't you just lie down on the sofa and close your eyes for a little while?" Gerald suggested.

Lucy nodded and sniffed loudly. "Okay, just for a little while."

She pulled her feet up on the sofa and made herself comfy, as Richard tucked a woollen throw around her.

Once she'd fallen asleep Gerald dropped his head into his hands. "I should have gone with my instinct last night, and not told her until today. I could hear her moving about all night; she needs to be getting as much rest as possible," he said glancing across at his sleeping daughter.

Richard nodded and sighed. "I know, but Georgina was pretty insistent. Did you manage to get any more information when I went out earlier?"

"No," said Gerald shaking his head. "They wouldn't tell me over the phone as I'm not a relative, and Georgina was sleeping in the day room, so I asked them not to wake her. Hopefully she'll call me back later."

"Poor Georgina, she's all alone at the hospital, unless Katie is there of course, but I don't really see that being a comfort to Georgina, from what Lucy told me she can't stand Katie." Richard said giving an empty laugh.

"It's a pity Jack isn't with her, but he stayed with Nate. Oh and poor Nate, I wonder if he knows what's going on."

Richard shook his head. "I doubt it, they've spent all his life trying to protect him, so unless the worse happens, God forbid, I doubt they'll tell him anything just yet."

Gerald got up from the sofa and paced the rug. "I really think Lucy should go, don't you?" he asked, stopping in front of Richard.

"Yes, but it has to be her decision Gerald, just don't push her." Richard reached out for Gerald's hand. "She's a sensible girl, and after some sleep I'm sure she'll see it's the right thing to do."

"I suppose, I just hope that she isn't too late."

Richard was right, as soon as Lucy woke up later that afternoon she knew immediately that she wanted, needed, to go and see Ed. She loved him despite everything and, even if it meant coming face to face with Katie, Lucy wanted to see him and make sure he was going to be okay.

Gerald was pleased that Lucy had made the decision, and when Georgina rang later to tell them that there was no change in Ed's condition, he let her know that they'd be arriving early the next day.

"So, what did she say Dad? Is Katie there?" Lucy asked tentatively, staring at her father with tired eyes.

"She just told me that there's no change really. Ed is still heavily sedated until they know if there is any brain injury, but the operation on his leg went well and they managed to repair both breaks; although apparently there are a few nuts and bolts in there that will be setting airport scanners off next time he goes abroad." Gerald smiled at Lucy, trying not to show in his own voice the fear he'd heard in Georgina's.

"And Katie?"

"I didn't ask sweetheart, and she didn't say. We weren't on for long. I told her we'd be there for about nine in the morning. Are you okay leaving here at six, you can sleep in the car on the way down?"

Lucy nodded as she chewed at her thumbnail.

"I'll be fine, as long as I can avoid Katie."

Richard pulled Lucy into a hug and sighed. "We'll do our best darling, we'll do our best."

As Lucy, Gerald and Richard rushed down the hospital corridor, all thoughts of Katie had disappeared. Lucy didn't care who was there, she needed to see Ed and make sure that he was okay. She'd gone over and over it in her head during the three hour drive, and she knew that she would have to tell him about his child, or at least tell Georgina should anything happen to Ed. But, she couldn't contemplate that at the moment, for now she just needed to concentrate on holding it together.

"Here, this is it," Richard cried as he opened a door that led them into another smaller corridor.

Racing down it Lucy could make out a small figure pacing up and down; it was Georgina. As they reached her, Lucy stopped. Suddenly she wasn't sure what to do, or, in fact, whether she should be there. Georgina quelled all Lucy's insecurities by rushing over and throwing herself into Lucy's arms.

"Oh Lucy," she cried. "I can't believe it."

Georgina started to cry, tears wetting Lucy's shoulder.

"Shh, it's okay, come on let's sit down," Lucy whispered, her own voice cracking with emotion.

Georgina allowed herself to be guided toward a row of hard, plastic chairs. Lucy sat and pulled Georgina down next to her, all the while still keeping a firm grip of her.

After a few minutes Georgina was calmer, her tears slowed down and her shoulders stopped shaking.

"How are things today?" Gerald broke the silence that had now fallen. "Is there any more news?"

Georgina shook her head. "No, he's still sedated, they're just changing his pain relief pump and doing some checks at the moment. His leg took an awful lot of the impact, and it was pretty smashed up, but they're more worried about his brain. He banged his head a couple of times and now his brain is swollen, so they can't tell how bad it is until the swelling has gone down. He's got a lot of cuts and bruises too."

Lucy clenched Georgina's hand tightly. "Is he going to be okay?" she gasped.

Georgina shook her head. "They don't know Lucy, they have no way to tell yet what damage has been done. Once the swelling has gone down they'll be able to do a scan, but until then we just have to wait. He had two fractures of the leg, one of which was pretty nasty, so they had to pin that, but otherwise his leg will be okay, eventually." Georgina looked exhausted as she pinched the bridge of her nose.

"Is anyone else here?" Richard asked, his eyes darting to Lucy.

Georgina shook her head. "No, someone needed to stay with Nate, and Jack had been down to the pub and had a couple of pints of beer when we got the call, so we thought it best if I came. He came over today with some clothes for me, but we've had to be so careful because of Nate."

"What does Nate know?" Lucy asked.

"He thinks I'm visiting an old friend in hospital and that Ed is back home working."

Lucy heaved a sigh of relief. "That's good," she whispered.

"We'll go and get some coffee, would you like one Georgina?" Richard asked.

"Please, that would be great."

As Gerald and Richard left, Georgina turned to Lucy.

"How are you sweetheart?" she asked. "This must be a terrible shock. I hope you didn't mind me calling you."

Lucy wiped the tears from her cheeks.

"I'm glad you did, but I wasn't sure I should come. That's why we didn't come yesterday, I didn't want to at first, but I just couldn't stay away."

"The fact you did shows me that you still love him. What on earth happened?" Georgina wiped a tear from Lucy's face.

"Didn't Ed tell you?"

Georgina shook her head. "No, he doesn't have a clue what's gone wrong. One minute you were happy, the next minute you'd gone."

"I know he's your son Georgina, and he's been in a terrible accident, but he's lying." Lucy paused as she wondered whether to tell Georgina the truth. What would it accomplish if she did?

"He's been devastated Lucy, I've never seen him like this before. Not even when Katie left." Georgina shook her head. "I honestly don't know what you mean by he's lying. Lying about what, how devastated he is?"

"No, he's lying about why I went. I found him in bed with Katie."

Georgina looked surprised, but not shocked. She obviously knew, Lucy thought.

"I think we need to get a few things straightened out." Georgina took hold of both Lucy's hands. "I don't know what you've been thinking, but there is nothing and never has been anything going on between Ed and Katie. He got home, and you were gone, just a note saying it was over."

Lucy looked at Georgina, puzzled by what she'd just heard.

"Whatever he told you, I promise you I didn't leave any note. I saw them together in Ed's bed, so the last thing I'd do would be to write a note." Lucy shook her head in disbelief.

"Lucy you're mistaken," Georgina insisted.

"No, Georgina I'm not. I suppose they've haven't told you about the baby yet, wasn't that why Ed was coming to see you this weekend, to tell you that they're back together and that Katie is pregnant?" Lucy looked away, not wanting Georgina to see that tears were brimming against her lashes once more.

"Oh Lucy, you're right Katie is pregnant, but it's Luke's," Georgina replied. "Lucy look at me, please."

Lucy turned to face her.

"What did you say?" Lucy gasped.

"Katie is pregnant, but it's Luke's child."

Lucy's heart began to beat rapidly, and her hands shook.

"But I saw them together, Katie and Ed were in his bed."

"Lucy, tell me everything from start to finish, about what happened that night."

Lucy relived every painful moment, from the phone call from Grace, to packing up her things and leaving, finally telling Georgina about seeing Katie at the hospital. At the end, Lucy was crying freely, holding tightly to Georgina's hand.

Once she was sure Lucy had finished, Georgina sighed and said. "Lucy sweetheart, I think you and Ed have been tricked in the cruellest possible way."

"What do you mean?" Lucy asked between sobs.

"Well Ed found out a couple of days ago that Katie has never split up with Luke. Her coming here was all a plan to make money out of Ed. You remember that I told you they were broke, well as I didn't seem to be coughing up any money they thought Ed might. When I was over there, I told Luke that Ed was single because I genuinely thought that he was. So, they cooked up the idea that Katie would come over and give Ed a sob story about Luke hitting her, she was supposed to be destitute and Ed was supposed to bail her out. It appears that Luke has been holed up in a hotel in Newcastle while the children stayed in America with the housekeeper."

"But Ed offered her ten thousand pounds, and she refused it," Lucy whispered. "Surely she would have taken the money if that were her plan."

"Ed found out that ten thousand is a drop in the ocean to what they owe, and apparently they guessed there must be a lot more where that came from, seeing as Ed offered it so readily." Georgina stood up and paced the floor, a hand held to her mouth as if to stop screams of outrage escaping.

"How do you know all this Georgina, how did Ed find out?" Lucy really wanted to believe it, but there was still the fact that he did actually have sex with Katie.

"Well, once you'd left she packed her bags from the B & B and landed on Ed's doorstep in the middle of the night, refusing to go back and refusing to leave until she had some money from Luke. Ed couldn't stand to be near her, he thought you'd left because of the situation, so obviously blamed her. But your leaving devastated him, and I don't think he had the energy, or inclination, to fight anymore, so he let her stay and he went to live at our house, and that's where he's been ever since - although she's done her utmost to entice him back over the last few weeks. Then on Friday afternoon, he nipped home to get some more clothes for Nate as we were coming home this weekend, and he caught them together. I believe there was a huge row and some pushing and shoving between Ed and Luke until the whole sorry plan came out." Georgina sat back down next to Lucy.

"It still doesn't answer why he slept with her in the first place, and why he didn't try to contact me until the early hours of the following morning," Lucy said with a grimace. "He can't deny that, I saw them."

Georgina thought for a second. "Did you say Ed didn't contact you until the next morning?"

Lucy nodded. "It was the early hours, about five I think, why?"

"I think that was the night he had to go to Callie. Do you know she's got cancer?"

"Yes, I went to see her."

"That was the day she found out. She'd been to see the consultant, and Ed told me she'd called him distraught, so he'd rushed round there, and he and Ellen stayed with her until the early hours, then when he got back you and Katie had gone. All he found was your note."

"The house was in darkness when I got back from Dad's, they'd not even eaten their take-away they were that desperate to be together." Lucy couldn't help the bitterness in her tone.

"Ed told me that, he said he'd just got back with the food when Callie rang, so he just dumped it and left."

Lucy knew Georgina was bound to stand up for her son, but she hadn't seen what Lucy had seen.

"*I saw them*!" Lucy insisted. "And all he could say was 'Oh shit', no pleading for my forgiveness, no apology, just 'Oh shit'," Lucy finished sadly.

"Why would Ed just let you go Lucy, he loved you, does love you. I know my son and I know that he would fight for you, he'd follow you, and I also know he's not a coward, he'd face up to his mistake not just curse that he'd been found out, that's something that ..." Georgina's voice trailed off as she fell silent.

After a couple of minutes Georgina asked. "What's Ed told you about Luke, Lucy?"

Lucy looked at Georgina puzzled. "Nothing much, he's a pretty decent footballer, he stole his wife, and he's his twin brother. I didn't ever ask, and Ed never told me, it all seemed too painful for him, why?"

"Oh Lucy, Luke and Ed are *identical* twins."

Lucy's hand shot to her mouth as she inhaled deeply. Fresh tears started to emerge as suddenly she realised that it wasn't Ed that she'd seen on top of Katie, but Luke.

"But Ed once told me they were nothing alike," Lucy cried.

"They are nothing alike in character, nothing at all; Ed's a good person," Georgina said. "As children they hated being twins, always insisting that they looked different, but they don't. Even their voices are the same, although Luke has a slight American accent nowadays. Tell me, what exactly did he say?" Georgina asked.

"Oh shit Lucy, nothing else."

"Not a lot of words to have to disguise your accent in, is it?"

Lucy shook her head slowly. "No, I suppose not."

"I'm guessing that it was all part of their plan that you found them, unless it was just a lucky break. Without you around, Katie probably thought she had more chance of seducing Ed, or at least getting more money out of him. I'm also going to bet that she wrote the note, Ed was so upset he wouldn't recognise it was her writing and not yours."

"What exactly did the note say, did Ed tell you?" Lucy asked.

"Oh, something along the lines of it was all going too fast and after seeing them together you'd realised that you could never replace Katie. Hah, she certainly like to big herself up, I must say." Georgina shook her head in disbelief.

"Okay let's say she did write a note, why didn't Ed ring me to say where he was?" Lucy still couldn't bring herself to believe everything could be resolved.

"I don't know sweetheart, you'll have to ask him that. Maybe he forgot, I believe Callie was in a terrible state."

Suddenly everything that Georgina said made sense it all fell into place. Lucy let out a loud cry.

"Oh God, Georgina, what if he dies? He'll never know that I'm sorry for not believing in him and that I love him." Lucy exhaled slowly.

"Well he won't, so you'll be able to tell him both those things." Georgina brushed away the tears from her cheeks. *"We cannot think like that."*

At that moment, a man pushed through the door, Lucy guessed from the stethoscope around his neck that he was a doctor. He smiled at the two women and ran a hand through his hair. The movement reminded Lucy of Ed, and she gasped as a sob escaped from the back of her throat.

"Hi there Mrs Bryce, well there's no change still I'm afraid, but he's stable which is a positive."

Georgina grasped Lucy's hand tightly.

"Do you know when he might wake up?" Lucy asked, her voice cracking with emotion.

The doctor looked at Lucy and smiled.

"This is my son's partner," Georgina explained. "This is Lucy."

"Hello Lucy, no we can't say just yet, but, not for a couple of days at the least." He went on to explain everything that Georgina had already told them, stressing that Ed wasn't in a coma, but taking a much needed sedated holiday, was how he explained it.

"A lot of sleep can do wonders for the body," the doctor said, smiling warmly at Lucy. "As for his leg, well he'll need a fair amount of physio once it's out of plaster, but I don't think it will bother him too much. He's had all his obs' done for this morning, and had his pain relief, and IV changed, so you can go and see him if you'd like. Just talk to him, but try and keep it nice and peaceful in there, although he's sedated he may still pick up a few sounds."

As the doctor disappeared, Georgina turned to Lucy.

"Off you go then," she urged. "Go and sit with him."

"No, you should go." Lucy shook her head.

"No darling, its fine. I know he's not likely to wake just yet, but if he does I'm sure it will be you he wants to see. He was coming home to see you when it happened, he'd got Richard's text message as he got to the cottage, and so pretty much had a cup of tea and then left again."

Lucy bit her bottom lip and wiped her tear stained face with the back of her hand.

"Really, he was coming to me?"

Georgina nodded as she also wiped more tears away. "Yes sweetheart, so go and sit with him."

"If you're sure?"

"I'm sure, now you're here I may go back to the cottage for a few hours, I desperately need a shower and a cuddle from Nate." Georgina stood up from her seat and stretched. "Jack can come over then, he's been desperate to see him."

"Are you okay to drive, I can ask Dad or Richard to take you?" Lucy said, aware of how exhausted Georgina must be.

"No, don't worry, I'll be fine. It only takes about 40 minutes, I'll be there in no time. So, go and see my boy and tell him that you love him."

Lucy walked quickly to Ed's private room at the end of the ward, she was eager to see him yet, just as she had been with Callie, filled with apprehension of how he would look.

She was also scared that when he eventually woke he would reject her, after all she hadn't believed in him. Pushing open the door Lucy inhaled and then exhaled, trying to slow down her heartbeat.

Ed's face was ashen against the stark white of the pillow, except for a dark, blue swelling around his eye and a deep red cut across his forehead. He still looked like her gorgeous Ed though, Lucy thought, the familiar feeling of love for him enveloping her body, and tingling her nerve endings.

She quietly pulled a chair across to the bed, and as she sat down Lucy took his hand gently, and kissed his fingertips. Ed stirred making Lucy hold her breath, but then his breathing settled back into a regular pattern, and he was motionless again.

Lucy's eyes, bright with tears, scoured Ed's face as she hugged his hand to her chest.

"I'm so sorry Ed," she whispered. "I should've known that you wouldn't hurt me. When you wake up I hope that we can put things right because I need you and love you so much. It's been horrible without you, so I'm not leaving your side until I know that you're going to be okay. Please be okay." Lucy's voice broke as she struggled to hold back a sob, anxious to remain as calm as possible. She brushed away the salty tears and kissed Ed's hand again, desperately hoping that he was going to be okay and not daring to think about the alternative.

Lucy had fallen asleep holding Ed's hand, when Jack sneaked quietly into the room. He shook Lucy gently by the shoulder while all the time staring at his son.

"Lucy," he whispered. "Wake up sweetheart, it's time you had a break."

Lucy stirred and lifting her head from Ed's bed, rubbed the sleep from her eyes.

"Hi Jack, are you okay?"

Jack nodded and bent down to kiss her cheek. "Hmm I'm fine, I'll be better when Ed wakes up, but generally I'm okay. What about you, how are you holding up?"

Lucy shrugged. "The same I guess, I just want him to be better." She darted a look at Ed. "What time is it anyway?"

"It's 4 p.m. You need to take a break love, your dad and Richard are waiting in the visitor's room for you."

Lucy gasped and put a hand to her mouth. "God I forgot all about them, I'd better go and check that they're okay."

"Go and get something to eat as well, I'll hold the fort for a couple of hours."

"Ring me if there's any change won't you?" Lucy's eyes were anxious as she scrabbled in her bag for a pen and some paper. "This is my new number."

Jack took the paper from her and put it in his pocket. "I will, but I doubt anything will change today. Go on and I'll see you later."

As Lucy went into the visitor's room, her resolve crumbled and as soon as she saw Gerald she burst into tears and ran to him. After a few minutes of sobbing Lucy gently pulled away.

"Okay now? Georgina has explained everything," Gerald said, leading her to a chair.

Lucy wiped her nose with a tissue that Richard handed to her.

"I'm sorry I left you both out here for hours."

"That's okay, we've been busy, haven't we Richard?"

Richard nodded and sat the other side of Lucy. "Yes, we've booked you into a B&B for a few nights, you and your dad. We knew you wouldn't want to go home, so have found one pretty close by that can fit you both in."

Lucy grabbed Richard's hand and squeezed it tightly. "Thank you so much, but what about you?"

"I'm going home, I need to help out at the surgery. Things are bad enough there as it is with Callie off, and now this," replied Richard shaking his head.

"Do they all know then?" Lucy asked.

"I spoke to Elspeth earlier, she's going to tell the staff tomorrow when they're back in after the weekend, but she's not sure about the patients. She's going to see what Dr Kindler thinks."

"I'll stay with you though sweetheart," Gerald interjected. "I don't want you to be on your own, particularly…" Gerald leaned in and lowered his voice, "in your condition. I'm guessing you've not told Georgina or Jack yet."

"No, I want to tell Ed first, plus I don't want them worrying about me, they've got enough on their plate."

Gerald nodded in understanding. "Okay, well why don't we get round to the B&B so that you can have some rest and maybe a bite to eat."

"We don't have any clean clothes though Dad, perhaps we should nip out and buy some."

"No need. Richard is the cleverest man alive and took the liberty of packing us both some this morning while we had breakfast – well I had breakfast, you refused to eat yours." Gerald smiled at his daughter as he moved her fringe from her eyes.

"I thought that you'd probably stay and that Gerald would insist on being with you, so thought it was a good idea."

"You are bloody amazing Richard, and I don't know what Dad or I would do without you. Okay, I'll just nip to the ladies and then we'll go, because the sooner I leave the sooner I can get back"

On her way back to the visitor's room a few minutes later, Lucy heard raised voices at the nurse's station; she gasped as she recognised the American twang. What on earth was that bitch doing here Lucy thought, with anger building inside her? As she reached Katie, Jill one of Ed's nurses spotted Lucy.

"This lady is insisting on seeing Mr Bryce, she says she's his wife?" Jill said looking at Lucy quizzically.

Katie swung round to see who Jill was speaking to. "Well hello honey, what a nice surprise." Katie appeared to force her lips into a thin smile.

Lucy placed a hand in the small of Katie's back. "It's okay Jill, I'll get rid of her. The family don't want her here, and I know I can say the same for Ed. Come on Katie, let's talk outside shall we."

Lucy pushed Katie away from the nurse's station, and along the corridor. Just past the door into the visitor's room, she turned Katie around and slapped her firmly across the face.

"Oow, you fucking little bitch, how fucking dare you?" Katie cried lifting her hand to strike Lucy back.

Lucy grabbed Katie's wrist. "Don't even try, because the way I feel about you at this minute, I'll rip every hair from your head and punch your bloody lights out."

"You wouldn't dare," Katie said as she pulled her hand away from Lucy's grasp and placed it against her reddening cheek.

"Don't dare me," Lucy hissed. "What the fuck are you doing here, Katie? Haven't you done enough damage to Ed, to us?"

Katie moved away from Lucy and lounged against the wall. "More to the point, what are you doing here? I thought after what you saw you'd have been long gone out of his life?"

Lucy noticed a flicker of disquiet in Katie's eyes; she obviously wasn't sure how much Lucy knew.

"I'm here because I love Ed no matter what, *so* what about you?" Lucy asked.

"For the same reason, the only difference being that he loves me and not you, so I think you should leave." Katie pointed toward the exit. "Go on, he won't want you here."

"How do you know that he loves you Katie, please tell?" Lucy placed her hands firmly on her hips, and glared at Katie defiantly.

"Because honey he told me, the night that we made love in his bed. The night he got me pregnant."

"Really, oh I see."

"Yes really, and he told me that he'd never stopped loving me." Katie smiled and moved closer to Lucy until she was toe to toe with her.

Lucy stuck out her finger and poked Katie in the chest. "And you are one lying bitch," she said shaking her head. "Did you really think that I wouldn't figure out that it was Luke in bed with you?"

Katie sighed and then started to laugh. "That's what Ed's told you is it, that it was Luke, not him on top of me?"

"Nope, Ed hasn't told me anything, he's not conscious, but Georgina has told me all about his fight with Luke, and that you never split up. The rest we both worked out between us. So it's about time that you told me the truth, what are you doing here and how on earth did you think you would get away with it?"

Katie folded her arms across her chest and sighed. "Okay honey, truth, well the truth is exactly what I've just told you."

Lucy laughed and poked Katie again. "Once more Katie, tell me the fucking truth, because I swear to God I *will* rip your hair out and punch your lights out, as promised."

Katie stared eye to eye with Lucy for a few moments. Finally she gave a deep sigh of defeat. "Okay the truth is honey I only ever wanted Ed's money. Luke and I are broke, and I thought that if I could get him to fall in love with me again then I could get him to give me the money that we needed. I just didn't count on you."

"So it was your idea, not Luke's?" Lucy asked incredulously.

"Well he didn't argue when I suggested it. I've got to admit honey, I was pretty shocked to find Ed in love with someone else - Georgina never mentioned you when she visited." Katie replied shaking her head.

"But he offered you money and you turned it down, why if you were so desperate?"

"Because ten grand wasn't enough, if he'd offered me eight times that much I'd have been on the next plane home." Katie laughed.

Lucy ran a hand through her hair, shocked at Katie's immorality.

"And what about Nate in all of this," she asked. "What were you going to do about him, were you okay about breaking his heart, just for his father's money?"

Katie shrugged. "Never thought about him, it was never about Nate, it was only ever about making sure my family don't go under."

Lucy stamped her foot and almost screamed, she felt so angry. "Argh, you absolute bitch, that poor, poor child. How on earth could you do that to him, come back into his life and then disappear again? He's your child Katie, just like Louis and Amelia, does that mean nothing to you?"

Katie didn't answer, but at least now looked uncomfortable.

Lucy moved away from Katie, frightened that she would harm her, as she had threatened to do. She realised that if Katie had no shame about hurting her own son, then no wonder she had no qualms about lying to Ed about Lucy's disappearance, even after she and Luke had been found out.

"You should go Katie before I lose control of myself, your plan failed, so just piss off back to America," Lucy whispered.

"But I need to speak to Ed," Katie protested. "I have to get some money from him, he's our only hope."

"What? You really think he'd lend you money after all this?" Lucy asked shaking her head. "Are you drunk or high?"

"Listen honey, I know you hate me and I totally get it, but my family need that money. I'll have another mouth to feed in a few months, Ed can afford it, he's a doctor for fuck's sake, and Luke's sure he won't have spent the money that Jack gave him from the houses. He only has Nate, he has to help us." Spittle was forming at the corners of Katie's mouth, she was becoming so agitated. "You can't stop me seeing him anyway, you're not even together anymore; at least that's one part of my plan that worked out. Christ you are one annoying little bitch, and Ed didn't even try to find you after you left, surely that should tell you something."

"Well that's where you're wrong, Ed was coming back to me on the night of the accident," Lucy replied calmly. "Ask Georgina if you don't believe me, she'll be back soon."

"Huh, that old cow will say anything to get rid of me. But, I will always be the mother of his child, and she can never change that, and that's a connection that you'll never have with him. You, you'll just be an old girlfriend that he'll think about from time to time." Venom flashed in Katie's eyes as she pointed a finger at Lucy.

Lucy smiled and instinctively placed a hand on her stomach, just as she'd seen Katie do all those weeks ago. Katie noticed Lucy's movement and shook her head.

"Don't tell me, you're pregnant," she said. "Whatever, it doesn't matter, I had his first borne and you'll always wonder whether he came back just for the child."

"You really think so, well you're wrong Katie. Ed doesn't even know I'm pregnant yet. He was coming back because I asked him to and according to Georgina, and everyone else I've spoken to, has been heartbroken that I left, unlike when you turned up and he tried to pay you to get out of his life. So like I said, just go, you're not wanted here."

Katie dropped her head and paced up and down for a few moments, until finally she stood still and looked up with tears of frustration pricking at her eyelashes.

"Look can you just ask him for me?" she pleaded

"No," Lucy said shaking her head in disbelief. "No, I bloody well can't. I'm sorry but you're going to have to figure another way out of this one."

"How though?" Katie asked her voice rising. "How the hell am I going to feed my kids?"

"Do what everyone else has to do, get a job and stop spending money that you don't have." Lucy held up the palm of her hand, as if to dismiss Katie. "Now if you don't mind take your stupid blow up breasts and go back to your own family, and let Ed and I look after ours."

As Lucy turned to leave Katie grabbed her elbow, spinning Lucy round to face her.

"Listen to me, it would be in Ed's best interest if you persuaded him to loan us the money." Katie spat the words at Lucy.

Lucy pulled her head back from the space that Katie was invading.

"His best interest, how do you work that one out?" she asked.

"Because honey, if he doesn't I'll go for custody of Nate," Katie shouted.

A nurse, who was carrying something covered in a towel, appeared at Lucy's side.

"Everything okay here?" she asked Lucy.

"Yes, now piss off," hissed Katie pushing her.

"Katie, stop it," yelled Lucy holding onto the nurse to stop her falling.

"I'm calling security." The nurse moved back along the corridor.

She had only made a couple of steps when Katie pulled at her arm to stop her. The nurse, pulled off balance, flung her other arm above her head as her feet moved from under her. The towel that she was carrying flew through the air - and the contents of the bedpan that it was covering flew all over Katie.

As the rather smelly liquid dripped down Katie's face, she stamped her foot in fury.

"Shit, shit, shit," Katie cried.

"It appears so *honey*," Lucy replied, a huge grin spread across her face.

Security had eventually ejected Katie from the hospital. She was highly embarrassed, although it was difficult to decide what she felt most ashamed of, the smell of excrement or the blue hospital gown that she'd had to put on over her jeans. Lucy, Gerald and Richard had delighted in watching Katie leave between two security guards, her head bowed, obviously angry and frustrated that she'd failed to get the promise of any money. Jack, oblivious to all that had happened, emerged from Ed's room as Katie was being escorted out. Once Lucy had told him what had happened, Jack had wanted to go after her at first, worried that she would carry out her threat about Nate, but as Gerald pointed out, Katie wouldn't really want another mouth to feed, and it was highly unlikely Luke would want Ed's son living with him, so Jack relaxed and joined the others in laughter as Lucy regaled the tale of what was to become known as "Shitgate", once more.

Over the next few days, Lucy, Gerald, Georgina and Jack fell into a pattern of visiting Ed, with some eating and sleeping interspersed. The majority of their hours though were spent at his bedside, with either Jack or Georgina alternating with Lucy and Gerald. They lost any concept of the outside world, cloistered away in the small private room where the air was stale, the smell antiseptic, the light artificial and the hours long and tiring, but none of them wanted to be anywhere else.

Finally after four days, the doctors told them that the swelling on Ed's brain should have reduced enough for him to have a scan; a scan that would tell them whether there was any brain damage. Both Georgina and Lucy were with Ed when they took him away, and both of them felt bereft as he was wheeled out of sight, off the ward. Lucy thought her heart was going to erupt through her chest it was pounding so hard and fast, and she felt sick and clammy at the prospect of what they may be about to find out.

"How long is it now?" Lucy asked a weary looking Georgina.

"Just over an hour, they did say it may take a while. Why don't you go and get a coffee or something, you look shattered."

Lucy shook her head. "No, I want to wait until he comes back."

"Okay, but I'm worried about you. You're starting to look peaky, and I know that you're shattered. I wish you'd get some more sleep in a proper bed, your dad said you stayed here again last night." Georgina frowned at Lucy, whose eyes were framed in dark circles.

"I'm fine, I wouldn't sleep if I was at the B&B anyway. At least here I manage to get a couple of hours. They brought a camp bed in for me last night."

"Well you need to go back tonight because if you don't I'm going to ask the staff to ban you." Georgina gave a small laugh and then sighed. "Christ I wish they'd hurry up."

Finally another half hour later, Clare, one of Ed's nurses, popped her head around the visitor's room door.

"Hi ladies, he's back if you want to go back in."

"How did it go Clare?" asked Lucy moving toward the door.

"It was fine, no problems. I believe Mr Rahman will be up in about ten minutes to tell you about the results."

"Any clues?" Concern was etched across Georgina's face.

"No idea sorry, but he won't be long. I'll speak to you afterwards, in case you have any other questions."

"Okay thanks," Lucy replied.

"No problem, now try not to worry." Clare gave Lucy's arm a comforting rub, before disappearing back onto the ward.

And so another wait started, at which point Lucy thought she was going to scream. She knew that Ed wasn't the only patient, but as far as she was concerned he was the most important; why couldn't everyone else see that and hurry up.

Then finally Mr Rahman appeared in Ed's room, he was armed with a buff file, full of papers and notes about Ed. As he began to talk Georgina grasped Lucy's hand tightly, so tightly that her knuckles were white, and Lucy's hand went numb.

"Well, you'll be pleased to know that there is no damage to Edward's brain, and he's going to be fine. The oedema appears to be purely from the collision, nothing else. Edward's head…"

Lucy didn't actually hear the rest of what Mr Rahman had to say, she'd heard the most important part – Ed was going to be okay.

Georgina's voice brought Lucy back to the conversation. "So, if you start to reduce his sedation today how long before he wakes up?" she asked.

"Based on the fact that he's been sedated for about five days, I would say between 12 and 24 hours, but it may be sooner. It's just a case of waiting Mrs Bryce." Mr Rahman smiled warmly at Georgina.

"Okay, another wait it is then. We're used to that, aren't we Lucy?"

Lucy nodded. "Yes, we certainly are."

Neither Georgina nor Lucy wanted to leave Ed's side, now they knew that he would be coming round at some point. So, they both sat through the night as slowly and surely Ed started to come out of his sedation. He was still extremely groggy at first and didn't appear to know whom they were, but by the following morning, he was much more alert. He recognised Georgina first, kissing her hand and smiling widely at her. Lucy stood back to allow them some space until Georgina pulled away from Ed and beckoned Lucy forward.

"Look who's here sweetheart," she whispered.

Lucy needn't have been worried about Ed rejecting her. As soon as he saw her his eyes lit up, and a huge smile spread across his face.

"Hi baby," he whispered as Lucy moved forward towards him.

Lucy couldn't help the sob escaping as Ed lifted his hand and touched her face.

"Does this mean you're my girlfriend again?"

Georgina, recognising that Ed and Lucy needed time alone, quietly backed out of the room. With tears of happiness streaking her cheeks, she went to find Gerald and to call Jack with the good news.

Over the next couple of days, Lucy and Georgina mainly watched Ed sleep. After initially waking, Ed and Lucy spoke for a few minutes, mainly professing their love for one another until Ed drifted into sleep, still holding Lucy's hand. He continued to drift in and out, but was never awake long enough to have a lengthy, or indeed meaningful, conversation.

Lucy had now taken over from Georgina, who informed her that he was much more aware today. So, Lucy was waiting anxiously for him to wake as she knew today they would have to talk about what had happened.

As Ed stirred suddenly, Lucy moved forward and stroked his face.

"Are you okay, do you want a drink of water?" she asked.

"No thanks, I'm fine. I just want to look at you." His eyes, now much brighter, gazed at Lucy.

Lucy kissed his hand several times, unable to believe that he was awake after all the hours spent watching and wondering.

"Oh Ed, I'm so, so sorry that I didn't believe in you," she gasped. "You told me she wouldn't get you back, and I should have listened."

Ed shook his head. "Why did you leave, I've missed you so much. Was it because I didn't send Katie away? Your note just said it was too quick and that you knew you couldn't replace her, how could you even think that?" Ed stroked Lucy's hand gently.

He could see in her eyes that Lucy loved him, but he also needed to know why she'd left, when everything seemed to be so strong between them.

"God Ed, I'm so sorry, I've missed you too." Lucy sniffed and used the back of her hand to wipe the tears that were now on her cheeks. "I can't believe how Katie tricked me, how they tricked me."

"What do you mean, she tricked you?" Fury building up in Ed's voice, he gripped the bed sheet.

Lucy told Ed all about finding 'him' and Katie in bed together, and how she and Georgina had figured out what had actually happened.

"So you see, I should have stayed and talked to you about it, then we wouldn't have been apart all these weeks." Lucy kissed Ed's palm and then held it closely to her chest.

"Bloody hell Lucy, how would you know? Even Mum and Dad used to have problems telling us apart, how were you supposed to. I've felt like shit without you, I could kill them both." He coughed and reached across for the water on his cabinet, taking a long drink.

As he put the water back, Lucy said, "Even at the hospital, when I went to see Callie, she still tried to trick me." She smiled weakly at the memory.

Ed looked at Lucy with a puzzled expression. Lucy explained about visiting Callie and seeing Katie there. She also told him of Richard's call with Katie when she confirmed she was pregnant, and finally the showdown she'd had with Katie a few days ago.

"Christ, all that just because they need money. She's an absolute bitch, she must have answered my mobile while I was arguing with Luke, I think I left it on the table with my keys. Sounds like she got what she deserved though," Ed laughed taking hold of Lucy's hand. "And he's more of a bastard than I imagined. How can anyone be willing to let their wife sleep with someone for money?"

"He sounds like a total shit," Lucy commented, laying her palm on Ed's cheek. "God, I can't believe I may have lost you. What happened anyway?"

"It was a guy in a transit van. He was overtaking me and suddenly he just careered toward me. We both ended up in a ditch in the side of the road. The police think he had a heart attack at the wheel." Ed groaned slightly and touched his black eye.

"Is he okay?" Lucy asked.

Ed shook his head. "No, he was dead when the ambulance got there. Luckily for me I'm okay, except for that," he said pointing at his right leg that was hoisted above the bed.

"It's going to be fine though the doctor said. Are you sure that you're okay, no headaches or anything?" Lucy's face was full of concern.

"I'm fine," Ed chuckled. "I'm not going to drop down dead, I promise, and don't I always keep my promises?"

Lucy leaned across and kissed Ed tenderly.

"Bloody hell Luce, even in this state I can feel a stirring." Ed nodded toward his groin. "Do you fancy getting in with me?" he asked, although a little feebly.

Lucy laughed. "No, and there'll be no hanky panky until you're better."

"Christ, I'll have to make sure I stick to doctor's orders then. Have you seen Mum today? How is she doing, I'm worried about you both spending hours on end here?"

"She's fine, shattered, but she's okay. I don't think Luke and Katie will be on her Christmas present list though." Heaving a sigh Lucy leaned back against the chair. She thought about everything that had led to this point. "Katie obviously thought it was a miracle when Dad had the flood."

"Ah now, that one I can help you with. She did it, she caused the flood," said Ed wincing at the pain in his leg.

"How? And how on earth did she get into Dad's house?" Then suddenly light dawned on Lucy. "The day she borrowed my car to go to Newcastle."

Ed nodded. "Yep, she had your keys, let herself in and knocked a nail in the pipe."

"The nail, of course." Lucy fingered the now smooth scar on the palm of her hand. She lifted it to show Ed. "I cut myself on it when I was cleaning up after the plumber."

Ed shook his head in despair. "She rather enjoyed telling me about that when it all came out when I found them. She'd done it to take you away from the house so that *she* could get *me* into bed, but I spoiled the plan by rushing off to see Callie. That's why she called Luke, I suppose. Shit, when I saw Katie and Luke together I should have realised that she'd probably done something to make you leave. I've been such an idiot, not realising what they've been doing. There were enough clues." Ed shook his head and sighed.

"She's been clever Ed, and sometimes it's hard to think clearly when there's other things on your mind. Why didn't you call me though, to say you were at Callie's, didn't you wonder where I was when you got back with the food?" Lucy was still perplexed by it all.

"She told me that you'd nipped out for more wine, so when I got the call from Callie I just asked Katie to let you know that I'd had an emergency and that I'd call you when I could. I didn't want to say it was Callie because of confidentiality. I should have just made her leave when I did, but I was so worried about Callie." Ed shook his head and sighed. "And she took a risk that I wouldn't call you before you got back to my house; that would really have spoiled the plan."

"She obviously took a chance that even if you'd called me I'd still think that it was you in bed with her. If I had realised it was Luke, then so be it – she had nothing to lose. My head hurts just trying to fathom it all out to be honest." Lucy gently kissed his forehead. "Don't worry about it now anyway, she's been really sneaky and managed to trick both of us."

"I know Luce, but what I don't understand is why she didn't tell me that you found her and Luke in bed together? It was all over then, I knew they hadn't split up, so why carry it on?"

"Because," Lucy replied, "she realised that if you knew you'd probably have come to find me, and it was her last bit of revenge to keep us apart."

"You're right, she still wanted me to believe that it was your decision to go. She is one evil bitch! Thank God you asked to see me otherwise we may have never sorted things out." Ed winced and closed his eyes momentarily.

Finally, he spoke. "Anyway, I meant to ask, what was it you wanted to see me about? I'm assuming after what you thought you saw it wasn't to make up."

Lucy had totally forgotten that she had something important to tell Ed. Making sure he was okay and that they were okay had overshadowed everything else, and apart from her jeans feeling a little tighter over the last couple of days, she hadn't honestly thought about the baby.

"Well, I don't really know how to tell you, and I totally understand if you decide it's not what you want, so don't want to get back together. I know it's pretty soon, and people will probably talk, but I've got used to it now and am genuinely happy about it..." All the thoughts jangling around in Lucy's head came blurting out rapidly.

"Luce just tell me," Ed interjected.

"Okay, well the thing is I'm pregnant." Lucy froze waiting for Ed to respond.

"Say that again." He tried to pull himself up, but winced.

"Please don't be angry, I didn't do it on purpose. You know how I felt about having another child."

"*Lucy*, for Christ's sake please just say it again."

"Okay, sorry. I'm pregnant," Lucy whispered, her eyes shut tightly.

Ed was silent for a few moments and then his face broke into a huge smile. He pulled Lucy to him by her hand and kissed her gently.

Eventually, Lucy slowly pulled away.

"You're not angry then?" She looked at Ed with large eyes.

Ed suddenly knew what it must be like to win the lottery and your football team win the Premiership title, all on the same day. The woman that he loved was going to have his baby; they were going to be a family. He didn't care how soon it was, or whether people were negative about their situation. All he cared about was this beautiful woman in front of him, and the new life growing inside her, he cared about Nate, and he cared about their future together.

Eventually, his voice full of emotion, Ed answered. "Are you joking? I'm over the moon. I can't believe it! How far along are you? How long have you known?"

"Nearly eight weeks, and I've known for about six. That's why I wanted to see you, to tell you. I couldn't tell you before because I was so upset, I'm sorry," Lucy responded, anxious that Ed was annoyed at keeping it from him.

"Hey, I understand," Ed soothed. "I totally get it, why would you want me to know if you thought I was back with Katie, and that she was pregnant. Come here." Ed beckoned Lucy to him and kissed her gently. "I love you baby, and I can't think of anything better than having a child with you."

Lucy smiled, happy to be back with him and starting a life together. She kissed Ed back, and then nibbled his ear, breathing the words. "I love you too."

"Lucy, can I ask you something?" Ed asked breathlessly.

"Hmm," Lucy murmured now kissing his neck.

"What shoes have you got on?"

Epilogue

As her daughter ran around in circles, Lucy sighed contentedly and gazed at her. She was a beautiful little girl with dark brown hair in bunches and plump little arms and legs and her brown eyes were full of happiness. How lovely to be so happy just because you could run around in circles against the wind, Lucy thought.

"Careful Tilly, not too fast or you'll fall," Lucy called, smiling at the little two year old. "Oh quick look here's Daddy and Nate." Lucy pointed in the direction of Ed walking towards them, Nate dawdling alongside, dragging a bag behind him.

"Hello, how are my gorgeous girls then? Ready for some lunch with Daddy?" Ed smiled as he scooped Tilly up into his arms.

"My been chasing the wind Daddy," she whispered into his ear as she flung her arms around his neck.

"Have you? And what has Mummy been doing?" asked Ed, leaning towards Lucy and planting a kiss on her lips. "Have you been chasing the wind as well?"

Lucy shook her head and sighed. "No, Mummy has been making sure Granpy and Grandpops are all packed for their holiday. But as fast as Dad put things into the case this little madam took them out, didn't you monkey?" Lucy turned her attention to Nate. "Anyway, how are you sweetie? How did the football training go?" Lucy asked as he stared up at her with his enormous eyes.

"I scored a goal Mum, it was almost from the halfway line, wasn't it Dad?" Nate mimicked his earlier shot with an imaginary ball.

"It was brilliant Nate, the best goal you've ever scored." Ed smiled, full of pride.

Lucy looked down at Nate, feeling that now familiar swell in her heart every time he called her 'Mum'. She loved it as much now, as she did the first time he'd said it. "The best you've ever scored, wow. Well, I'm very proud of you," she said, ruffling his hair.

"Anyway madam," Ed now turned to his daughter. "Why were you taking all the clothes out of the suitcase then?"

Tilly's dimples appeared in her cheeks as she smiled at her father. "I not want Granpy and Grandpops to go on ayoplane."

"Oh dear," said Ed. "I having a feeling it's going to be a nightmare when we take them to the airport."

"I know, she's going to be hysterical." Lucy sighed. "Perhaps we shouldn't come, what do you think?"

Ed kissed Lucy tenderly and smiled. "Oh you'd better because I can't go to South Africa without you three. It would be horrible, I'd miss you like mad."

"What…what do you mean?" Lucy asked open mouthed. "We're going too?"

"Yes my beautiful wife we're all going too. It's all arranged I've got a locum in at the practice, Callie's going to work full time while we're away, and she's arranged for Gladys to help out, I've arranged for Nate to have an extra week off school, and we are going to have the best time ever for three whole weeks. How does that sound?"

"But are you sure Callie is well enough to be working full time, I know she's in remission, but she's only been used to working part-time since she was ill?" Lucy asked, concerned for her friend.

Ed smiled and nodded. "I've checked and double-checked with her, and she insists that she'll be fine. Dr Kindler is going to keep a close eye on her, as is everyone else. You know what she's like, she's been chomping at the bit to come back properly for ages, so she's thrilled."

"So, are we going with Granpy and Grandpops or not, Dad?" asked Nate jumping up and down.

"Yes, we are. We're all going to see Auntie Sophie."

"God did I ever tell you how much I love you?" Lucy asked, hugging Ed tightly.

"Often, but I tell you what let's get these two to bed early tonight and you can show me how much." Ed laughed as he kissed Lucy.

"Okay," she giggled and looked down at her shoes.

If you enjoyed "Lucy Steps Out" then why not try my first book.

Guess Who I Pulled Last Night?

"Love this book! It explores the trials and tribulations of three best girlfriends in their early 30's...we've all been there and done it, so we can relate to it. In parts it made me laugh out loud, in parts it made me cry, as life in reality does. If you're a Jill Mansell fan you'll enjoy this book. I was really pleased with how long it was, because I was enjoying it so much I didn't want it to end. Looking forward to more novels by the same author. "
This funny and charming romance that tells the story of three twenty-something friends and how they cope with the trials and tribulations of life; always finding comfort and loyalty in each other.

Charlotte is scatty and engaging and after having her heart broken 3 years earlier by cheating, Capri driving, Grant she's now looking for love again believing that finding Prince Charming will make her life complete; but is the arrogant but frustratingly sexy Irishman, Niall Devine, that man?

Bets is the glamorous good-time girl and beauty salon owner who secretly yearns to settle down. She is the life and soul of the party with plenty of notches on her bedpost but since flirting with hunky Stuart all summer she wonders if he may be the one that she finally commits to.

Kerry, of the impressive cleavage, is the only of the trio to be married and a mother. She should feel satisfied and content but feels like she's missing out and losing her identity. Suddenly she's turned in to the bitch from hell, alienating all those around her, including Charlotte, Bets and her devoted husband, Kelvin.

This is a charming story focussing on friendship and love, but exploring some difficult and sensitive issues in its course. It has humour and wry observations and some surprises along the way. It will make you laugh out loud, smile, cry and desperate to turn every page.

http://www.amazon.co.uk/Guess-Who-Pulled-Last-Night-ebook/dp/B00C7FH7J8/ref=cm_cr_pr_pb_t

Made in the USA
Charleston, SC
17 May 2014